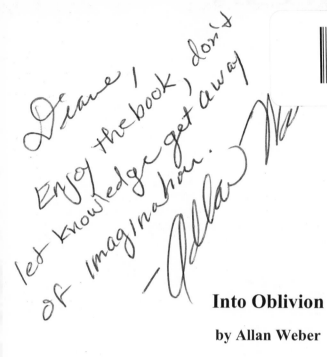

Dear [...] !
Enjoy the book, don't
let knowledge get away
of imagination.
/Alla

Into Oblivion

by Allan Weber

"What binds me has been slain, and what surrounds me has been destroyed, and my desire has been brought to an end, and ignorance has died. In an aeon I was released from a world, and in a type from a type, and from the fetter of oblivion which is transient. From this time on will I attain to the rest of the time, of the season, of the aeon, in silence" –**Gospel of Mary**

Preface

The Ancient One decided to allow his children to leave their planet and spread their wings. Thousands of millennia had passed since he brought them into existence but now it was time for them to find out who they actually were. He knew that some of his children would doom themselves for eternity while others would prevail and orchestrate his plan. He encouraged them to bring other sentient races with them either to their doom or salvation. Still, everyone had a choice. And what was the right choice, was there enough wisdom in the universe to make a *right* choice? In the early dawn of time, he was not offered a choice but was trapped to reside within this galaxy while his brethren resided in others. Now there were hopelessly separated by enormous distances with their galaxies hurling at tremendous speeds away from each other towards oblivion. The Ancient One hoped that he had made wise choices since then, but only time will tell.

Chapter 1 - Awake

"Mother," he thought when he heard a voice inside his head.

It was not what the voice said that was important but more of how it sounded. He didn't even comprehend what the voice was saying. Conscious thought had yet to arrive, but he did hear the voice. Slowly and quietly his mother's voice repeated the same message to him. The voice was reassuring, gentle and kind. It relaxed his mind where no thought had occurred in years.

He started to arrive at consciousness, when he began to understand what his mother was saying, "Jacob, this is your mom; you are waking up from a long, long sleep. But don't rush, take all the time you need."

Well he planned on taking his time. He didn't know where he was or how he got there. He didn't even know if he even cared. There were only images that began to plague his mind. Feelings of loss, grief, and desolation swam among the vague and disorganized images. He began to wonder why he had to wake up, he felt so peaceful. After all, he felt secure at the moment, and he didn't trust waking up on what he might find. Where was he? Was he in his mother's womb? No, his thoughts though very vague seem mature in nature. His mother's voice came to him again, repeating the same message.

He couldn't feel his toes, or his legs for that matter. His hands and arms also appeared absent. He felt nothing but his mind was beginning to emerge from a very dark place where his mind had slept for a long time. He didn't quite yet know where he was, but those bad feelings he felt, made him aware of the dreadful truth about his mother. He began to remember his mother's body drifting away from their spacecraft, while he was standing next to a portal window watching. It was only an image at first but his memory of the death of his mother flooded his consciousness. His father held him steadfast, while he was squirming to get away to save his mother. He watched her often over the years from various portal windows; she looked like an angel drifting from one place to another, without an apparent care in the world. She was an incredible engineer but also was well adapted to space walking. She spent hours outside the spacecraft along with her mechanical space buddies fixing this and replacing that. Her "space buddies", SAMs (Space Assistant Modules) $\alpha 1$, $\beta 2$ and $\pi 3$ spent more time with her than with anybody else of the crew. Almost all her trips outside were uneventful and routine. But on this one dark occasion, a wayward space rock hit SAM $\pi 3$ somehow causing it to ignite its main thrusters and mistakenly crash into his mother. The crash killed her instantly and caused her tether to break loose from the spacecraft. SAM $\pi 3$ was damaged beyond repair and also drifted off into deep space.

His father told him, "I'm sorry son, she is already dead; there are no life signs from the monitors of her spacesuit."

Jacob was only a teenager but at that moment he hated his father and struggled mightily against his grip but to no avail. He wanted to save his mother at any cost, but deep down he knew that his father was right after all he was the ship's doctor. Later his father told him that it took all his strength to hold him still. Jacob wasn't sure if he would ever forgive his father for restraining him. He understood years later that any action he or his father would have taken would have been futile, even in attempting to retrieve his mother's body. Her body was drifting away at an unrecoverable speed and in the opposite direction of the spacecraft's course. And none of the other SAMs had been primed for release from their storage bays to be of any assistance. For some reason, he still had not quite forgiven his father for that dreadful moment in his life.

So why was he hearing his mother's voice? He opened his eyes slightly, but saw nothing. He struggled but managed to open his eyes further, but he was in total darkness. Again, his mother voice came across.

"Jacob, this is your mom, you are waking up from a long, long sleep. But don't rush, take all the time you need."

Jacob was aware that his ears were actually hearing his mother's voice. Then, he remembered, it was a recording that his mother had made for him just for this occasion, waking up from a cryogenic sleep. It was not his mother's idea but his and she was more than willing to comply. They had recorded it prior to his mother's lethal spacewalk. Oh, how he loved his mother since she complied with most of his requests. He was beginning to be aware that his space hibernation was rather long, about 40 years if he had remembered correctly.

A very faint illumination began to appear in his cryogenic chamber. If hadn't been aware of his hibernation, he may have thought it was a sophisticated coffin in which he was buried alive. Worse than that, he became aware of fluid leaving his lungs and being replaced with oxygenated air. The natural reflex of coughing began to return to him, which had been inhibited over the years. Dramatically, his cryochamber opened and he was mechanically manipulated into sitting a position. Waves of coughing episodes came over him. It was unique experience to his conscious mind, but it felt oddly familiar. His father had told him that waking from cryogenic sleep, may trigger his subconscious memory in his birthing, which in many aspects was similar to the present.

He had instinctively had closed his eyes, when his chamber open. He struggled to open them. Mother's voice came over the speaker, "Relax and keep your eyes closed. You will be ready to open them in a few minutes. The illumination in the room will be very low, when you do. If you really need to do something, see if you can start moving your fingers and toes. But don't be disappointed if you can't feel them yet, it will take some time." Again, his mother's voice was soothing and relaxing.

Instead of trying to move his fingers and toes since at the moment he would be useless, he concentrated on his breathing. The episodes of coughing began to dissipate and his breathing became deeper and rhythmic. Even though, his mother was gone, her voice still had a calming effect on him. He started to relax and breathed deeply and evenly.

He let his mind wander, where was he? He realized that he was on the same spacecraft that has been his home his entire life. His spacecraft, SIL11 (Space Intelligence Locator), was one of 18 deep space missions to seek out sources of artificial radio waves, which promised the possibility of finding intelligent life. The SIL11 was rather a large vessel for its time, a little over a half a kilometer in length, it was designed for interstellar space travel and little else. The longtitudal axis was shaped as a long pencil with three anti-matter engines arranged as a triangle attached at the end. Large panels which were the crew's working and sleeping stations slowly turned slowly to create a very low gravity that could be adjusted up to normal earth gravity. One of those panels was a large dome-shaped arboretum.

4

What the crew found on their mission were remnants of an old civilization that had either left their dying planet, or was wiped out by some natural or unnatural force. Their mission had been a failure and the surviving crew were tucking their tails between their legs and heading for home, Earth. They didn't find any actual intelligent life but there were trillions of megabytes was left by a civilization that was yet been deciphered. In addition to the failure to the primary mission objective, there had been a horrific event that resulted in the massacre of six crew members and the destruction of the only shuttle craft available to the SIL11, all by a deranged fellow crew member, Tom. The psychotic break was totally unforeseen and from an unlikely source, Jessica's brother. It occurred when the last shuttle mission returned to the SIL11 from Leon's; planet. Of course, none of this would matter, if there was no home to go to.

His eyes slowly opened, viewing his dimmed but familiar cryogenic room. He was aghast at the size of his legs and arms. His appendages had dramatically shrunk and were a far cry from the limbs that he had remembered. When he went into hibernation, he had a robust physique with an Earth weight of 102 kilograms and had height of 185 centimeters. He knew his present weight was no more than 70 kilos, but he hoped that his height hadn't significantly changed. He knew he was in for few months of physical therapy to regain his former self before even attempting the full gravity pull of Earth. He looked at his toes and tried to move them. No luck there yet, then he tried his fingers. There was a small but perceptible movement of his index finger reaching for his thumb. Closing his eyes, and concentrating he again repeated the motion, this time he felt a light sensation on his thumb from his index finger briefly touching. Relief washed over him. He began moving other fingers and eventually his toes. Now his arms and legs were another matter. They felt like tons of liquid lead, he could move them but was unable to raise his arms and legs appreciably against the 0.3g artificial gravity. As his mother said, it will take time.

He continued working his muscles, which of course had atrophied over the long sleep. They were of course electro-stimulated while in hibernation, but that did not prevent the substantial loss of muscle mass. He again recollected his time on the spacecraft. He knew of no other home. He was born here, light years away from his parent's home. He knew every inch of the spacecraft and well trained on its functions. Crew of eight had left Earth; all but one of the initial crew had died while 5 out of 8 spacecraft birthed offspring was also returning to Earth. The one of the initial crew that survived was his father, who at 62 Earth years was the youngest of the initial crew. The rest of the crew was his twin sister, Sarah and two other women, Jessica and Christina. There was one other male crewmember and that was Todd, his sister's husband. All were in cryogenic sleep now. He had been appointed captain by the former captain, so it was his duty as captain to be awakened first. But over the weeks ahead, all would be awakened.

He feared for his father, with his advanced years will make it hard for him to awaken. Hell it was hard on anybody, but in truth his resuscitation may not be successful at all because of his advanced age. There was little data on the resuscitation of the elderly, so only time will tell. Despite not forgiving him for the loss of his mother, he still loved his father very much. He was the only university educated doctor on board, and carried out his medical duties with personal warmth and empathy. He had trained his sister, Sarah to take over medical duties if he had failed to resuscitate. He spent hours with Sarah, teaching her, there was a small pang of envy he recognized directed at Sarah. The jealousy was there but of no real importance, after all he was captain. He needed to rid his jealous feelings toward Sarah, since she was scheduled next to be awakened and he didn't want any petty feelings to create a wall between them.

Sarah was very intelligent woman, and passionate about her medical training. She knew by heart most the medical texts that were stored on their dad's computer and on the ship's library. Jacob was sure that she would handle this waking up business much more easily than he did. The science and medicines she knew backwards and forwards, but her intimate knowledge of people was another matter. It was a shame that dad's touch with patients had not rubbed off on her. Dad knew how to calm his patient's nerves, and to reassure them that he was on their side with whatever affliction affected them. Whereas, Sarah would tell you what's wrong, what's the best treatment and throw in the probability of success, but that's about it. She didn't appear to want to invest emotionally in her patients. To be fair, Dad had much more practice as a hospital intern, while Sarah has had little or no bedside experience. Besides, Dad was always around for the more serious injuries or afflictions. But Dad hadn't saved their mother or the captain's wife from pancreatic cancer. Sarah was not very emotional in other parts of her life as well. Though Todd was her husband, she seemed to show little affection to him or for him. There was no apparent playfulness in their relationship. It appeared to him that their marriage was only more or less a necessity to propagate their species, and not much else.

Todd, to his credit, was amazing with her. Always treated her well, and defended her when he knew that Sarah was at fault for one thing or another. Maybe, he felt lucky, since Sarah was smart, sexy and beautiful. But to Jacob's eyes, it was more than that; Todd did love his sister unselfishly and without any guarantees, bless his soul. Their relationship had great potential of his sister would open her eyes. Jacob did love her sister too, but he had rather not just let anyone know about it.

A platform with a container with a straw protruding from it was mechanically raised to his lips. He heard his mother's voice say, "Take some sips, my hero, but only very slowly. Again, take your time."

Jacob hadn't realized how thirsty he was until just then. His mother had impeccable timing; of course, the awaking procedure was fairly well defined and really had nothing to do with her. Jacob gave credit to her anyway.

"Thanks, Mom." He mumbled. His mumbling was so badly jumbled that his ears couldn't understand a word he said. He stretched his lips and began moving his tongue around. He didn't want to drown on his first swig. He sucked gently on the straw and refreshing liquid poured into his mouth. He had to consciously stop breathing and swallowed some the liquid down. The rest of liquid harmlessly drooled down this chin and neck. His next sip was more successful, and the one after with even more success. He had to resist the temptation to suck the container dry. The nourishing liquid was slightly sweet with a pleasant nutty taste.

Jacob took a few sips of the nourishing liquid, which was a sweetened almond drink. Something he chose before going into cryogenic sleep. He pressed a button near his right hand, and mechanical arms began to gently grab his arms and legs and slowly began to move them about in small circular motions. Again, there was a defined procedure for waking up his larger muscles. It felt rewarding and painful at the same time. He hit the button again for a brief pause, then again hitting the button for more stretching and exercising. He cycled through rests and exercises when his mother's voice interrupted. "Hey my hero listen to me, remember to take your time!" she said emphatically more so then anything she had said before

He'll do as she asked but at the same time Jacob reached out with his other hand, and turned off the speakers and mumbled again, "Thanks Mom!" That time, his ears had understood what he mumbled then he went back to his exercises.

Chapter 2 - The Twin

After a couple weeks of rehabilitation, Jacob could walk about slowly but more certainty and confidence then when he took his first few steps after waking. He felt like he was 1 year old again when he began his walking, taking his first baby steps again.

Jacob was able to eat and drink on regular basis. Even his plumbing, seemed to be ahead of schedule. He was back up to 85 kg and his mind began to clear. He almost achieved a regular schedule of waking and sleeping, but dreams occasionally haunted him, especially apparitions of former crew members, which resulted in some wakeful sleep periods.

It was now time to wake his twin sister, Sarah from her long cryogenic sleep. Each cryogenic tube was in a separate room, this was done to increase the probability of someone surviving an unforeseen event that may paralyze specific section of the ship. If all the cryogenic tubes were in one room, a single event could have wiped out everybody on board. Each cryogenic room was then converted to its occupant's quarters without much effort.

Jacob initiated the awaking procedure, and found a chair nearby to wait out the process. It took him hours for him to be fully conscious, exercising and taking in fluids, so he planned for the long haul with his sister.

Sarah heard her dad's voice, "Sweetheart, you are coming out of cryogenic stasis. Relax take your time."

Why didn't her dad just leave her alone! She was quite relaxed already and really didn't want to wake up. She let herself float back into unconsciousness, but again she heard her dad's voice calling out to her with the same message. She didn't understand why if she could take her time, why wasn't her dad not letting her fall back to sleep, for God's sake!

She knew she would eventually relent to her father. She loved him more than anything else in the universe. Again, her dad's voice repeated the same message. That was odd; he was very well-spoken with a great wealth of vocabulary, so he wouldn't keep repeating the same exact message. Some memory came back to her, this was an irritating recorded message, not her real father.

Her head appeared to be in the clouds flying above the ground. With the occasional cloud break, she saw some of her memories. Her mother left her when she was a teenager, dutifully doing her tasks outside the ship. But on one ill-fated day, her mother left her forever. Thank God, it was her mother and not her father. It was a terrible thing to admit to, but her father had been her world. She would have been lost and alone if it had been her father who had left her. She mourned for her mother as expected but not to the degree of her brother, who had been lost without her.

She was married with Todd, a handsome man in her eyes and the only choice she had for a mate. Besides, she wanted to show some superiority over Jessica and Christina by lassoing Todd in before Jessica or Christina had a chance. Sarah thought how awkward they now appeared, stumbling over each other to gain her brother's attention. Oh yeah, her brother, more than likely, had begun her waking up process and was probably waiting in the room with her. There had many deaths on this ill-fated mission. Her brother could have been one of its victims, but she hoped that she would hear his voice again.

She read all about the cryogenic processes in her father's books and the computer library. She studied the real-life process again with her own awakening. It was one thing to read it, but it was quite another to take part in the process. After all, it was her medical duty to awake all the others, except Jacob who probably was already awake. She wanted to know everything about the process she could possible know, before waking the others. So her brain was now in full analytical mode, no room for her personal feelings as of yet.

She batted her eyelashes, but could not see. That was predictable, since she knew her cryogenic room would be in total darkness, until at a certain point of the process. But what point in the process was she at? She should know the procedure better than this. But again, she reassured herself that her cognitive abilities would improve over time.

Her cyrotube opened and she was in the sitting position, as with Jacob she had spasms of coughing. She kept her eyes closed and starting testing her smaller muscles against the 0.3 g gravity.

"Hey sis," her brother's voice said, breaking the comforting silence. Relief did wash over her, knowing at least her brother was still alive.

Adding to noises, her father's voice piped in, "That's my girl, you are doing great!"

She mumbled something unintelligible just to let Jacob know that she had heard him. In response to her father's voice, she like her brother just turned off the speakers.

Jacob interceded jokingly, "Dad wouldn't like you turning him off like that."

She knew Jacob was attempting and failing in little humor. She just shook her head. She wasn't sure if she had much of a voice yet and didn't want to talk at that moment anyway. She concentrated on mechanical exercising arms, stretching and moving her legs and ignored Jacob. The plan was to awaken, Jessica and then Christina, the chief science officer and the ship's chief engineer next. But Sarah really wanted to wake up her dad and Todd, her husband, up next. She grinned to herself, on the possible facial reactions from both Jessica and Christina if she had done just that. But her straight-laced brother wouldn't allow it, nope, no way.

She received her drink of refreshing lemon water and began to open her eyes. She glanced over to where her brother was sitting. He had lost a lot of weight. His face was taut but had some color. He looked rather well considering sleeping for over 40 years. She looked down at her own legs and arms. She was skinny as a spider monkey; if she wasn't careful she felt that she could slip through some of the ship's small cracks and crevices. She had not really seen a spider monkey before but slowly remembered seeing various pictures of them in her books. It would take her a couple of weeks just to be barely functional, and about a month to be normal again. That was the problem with being cryogenic stasis for an extended period of time.

"How's the status of the ship?" she asked Jacob. She wasn't sure if she was at all understandable yet. But her brother piped up rather quickly, "All is nominal, there are a few glitches outside the craft but Christina will need to look into it when she is mobile."

Jacob knew he was in no shape to venture outside himself, and no desire to do so. He admired both Christina and his mother, the engineers, allowing themselves to drift around in empty space but he had no stomach for it himself. Sarah nodded as though she agreed with his assessment.

"So all ship's functions are normal, did you send a message to Earth yet?" she asked.

"Nope, not yet. I wanted some reinforcements with me before delivering our failure to the rest of humanity," he retorted, "besides we have tons of time for that, no use to rush bad news."

"Hey, we didn't fail! We retrieved immense amount of data from a civilization that did once live on that planet," she replied. Sarah startled herself at the strength of her voice and it caused another round of hacking and coughing.

Jacob smiled and said, "You will need to be able to wake up the rest, so take your time about getting around. I know you and there is not one ounce of laziness in you."

He paused and then continued, "Do, you need anything else from me?"

Sarah shook her head, so he got up and left the room.

She thought about asking Jacob about waking up Dad first, but she wasn't ready for that conversation. She was sure that Jacob would be a stickler to the agreement they all reached before they all went to sleep. But, the rest of them weren't awake; it was only her and her brother at present. She allowed time to get comfortable with her familiar surroundings, as the room lighter became brighter. She continued to work her smaller muscles and the machine to the rest. At this stage of waking, it was easy to daydream. She studied a light brown plague on her desk with gold lettering that ad had made for her. It stated:

Dr. Luther Wilson from the University of SIL11;
Bestows onto
Sarah Wilson,
diploma of Doctorate of Medicine.
with all the rights, privileges and honors herein.
Date: on Sarah's 21st birthday.
Signed: The SIL11 crew; Jacob, Todd, Jessica, Christina and Luther.

She grinned, it was pretty silly. It was not a legal document but it stirred her personal satisfaction on the labors of becoming a functional doctor. So, she prominently displayed it. There were books scattered throughout her cryogenic room, now her quarters, and shelves of hundreds of other books. Most of her and dad's medical texts were in the infirmary but of her dad's fictional books were here. Like her dad, she was a collector of books but unlike her dad, whom likes all kinds of books, she preferred classical and esoteric fiction, and children's books. There were also the required family pictures adorning the walls, mostly of her and her dad. It was a library room with little room for of any other decorum.

10

She was glad there were no immediate or urgent issues regarding the ship. They must have travelled unnoticed for these last 125 light years. Jacob seemed to be in no hurry in contacting Earth, despite beginning to travel through the solar system's outer limits, the Oort cloud. They were decelerating and at some point triggered Jacob's awakening. Jacob, her captain and her slow witted brother had the task of waking her up. If had been left with some of other crew members, she may have never been woken up. She was not particularly popular among the crew, but she intended to be most influential. Her father insisted that she should become a better team player for the crew in every possible way. She did relent to him to some extent, after all it was Dad and the team was a necessity, but all teams had all-stars and she was going to be one.

Chapter 3 - The Signal

Jessica called Christina on the headset, "Hey out there, any possibility of getting the Microarray Detector System checked out for damage?" "I know you'll be in the vicinity."

"Really? 500 meters is in the vicinity?" Christina retorted.

"Look Christina, I wouldn't ask if it wasn't important," said Jessica.

"Yeah, but so is this list from the captain, I believe he still outranks you."

"Yeah, but just barely," Jessica laughed. "Anyway, if you want, I can talk with the captain."

Christina grimaced. She didn't want her talking to the captain, but at the same time she didn't want Jessica get the idea that she could just boss her around any time that it suits her.

"I'll tell you what, Jessica, I have 2.5 hours of oxygen left in my spacesuit, if I have enough energy after this last task, I can give the Microarray a quick visual inspection. Anything more involved than that will have to come from the Captain."

"Understood, Christina, over and out," Jessica signed off.

Jessica was flabbergasted. According to the MDS (Microarray Detector System), the two planets, Juno and Hera were beginning to shrink at an alarming but differing rates! Both of these two planets were presently within 10 degrees of one another in relation to the sun, but still at least 200 million miles apart. These planets had been discovered rather late in human history. Juno was discovered sometime in 2020 or 2021 where part of its orbit encountered the Oort cloud, while Hera, discovered in 2045, which spent all its time within the Oort cloud.

"What the hell?" she mumbled to herself. There was no rationale, natural or unnatural for what she was seeing. She wanted to find out if the MDS was damaged, which would be the mostly likely explanation for the data she was receiving. At the present rate, both planets would be singularities by the time SIL11 neared Neptune's orbit. What was even more astounding was that two planets would suffer from the same phenomenon at the same time and their masses were also diminishing without some energy release. There was no energy being released from the planets that the MDS could pick up. She had to report this to captain and the entire crew of the findings, if the MDS was operating properly, but only after dismissing equipment failure as a cause.

She didn't mind immersing herself in all this data. It was a usable escape. All she wanted was to be was an effective and accepted crewmate. The latter was more difficult to attain than the former. She was marked of course, the outsider, and she harbored bad seed. Her brother had killed six members of the crew, after he suffered from some sort of psychotic break. Her brother in turned was killed by the previous captain. Most of the crew except Jacob and Luther looked at her with uncertainty and apprehension. She grieved for all of them, 4 of them were from the original crew, and two were offspring. Four of them belonged to a single family, two parents and two young brothers. The father and the young brothers were killed on board the SIL11 shuttle by her brother's hand. The former captain had finally stopped him by killing him, but it ended in costing him his life as well. Her mother could not bear it, and committed suicide several weeks after her brother's death. It was a horrid nightmare, she couldn't sleep for months after the massacre. She was utterly alone. There was no warning of her brother losing grip on reality. No one ever found out what set off her brother like that to go on to a killing rampage that including both a 12 and a 14 year old brothers.

She didn't know if the crew would ever forgive her for the crime of being related to this psycho killer. She herself wondered if she deserved any forgiveness. It was her brother after all maybe she too will have the same psychotic break, or have children that inherit the mental illness. Jacob did not look at her as an outsider though, but only a viable part of the crew, same as everyone else. It's possible that Jacob is using a façade to mask his mistrust for her, but he seemed totally genuine regarding trusting her. She needed that reassurance from her captain, to survive this mission. Luther was silently outraged at the attitudes of the crewmembers towards Jessica and went out of his way to comfort her. Luther reminded her of her own departed father, but she knew full well that he was not her father.

She even toyed with Jacob, trying to seduce him in front of the others, specifically Sarah and Christina. She was considered very sexy and seductive, perhaps not as beautiful as Sarah and not as cute as young Christina, but she definitely had her charms and she knew how to use them. It made the game more interesting when Sarah and Christina felt uncomfortable or down right angry, even though Jacob had turned down her advances.

As long as Jacob considered her part of the crew, the rest really didn't matter. She was toying with Jacob to laugh as Sarah's and Christina's displeasure. Maybe it will personify her a bit, even as an evil seductress, it was better than the bearer of bad seed or a possible psycho killer.

Currently, these observations from the MDS were all the distraction she needed.

"Jessica, the MDS appears nominal, no damage," Christina announced over the headset. "I'm coming in, better be ready for some explanation for trying to reprioritize my engineering schedule!"

"Sure, Chirstina, I can tell you about my observations but an explanation, well that's another matter, I'll explain when you come back in. Over and out."

Christina headed for the airlock. She checked her oxygen level, about 15 minutes left. She was pushing herself too much, cutting it too close and all that when she wasn't at her prime yet. Accidents happen that way. Damn that Jessica, checking the MDS had better had been important. She was tried, her body wasn't yet up to snuff for these long outside spacewalks. However, she was improving, she only had been outside for 1-2 weeks. The first outside trek lasted a fierce half hour but now 4 hours was normal, with oxygen only lasting 6 hours maximum, she was getting close to that maximum. Today was the day that she finally had reached that maximum, she was looking forward to a nice meal and long nap when she got back after speaking with Jessica. She didn't really look forward to speaking with Jessica however; she always was condescending to her. Both Jessica and Sarah considered themselves more intelligent than her. She considered both Jessica and Sarah, as prima donnas, each trying to outdo each other. Of course like most of the crew, she didn't trust Sarah and really didn't like Sarah, since she was just a royal bitch. She was the youngest of course, no use in denying that but she could kick both of their asses, even now with her skinny post-awakening legs. A few more days like today would bring her closer to her ideal shape, if didn't kill her first. She wondered if Jacob had noticed her improving shape.

13

She grinned to herself as she reached the door of the airlock, fantasizing about his different shapes in and out of his trousers.

"OK Jessica, what's up," asked Christina. She was tired and didn't want to trade salvos with Jessica right now.

"Thank you so much Christina for checking that out for me!" Jessica responded somewhat condescendingly. "But I think, we should discuss with the captain about doing a full-fledge diagnostic on the MDS. Maybe I'll hail the captain to come down here before discussing it."

"Look Jessica, I'm tired, tell me what you know. After all, repairs should be discussed with chief engineer first before involving the captain."

"Well, I was trying to estimate the local time here in our solar system, by looking at both Juno's and Hera's orbits and calculating the time from the last position when we had left the solar system. You know, it hard to gauge when travelling near light speed."

"Yes we all know that. Could you please get to the point!"

Jessica sighed and shrugged her shoulders. Jessica thought this woman, Christina, was sometimes quite impatient. "That's when my understanding of physical laws went out the window."

"What the hell you mean?" asked Christina.

"Well both Juno and Hera are both shrinking."

Christina went silent and looked quite perplexed.

"What do you mean by 'shrinking'?" Christina asked.

"Just that! The planets are shrinking in size and luminosity. But the 'shrinking' does not result in a concentration of mass, and there is no detectable energy release to compensate for this loss of mass. Considering the amount of mass being lost, it should exploding with energy."

"There goes another law of physics," Christina retorted, "How could that happen, science officer?"

Jessica was taken back. She didn't like labels for people, such as, "chief engineer" or "science officer", or "psycho". She gazed at Christina. Christina was physically spent, you could easily assess that by looking at her eyes and posture. Christina did nothing to hide it either. She decided to ignore the label and the imagined slap across her face.

"You know as well as I do, there is no rational explanation, natural or unnatural that would cause this. The most logical explanation is the MDS malfunctioning." She stopped and remained quiet, watching Christina think about what she had just said. Christina would most likely think that she was just crazy. If the shoes were reverse, she might think the same thing.

Christina looked up at Jessica's awaiting eyes. "Jessica, could you keep monitoring this 'event' to gain more data. I'll invite, Jacob, Sarah, Todd to a meeting with us to discuss after I have had meal and a sleep period. And I'll schedule a full diagnostic of the MDS regardless the outcome of the meeting. Could you ask Sarah to check your data, so that it can be confirmed before notifying the captain?"

Jessica grimaced, "Sarah? Couldn't you take a look at it?"

"Sorry, I'm spent. Sarah will be able to confirm your data, Right?"

Jessica frowned. "Yes, you're right. Go get some rest, Christina. Sarah should be able to help, if I can pull her away from her husband. You know reunions can take some time."

Christina smiled and went straight off down the corridor to the galley. Maybe she would accidently run into Jacob and start a reunion herself.

Jessica decided to put off hailing Sarah for now. As she said, reunions take time, and maybe Sarah would be in a less bitchy mood than normal if she had her fill of Todd. Todd had only been awaken for about a one week, but Sarah thought that he would be of some use in bed now with some coaxing. The last remaining crewmember to be revived later that month would be Luther, the last old timer. She liked Luther, maybe his experience and wisdom would help this young crew endure and face whatever challenges comes next, and put away their concerns about her and her sanity.

She returned to the computer screen, for the latest measurements of Juno and Hera. Hera still continuing to shrink as before, but Juno had rapidly reversed the pattern and began to increase in size. She must be going crazy, or somebody had a notorious sense of humor by trying to make her think she was going insane. She was NOT insane in the least, she decided.

Over the next couple of hours, Hera also reversed itself and began to expand and Juno was more than twice its original size. After its expansion of being 3-fold larger than the original Juno, it again reversed itself and began to shrink. When the two reached their original sizes, they both stopped shrinking or expanding and stabilized at their original sizes. Jessica continued to monitor them, and then decided to call Sarah.

Sarah had managed to revive most of the crew, and was enjoying fruit of her labors by spending a few luscious hours with Todd, alone and without distractions. She deserved it. Even though Todd wasn't totally his normal self, he was enough to quench some of her sex-starved urges, but definitely not all of them. That was before Jessica hailed her with a second urgent request. She ignored Jessica's first call, but it went against ship's protocol for not responding to a second urgent request. Maybe it was just Jessica's way to get her all riled up. Well, it was working, that damn bitch didn't know when it was better to leave her alone.

"Well, what is it, Jessica?" she growled into the computer's microphone.

"Sarah, we have a situation down here. I have been retrieving some very unusual data down here. I need the data verified, before we have an all-hands meeting with the captain regarding this situations. I'll explain once you get here."

"Is this some practical joke, is this just your way of getting me out of Todd's arms isn't it?"

"No, no joke. Christina is setting up the meeting for the awaken crew as we speak."

15

Sarah paused which created an uneasy silence between them. Did Jessica finally lose it? Did she have that psycho gene all along? Sarah didn't like her in the least; of course, Jessica knew that she didn't trust her.

Jessica responded again smugly, "If you think I'm nuts, come down armed or bring that husband of yours. He should be able to keep you safe!"

Damn her again, Christina thought. She was putting her on the spot. It would be interpreted as a failure on her part to cooperate with a functional crewmember because of *her* mistrust, therefore, *her* problem. Even though most of the crew did not trust Jessica, she would appear weak and mistrustful. She could not let that happen and allow Jacob to view this as her problem and not as Jessica's problem.

She replied calmly to Jessica, "Whatever gave you that idea? I'll be down in a few minutes." But before leaving, she told Todd that she would ping his communicator to let him know that she was OK within the next 10 minutes.

After hearing Jessica's crazy story, she needed to see the data for herself. She initially agreed with Jessica that it most likely scenario was the MDS malfunctioning. But in her experience, the easiest explanation is not always the right one. She felt somewhat stupid when she pinged her husband's communicator. She couldn't quite hide the communication totally, but Jessica ignored her and didn't comment. Jessica was quite infatuated with this phenomenon anyway, and probably thought Sarah's mannerisms were of no importance. These data seemed to come right out of a fairy tale, then halfway through the data, the fairy tale got even stranger.

"Sarah, the two planets are at it again. Look at the incoming data yourself, since you are here anyway."

Sarah studied the incoming data. This craziness must be contagious, she seeing the same thing as Jessica. Not just the same type of phenomenon, but exactly the same event. Both planets, Juno and Hero were shrinking fast again and with Juno shrinking faster than Hera. These were exact rates that Jessica had first observed. Exactly!!

"I feel like I'm Alice in Wonderland here, what is going on here, Jessica?"

"Beats me, but at least I'm not crazy, unless you are too!" she smiled at Sarah, which Sarah failed to return.

Before the all hands meeting got underway, both Sarah and Jessica had observed the complete same exact pattern of Juno's and Hera's size shrinking and expanding that Jessica previously observed. They continuously observed this phenomenon and recorded all aspects of the events.

They met in the galley so a scheduled meal would be available to any crewmember at that time. But nobody was eating, but some synthetic beer was being consumed. Jessica nor Christina drank, but Sarha was getting quite a belly full along with her brother. Todd would have normally joined in but he wasn't quite himself yet from the cryogenic sleep, and synthetic beer didn't have its normal appeal quite yet. He was supposed to be off duty now, getting some well-deserved shut eye. Sarah had been quite insatiable today which doubled his fatigue. He hoped he could manage to keep his eyes open.

Jacob spoke first. "OK, Christina was is this about?"

"Captain, I'll let Jessica explain, she was the one to first observe this phenomenon."

Jessica methodically went through the timelines of the different events from MDS and the corresponding measurements of mass and luminosity from the first sighting and the second. Sarah was simply nodding her head while Jessica was reporting.

"So captain, we thought the most likely explanation is a malfunction of the MDS."

"So sis, do you concur with Jessica about these occurrences?"

Sarah spoke up, "From the data Jessica gave to me and the data that I saw firsthand myself. Yes, the descriptions of the phenomenon are very accurate. But I don't know about the explanation, but I do see merit in eliminating any possibilities that we can."

Jacob turned to Christina, "I assume that you have already scheduled a full diagnostic for the MDS? How long it will take, Christina?"

Christina smiled, "Of course, captain, about 6 hours of spacewalking and 2 hours for collating the data. "

"Where are we on the other engineering assignments?" Jacob asked.

"Well, the priority list has been dealt with as best we can. There are no red flags at the moment. We do have some secondary tasks at hand, but we can postpone them for a day or two."

"Then start on the full diagnostic immediately." Jacob turned to the group rubbing his chin in deep thought and keeping his eyes lowered. "Good work everyone," he paused and then added, "But I tend to agree with my sis with this one and I'm sure that most of you as well. It is unlikely, that MDS malfunction would explain all the observations; however, I also doubt that laws of physics have been tampered with." He raised his head, "Jessica and Sarah, continue to monitor and record in detail these phenomenon and Jessica start looking into the reams of data that we had collected from our 'dead' civilization and see if the phenomenon is forging a pattern that may be recognizable in the other data set."

Jessica replied, "Why do you think the two would be connected?"

Jacob shrugged his shoulders, "No science, just a hunch."

Jacob paused for a moment, to ensure that all eyes were on him. "Best explanation is that our instrumentation and/or our own eyes are being manipulated somehow to produce this phenomenon, possibly some kind of signal. But I for one would like to know from where and from whom this signal is coming from. Maybe our 'dead' friends had also stumbled on such phenomenon before we did. It would be wise to check all possibilities."

Chapter 4 - Luther

Luther was beginning to feel a little like himself. Of course, he knew the effects of cryogenics would be exaggerated on older individuals, but 62 years of age wasn't that old but right at this very moment, he felt like 100 plus. It has been a month since his dramatic "come back from the dead" act. He still hadn't been much use to anybody, his children, Jacob and Sarah were glad to have him back, but the rest of crew, looked at him as a historic relic, interesting but one who took up too much space and was an added drain on their resources. So far, he had to agree with them, he had been no use to anybody.

Sarah, his attentive daughter had visited him every day. She filled him in on their astonishing discovery of using planetary bodies as a way to communicate. The phenomenon occurred over several hours, then a pause for a couple of more hours after the planetary bodies returned to their original size and luminosity. This exact cycle was repeated. Then a new series of planetary gymnastics occurred which as before was followed by a brief pause, and then again, the new series was repeated exactly. Each of these series represented some alien "alphabet" or "phrase." Jessica had training in linguistics was working feverishly on the alien alphabet but as of yet had not broken the code. She felt with more "alphabet" coming in, she should be able to draw some basic conclusions regarding their language. But no alien language is easily decipherable. Most languages on Earth of course are much easier to interpret since they all draw from the same references; i.e. mother, family, sun, moon, water, walk, eat, sleep, etc. But this new alien language did not have any of those common references.

The original plan was for Jessica and her team to decipher any language spoken by the aliens they were visiting if possible, whom lived at the source of the radiowaves. If the civilization no longer existed, to decipher what they could retrieve from the source after coming out of their deep sleep. Our course, there were two problems with that plan; one Jessica did not have a team because of Jessica's brother and there was another competing more compelling communication that needed deciphering. The entire crew now believed that the planetary phenomenon was a means of communication, which was first suggested by his son. His son gave this communication high priority since it was current and directed at them, and the crew believed in him.

Luther thought Jacob was a little hard on Jessica, assigning her both the linguistics of the "dead" civilization and the new "planetary gymnastics" languages. Sarah was spending time with Jessica and was trying to assist where she could. But she was not a linguist at all; she was terrible at learning any simple foreign language such as French, Spanish or German. Math and science were in her genes, not linguistics. On the other hand, he might be able to assist. He was fluid in 3 other European languages other than English. But learning new languages was easiest for the young, where their brains are more pliable and acted like sponges rather than his current concrete brain. But his experience may help him overcome some of this age disability. At least, it was some possible way to become useful.

Sarah was becoming a better doctor now, then before they went into hibernation. She was listening to his complaints entirely now, demonstrating patience where she lacked before and adequately suggesting not demanding specific therapies for him, whether it was pharmaceuticals or physical therapy. The crew was in good physical condition, which could be attributed somewhat to Sarah's medical practice. But she was not a psychologist or psychiatrist and neither was he, and the psychological effects of the crew's massacre must have weighed heavily on the shoulders of the surviving crew. Nobody addressed it, or even acknowledged potential effects on the crew's mental health. It was a small infection with all the potential signs for spreading systemically. Luther was most concerned with Jessica. It was quite apparent that Jessica was drowning herself in her work, either to eliminate the great guilt she may have felt for her brother's horrendous act, or disengage from the rest of the crew as much as possible, since most of the crew still didn't trust her, especially his own daughter.

The twins had done well for themselves, a captain and doctor. If had not lived another day, he would have been pleased in what they had been accomplished. Yet, even now, he mourned. His dead wife was floating in different part of the galaxy, lights years away. He wondered whether she would be ever recovered by an alien spacecraft and she would still be influencing others. She was the rock of the family; Luther attributed most of the twin's accomplishments by inheriting her determination and willpower. She had been the center of his universe for so many years. So what's next for him, he wondered.

Luther began his morning exercises. The twins were coming down to see him and he didn't want to appear idle. His morning exercises; include working his upper body and then some swimming or cycling after an hour break. He was lifting rather light free weights of 10 and 5 kg weights and tried to slowly gain in the number of repetitions. Sadly, he was only up to 10 repetitions for most his exercises.

"Dad, Jacob is here with me. We are just outside your doors, can we come in?" Sarah announced over the intercom.

"Of course." He responded. At least he had worked up a little sweat before his children came in.

He smiled at his twins. An unshielded glimmer of pride broadened his smile. "What can I do for the two of you?"

Jacob laughed. "What do you mean what you can do for us, it's more like what can we do for you?'

Sarah interjected, "Yeah, remember you're the patient right now."

"Sarah, you know better than most, doctors are the worse patients. It would be better if you didn't treat me like patient any longer. But I do admire persistence." Luther responded. "Anyway, I feel fine and I'm starting to get my strength back."

"Dad, how well are you eating and sleeping?

"If you must know, Sarah, I'm beginning to eat rather well and will be putting some pressure soon on those stores of food on board."

"I doubt that. You didn't answer the second question though. Sleeping?"

"Sarah how much sleep do you think I need. I slept for years already, don't think I need a lot of it right now, especially since I'm not busy," Luther responded and smiled back at the Sarah. He lied of course, nightmares of the crew massacre haunted still him more often than not.

"Dad, it's great to have you back!" Sarah said affectionately.

Jacob went to his bed and sat on it, then turned to his father. "Are you ready to begin duties?" he said somewhat coldly.

Luther looked at his son and began stretching by grabbing his right elbow and pulling it to his left. He smiled and said, "Yes, captain. I'm ready"

"Jacob what is wrong with you! He is recovering from a major trauma. He doesn't need your duties quite yet except to get healthy. Dad go over to your chair we will go over your exercise routines, I would like to add some new ones in the afternoon session."

"Sarah, stop babying Dad! We are badly short of personnel and he needs to begin to do his part," Jacob said firmly.

Sarah just glared at her brother and she thought about arranging some of his teeth on that pretty face of his. Jacob turned to her sister with unwavering eyes, steady and penetrating. Jacob knew he was not backing down to his sister and definitely not in front of Dad. Luther chuckled to himself; some things don't ever change even if space and time does. He didn't want to damper this family reunion, so he gently put his hand on Sarah's shoulder.

"It's OK Sarah. I want to pitch in!"

Sarah just continued to glare at Jacob. "You bonehead, this is our Dad!"

Jacob smiled faintly and said rather nonchalantly to Sarah but quietly, "Doctor, you're dismissed."

Sarah huffed and stormed out of Dad's quarters, never taking her eyes off her brother. "You'll regret that!" she murmured and slammed the door shut.

Luther turned towards his son. "You know you could have handled that a little better, I would think. She always has been quite emotional when she doesn't get her way. Anyway, I do agree with you. What did you have in mind?"

Jacob turned to look at some of father's relics sitting on his desk, a couple of leather bound books, a clock that actually need to be "wound" up, whatever that meant, and an actual still photo of his mother in some kind of glass display case. But his eyes were far away as he sat examining the pieces. Luther could tell that his son wanted to tell him something, but he did not quite know how.

"Dad, I just wanted Sarah out of the room. I'll take whatever she plans for me."

He paused and then looked straight into his dad's blue eyes, "We are not getting any signals from Earth. None whatsoever! Dad, have we come back from one 'dead' civilization to another?"

Chapter 5 - The Silent Planet

Luther pondered on the news from his son about recent events. Their discussions ranged from his news of Earth to his new duties on board, which concluded in little over an hour. Jacob did ask him not to disclose what he found so far to the crew, until he could confirm his findings. He protested that the crew had a right to know the current situation with Earth. Earth at the time of launch would have had a plethora of radio transmissions streaming into space. Now, Jacob could only measure slightly higher transmissions than background. They were nearly at Neptune's orbit and they should have been able to pick up those radio transmissions from Earth. The SIL program had been set up so that returning SIL spacecraft could pick up a clear signal from the SIL command center for the program anywhere near Saturn's orbit. The command center's signal would be coming from the Moon, in an effort to isolate the signal better from noisy Earth for the SIL vessels to receive, at least, that was the plan when they left, a few centuries ago. But according to his son, the moon was also silent.

There were other explanations for the silence since they had been away for centuries. A new technology could have been discovered which made radio signals obsolete. Or they were threatened by a hostile alien species, and invoked radio silence to hide their existence. But in Jacob's mind the most likely explanation was still that the human civilization had not survived. It may be the most likely explanation but Luther didn't want to believe it as quickly as his son had. He was by no means ready to give up on the human race.

His son wanted to keep the crew busy on various projects and felt that the planet gymnastics phenomenon was a good distraction. Christina had confirmed that the MDS was working nominally. She did replace a few damaged components, but the array was 97% intact and functional. She continued her assessment of any damage the ship may have incurred while they were in cryogenic sleep and made any necessary minor repairs. Jessica was working on the "language" that the planets were speaking and had informed everyone that she had made some headway. Sarah who was assisting her was even more optimistic that they would have a breakthrough in the next couple of weeks and thought Jessica was being modest about their progress.

Jessica may have been modest about their progress. But she wasn't necessarily modest in other respects. She dressed provocatively with very short skirts showing off her skinny and beautiful legs and kept her blouse unbuttoned to expose some remarkable cleavage. There was no dress code aboard and even if there was it was doubtful that any the crew would adhere to it. Even though she didn't outright boast about her intellectual abilities to go along with her impressive looks, she quietly demonstrated her intellectual superiority to impress the crew. When she had an opportunity to be with Jacob alone, it was all Jacob could do; not to plush, get nervous or just run away. Jessica loved teasing Luther's son. He had better watch out for her before he was putty in her hands.

Jacob did agree with Luther about the need for his assistance with the decoding of the alien data from the "dead" civilization. But Jacob wanted Luther to assist Todd first. Todd had been assigned agriculture duties in their modest but functional arboretum on board the spacecraft. Todd even in his own admission wasn't the brightest among the crew, but he was quite strong and liked working with his hands, when they weren't on his daughter. Luther didn't precisely know what Sarah had seen in Todd, but Sarah did not have a choice for mates, so they got married. He was no pretty boy by his assessment but he was tall, strong and quiet. Sarah probably liked this last attribute the most. He didn't complain and she never got any grief from him when she wanted something. And Sarah always wanted something. Todd was having some difficulties with equipment for the artificial sunlight and the irrigation system. Jacob had told him, they needed to start growing their own food as soon as possible especially if Earth was not an agricultural paradise any longer. It would be good to get out of his quarters and be somewhere not so enclosed. The arboretum was small, but it was still about 10 acres in size which did make it overwhelmingly the largest single working section on board the SIl11. Jacob had told him that initially he wanted him to assist in its repairs and decide on the most appropriate crops to grow, while Todd did the physical labor. But Luther knew he would need some physical strength more than he had now, so he picked up his weights and began his now late morning exercise routine.

His intercom broke the silence when he finishing his last routine, "Dad, can I talk with you?"

It was Sarah of course. He should have expected her coming back.

"Sure come in Sarah, but your dad is a bit smelly right now."

Sarah didn't hesitate and entered her dad's room. "How were your exercises?" she asked smiling.

"Not bad, what can I do for you?"

"Have you been working out all this time? I think that is too much right now. And don't listen Jacob, you shouldn't be working yet. He might be captain but I'm the chief medical officer and I don't think you are ready."

"Listen Sarah, I need to work. I want to contribute to our crew. Besides, Jacob has asked me to assist Todd in growing some food. It would be nice to get to know my son-in-law better, don't you think."

"What the hell is Jacob thinking!!" Sarah lashed out. "You are not able to do that type of physical labor as of yet!"

"Sarah, you got it wrong. He only wants me to help fix the equipment and plan for the crops. He wants Todd for all the physical activities."

"Todd is more than capable of growing some simple plants," she exclaimed.

"Look Sarah, Jacob must have his reasons. He is the captain and I'm part of the crew. I have to follow orders and do my duty. Please do not interfere by telling Jacob that you decided that I'm unfit for duty, young lady!"

Sarah became quite and withdrew. Her father had raised his voice to her in disagreement, which was a rarity. She had a slight pang of regret that she had unintentionally challenged his pride. She needed to let her father know that her anger was not targeted at him but to that brother of hers. Besides, she had not come to discuss his fitness for duty.

"Sorry dad. I won't dream of challenging your abilities to do your duties, if that is something you want to do," she meekly answered. She paused and brought up her finger to her lips, tapping them absent mindedly. "I know you haven't exercising all this time, what did you discuss with Jacob?"

Luther looked at her daughter. Ah, the real reason she had come to his quarters. He had to be careful not to let anything slip since it was captain's orders regarding the secrecy of Jacob's findings.

"As I said, we discussed what my duties are. He wants some food growing soon and Todd by himself is struggling a bit."

Sarah sighed, "Yeah, we all have too much to do. Jacob is putting a lot of pressure on the crew, to get things done. He had also asked Jessica to look into some data files from our mission as well as decoding that Jessica and I doing. But to be honest, she hasn't looked at those older data files. I know since I spend most of my time with her. So why is it that you get to spend time with Todd and not me!"

"Come on, Sarah. If you and Todd were together, neither one of you would get a lot of work done. Besides, you brains are needed elsewhere."

Sarah smiled. "So, what else did you discuss with Jacob? And why is growing crops so urgent all of sudden.

Her father answered, "You will need to speak with Jacob about the second question." He paused and stretched out his arms, then looked back at his daughter.

"Can't I just speak with my son? I wanted to know how he was holding up with command duties. And we briefly spoke about your mother," Luther lied. He hated lying to his daughter but sometimes she would not give in.

Sarah looked his father. He was hiding something, but she knew he had already made his mind about not sharing any further information.

"OK dad," she responded and started for the door.

Luther spoke out, "Hey Sarah, weren't you going to introduce me to some new routines for my afternoon exercises?"

She turned and smiled at her father. "OK, dad, no problem." And she came back sat next to him. "Let's get started."

Chapter 6 - The Warning

"We agree then?" Sarah asked Jessica.

They had been reviewing all the data from MDS regarding Juno and Hera which had accumulated over the last several months. There were several Personal Computing Devices (PCDs) that lay on the large table in the science lab. Sarah had several old fashion notebooks with ball points that were laid out as well which she had been writing notes, an old habit she learned from her dad. Jessica stuck with her PCDs as would most people. Even though the message was not entirely understood, its basic message had been translated. Jessica was thinking to herself that maybe they should have more clarification on the entire message before telling the crew. Of course, Sarah disagreed. The message importance was too high to wait for further clarification which may never come. Both Juno and Hera had returned to their normal size and luminosity with no more "planetary gymnastics" occurring, the message had ended. Without any more signals, it may not be possible to clarify the message anymore.

"OK, Sarah, on one condition, that either you or I speak with captain first to let him in on it before telling the rest of crew."

"You go ahead and tell him. It's most of your work anyway and my brother and I are not really on the best speaking terms right now."

Jessica looked perplexed. Sarah really didn't like the crew going to her brother unless she or her dad was involved. Jessica knew that Sarah had control issues regarding her family, which was unfortunate since it elevated her to be a royal pain in the ass.

Jessica grabbed one of her PCDs and turned towards the door. "Sarah, if you don't mind, could you schedule a crew meeting in the next day or two. I'm going to speak with the captain after a shower and quick nap."

"Not a problem," was Sarah quick response. Jessica then left the science lab.

Jacob initiated his daily exercises by lifting his routine weights. He was gratified to see improvement in his muscle mass and tone since he had been awaked. But exercising was more than that to him, it was his escape from the all the problems and trials that his command put him through. He turned down lights and put on some classical music. The weights gave him just the right amount of discomfort to not entirely focus on SIL mission but not enough discomfort to not allow his mind to wander too far. Sweat had begun to bead on his skin and glisten in the dull light when the intercom interrupted him.

"Captain, this is Jessica may I speak with you?"

Jacob wished he had the luxury to put on a "Do Not Disturb" sign on his monitor just outside his door like to the rest of crew. The crew was allowed to isolate themselves mostly for sleep periods or personal time and would only be disturbed if there was an emergency. Everyone respected those signs since everyone wanted undisturbed sleep or uninterrupted personal time. But he was the captain and he had chosen no such luxury. Yes, at times, he regretted his decision but it was not in the best interests of the crew, the ship or the mission to have chosen otherwise. He wasn't really ready to receive Jessica, he needed a shower.

"Can this wait?" he asked Jessica.

"Captain, yes it can wait. But I really think you would want to know this ASAP."

"What is it?"

"We have decoded the signal and the message therein."

Jacob immediately opened his door and allowed Jessica to enter.

Jessica at times dressed very provocatively and this occasion was no different. She wore a skirt that was a bit longer than her typical short skirts but it had slit on the left side that went up nearly to her waist. She was wearing a white blouse that was tied in knot below her firm breasts that exposed her flat stomach and her pierced belly button. She was of Asian descent with slightly tan legs and breasts. She had large, beautiful and knowing eyes. There was little doubt there was a formidable intellect behind those eyes and they were not to be taken lightly. Jacob was unknowingly scanning her body when she spoke up smiling, watching him. Jessica had gotten the reaction she was hoping for. "Captain?"

Jacob pushed his hand through his hair. He couldn't allow Jessica distract him. "What is it Jessica?"

"Captain," she said with a knowing smile, "Your sister and I have decoded the signal and it does give a definite message. I don't know all the details of the entire message and some of it, we may never understand."

"Yes, yes, Jessica. I understand but you seem certain about the core message?" Jacob thought that Jessica was way too conservative on some things especially when it was about her work, but other things she was just the opposite.

"Yes, captain."

"Well, what is it?" said Jacob impatiently.

Jessica gave a brief sigh. Her eyes had not moved from watching Jacob's sweating body. She much admired the muscle tone in those arms and shoulders. Sex was not discouraged on board when actually it was encouraged in order to propagate their species but opportunities for her had been rare despite her charms. Jacob would be a very suitable and delicious partner. She smiled slightly.

"Captain, the message is simple and it says, 'Do not go home, there is a trap awaiting you.'"

Jacob forehead creased. He reached for small towel and began wiping away some his sweat. He was quiet for a moment.

"It there anything else to the message, Jessica?"

She went to his bed, where he was sitting and sat next to him. Not just next to him but very close to him. If she was any closer, she would be in his lap. Jessica would have preferred that and she was beginning to think how restrictive her clothes were making her feel.

Softly she whispered. "Yes captain, they also congratulated us on discovering the signal and deciphering it, it seemed that they were encouraged by it, like a parent encouraging a child to talk or walk. It is somewhat condescending, but I don't think that was their intent."

She paused and took the towel from Jacob to wipe the sweat from his forehead and face.

She added, "The message also attempted to describe who and what they are and where they come from. But the message started to be very confusing and my lack of understanding of the language prevented me to clarify it."

He finally looked up to her eyes. She hoped that he wouldn't get up abruptly and walk away, she was enjoying being close to him.

"OK, Jessica," He said softly looking into her hypnotic eyes and then down to her moisten lips, "What is your best guess on who they are and where are they from?"

She bit her lip and looked deeply into his eyes.

"They call themselves the 'Dimensionless Ones' or another possible interpretation 'our guardian angels,' or other numerous interpretations. It is obvious they are a highly advance race but they really don't seem to restricted by time or space, as though it doesn't exist for them or it is of no consequence or barrier for them. But I could be way off base in my interpretation. Maybe they saying 'they would like popcorn with the movie.'"

"Nonsense Jessica, I   yes, I trust your interpretation. But…" he said with a bit of a stutter as he looked down to the rest of her. She was very inviting. He thought to himself that he hasn't had sex since he had awoken and his body was crying out for relief. "But…damn I don't trust the rest of you." He grabbed her head and pulled her to him with his lips pressing hard on her wet inviting lips. She instinctively allowed her tongue to lightly touch his. His hands reached under her skirt to pull down her panties, but of course, she wasn't wearing any. He slide his fingers between her legs and with his other hand tugging at the knot of her blouse, which easily came undone since her blouse's buttons were unbuttoned. She arched her back and and smiled at him invitingly. She reached up smiling stroking Jacob's chest gently and slowly. Jacob had one last thought before engaging with her, 'I'm going to regret this.' All Jessica thought was, 'This is going to be so delicious!'

When they had exhausted themselves, she promptly got up and dressed. This time she buttoned her blouse and tucked it in her skirt. She also zipped up the slit that was part of her skirt. She looked at him and smiled, "Core message was no doubt a warning. What do you make of it, captain?"

He became aware that he was naked and reached for his underwear and shorts. "It is quite apparent that they are advanced but the real question was, were they benevolent or otherwise?"

"Captain, your sister is setting up a meeting to discuss this finding to discuss with the whole crew, as I briefed you, so we can discuss possible interpretations then, don't you agree?"

Neither Jessica nor Jacob wanted to discuss what happened between them over the last few minutes. It seemed they understood that the encounter was energetic and exhilarating but was strictly physical with no lasting emotional ties.

"Jessica, I would prefer if nobody knew about the details of our meeting."

She smiled, "Of course captain," as she started for the door. "Your sister already knew I was coming to see you of course, she may want to know more."

"Jessica, you can leave out any specific details. Don't you agree?"

"Yes, Captain." She smiled mockingly at him, then turned and left.

***

Both Jessica and Christina were waiting in the mess hall for everyone to show up for the crew meeting that Sarah had called. An uneasy silence wavered in the room as neither chose to start a conversation with the other. Jessica was going over points she wished to discuss with the group on her PCD, while Christina was checking ship's logs on her space excursions in the past couple of weeks.

Christina knew that the crew in general was shorthanded and overworked but she felt it even more so for herself than anyone else. Not even Jacob's mother had put the number of spacewalking hours in as she had in the last 3 months. She was disappointed that the captain had not assigned Luther to her. But she understood that Luther was not physically adept presently to attempt any spacewalking, but she could really use another pair of hands outside the ship, human hands that is. The two remaining SAMs were helpful and were being used at their full capacity but they were brainless and needed specific instructions at every turn. Besides, she spent too much time out there, when all she wanted was to be near the captain. He was always kind and understanding with her. She wished at times that he wasn't so gentle with her, and would be playfully rough, yeah even some rough sex with him would be welcomed. He took notice of her of course, but here with Jessica, she was like a small candle trying to pry his attention away from a lighthouse. Christina dressed a little more flamboyantly than usual. She put on a light blue wrap that exposed her bare white shoulders. She had small breasts, so no use in drawing his attention to them. She wore very tight jeans that accented her fine figure. She was short with Jessica towering over her, so Jessica's figure dwarfed hers. She cleansed her smooth face and had put makeup on, not a lot just a little. Her curly red hair was short but skillfully arranged in stark contrast to Jessica's long sleek straight black hair. Christina knew nobody was probably better fit than her. Spacewalking was demanding physically despite being zero gravity. Jessica probably assumes there was an underlying competition between herself and Jessica for the captain's attention. And she knew that the meeting was another spotlight for Jessica in obtaining his attention. There were rumors that Jessica and Sarah had decoded Juno's and Hera's signal. Christina hoped she would soon get her opportunity to attract some his attention.

"Hello ladies," Luther said as he entered the mess hall. Both women turned to him, but Jessica spoke first giving him a playful smile and said, "Well doctor, you are starting to look good, a little spring in your step and color in your face. You look wonderful."

Luther responded smiling, "I'm sure you tell all the gentlemen on board that."

27

Luther then turned to Christina, "How you doing?"

Christina responded, "I have the entire outside surface of SIL11 memorized. And most of dreams seemed to be about normal human activities in zero gravity."

"And which 'human activities' are you referring to?" Luther murmured with emphasis on 'activities'.

Christina blushed but playfully said, "Wouldn't you like to know, you are dirty old man, quite different from your son."

Both Luther and Jessica gave a short laugh. Then Todd and Sarah entered the hall.

"What's so funny?" Sarah asked.

Luther responded, "Oh we were discussing Christina's activities outside the ship." All three, Jessica, Christina and Luther knowingly smiled at each other. Luther looked at Todd and asked, "I guess we are going to be working together," changing the subject.

Todd glanced his way and mumbled, "I guess so. The help would be welcomed." Silence followed, Todd had nothing further to add. Todd was not much of conversationalist and Luther wondered what kind of company he will be when they would be working together. Luther had never had too much opportunity to interact with Todd before this opportunity. Luther was hopeful he could draw more out of him when they work together. Perhaps, Sarah presence hindered him in spontaneously interacting.

Jacob strolled into the hall carrying his PCD.

"Hello everyone, sorry I'm late," Jacob said and then added, "Jessica the floor is yours, if you would please tell everyone about the message."

Jessica reiterated everything that was discussed with the captain the day before, adding some details here and there. She concluding with, "I couldn't have done this alone, Sarah has been a big help in organizing the signals and assisting in developing a language for the Dimensionless Ones."

Sarah nodded towards Jessica in acknowledging her expressed gratitude. Everyone else was motionless with no expression on their faces, more stunned than anything else.

Luther rubbed his chin and finally broke the silence, "Let me get this straight, the signal from the gymnastics with the planets was a message, and this message was a warning directed towards us specifically."

"Yes, dad," Sarah responded. Jacob interjected, "We do not know for certain if these Dimensionless Ones are benevolent or hostile themselves."

"Captain," Sarah started with a strong emphasis on the word 'captain' which everyone noticed. "Why would they want to warn us if they were hostile?"

"Perhaps, they are attempting to deceive us," Jacob added.

Luther spoke out, "Son, is there something else, we, your crew, should know?"

Jacob jerked up and directed his stare at his father. Dad promised me his secrecy if I confided in him, he thought. Dad was good at keeping secrets but he hated doing it, maybe this is his way of letting me know that he didn't want to keep his secret anymore. He pursed his lips perhaps it is best to tell the crew about his findings, besides his father had opened an aromatic flower that could not be hidden, since its pungent scent was going to everywhere and now to everyone.

"Yes, there is," Jacob began. "Since the MDS was operating nominally now after Christina's complete diagnostics and since the Juno and Hera had ceased their so-called transmissions, I directed the MDS to our home. I know we are too far out for timely verbal transmissions but I was just curious about its noise level." He paused and scanned the faces of his crew, it was his signature for insuring everybody's attention. "I'm afraid I don't detect any radio transmissions from there, yes our Terra system, both the Earth and Moon are quite silent."

Todd spoke right out, "What do you mean 'silent'?"

Jacob responded, "Our earth has been a hot bed of radio transmissions for a couple of hundred years prior to our departure. But as of now, it is not transmitting."

The remainder of the crew knew the implications of these findings. Nobody else spoke out, mostly stared at their hands and then glanced at the faces of their fellow crewmembers. Sarah stood up and started to leave, she had streams of tears coming down her face.

Luther reached out to grab his daughter's hand. "Please stay," is all he said as he looked into her face. She seated herself to her father and began to cry uncontrollably. The rest of the crew was somber with most having moist eyes of their own.

Jessica struggled to remain calm but said in a low voice, "There could be other explanations than the one everyone is thinking."

Luther said, "I agree. I don't think everyone should jump to the conclusion that our civilization is no longer there."

Christina didn't know what to think. She wanted to leave to ponder on all this new information. At least, Jessica is not leaving with the spotlight on her. The entire crew seemed confused and lost. Jacob adjourned the meeting and the crew agreed to reconvene in a couple of days.

***

Christina took the long way back to her quarters. She stopped at the portholes along the way to look at the vastness of space. Even though, she was constantly outside the spacecraft, she never got tired of the stellar view. Besides, when she was working, most of her attention was given to her tasks without too much awarding herself by scanning the star-filled skies. She reflected on the news she had received at the meeting. It was overwhelming at first, but as with all tasks, you ask yourself what's important and started out with some simple basic steps. The crew had to decide if they were going to trust the message they had received from the Dimensionless Ones or not. If the crew did not trust the message, then they should proceed with caution directly to Earth and see what has happened to their home planet. If you did trust the message, maybe you stayed away from Earth directly but combed the rest of the solar system for clues of what may have happened to their home. When they had left Earth, there was not only small colony on the Moon but one on Mars as well. Industrial conglomerates were investigating the possibility of mining the asteroid belt and Corporate became an entity on Earth.

Corporations had become the most influential entities on Earth. History tells us that nations or countries were at one time, lead the world, Christina thought, but it was now industrial giants. It did bring in a period of peace and prosperity where incessant wars had finally ended. Wars were not profitable and were a waste of resources. But, people had lost their individuality. It was a type of enslavement where only corporations ruled the world, and individuality was ignored.

Corporations had come to realize to keep profitable and sustainable, that their shortsightedness on resources needed to be replaced with long term plans. They collaboratively formed a research group called Corporate and started to pay attention to the environment and even attempted to heal the Earth where needed. But during their cooperative research, they discovered that Earth, not matter what actions they took, was a finite home and someday Earth would not be able to sustain human life, at least not at capacity it was at presently. So, Corporate decide that a new home was needed and looked to the stars for answers. It was known that there were sources of artificial radio transmissions, difficult to discern but advances in radioastronomy had allowed them to identify many of these sources. These artificial radio sources may be the clue of advanced civilizations which may also have realized that their home planet was not going to be forever. So the SIL missions were planned rather hastily. It was not known when Earth would begin to show its inability to sustain the human species but some scientists believe those signs were already present. Some scientific clues suggested that the end will be much more sooner than later. In addition, they had to overcome a major hurdles, the vastness of space and physical laws that pertain to space travel.

With cooperation between corporations, technology advanced at a much accelerated pace. Even though, the speed of light itself was a limit, technologies did begin to rise that would allow spacecraft to attain velocities between 0.9 and 0.97 that of light speed. Of course, it took years to attain such speeds as well as years to slow down from them. Years before Jacob had been awakened; the SIL11 had already begun its deceleration. It was planned that the planet Saturn was going to be used to brake the SIL11 and slingshot it to Earth. If they were going to take a chance on the Dimensionless Ones, they would have to modify their flight plan. Jupiter was on the opposite side of the solar system, so for braking they would need to use a different gas giant, Uranus perhaps, but would make the trip considerably longer.

Christina believed in the Dimensionless Ones. A species that could not only fool humans but manipulate equipment the way they did and at a vast distance could easily choose other ways of causing harm to them. But they wanted to warn them discretely and took great stride to do so. It possible that these manipulations and mass hypnosis were minor tasks to them, like a child grapping a balloon string and then changing the balloon's position. It did bring up another interesting question, was who were we being warned about? The Dimensionless Ones had failed to reveal that in their message.

Her quarters were the last quarters nearest the engine compartment with the airlocks hatches for her routine spacewalking as well as the hive of SAMs on the other. She was passing this hive on her way to her quarters, when Jacob whispered at her back, "Christina?"

Christina stopped and quickly turned. Christina licked her lips in anticipation; the captain along with the rest of the crew was rarely down in this part of the ship. She was very aware of the fact that they were finally alone together.

"I was getting concerned about you. You took your time getting back," Jacob said.

"Don't worry about me Captain. I like to walk when I think. And there was a lot to think about after that meeting," Christina replied.

"Would you like to come to my quarters? We are almost there." Christina added with hope. She was being much more forward than usual with the captain, but opportunities were rare for her.

"Yes, there is a lot to think about. Yes, I'll come in for a bit."

"Splendid," she said and lead him to her quarters. Her quarters were almost as large as his. But hers was mostly taken up by her massive bed, where numerous pillows laid haplessly about. She had fragranced silk sheets, a bright chandelier and fan above her bed. There was a small desk and chair from her dad, and an old style dresser from her mother, but there was not much else in the room. She did have small bathroom and large closet on one side of the room, as did everyone else's room. She went in and purposefully blocked his path to the desk and chair. He looked around and sat on the edge of the bed.

Christina smiled mischievously, "Now captain, what can I do for you?"

Jacob noticed her smile and this is not what he had intended. He really wanted to talk to her about the meeting, and get her views before they were polluted by others. He admired her ideas and thoughts for their insightfulness, singularity and simplified approaches; but others so easily corrupted them before she would voice them especially by the time they got to him. He had grown up with her and knew she had great insight but she was too easily coerced by others. He wanted her ideas in the raw form. Looking around, well maybe she does have a raw idea in mind, Jacob thought, and it had nothing to do with the recent meeting. Before the long space sleep, he had spent a few wild nights with her that was mutually satisfying. As she removed her shirt and unbuttoned her slacks, it was obvious to him that she wanted a repeat performance. Maybe afterwards, Jacob could get Christina to tell him about her ideas. Of course, there would be hell to pay as well if Christina and Jessica discuss their recent romantic adventures.

After their energies were spent, Christina began telling him about her ideas about the Dimensionless Ones and why she believed in them. Jacob nodded his head in agreement.

"Of course, Christina, to do that we would have to change course to Uranus and away from Saturn," Jacob remarked, "this may add a year or two to our mission. The rest of the crew may not like that."

She laid on her stomach, with her head his shoulder, playfully caressing the few chest hairs he had. "I'm wouldn't be that concerned about the crew. I'm sure they will all eventually go along with whatever you decide. The crew for most part except maybe your sister has faith and trust in you," she answered.

Her head slid down his arm, and she rolled on her back staring at the chandelier above. "To be frankly honest, Jacob, I'm more concerned, no, that's not the word, more like terrified about whom or what are we being warned about? Who else is out there? Maybe all our SIL missions are giving us unwanted attention from some of our nastier neighbors. "

"No Christina," Jacob responded, "our biggest nightmare is that our planet and civilization may now be dead, and we may be the only ones left."

Chapter 7 - The Next Generation

Jacob thought about the message from the Dimensionless Ones. If they were going to believe in the Dimensionless Ones message, the crew had to be all in and the crew would have to go all out. First thing that needed to be addresses was that travel had to continue without detection, so they avoided transmitting any unnecessary signals. The power to the SAMs transmitters and space suits themselves were minimized so that just enough power was provided to transmit over very short distances. No transmissions to Earth, or its colonies on Mars or the Moon were sent. Second, they needed to change course for Uranus, the so-called ice giant which at one time was thought to be coldest planet in the solar system; however, that was prior to the discovery of Juno and Hera. They had passed beyond Neptune's orbit, but Uranus was still about 6 billion miles away and moving away from them at a velocity of about15,000 miles per hour, but at their current speed of about 0.002 of the speed of light, it would add about 6 more months before reaching Jupiter's orbit, but they were also still slowly decelerating so it would longer still.

They scanned Hera and Juno for any other messages on a weekly basis but these frozen planets had returned to their permanent acquiescent state, while becoming more and more distant. Jacob had now turned his attention and the ship's MDS to their inner solar system. The inner planets relative distance from the sun was making it difficult to pick up any specific minor signals, but Jacob had lots of time on his hands to sort out any artificial signals, for the time being until they entered Uranus space.

Both Sarah and Christina had also had more time on their hands, since both the ship and crew were operating nominally. They were both more or less on constant call for anything that might come up with either the crew or the ship, but in the meantime Jacob had assigned them both to agricultural duties to help Todd. He reassigned his father to assist Jessica in decoding the information that they had obtained from Gamma Leonis system, the one with the deceased civilization and became known as the "Leons" to the crew.

Sarah was quite content to spending time with her husband and toying with him. She felt like a natural leader but any attempts with supervising Christina were met with dismal failures. She had to be careful with Christina, since Christina had more than apparently been sleeping with her brother, and may become more influential with him even more so than her father. Sarah had seen Christina leave Jacob's quarters at various times. Adding Christina to the agricultural crew might be Jacob's poly to spy on her.

Their first harvest of green vegetables, tomatoes, corn and wheat had commenced, even some chickens were ready for slaughter. Of course, Todd would do the slaughtering. Her father had managed quite skillfully to overcome all the challenges that Todd had encountered in the initial plantings. He also skillfully managed to let Todd think that he had come up with most of these solutions himself. Sarah smiled to herself; her dad had really instilled a great sense of confidence in Todd, not only in his job and normal daily activities, but in their bed as well. Sarah had just confirmed yesterday morning that she was now pregnant, the first of the third generation on SIL11. She hadn't told anybody, not even Todd about her condition as of yet, but she would when she starts experiencing the typical physical attributes due to pregnancy. First, she would tell Todd and her dad, and then the rest of the crew. She was sure that everyone would be extremely happy for her since it would a big event for the crew. This upcoming harvest was blessing in her eyes; she felt now that she could nourish her unborn properly by ingesting normal quantities of organic food during her pregnancy. Despite having Christina, the spy around; she was quite happy with her assignment. But she wasn't going to let Jacob rest easy on his decision though, and complained to him about having to work with his whore. She didn't want to become predictable in the eyes of her brother.

***

Again, Jessica relied on her work to divert her attention from her present situation. Her work was to decipher as much as possible the Leon's database. This database was entirely different than the simple message from the Dimensionless Ones, but she had a lot of data to draw from. Unlike the Dimensionless Ones who presented themselves simplistically as possible so that an inferior intelligence could conceive their language, the Leon's had no such intention, either you got or you don't. They were not into any "hand-holding"; and they might have believed that if a race could not decode their language, then that race didn't deserve its content. They were as smug about their language as where French of ancient Earth.

Jessica was pleased that Jacob had assigned his father to her. He was mild mannered individual with soft-spoken intelligence. He was talkative, but he was polite and unassuming with a good dose of candor and transparency. He was not afraid of her and lacked any nervousness when he was around her. He was a breath of fresh air when compared to her former work companion, Sarah, his daughter. Sarah on the other hand, seemed always nervous around her, probably because of Sarah's belief that Jessica might turn into her brother, slaying anyone nearby. Sarah was tolerant of their situation and even respectful of her but there was always an underlying tension between them. But Luther was actually fun. He had a very self-depreciating humor that made him absolutely adorable. Jessica could see all the good qualities in Jacob coming from this man. Just to keep you off guard, he shyly and quietly showed his formidable intelligence when you least expect it. Definitely a man to be reckoned with, if ever he became your enemy, Jessica thought. But Jessica had no intention of that, matter of fact, just the opposite. She needed allies when dealing with the rest of the crew and Luther would be a tremendous ally and friend.

So her work was able again to mask her biggest concern. She was rather late for her period and she was never late. Yes, she needed to do her part, in repopulating the species but not right away, she had her work. She only had that the one episode with Jacob. And rumors of Jacob and Christina were everywhere, and neither of them rebuffed those rumors. She was not upset with Jacob or her situation. Jessica thought that Christina was right for him; since she was an embodiment of Jacob's mother. He did miss his mother tremendously after her tragic accident, even now. It had driven a wedge between Jacob and his father, Luther from some time, until Jacob decided to grow up, and allow old wounds to heal. But now he was as vulnerable to Luther's charms as anybody else. Christina definitely did not treat Jacob like his mother for their mutual sexual benefit, as she couldn't have enough of him it was said especially by Sarah. Of course, Sarah had no misgivings about spreading rumors about Christina. It was obvious Sarah didn't care for Christina that much, but Christina didn't care much for her either. Of course, she didn't care for Sarah either, Jessica thought.

She would have to make an appointment with Sarah to shut her up. Sarah, the doctor, would now be on the hook for a patient-doctor confidentiality, which despite Sarah's flaws, she would never abuse or gain an advantage with it. Jessica was quite certain of that. She didn't want everyone especially Christina thinking different of Jacob either, after all, she had practically raped the poor fellow. She didn't want any discord among the crew that centered on her. Most of the crew distrusted her or were worried that she may crack as her brother did. Damn her luck, she thought, it was only one time with Jacob.

Jessica conceived a plan to deal with her situation but she needed Luther's assistance. Maybe, she could convince the crew, that Luther was the father. Sarah would probably know the truth of it, but there was that patient-doctor confidentiality again. He was much older but he seemed to display a lot of vitality and hopefully he had some virility too. Of course she would have to seduce him and let him believe he was the father as well. She did like him and when it came to sex she wasn't necessarily that choosy. But she hated to deceive Jacob, but she resolved that conflict by promising herself that she would tell him someday. She just didn't know when. Jessica and Luther worked together much of the time, so there would be plenty of opportunities for her, but she needed Luther to copulate with her as soon as possible for the deception to have the best chance to work.

On her next work shift after a good rest period, shower and breakfast, she dressed up in her black skirt with the long slit up her left side and she wore no bra. "That should be obvious enough," she thought. Luther began to kid her about her outfit, "You are going to cause me a heart attack, with those skimpy outfits of yours, Jessica," he would say. But before they began to do any work, she locked science lab door. She watched Luther's eyes respond as she began to undress in front of him. Once she was undressed, she kneeled in front of Luther and began to unzip his trousers. Then she pulled them down, and to her amusement she found Luther quite stiff. She put her lips around his engorged member and thought to herself this will be easy. Once he was wet, she stood up and leaned over the table with her vagina exposed. Luther whispered, "Oh my, it's not my birthday, but I've been waiting for this kind of present for quite some time."

Once he was done, she stood up and she put her skirt back on, this time with slit zipped down and added a bra under her blouse.

"Should we go back to work?" she asked Luther.

"Men are not as easy as you may think, Jessica," Luther playfully said.

"Of course they are, and I don't mind giving them what they want," Jessica retorted playfully as well.

But Luther stood in front of her with his smile never leaving his face. "How long have you known" he asked her.

"Know what? That you are dirty old man?' she flirted.

"No I'm afraid not, how long have you known that you're pregnant?"

Damn that man was all Jessica thought.

But Luther again showed his charms to her. He agreed not to tell anyone about her pregnancy and wouldn't mind her suggesting that they had a possible sexual encounter or two with another crew member. Maybe it would diminish his persona as being the old man of the crew. Anyway, he wanted to protect his son as well as she did, even though he didn't take all this as serious as Jessica did. Luther came up from behind her.

"I'm a little out of practice," he whispered to Jessica, "I think will have to do this a few more times"

She smiled and turned to him. "I would like that," she told him, "But you will have to keep up!"

***

Jacob awoke with Christina in his bathroom again. He wasn't sure what she was doing, it was quite quiet in there.

"What's up?" he asked her rolling onto his back. He got no response. The door to the bathroom was closed and he heard very little activity coming from within.

"Hey did you hear me? Are you OK?" raising his voice, so she could hear him.

She danced out of the bathroom with a large grin. Her cheeks were wet but her eyes were bright and cheery. She had a small object her right hand but she was bouncing around so much that Jacob could not make out what it was.

"Captain," she said in a fake respectful voice. "I will need to inform you, that a new crew member will be coming on board." She raised her urine dip stick to his face to show its positive result.

"This will be the first of the third and new generation to be welcomed on board," Jacob responded and smiled at her. "How many of them do you want?" he added.

"How many what?"

"Babies."

She laughed and jumped on him. "Is that a challenge? Maybe it will be twins or even triplets this time; after all we are pretty good at this. You know my grandmother was a twin!"

"I'd rather do this, one at time," Jacob responded to her. "Just like so," he whispered as he covered her mouth with his lips and he rubbed his enlarging member against her colitis.

36

Chapter 8 - Others

A month later, Sarah had called a dinner meeting, to share everyone the news about her pregnancy. To her surprise, Christina told her that she also wanted to inform the crew of her pregnancy as well at the same time she did. It was definitely time to celebrate the additions of new crew members. Sarah also new about Jessica's pregnancy as well, but she was very secretive about it. Since both were her patients, she had no choice but to respect their wishes. She had overheard Christina and Todd speaking about her dad possibly being the father of Jessica's baby. She guessed that her dad wasn't as frail as she once thought. She needed to stop being such a ninny to him anyway; he never liked being treated differently from everyone else. She wasn't sure how she felt about having another brother or a sister, but of course she would never accept Jessica as her stepmon.. Dad would never insist on such an acceptance on her part, though she would smile at a potential reaction from Jessica by inadvertently calling her 'mom'. She may have to begin to trust Jessica now and her new offspring. The bad seed theory needed to be tossed and forgotten.

She purposely mislead everyone to think it was a celebration of their new harvest by serving fresh roasted chicken with bread, potatoes, salad and green beans. It was a bit of subterfuge but everyone would enjoy a home cooked meal. But this was going to be a celebration of life, and after such painful losses during their mission; it will put a positive stamp on their mission going forward. Of course, her dad and Todd knew about her pregnancy already but as far as she could tell none of the other expecting mothers had told anyone of their news. Jacob had not mentioned to her about being a first time father and her dad never mentioned anything about him re-entering parenthood either, despite having a thawing of their relationship with Jacob of late and her close relationship with her dad. But it was like dad to adhere to Jessica's wishes of secrecy and keep quiet about the whole affair, and maybe Jacob was waiting on Christina to announce the news and didn't want to spoil it for her. She didn't think Christina would withhold such information from the expecting father, after all she was quite infatuated with her brother.

Sarah and Todd were disappointed that wine wasn't on the menu, since it was celebration. But the grapes weren't quite ripe yet. Sarah thought that someone might have some private stock of liquor that they might be willing to share to enhance the celebration and there is always synthetic beer. Jessica, Christina and herself would probably abstain from any alcohol, and let only the expecting fathers celebrate with drink. Todd had interesting thought he shared with Sarah and that was to invite everyone to an old-fashion foot stomping of grapes in the next week or two, but when he mentioned the idea to others he didn't get a lot of support as of yet. He didn't know why people would distain at such an idea and why it would have an "icky" element attached to it. After all, the food that was being served this evening was fertilized largely by human excrement, all of it their own. He planned to ask everyone again this evening after certain amount of eating and celebrating. It was possible that they would be more inclined to agree with his proposition later in the evening.

All three women had dressed up for the occasion. Sarah wore a long black dress with matching black high heels that was modest but stunning at the same time. Christina wore a white wrap with bared her shoulders accompanied by white pleated skirt that hung just above her knees, and of course Jessica was again the more provocative one with bareback short purple dress with plummeting neckline that adequately exposed her full breasts. They all felt beautiful and for now they looked beautiful. In a few short months, however their views on themselves would change drastically to a more plump variety.

Sarah had done the cooking but everyone pitched in setting up the table. They sat at the table now as three couples. She and Todd took one side of the table while her brother with Christina took the other side. At the head of the table, her dad and Jessica squeezed in together. They didn't have everything for a typical home style cookout; like butter, pepper and milk, but it will be one the best they had since leaving Earth. For dessert, they had strawberry shortcake minus the whip cream, which nobody seemed to miss.

During dessert, Sarah stood up and stuck her glass with a spoon to gain everyone's attention.

"Todd and I have some wonderful news," she exclaimed, "we are adding another crew member in about 8 months."

Everyone clapped for both Todd and herself. Todd was beaming and said, "to celebrate I would like everyone to participate in the grape stomping chore next week; it's time to get earthy again."

Christina and Jacob laughed and agreed. Luther whispered into Jessica ear, and Jessica replied with a grin, "The both of us would love stomp around a bit!"

Todd just sat there beaming as he did before, nobody wanted to see his smile evaporate and disappoint the new expecting father. Everyone liked Todd, since he came across as an exuberant child while most ignored their own inner child.

After Sarah sat down, Christina stood up and said, "I want to double the celebration, I am carrying our captain's baby, he or she will be here in about 8 months as well."

Jacob stood up laughing and took Christina's hand into his own and announced, "Tomorrow is a day off for all expecting mothers." Jacob extended his glass of water as a toast to his sister. "Wow," he said to her, "A father and an uncle all at once."

Before Christina and Jacob sat down, Jessica stood up and looked everyone eyes, one by one. Then she settled on Jacob's eyes. "Captain," she said, "I'm afraid you will have to be without half your crew tomorrow, since I'm also expecting."

Before Jacob had time to respond, Luther grabbed his son's shoulders firmly and said, "Not only will you be a father and an uncle but a brother again as well."

Luther lied but it was best lie he had ever mustered. Jessica will tell him one day and then he will apologize to his son for lying.

The crew celebrated eating fresh food with synthetic beer for all the new expecting dads. It was the best meal that most of this crew has ever had. Luther may have been the one exception since early in their flight to Leonis system, they had large dinner parties as well but the rest of the current crew wasn't even around at that time.

***

The crew settled in with their daily routines after the grape foot stomping event. For the grape stomping occasion, Luther had brought a private stash of brandy and the gentlemen ended doing more foot stomping than probably necessary. All three were asking Sarah for some pain meds the next morning. She turned them all down on the spot, telling them she was saving pain medications for more dire needs such as upcoming labor pains. They accepted her decision without any comment but moaned most the next morning anyway. Sarah almost caved in just to shut the lot up but decided to let them suffer.

Todd, Christina and Sarah took care of the new plantings for the next harvest. They replanted their more successful crops such as corn, potatoes and tomatoes and added a few new ones such as peas and asparagus. Christina as the same time made sure the ship was running optimally not just nominally. She had gradually been increasing the rotational speed of the living quarters around the core of the ship to near normal gravity so that no one would notice the gravity change. Since all the women were pregnant, the remaining speed to reached normal gravity was achieved all at once but since they were at 90% of normal gravity anyway, the sudden increase wouldn't cause any hardship on anyone. Some studies suggest that fetuses were meant to develop in normal gravity, and her captain of course didn't object. Sarah also had added duties of her own by giving Jessica and Christina as well as their fetuses added medical examinations. Luther had insisted on becoming Sarah's own private doctor. Sarah knew she would be a terrible patient, as most doctors were. She kept asking for this test and that test from her dad, when there was no clear clinical reason to do so. She told him of her nausea and abdominal pains, and responded to her that those were quite common. Dad just smiled at her and basically ignored her constant bitching and attempted interference. He reassured her that she was doing fine. Matter of fact, all the mothers were progressing normally with their pregnancies.

Jessica and Luther delved into the reams of data left by the Leons. Luther had discovered a series of signals that had been recorded by the Leons. That signal was not part of or native to Leons language but had matched part of the signal to what they had received from the Dimensionless Ones. Apparently, the Leons had also been in contact with Dimensionless Ones themselves in their more recent history. Something that Jacob had suggested months earlier. The part of signal was the Dimensionless Ones description of themselves that lead Jessica and Sarah to refer to them as the Dimensionless Ones or the guardian angels. This discovery helped Jessica and Luther to begin translating some of what the Leons reactions to Dimensionless Ones signal. The Leons simply referred to them as "Angels" or maybe "Demons" it was unclear which one as of yet, but they were perceived as spiritual or surrealistic beings. So at this point, Jessica and Luther could not shed any more light whether the Dimensionless Ones were benevolent or malevolent. The Leons had received the signal as a radio transmission but without a source. No matter where they directed their listening devices, the radio transmission did not change in strength and amplitude which indicated that the signal had no true source. The Leons seemed quite incredulous at this phenomenon. Jessica and Luther began to center their attention on these particular databases of the Leons, since the Dimensionless Ones had contacted the SIL11 also in a miraculous way and now its crew had put their faith in them.

Jacob concentrated on detecting signals from the inner planets of the solar system. Since, it was there most likely that the human race would leave a trace of what had happened if there was any trace to be found. Periodically, he turned the MDS array at Hera and Juno. But they remained acquiescence; he concluded that the Dimensionless Ones were done with those planets. But he continued to monitor these planets just to be sure. He occasionally pointed his array to the various gas giants; Neptune, Uranus, Saturn and Jupiter. Jupiter's juxtaposition from the sun had the most interference, and was most difficult to detect even thought it was by far the largest planet. Neptune was now also getting quite distant from them as well since they were approaching Uranus space. Saturn was easy to monitor but there was nothing out of the ordinary with this ringed planet. The asteroid belt was a more likely target for human activities, so began charting the asteroid belt for signals but it was a vast region space and would require quite some time to complete the assessment.

Then there was their target, Uranus. Uranus was a uniform blue disc to the unaided eye at their current distance, with two of its major moons, Oberon and Titania visible to the unaided eye. Titania was quite bright sitting in Uranus's foreground while Oberon was in more in the background and much dimmer. Uranus tilted ring system was also becoming detectable. Charts of Uranus's minor moons and minor rings were not as well defined as with Saturn's, which will cause some added headache in navigating the system during their braking procedure. Jacob knew they were coming into Uranus space at tremendous speed and any navigational mistakes would cause dire and unrecoverable consequences. The SIL11 was to use the planet's atmosphere and several of its less dense rings to decelerate. They didn't have the fuel at this time to decelerate on their own. The original plan was to break in a Saturn fly-by but their current circumstances dictated otherwise, so they were using Uranus system. They would also slingshot out of Uranus's gravity pull for a course to inner planets but away from Mars and Earth, quite possibly to Venus. It was their intent to keep the sun between them and Earth until they got a better idea on the status of the human race.

Jacob was now spending more of his time on Uranus, to better define the charts that he had on this system and plan his navigation course accordingly. Again, there was no room for error and tolerance limits for course adjustments were very narrow. The PCDs were quite capable of doing the navigational calculations; but those calculations were only as good as the data that was available. Every day, he would bring a crewmember, a different one each day to go over and confirm the data he was collecting from Uranus, its moons and its rings that day. He figured they all could use a brief break from their usual assignments. He would also take breaks from his navigation and scanning, to meet with Jessica and his dad to see about their progress on the Leon's databases. There was a lot more excitement involved in decoding the language than the mundane collection of moons' positions and measurements of rings' position and densities. Their task involved much more deductive reasoning to tease out alien concepts. Jessica and his dad needed to think like a Leon in order to speak like one. They were the best two on board in the field of linguistics. Despite the common sexual attraction between them, which he didn't fully comprehend or wish to, they were more than mature enough not allow it to interfere with their duties. He considered the SIL11 quite lucky to have two such intelligent people on board to deal with this problem, when he could have more easily had none.

As the days went by, Jacob spent more and more time on Uranus system then with the other planets or asteroid belt. He would have more time for them when they had finished their slingshot maneuver around the Uranus system. But he still allowed a little time for a quick look at each of the other gas giants each week.

It was one of those times early in his shift when he glanced at Saturn briefly that the MDS received a strong signal. Not only was the signal artificial, but it was verbal human message directed toward the Moon and Earth. The message read:

"This is SIL7 we are 2 million miles away from the Saturn system. We will begin our braking procedure soon. We are attempting to contact Corporate, do you read Corporate? We have met some new friends." The message repeated itself over and over again. It would be at least 2 ½ hours before SIL 7 would hear the response from Corporate if Corporate still existed, and Jacob wouldn't hear that response just a little later in about three hours.

Jacob was stunned. Jacob thought to himself oh my god there are others! His first impulse was to break radio silence and respond to SIL7. But he restrained himself and began to think through the discovery and consider what consequences there may be for any action he may take or may not take. This was too big of a decision for him to make until he conferred with the rest of the crew. SIL7 was following standard procedures as expected while they, SIL11 were not following procedural guidelines, but proceeding on the whim of angels.

Chapter 9 - Uranus

Jacob set up an all hands meeting for that evening. Dad, Christina and Sarah had all tried to persuade Jacob to let them in on the topic or issue, but he refused. He wanted everyone's opinion and at the same time. Besides, it was fairly straight forward what he had to report. He predicted that proposed actions or lack of actions would be quite debatable among the crew. He did not want to start the debate until everyone was informed and allowed express their opinions. This was especially true for Christina, where no one will have an opportunity to modify Christina's opinions before he heard them, which along with his dad's, he respected the most.

The crew had established daily routines, so when they came to this quickly called meeting, they were in different stages of alertness. Jessica and his dad were wide awake and ready. Christina on the other hand was tired and hungry, a state that she was more familiar with each passing day of her pregnancy. Sarah was grumpy also more common with her pregnancy along with her somber husband. Jacob was afraid he had to awaken them both for this meeting. He was also sure he was going to get a few angry stares in his direction from his sister. To his surprise, Todd had brought an unopened and unlabeled bottle with him.

He told the crew about the detection of a message he had discovered near Saturn from another SIL spacecraft, the SIL7. That particular SIL spacecraft originated from Asia in what was formerly known as China and Mongolia; it had left a decade or so prior the launch of SIL11. Its mission was to search out an area about 180 light years away. He repeated their message verbatim to his crew. The crew of the SIL7 was following specific procedures that was universal and in place for all incoming interstellar SIL space vessels. Of course his crew wasn't following those set standard procedures.

"I imagine there was no response from Earth or the Moon." Luther spoke out directly.

"A signal from Earth would take nearly three hours to reach us at our current distance, but that was 5 hours ago. And there has been no response from the Terra system as of yet," Jacob answered.

"Why haven't you responded to SIL7? Our prayers have been answered we are not only survivors," Sarah asked excitedly.

"Once we break radio silence, our position could be determined by anyone or anything in our solar system. Wanted to see what the entire crew thought of this new development and what would be a best course of action," Jacob answered her sister.

Jessica piped in quite abruptly, "I wonder who their 'friends' were?"

Jacob responded, "Best guess they would be ambassadors from somewhere in Hyades star cluster, the region of space that the SIL7 was scheduled to explore,"

Jessica jumped in, "That's extremely exciting, and I would agree with Sarah we should contact them immediately. In addition, we should head back to Saturn without braking at Uranus to keep up our speed and have a reunion with them sooner than later."

Sarah and Jessica started to talk at once to one another, using their imagination of what the new alien species looked like and what their civilization had accomplished. Neither expected any opposition to what they were suggesting.

"I disagree." Christina exclaimed trying to be heard over the top of the other two women. The two women turned toward Christina with questioning faces and wondering who dared to interrupt them.

"What are you talking about?" Sarah interjected with a bit of distain for the interruption between Jessica and herself."

"Easy Sarah," Jacob said, "I wanted *everyone's* opinion. Go ahead Christina, what are your thoughts?"

"What about the warning, nothing has really changed. Why are we going to change our plans? We agreed the only reason to change plans, would be that if we found that the message from the Dimensionless Ones turned out to be a farce or a hoax. I, myself, see no evidence of that. When we decided to change course to Uranus, we became committed to specific course of action. Why do you want to change now on such short notice?" She paused and put her hand gently on her enlarged abdomen and added, "I think it would be reckless in abandoning our plans now, and I would fear for our very survival."

Jacob looked up at Christina with a great deal of pride. Those were his thoughts exactly.

Sarah spoke to Christina in soft but firm tones, "Hogwash, that was before when we thought we were alone." Then Sarah in a loud and excited voice, added, "We just found out that WE ARE NOT ALONE!"

Luther then stood up and softly spoke, "I think that patience would be the wisest course of action."

Jessica drew in his hand to hers but he continued to speak uninterrupted. "Do we really want to announce where we are right now? What would that change?"

He continued, "The crew of SIL7 may have never received a warning, or signal as we did, or they may have rejected it outright and continued on their planned trajectory."

"If they rejected the warning, let see what repercussions may befall to them. If, after a reasonable period of time, there were no consequences then we can announce to them our position."

Jessica asked Luther, "What are you worried about?"

Luther answered, "After spotting one single prey, a hidden intelligent predator may lie low longer to make other prey more comfortable by allowing them to observe the presumed safety of the single prey and draw them out from their places of refuge. Then the predator can make a quick assessment for the easiest kill which may no longer be the first observed prey."

"Dad, what predator are you referring to?" Sarah asked.

"You haven't been listening, the *hidden* predator is the most dangerous," replied Luther.

Jessica gently squeezed Luther's hand and appeared to wonder at his response, and began doubt her support for Sarah's course of action. Then she also, lifted her hand and protectively laid it on her enlarged abdomen.

Jacob turned to Todd, "What's your opinion?"

Everyone fell silent to listen to Todd. He stood up, uncorked his bottle, and took a swig of the contents. "This is first vintage of our new wine. I think everyone needs to take a swig. It's the best wine I ever had but it also my first. He turned towards to the Captain, in my humble opinion we are probably screwed either way." He lifted the bottle and offered it to Jacob.

Jacob took the bottle and took long swig of the bottle and then handed to Christina, "Todd that may be the best assessment spoken here today," Jacob paused and smiled to the rest of the crew, "it is the best wine I've ever tasted as well."

Everyone took a swig and agreed with the general consensus to continue radio silence. Everyone that is, except for Sarah. The sweet wine turned sour in her mouth, thinking that everyone else was brainwashed by Christina. But again, she relented. Someday, she will take action on her own and show everyone what fools they have all become.

***

Most of the crew would rather be sleeping during the braking maneuver around Uranus; but Jacob wanted everyone awake in case of an unforeseeable mishap. Only Luther had any real experience with the maneuver, but that seemed like a lifetime ago to him. Everything and everyone need to be strapped down and secure. It was going to be a very bumpy ride. Jacob had the perfect course planned with an accompanying safety margin, but that's usually when a plan goes awry just when you think it's 'perfect'. He had a safety margin, but with an adequate margin that part he was unsure. He will have a better idea on his margin after it's all over one way or another. He agreed with Sarah to give all the expecting mothers a low dose of a mild sedative, to calm their nerves and prevent any undue stress to their unborn fetuses. Luther was his co-pilot, and Christina his navigator. Christina would only agree to the half the dose that Sarah and Jessica had received. She couldn't afford any mistakes either. Both Luther and Sarah tried to convince her that the half the dose may not be sufficient, but to no avail, and Jacob was rather relieved to have her fully awake anyway. He was already at disadvantage not to have Jessica and Sarah fully alert.

Todd knew he had no vital part in this roller coaster ride through the Uranus system. He had secured the growing crops but most of the plantings were still rather young and resilient. He would have rather been useful to Jacob and the crew, but he didn't have the training to help pilot the ship. Of course, he was told he lack the 'skill sets' necessary for that sort of training. Another words, he was brainless as he often gets reminded on way or another. That might be an exaggeration but he has been told he hasn't the sharpest tack on board. He felt confident that he was smarter than the average Joe on what was once Earth, but here on SIL11 the bar was set very high. He accepted that he wasn't the brightest on board. Everyone else tried to lay claim to that distinction, but it only led to petty fights and pointless bickering among the crew. He was liked and accepted by the rest of crew and didn't have any animosities towards any other crew member. He knew he was somewhat the polar opposite of his mate, Sarah, whom wouldn't be comfortable without some fireworks. He admired her for standing up for what she thought. Matter of fact, he loved her for it. He desperately was hoping that their new son or daughter would have Sarah's intelligence but in the same breath, the child would have his disposition. He was certain the whole crew would be at least in agreement with this specific assessment.

He had been much more pleasant than he expected to work with Sarah's father. Luther was not what he had expected. What he didn't expect was a father who was soft-spoken and thoughtful. He had a wry sense of humor and didn't mind laughing at his own daughter's or son's antics or even, no especially, himself. Unfortunately, the captain reassigned him and he got both queen bees; his wife and Christina. His feelings about the reassignment might be misinterpreted that he preferred Luther over his own wife. Yes, it might have been more relaxing with Luther, but he loved his wife and didn't care about how anybody else felt about her. Sarah was only one on board that made him feel special, and he was ready to defend her even when she was wrong. Of course, she would say that never happens, so he thought. He enjoyed treating her special as well, never questioning her requests and always ready to comply. Some of the crew may have viewed him as a dog harnessed by Sarah's leash. Let them think whatever they want. All that mattered to him was that he and Sarah were happy.

Todd had a couple of hours to kill, before the mandatory restrains were put on everyone. The crew would lose gravity, and become weightless. The rotational mechanism along the entire axial length of the ship, including his miniature farm, and crew's quarters, crew work areas were to be stopped and locked down. The captain did not allow anyone to go into sleep stasis in their cryochambers, but he didn't disallow some shut-eye for him if he could somehow manage it. Sarah was already on the bridge giving the expecting moms some sedation. He on the other hand, had a different approach as he uncorked one of his wine bottles in his and Sarah's quarters. He started toasting everyone and to everything. He first toasted the SIL11, the only home he had ever known, then he toasted Sarah, his wife and his unborn child. He followed that with a toast to his captain, hopefully he will be able to pull them through. Then he raised his wine glass to the rest of the crew; Luther, Jessica and Christina. He decided then to toast the Dimensionless Ones as well as the crew of the SIL7. He also made a small toast to their new found friends on board the SIL7, and hoped they would turn out to be real friends and not some kind of Trojan horse.

He poured the few remaining drops of wine into his glass. He smiled and hoped he had not forgotten anybody. He decided that just in case, he would toast the mythical Uranians and beg for their forgiveness for trespassing into their system.

He stumbled up to the bridge where everyone else was preparing for the expected nightmare over Uranus. He nonchalantly went over to his wife who was discussing something with her dad and gave her a big kiss. She looked up straight at him, and gave a little laugh. "So you've been drinking a little bit."

"Well, maybe not a "little" but I was able to give a toast to everyone and everything."

Sarah grabbed him and hugged him. Luther calmly looked up at the two of them and said to Todd, "Congratulations, you're the only one on board who knows what to do."

Sarah guided Todd to his safety seat and began strapping him in and whispered in his ear, "This may take a while, so sleep it off, so I can get you all refreshed and in our bed when this is all over."

Todd looked up at her and touched her face, "Please don't forget about me." He then closed his eyes and instantly fell into a leisurely slumber. He began to dream about laughing Uranians pointing to a dim fireball burning up in their cloudy sky.

Chapter 10 - The Aftermath

Sirens were wailing and warning lights were flashing everywhere. But Jacob knew that SIL11 had made it through without substantial damage. He looked on his PCD to access if they were still on their planned course. Jacob was satisfied with the projected course to Ceres in the asteroid belt with them continuing on to Venus. The deployed heat shields had protected their large ship in the Uranian upper atmosphere. The shields were retracted once the SIL11 had sling-shot its way beyond Uranus's gravity.

"What have you done to my ship?" wailed Christina. Jacob guessed that the sedative was not quite enough for her, which was too bad.

"So you're the captain now," Jacob laughed. "You'll have to make the final assessment on all our systems. But I can tell you that navigation, engines and environmental controls appear to be working nominally. Crew's quarters and work areas appear to have suffered only minor damage. However, I can't seem to be able to start their rotation. The MDS also appears to be functioning. We do have a hull breach in the engine room, but I have locked down that compartment and it has not affected engine's performance, at least not yet."

Both Christina and Jacob were examining and then recording all the causes for the sirens and warning lights. Most of the warning lights were proximity warnings when they cruised through Uranus's multiple ring systems.

Sarah broke in, "The crew appears to be fit and without injuries, even my fine husband has woken up. Also appears that all fetuses are nominal as well."

"Easy for you to say," interrupted Jacob, "but I feel like a grape that had been stomped on by entire crew."

Todd broke in, "So are you getting fermented too?"

"Not as fermented as you, my friend," Luther replied.

Jacob held up his hand and spoke loudly, "Listen people, don't think that we have got off scot free. There is no gravity as of yet. And we have a major hull breach. Fortunately, it's in the non-pressurized part of the ship. I want everyone to go to their quarters using the handholds on board, clean themselves up, take a nap if you can, get something to eat, but then we need to get busy."

Everyone was quiet listening to him except Christina who was still attempting to silence all the alarms.

"Then I want all of you to report back to me in 6 hours for new duties. Todd, that's 4 hours for you since you have already slept."

"Hey wait a minute Captain," retorted Todd.

Jacob waved him off. "Now, all of you go."

One by one, the crew made their way to their quarters. Using the handholds to travel along ship was actually easier than walking, but also more apt to cause injury. So, the crew took it easy. Christina stayed with her captain and her lover.

Jacob looked over at Christina, "Are you OK?"

"No problems, here."

"We'll get you some well-deserved sleep once you tell me why there is no rotation what else might be wrong with our ship," Jacob responded to Christina.

"Yes, captain."

"I'm going to attempt to re-establish our signal from the SIL7 and see if it's still broadcasting and whether they had received any response signal from our Terra system."

Christina had just managed to turn off the last wailing siren. "I'll have a list prepared for you in 2 to 3 hours, captain" she said as she unleashed herself to go about the ship for general inspection.

"Take it easy, just remember what you carrying."

Christina laughed, "I'm weightless all the time, this is a lot easier than walking. I'll be putting on my garb and going outside. I'll let you know what I find."

Jacob looked up at her and softly whispered, "I love you."

Christina face lit up and ignited a radiant smile. She did a somersault and plunged herself down one of the corridors and yelling, "You are now in a heap of trouble, my love."

***

Todd didn't feel that hungry but he knew he must eat something before reporting to the captain. Who knows how long it would be before he got another meal. Sarah was sleeping in their quarters after a brief tussle with her in bed. She was worn out, and actually set a reminder on her PCD to be woken up in 4 hours, which is something that she rarely does. Todd decided on a piece of chicken along with a couple of eggs, small hill of potatoes and some country style gravy. Of course, the whole meal would have to be served in plastic squeeze bags without the assistance of gravity.

Jacob floated into the room while he was squeezing some chicken meat into the gravy bag.

"Captain, I thought I had another hour before reporting for duty."

"Don't be ridiculous, I'm here for some food, not to chastise you!"

Jacob shook his head. That did not come very well. He was tired and hungry as well.

"Hey Todd, that does look good. Could you make me some of that?" Rank does have some benefits on occasion, Jacob thought to himself.

"Right away, captain."

"You missed one hell of a ride that most of us would have rather missed."

"That's what I hear. But I didn't miss all of it though, nobody can sleep that long"

Todd sat down steaming bags of food in front of Jacob. "There you go, sir."

"Come on Todd. None of that 'sir' business with me, OK?"

Todd smiled and returned to his plate and started working on his egg bags. "How's the ship?"

"As well as to be expected, I guess. Christina has not logged in all the minor damage as of yet. The only major damages were the servo gears for rotating the work areas and quarters as I mention before and very large gash on the port side of the engine room."

"I'll need you to get the manuals out and start inventorying the parts we will need to repair the rotational mechanism. I'll provide you with Christina's technical report on the servo gears." He paused then continued, "But stayed seated, eat your meal, and tell me how my sister is doing. My sister and I haven't spent a lot of time together lately."

"Don't worry captain. Despite not getting her way as often as she would like, she is quite happy. She would not want you to know that, so please, please, please, don't tell her I told you that. OK?"

Jacob smiled, "Not a word, Todd."

Todd added, "She is very much looking forward in having a family. I hope I'll make her proud, a worthwhile dad."

"Just remember Todd you are going to be a dad for your child not for Sarah. She already has a dad. I have no doubt that if you are just yourself, you'll make a wonderful dad. On the other hand, I'm not sure what kind of father I'll be. Never been a dad before and being captain wouldn't allow me a lot of spare time to spend with my new son or daughter."

"Jacob, are you kidding, you have the perfect blueprint, look at your own father. Hell being a dad is in your genes."

Christina came spiraling into the room with practiced deftness and ease.

"What's up boys?" she asked.

"Just telling Uncle Todd here, some of ship's damage," Jacob responded. Could you send over your report on the rotational mechanism for the crew's work areas and quarters to Todd here, so he can start gathering up the parts that we will need."

Christina nodded, "OK."

Then Jacob nodded, "I'll fix you a meal, and the both of us can get some shut eye, no arguments Christina, and that is an order."

"I'm ready for sleep, you won't get an argument from me this time," Christina replied, "after a pause, she said with some practiced distain, "Captain!"

49

Jacob had assigned the entire crew to fix the servo gears for the rotational mechanism. It was fortunate that the ship carried all the necessary parts. All SIL spacecraft had enough parts to almost build another SIL spacecraft. Only one of the five servo motor was totally destroyed and had to be replaced, while others needed a few minor repairs and most of all a thorough cleaning to remove debris from servo motor gears. Both Jessica and Luther stayed on board to monitor the entire crew's life signs and progress while they were working in the vacuum of space. Christina was in charge outside and was vigilant of the rest of the crew, since no one else had been in space since waking up. They all had training and certification prior to cryostatis of course, but that seemed like eons ago.

Christina thought Sarah might object being out in the vacuum of space, considering her present condition. But Sarah didn't mind the work especially working alongside her husband, since she was weightless whether she was inside or out. Christina had to hand it to Jacob; the crew worked very well together which was a sign of acceptance for his style of command. But she also had to give credit to the crew to submit Jacob's command and overlook the shortcomings of others when working together.

In two days' time, the huge rotational mechanism with all its servo motors began to turn. Jacob allowed the rotation to increase in speed at very slow rate at first. One reason for this was to allow the crew to briefly get use to gravity again, avoid any shock to the fetuses (even though both Sarah and Luther surmised that it was only a very small risk) but most importantly to ensure the repairs were sufficient and no other undiscovered damage could ruin all their work. But again Christina was flawless in her assessment of the damage and the rotating mechanism was working smoothly. Once Jacob made that assessment he sped up the rotation so that they would be back at normal gravity. There was no need to slowly to increase gravity, they were all rather fit from being in normal gravity prior to their flyby of Uranus.

The crew also patched the breach in the engine compartment. The main purpose of repairing the breech was to reduce the stresses on the hull as a whole in that part of the ship. Soon, everyone was back on their normal duties. Christina though did not return to the farm as she continued to venture outside the ship to make all the required minor repairs. Sarah monitored Christina's pregnancy closely for any deleterious effect on the fetus from her constant spacewalking. Jacob had limited her spacewalks to 4 hours every 24 hours, but he knew she was most capable and appropriate crew member in the making the repairs, whether he liked it nor not.

Jessica and Luther went back to milling over the Leon's database files. Sarah and Todd went back to the farm. To their relief and to everyone else's, there was no damage to the planted crops or any of the agricultural equipment. Jacob went back to MDS to see if he could again monitor the signal from SIL7 and see if there was any response from Earth. The crew had months ahead of them, before entering into asteroid belt and possible answers about their home.

Chapter 11 - Tandoorians

"So Jessica, if I understand you correctly, the Leons were not extinct at all but left their dying planet nearly 10 centuries ago," Jacob blurted out from behind his PCD during one of his visits. "Not only that but they were influenced by "angels".

"Luther and I have been beginning to call them by their real names, the Tandoorians, after all their planet was Tandoor. Yes, some Tandoorians called our Dimensionless Ones, 'angels' but other Tandoorians especially the Southern sect had called them 'devils'."

Jessica and Luther had been quite successful in deciphering the data files from what the crew had affectionately called the Leons, but this ancient people had referred to themselves as Tandoorians. Their long history was summarized in the following way by a couple of scholars from the Southern kingdom:

Their planet was one of four that circled the more minor star of the Gamma Leonis binary system. It took 11 years to orbit the smaller star of a stellar binary system. Both stars of the binary system were older and much larger than their Sun with Tandoor orbiting the less massive star. It took about 7 Earth years for the planet to orbit their sun, but Tandoorian day was very unusual lasting much longer than a Tandoorian year, nearly 180 years. Life including intelligent life migrated where dusk and dawn was eternal. In addition, the tilt of Tandoor on its axis was consisted throughout the Tandoor year, therefore, the southern half was cooler, where life could exist during a Tandoorian day. The southern hemisphere was cooler, but a massive ocean existed covering most of this hemisphere. A small land mass did exist in the deep south which could sustain life during the day, but it was quite hot comparatively to the East's dawn and the West's dusk. No life existed on the northern hemisphere during a large part of the Tandoorian day and no life could survive the dark side of the planet during its long night. Tandoorian history seemed to indicate that the planet at one time spun on axis a much higher velocity, which resulted in life existing on much of planet's surface. It was unclear what caused the unusual days and locked seasons on Tandoor when the databases were being written over a thousand years ago.

The borders of the Western and Eastern kingdoms were always changing with the rotation of their planet. However, it was always eternally cloudy on Tandoor, so there was no distinct sunrise or sunset on the surface. Their borders were defined not geographically but by how far from the calculated sunrise or from calculated sunset. Thousand kilometers on either side of the sunset, was the Western Kingdom, and fifteen hundred kilometers on one the bright side of sunrise and 1000 kilometers on the dark side of sunrise was the Eastern Kingdom.

However, sometime in Tandoorian history, a small sect from the East traversed the southern ocean, exploring this small land mass far in the south and colonized it. But after 80 years when the small land mass entered the long night, the colony perished. After a few Tandoorians days, people again sought out the southern continent to colonize it but this time, arrangements were in place with the Eastern kingdom which allowed them to come back during the Tandoorian night. The Eastern kingdom ceded a part of their kingdom, which was 1000 to 1500 kilometers on the bright side of sunrise. This land was typically uninhabited for the most part but life could be sustained there. Life was definitely no picnic there in the ceded Eastern land, but colonists did manage to survive and claimed their independence from the East.

Every 80 years, southerners were on the move, either to their southern home or back to bright sunrise of the East.

Political system of Tandoor were made up of three monarchies; the East, the West and the South. These kingdoms were ruled by kings and queens, but a Council of the People was in place for each kingdom to govern their rulers. If one ruler chose to go his/her own way without the well-being of their subordinates in mind, then the Council would have no choice but to legally eliminate the ruler and substitute a new one. Only three-fourths of the council would have to agree on such a motion. That action was rarely taken but its intent was to keep the rulers in line with their constituents. The successor of a king/queen would be the youngest of their offspring, if there was no offspring, then a new king/queen was appointed by the Council but the appointed could not be a council member or their descendents. Kings and queens were not necessarily the most sought out positions, since either their life spans were much shorter than the average Tandoorian or they were only puppets of the council. But if a ruler did well in the eyes of the council and the people, they had absolute control and power, and was usually awarded with a longer than usual life span and luxuries that normal Tandoorians only dreamed about.

The Southern kingdom though very small had a profound effect on the political landscape. The East and West sects were basically similar in population and area, so a disagreement between them could only be resolved by whose side the Southern kingdom supported. Despite most Southerners being originally from the East, the Southerners were fiercely independent and typically supported only the side that would only bolster Southern interests.

Wars were very rare on Tandoor and usually ended quickly. Kings and queens typically were rulers with genuine interest in the people's overall well-being. However, there was much corruption surrounding the Council throughout Tandoorian history. For example there was a small revolution that occurred in the Western Kingdom, when a popular ruler challenged the logistics of a new Council of the People that came to power which was full of corruption and state thievery. The Council was indignant and threatened to eliminate the kingdom's queen. However, the common people loved their queen and the Council chambers were stormed by an overwhelming number of common people who slaughtered the entire Council. However, those incidents appeared rare in their history, so much of the time their corruption went unabated. The Council was elected by its people every Tandoorian year but this council had also to be approved by the previous council, and the current king/queen. This process had led to a lot of deal making between the various sides. It was thought that this process may have incurred much corruption that existed in the councils, but no solutions were raised by the council or by the ruler.

The Tandoorians were aware that the rotation of their planet was slowing down even more in a last few centuries, and it would eventually stop altogether sometime in their future. In addition, the atmosphere of the planet was beginning to thin. It was apparent that their planet was dying. Other planets of their binary star system were uninhabitable, so colonization outside Tandoor was not even considered by the Tandoorians. There was some interest in reaching for other star systems especially in the Southern sect but both the Eastern and Western kingdoms were more interested in going underground. The northern hemisphere had a natural labyrinth of tunnels and massive rooms underground and the two kingdoms in the North were aligned in developing this complex. Like Earth, the planet's crust sat on molten rock but

52

unlike Earth, the molten mantel was beginning to cool. The southern hemisphere was mostly underwater with no labyrinth complex of tunnels on their small continent.

It was surprising that it was the North, in both the Eastern and the Western kingdoms that got transfixed on the radio message that the Southern Kingdom had been receiving from unknown source. The Southern Kingdom shared their information with the other two kingdoms and it was confirmed over and over again from various receivers all over the planet that the signal did not come from fixed point in space but seemingly everywhere. The message was an invitation to help the Tandoorians survive their dying planet. They would help the Tandoorians built spacecraft to abandon their dying home planet and travel to a new home. They had indicated before that they have helped other civilizations survive their dying planets but not all civilizations took advantage of their invitation. These signals were difficult to interpret about exactly where they were going to but it brought great interest in the East and West. Typically, the Southerners were the more adventuresome but they were highly suspicious of these signals. Whereas, the East and West and called them "angels" who sent a signal to save their species, the South looked to them as "demons" which would condemn their race to slavery or even annihilation. None of the sects had enough information to determine which viewpoint was correct, but the South was very leery of these outsiders.

After couple of Tandoorian years, the Tandoorians from the Eastern and Western kingdoms accepted the idea of abandoning their doomed planet. When the joint announcement by the Eastern king and Western queen was made to the entire northern hemisphere, the angels' radio transmissions had reconvened, sending instructions for building their type of spacecraft. But the Southern kingdom rejected the offer and refused to leave their home planet. So when the two peoples of the East and West had finally built their ships and left the planet, the Southerners had decided to remain.

A period of very active solar storms started decimating the remaining thinning atmosphere of Tandoor after a couple of decades from the East's and West's departure. The South began to regret their decision not to leave the planet and turmoil broke out among the people. The insurrection from the southern people resulted in slaying the Council and its puppet queen. The infrastructure for its society collapsed and lead to anarchy among its people. The alternative of the underground complex in the East and West were years from completion but few sought out these tunnels. The solar storms were making the entire surface of the planet uninhabitable over time. When civil order was finally restored to the southern kingdom and work had begun on building the spacecraft for them to leave Tandoor as well, it was too late. Their own mistrust and panic had doomed the Southern inhabitants.

Many centuries later, the crew of the SIL11 had come into Tandoorian space. There was no civilization left in the northern hemisphere. The crew found Tandoor mostly uninhabitable, but a few life forms were found near the southern pole. No intelligent life was found, despite considerable effort by the SIL11 crew. But they were able to find some database archives in the Southern's home during the Tandoor night, which now related this Tandoorian story. Luther wondered if some Southern inhabitants were able to survive but the SIL11 crew was not able to find any signs of them. They had not combed in the entire natural underground of the planet, maybe a few Tandoorians still survived in that labyrinth. If they did, Southerners would have been quite resilient and resourceful but eventually Tandoor would become their tomb. Jessica was more wondering of what had happened to the northern people. Where did they go? Did they find a better fate than what had fallen on their Southern brothers?

Jessica and Luther spent hours going over some of the details of the Tandoorian story and discussing some of its ramifications as it related to their particular situation. One thing that was still not clear, were the Tandoorians' angels truly benevolent? They briefed the entire crew on the Tandoorian story and allowed the entire crew access to their notes and to the actual data files themselves for their own interpretation. However, none of the crew took them up on their offer. The entire crew seemed to believe in them, including the captain. Anyway, none of the crew had much idle time on their hands to allow such a luxury as going over other people's work. But it was a topic for many conversations among the crew in the months to follow.

Chapter 12 - Yama

Jacob, after the Uranus flyby, began his search for the lost SIL7 signal. SIL7 would have been entering Saturn's space during their flyby of Uranus. Both ships had orbited their respective planets to slow down their momentum, resulting in numerous blackouts of the SIL7 signal and eventually loss of signal entirely. It was decided by the SIL11 crew not to inform SIL7 or anybody else out there of their position or even their existence. But Jacob wanted to know if the SIL7 was still broadcasting which would be following standard protocol after its flyby of Saturn.

It was not long after, the Jacob had managed to detect the signal again from the SIL7 spacecraft, still reporting a similar message, "This is SIL7, we have completed our braking and course correction with our Saturn flyby. We are attempting to contact Corporate, do you read Corporate? Does anybody within the inner solar system read us? Mankind has some new friends."

Obviously, the Terra system had not responded to their signal. There was no indication in the message whether the SIL7 had sustained damaged during their Saturn flyby. Jacob assumed that their ship had sustained only inconsequential damage and they were continuing their mission. Jacob tuned the MDS array to focus on the SIL 7 and the Saturn system, to gauge SIL7's new course and speed. He was able to track most of the major moons in Saturn space and the SIL7 itself. According to his calculations, the SIL7 had accomplished reducing its velocity to a fraction of what it was and they were on course to intercept the Earth.

Jacob had a sigh of relief when he gathered this information, he felt better about the well-being of his comrades. He noticed Titan in Saturn's foreground, one of the largest moons in the solar system which the SIL7 had begun to pass. To his absolute surprise, there was a very large object that was orbiting Titan in a very low orbit on the opposite side from SIL 7. It was nearly 1/10 the size of Titan itself and possibly a small satellite of Titan. If he was just leisurely scanning Saturn itself, he would have been easily missed this new object. There were no records of a Titan satellite, but it was close enough to Titan to be its moon.

Jacob decided to keep MDS array on SIL 7 and Titan for a while longer and record what he could, while he grabbed a bite to eat. He had previously arranged to have a meal break with lovely Christina, and it was going to be another hour or two until SIL7 had passed Titan sufficiently to not allow simultaneous viewing of Titan and SIL7. It would allow time to collect information on this new object after all he was still a scientist at heart and didn't want to pass up a chance in gathering new information about their solar system. This new moon would probably be old news to mankind, if there was still a civilization out there. Of course, once SIL7 had passed Titan, all their focus would return on the spacecraft.

Christina, his future wife, was preparing a meal for them both. Soon after the announcement of her pregnancy, he decided to marry her. He was not marrying her because of her pregnancy but instead for the love that he actually felt for her. She was all that he ever wanted in a wife and now a mother for his future son/daughter. She was intelligent, capable and for no reason that was apparent to him, she treated him like a king. She fulfilled his every request, wish or whim. He knew eventually he would eventually fall off the pedestal, but for the time being, it was hard not to take advantage of it as long the pedestal didn't get too high. You don't want the pedestal oo high, since he knew he would fall off it sooner or later, or more likely pulled off its top. So he trtied to some extent, to keep the pedestal short as possible, with less chance of really getting hurt.

He felt great joy with Christina and that he would be extending his family. He knew dad would have expected this to happen and would be happy for him. He hoped his sister would be happy for him as well, but she was quite blind about other people right now, since she and Todd were also expecting an addition to their family. He was quite happy for his sister, and even with her apparent apprehension about being a new mom. This apprehension was more or less a facade for her, so she wouldn't come off as a giddy girl about the whole affair. She was radiant when spoke about her pregnancy however as well as her future family, so this disguise for the most part was a dismal failure. His decision for marriage was made even easier for him, with Jessica apparently taking up with his father. He hoped that his dad's health would hold out for him for a while, so he could enjoy Jessica and be a father again himself.

He wondered if the SIL7 crew was larger than his own and what tales of exploration they would share. It appears from their transmissions that an alien intelligent life form, so-called 'friends' were travelling with the on their voyage to Earth. He had to agree with Sarah and Jessica on that point, that it was very exciting. SIL7 would definitely have a larger tale to tell then the his crew, but neither of their stories were yet completed. SIL7 was now finding out that their home Terra system is silent and their mission may all be for not. But they were approaching Earth and may discover new things; new technologies for communication, or maybe the human race had left the solar system or had gone into hiding.

Of course, he and his crew except for his father had never been to Earth. The entire crew had spent hours on ship's computers to get a feel, or a taste of what Earth was like, going over Earth's geography, Earth's history and its science. But they mostly spent their spare time on human history and literature. Fictional tales were very popular among the crew since they showed only a snapshot of humanity, which was rich in detail and seemed more alive, with humanity coming right out of the pages. Sarah and he had spent time with dad and mom, when she was still alive, asking questions about Earth. They were captivated with stories of their parents. Their stories were for the most part; were pleasant with happy endings. But in truth, even though human history was quite remarkable, the darker side of humanity was always present and was typically present is some form or another on the pages of fiction. A battle of good and evil was at every major turning point of humanity. But many times, the branding of good and evil was at the hands of the victor. War, in itself, typically devastated both sides, but the victor managed to put blame on the other side and label them, the evil aggressor. So at times, the boundaries of good and evil were often blurred and concepts of good and evil were often difficult to interpret. Fictional novels tend to define these concepts early on in their characters clearly, not allowing for other interpretations. That might be reason for their popularity among the crew, they could enjoy reading about humanity without focusing on who was right or wrong.

Christina was all smiles. She had made them chicken enchiladas with fresh jalapenos, a recent crop. He would thought that Christina may have avoided such spicy food, but often these days she had a hankering for strange foods. At least, this meal was appealing to him.

"You're a tad late. Observing anything new from the MDS?" asked Christina.

Jacob grabbed silverware and retrieved a glass of water and turned to Christina, "Want some water?"

"You bet, but use these larger glasses. I'm sure we'll get quite thirsty with all these jalapenos."

A brief silence followed, in which Jacob had forgotten about her question with MDS and focused his attention on the simmering enchiladas.

"Well?" she asked.

"Oh," Jacob responded with some mild guilt. "Yeah, I may have discovered, or more likely rediscovered a satellite circling Titan, the SIL7 is approaching Titan when I came down."

"Why on heavens didn't you just call me and we could have postponed our meal. That sounds quite exciting!"

"Not really that exciting, a small rock orbiting another small rock; besides I'm recording everything while the SIL7 is nearby. I much rather watch myself devour these enchiladas. We can always go back and observe the footage."

Christina smiled. "You always had a healthy appetite, you're not going to get fat on me when we grow old together, are you?"

Jacob quickly quipped, "You're getting fat first. Just look at yourself."

"You know that's not fair at all," she responded.

"Well then just let me eat!"

"Do you mind after eating I come with you and see this for myself? I have already logged in my 4 hours of spacewalking today. That's all I can do, you know, *captain's* orders," she said with a bit of emphasis on 'captain's'.

"Sure come on down, and take a look. Maybe then I can coax you into our bedroom and not for sleep, after all you aren't that big yet."

"We'll see," she teased, "depends on if that is under *captain's* orders."

They entered the bridge, and when over to the MDS console. Jacob was shocked the SIL7 had simply vanished from his screen. He listened for its transmission of returning home but was only rewarded with silence for his attempt.

"Where did the SIL7 go?"

Of course, Christina was a bit confused, she saw the new object that Jacob had identified earlier as a satellite of Titan.

"Isn't that it?" pointing to the screen.

Jacob was again dumbfounded. "No this signal is way too large for it to be the SIL7. And there are no transmissions. I don't have any idea what happened."

Jacob made a slight adjustment to the MDS, to view Titan which had fallen off the screen, which he had expected. There was no longer a satellite circling Titan.

He turned to Christina's face, "I'm afraid that I did not discover a new satellite of Titan. It's some kind of alien ship. I think it left Titan's orbit to follow the SIL7. Let's watch the playback."

He accessed the earlier recording of the SIL 7 and misidentified satellite of Titan. He and Christina watched the SIL 7 leave Titan's space with the unidentified alien spacecraft leaving Titan's orbit to follow. The spacecraft was gigantic in size, larger or comparable to many of the moons in the solar system and vast majority of asteroids. It also was extremely mobile and fast, it quickly narrowed the gap between it and the SIL7. The previous transmission of proclaiming their successful slowdown was interrupted by a new message which did not repeat itself:

"A large vessel is approaching us from behind. We have established a visual on the alien vessel, and our new found friends have recognized them and are now terrified. No incoming message from the vessel has been received, and they are matching our course changes and rapidly closing gap between us. I believe they have hostile intentions and so do our friends. No response to our communications. Yama may have found us, our tiānshī may have been right. I have doomed the representatives of our new found friends, the Leserrians and the brave crew of the SIL7. This is the Han Chen, captain of the SIL7. Pray for our hun."

There was an overwhelming silence that followed and the blip of SIL7 vanished without a trace. The alien spacecraft slowed, and turned back to Titan. Which was what Christina and Jacob was observing when they first entered the bridge. They watched the spacecraft return to Titan and again established a low orbit around Titan. They both knew the general translation for the Chinese words; Yama, tiānshī, and hun; i.e. Ruler of Hell, angel and soul.

Christina turned to her husband to be and murmured slowly, "Good thing we listened to you and our 'angels'."

Jacob shook his head and whispered as though he didn't want the alien vessel to hear him even though they were hundreds of millions of miles away, "Ruler of Hell? Has Lucifer come to visit our solar system? I had thought all along that he was already here."

Chapter 13 - Chiron

Jessica grasped Luther's hand as they were waiting for the others to join them. Jacob had called an emergency meeting for the whole crew. Jessica and Luther were deep in sleep when the call had come, but yet they were the first to arrive. Of course, they had dressed rather quickly and did not prepare themselves appropriately to be viewed in the public eye, but the captain did say now. They were planning to return to their bed once this meeting was over, so neither one of them cared how they looked.

"I wonder what it is this time." Jessica asked Luther. "I'm starting to get real nervous about these unplanned meetings."

"Don't know and I would have to agree with you. The last time, my son called a meeting like this, he informed us that our home, Earth was silent or worse."

Luther was a bit flabbergasted how this beautiful lady, Jessica had got hooked on him. It was first an arrangement that Jessica orchestrated. But their relationship was well beyond that. Luther continued to socialize with his son, his daughter, his son-in-law and soon to be his daughter-in-law, Christina, but he found himself more and more in Jessica's company. He was hardly alone anymore and was finally accepted by everyone as not just part of the crew but to be part of everyone's family. He wouldn't believe after he woke up that he would be in these circumstances, not even in his wildest dreams. Not only was Jessica a ravishing woman with an insatiable appetite for sex, but she was a great partner, listener and storyteller.

Luther did consider himself old-fashion even for his generation, still reading books with printed texts and promoting actual conversations when possible. His apparent desire for real face-to-face conversations had attracted his deceased wife to him, whom also desired these face-to-face encounters. His generation and his parent's generation had allowed the art of conversation to apparently die a slow death with all the device media applications and "talking" had become a memory of much older generations. But this younger crew had resurrected this art which not only resulted in his enjoyment with this lost art, but found it delightfully challenging as well. And Jessica was one of the best among the crew in this art once she accepted you in her world.

Jessica allowed Luther to share some of her deepest secrets, such as her own belief that she is still somehow responsible for the crew's earlier massacre. She let down her mask of serene eyes and expressionless face to him and allowed herself to be vulnerable to him. He listened intently allowing her feelings of regret, loss and isolation wash over him, since he needed to not only hear what she had say but how she was feeling when she said them. He felt a responsibility to her for opening up to him and she endured the constant comments and looks from the other pregnant women. He saw through her crystalline glass that protected her from the outside world. At times, she appeared to be only a child, alone and afraid. But Luther was not going to fall into her trap, since she was exceedingly intelligent as well.

He didn't think he would ever love anybody again after his wife had died. As days went past, he found himself growing ever fonder of Jessica and caring for her. It was not the same love as he felt for his deceased wife, since it was different with Jessica. But he could foresee it growing into undeniable love and hoped that Jessica felt the same for him.

The crew was assembled when his son came into the room.

"Hello everyone, thank you for coming on such short notice, but I thought this was important enough for everyone to hear as soon as I found out myself," Jacob started.

He paused to confirm that the crew's eyes were all on him

"About two hours ago, I was observing the SIL7 approaching Titan and I wanted to re-establish our connection with their message. Their message had changed slightly to include a successful fly-by of Saturn but it was quite apparent that no one had answered their message. A large object in low-orbit around Titan escaped Titan's gravity and began to follow the SIL 7. When this object had closed the gap between it and the SIL 7, another different message was broadcasted. I have the recording which I will play for you. Soon after this message, the alien vessel came within 80,000 kilometers, then the image of the SIL7 simply vanished. The large object then simply returned to its low orbit around Titan. Here is the recording."

He played the entire message from the SIL7 to his crew.

"If you don't know, a Chinese translation of Yama means the ruler of the underworld and tiānshǐ means angel. It was odd that in the translation the Chinese words for the ruler of hell and angel was retained while the rest of the message is in English. But I would hazard a guess that tiānshǐ was ignored by the SIL7 and may have been the same as our Dimensionless Ones," Jacob concluded.

Luther remarked, "Hun is the Chinese word for spiritual soul, if I'm not mistaken."

Jacob answered, "You're correct, dad."

Christina piped in, "I would say that the Yama not only destroyed the SIL7 and killed everyone on board, but it had laid a trap for SIL spacecraft. And again, Yama is now waiting for the next SIL spacecraft to engage in their standard Saturn fly-by."

Jessica asked, "Do you know anything else of this Yama space vessel? I know we are at a tremendous distance from them but anything may help us defend ourselves, if it comes to that."

Jacob replied, "I know only four things about this vessel. None of them are good and they are too distant for any other details. One, it is extremely large about 600 km in diameter, two, it is very fast and agile vessel since it took only minutes for it to close the gap between them and the SIL7, three is must have very superior weaponry since it apparently destroyed the SIL7 at a great distance of approximately 100 thousand kilometers away and lastly, they are extremely aggressive with hostile intent."

The crew went silent. Again, each were in their own thoughts and deciding what each of them should say. Sarah finally broke the uneasy silence, with more of a plea than a question, "Is there any other possible explanations at all?"

Jacob and Christina both shook their heads. But Jacob added, "Does anybody else have a logical explanation for these observations? I do have the whole incident recorded, in case anybody would like to take a look."

Luther responded to his son, "I guess we follow your plan to continue radio silence and stay away from Earth for the time being."

"Yes, I agree dad. It does seem to be the prudent course of action. We are on course for Ceres in the asteroid belt. Does anyone else have a question or a comment?"

"Why Ceres?" asked Todd.

Jacob replied, "Ceres is far from Earth on the other side of the sun. It is the largest rock in the asteroid belt. According to Earth history, there were discussions about mining the asteroid belt and establishing outposts on these rocks. But we won't know for sure, until we get there. And I would say that Ceres is our closest chance to find clues regarding the fate of our human civilization. We also are getting rather low in water and there is appreciable amount of water on Ceres, but I do hope we discover some water sooner."

Todd's question was the last question from the crew, and the meeting was quickly adjourned. Luther asked Todd if he would like a have a syn-beer with him. Todd graciously said no, but countered by sharing a bottle of wine. Sarah looked over at the both of them and slightly nodded her head to Todd as if Todd had asked for permission. She wanted to be alone anyway.

Sarah turned away and walked down the length of the ship, peering out of the space portals as she walked. She wondered how could she been so wrong about contacting the SIL7. It was clear to her, that if she had been in charge, the whole crew would be fighting for their lives right now. Her pregnancy must be affecting her ability to make wise and correct choices. She couldn't allow this type of fiasco to happen again, or she would entirely lose her ability to influence the crew. She must make the smartest choice, clearly convey those choices to the crew and most importantly be right. She understood that she had dropped a peg or two in the eyes of the crew. It maybe sometime before she could influence the crew, so she needed to be less rash and more prudent in her choices. She had time. They were still months from the inner solar system and months before new members of the crew were to be born. She had time, for now she would spend her time with her husband while growing everyone's food.

***

Jacob knew that Ceres contained a large amount of water but the SIL11 would be needing water prior to reaching Ceres in his estimation. There were other much smaller asteroids between them and Ceres, and one of them would have to suffice in regenerating some of their water supply. Todd and Sarah have had bountiful harvests which everybody of course enjoyed, but the aggressive farming has had a strain on their water resources, which not only supplied water but was also used to generate breathable oxygen. There was no need to wait for Ceres, he would rather resupply their water now then later. After all it was most vital resource on the ship. He began surveying the planetary bodies that were close to them and used the MDS gauge the amount of harvestable water on them. Most asteroids had frozen water supply but only a fraction of those had water that was accessible, especially for the machinery available on board the SIL11. He hoped his theory that man had colonized the asteroid belt for harvesting vital resources was true, and he would be able to identify clues of their existence here. Orbiting space stations around Earth and colonies on the Moon and Mars would have been easily detected by the Yamas, but scattered colonies throughout the asteroid belt, he believed may have gone undetected or just ignored.

Jacob identified a planetary body that would suit their needs and did not significantly deviate from their present course. It was a not a true asteroid but a centaur, called Chiron. This centaur itself did not have retrievable water but it had two small rings associated with it which were rich in ice and harvestable. Its distance was between Saturn's orbit and Uranus's and if they slightly adjusted course, they would be there quickly enough. This asteroid may not have the potential for human colonization as did the asteroids between Jupiter and Mars, but Ceres had that potential and it was already a planned destination. He would need Christina's expertise in designing a strategy in retrieving water from the rings. But the best thing about Chiron it was less than three weeks away and as luck would have it, it only deviated from their present course by a mere 200,000 kilometers. In his eyes, Jacob found this to be a win-win situation. A sudden significant course alteration may be detected by the Yamas, but this minor change would most likely go unnoticed by even the most sophisticated detection systems. Their flyby of Uranus did not attract their attention. His recent scans of the Yamas detected no changes in their position, around Titan or its orbital speed. Best chance of going unnoticed is changing course now to minimize course alteration.

Jacob decided to adjust their course, and then he would talk with Christina and the rest of the crew afterwards. It was a dangerous course of action, not consulting with the crew first, but he was captain and they all needed water and breathable air.

Chapter 14 - The Water Harvest

Christina thought to herself, 'this was going to be royal headache', yes it was doable, but hardly easy. The plan was to fly in parallel with one of Chiron's rotating rings and gather boulders that contained a high amount of ice and then disperse the boulder debris during the operation. Even though Uranus flyby had significantly reduced their speed, the ship was still travelling much faster than the rotation of Chiron's rings. Water was absolute necessity for interstellar flight, so the SIL spacecraft was designed with large water storage bins and a system to harvest ice from either the surface of the planet or while in flight. Nobody on board had actual experience with either operation, and was just a read in flight operating manual. Surface harvesting was inherently a lot less risky than a surface operation, but their current situation would now allow for any landing. Besides Chiron had small amounts of ice on the surface but the curious ring around Chiron was rich in this necessity. The manual had established methodologies for water harvesting but at speeds that were 100X lower than their current speed. But she could see that Jacob was trying his best to mask their spacecraft activities from the Yamas, which was his highest priority. Hopefully with some superb piloting by Jacob, the SIL11 may come out unscathed and bring in a modest harvest of ice. But coming out of this undamaged or unharmed seemed somewhat unlikely to Christina. It was like walking next to a landslide and capturing small rocks with a small but nearly indestructible butterfly net. What bothered her most was that he didn't ask the crew for their opinions. He had already decided on this and then asked her how to do it. The nerve of that man, Christina thought. To his credit, Jacob logged in as many hours of spacewalking as she did for preparing for this maneuver. She had programmed the SAMs to be outside during the harvesting, but Sarah, Todd along with herself will be inside negotiating the large automated harvesting nets. Christina had given both Sarah and Todd a crash course in harvesting operations and supplied them each a copy of the flight operations manual for their reading enjoyment. Both picked up on the operations on nominal speeds but there were no simulations for the speeds that Jacob had intented. Jessica was to identify those rocks utilizing MDS of a suitable dimensions and composition with sufficient water content. The rocks need to fit into three of the spacecraft's rock crushers with worthwhile volume of water of >25% but with a low content of hard metals such as solid iron or nickel. The rock is to be pulverized into small granules and heated above 110°C to vaporize the water. The water is then sucked into the ship's condensation tubes where the impurities eliminated. The dehydrated granules will be dumped simultaneously during the operation. The plan was to collect enough water to fill the ship's storage tanks to half capacity, approximately 3000 cubic meters.

Luther was to be Jacob's navigator. Even though in truth, Jacob's PCD would be able to navigate the ship from his programmed parameters. Luther was there in case Jacob had not thought of everything and to prevent Jacob from being distracted while he piloted the ship to execute minor course corrections.

Chiron became to show itself and visible to the naked eye as the SIL11 approached. The day side of Chiron had a dull blue aura, and even departed Uranus had more reflective light than this dark world. However, its two rings stood out brilliantly in comparison to the centaur itself which highly suggests of high water content within the rings. Jacob had the SIL11 approach in parallel with the asteroid's rings. At any significant distance, the SIL11 would appear to be part of the ring. They would travel along the ring's margin to avoid a real navigational nightmare, but navigating in the margin was going to be intense in any case. They would stay equatorial to the rings until they had harvested enough ice. He did not have the ability to exactly match the SIL11 speed with the ring's rotational speed, but he would minimize SIL11 speed as much as what was allowed.

Jacob thought the SIL11 was as ready as it could be. He ordered the entire crew including himself a long stint of rest and relaxation two days prior to arriving in Chiron space. Sarah and Todd prepared a huge supper, which was attended by everyone. However, Jacob disallowed the consumption of wine or syn-beer for anyone. He had to endure only some minor protests from Todd, but the rest of crew readily complied. Jacob had stopped the rotation of the crew's quarters and work area, including the farm. The farm was faced farthest from the ring, to minimize risk of unwanted collisions with the farm, not to say that any collisions were wanted. This required the crew to become weightless again.

The harvesting nets were a technological marvel. These nets were made of intense electrostatic fields strong but flexible and could take quite the beating while still maintaining function. These nets were extended out with mechanical arms that could also endure significant impact and collisions. The function of the arms and nets was to collect the boulders and rocks that contained ice, it sounded simple but it was by far the most difficult task. One of Chiron rings was orbiting at much higher rate of speed that the other, so that ring was chosen for the maneuvers.

Jacob eased the SIL11 next the targeted ring. Everyone was prepared and the operation began. Christina had underestimated the task, she thought it was like collecting rocks with a butterfly net during a landslide while standing still, but it was more like trying to catch bullets from a rapid fire machine gun also with a butterfly net. They had estimated a success rate of about 5%, so it was slow going but doable. But Jacob was piloting the ship flawlessly, and was patient with the collection process. It would take a few orbits to collect the necessary water. The ship was sustaining some minor damage from some unavoidable collisions.

Luther was observing the details of Jacob's constant course corrections. He was awed with the precision and accuracy that his son was guiding their ship. He was thankful that it was his son and not him doing the navigation, thought Luther, he doubted if the SIL11 would have survived with his piloting even though he was an experienced pilot. He would have surely plunged the SIL11 into a rock the size of their farm with ease. He noticed that Jessica was quite adept in rock identification and supplied sufficient targets for Sarah, Todd and Christina, yet Jessica still had sufficient time to send him a message to the navigation screen on his PCD:

"Luther, something or more like someone is following us."

She connected his PCD device to the MDS locating the new object. She inquired if it was acceptable that he investigated this new object while she continued to identify the proper rocks for harvesting. She had already made arrangement for a small set of scanners to be available to him, while the rest of the scanners were focused on her task of identifying ice-rich rocks. He sent her a quick affirmative response and turned his attention to the object. This object had matched their current speed and course. No natural object would be able to navigate this maze as did the SIL11 or match its current speed. The new object had increased its speed slowly to bring close to the SIL11. There were no aggressive maneuvers from the object such as attempting to overtake the SIL11 or any weapons launch.

Luther sent a message to Christina's PCD asking how much water they had collected.

"Be patient, Pops. We are almost there, another 500 cubic meters and will be set," Christina answered warmingly.

"Don't stop what you are doing, but we are being followed," replied Luther. "I don't think it's threatening us, but it is very exciting as long it's not the Yamas or some other unidentified hostile race. I don't want to distract the captain while he is piloting the ship but as soon as you think we have enough water, we should probably move away from this asteroid and see if it follows us outside Chiron space. Then I will notify my son immediately"

He paused then added, "Pops uh? Not even my own kids call me that. But I think I like it."

"Sounds good to me, Pops" Christina answered, "Maybe an hour at most should do it."

Luther watched the new object over the last hour as it ever so slowly decreased the gap with the SIL11. He still was executing his primary role with his navigation, which was going quite smoothly. But he couldn't let up; the crew was depending on him so he did not spend too much time on the new object. But here and there when he managed to observe the new object and collect some data on it. The object was small about 200 meters in length. Luther could only surmise what the intent of this new object may be; quite possibly to gauge whether the SIL11 as a possible threat or figure out what operation the SIL11 was performing in the ring system. Luther began to pick up a weak audio signal coming from the object. Luther concluded that the object was some kind of spacecraft and it was specifically signaling them. Luther again sent a message to Christina, "I'm going to have to notify the captain, it's signaling us with a very low signal strength."

"No problem, we have reach 98.8% of what we came for."

She used the intercom to announce to the crew.

"We have reached our targeted amount of water, good job everyone."

Jacob broke in, "I am slowly turning the SIL11 and resuming our course to Ceres, and I echo Christina's sentiment, Great job everyone!" Then he added, "I am beginning the rotation as well, we should be at 1 g in within an hour."

Luther moved over to where his son was strapped in, "Fantastic flying son, you're the man."

"Thanks, dad. My neck has all kinds of knots in it. Maybe Christina will massage some of them out, or I could ask Sarah for some muscle relaxants."

"Son, there is something you should know. There is an object following us for the last 2 hours and it's signaling us on a very low strength transmission."

"How come I wasn't immediately informed," Jacob said raising his voice.

"My job was not to allow any distractions, while you were piloting the ship. Neither you or I wanted to be pulverized."

"Is it still there?"

"Yes it is and it's trying to communicate with us. What do you want to do?" Luther answered.

Jacob unstrapped himself and went over to where his dad PCD was, monitoring the object. He asked Jessica on the intercom to turn over more of the MDS to Luther's PCD to monitor the new object. She responded she would turn over most the MDS except a few scanners for any possible stray rocks that may be still on the SIL11's course.

"Before you do, can you get a quick assessment on the Yamas spacecraft circling Titan?"

"Yes, sir, just a moment please."

Jacob turned to his father, "Just being cautious."

His dad just smiled at him. He shouldn't have raised his voice to his dad. He was right, as usual.

Jessica answered over the intercom, "No change in their position or speed, sir:"

"Ok, thanks Jessica. Over and out."

"Well dad let's see what they are telling us, shall we?"

A Russian pilot had sent the signal from its shuttle. The computer hesitated with the translation at first, since the language had changed over the last few hundred years. But the basics of the language had not changed significantly enough, so the computer was only momentarily silent.

"Hello, this is Petrulov of the Chiron outpost. From my observations, I think that you are a returning SIL spacecraft. Is this correct?"

Jacob smiled to himself. "We'll answer him but use the same low energy transmission as he was using. It could not be much stronger than the transmissions with the SAMs," Jacob said to his dad. "This will keep our silent running intact. I believe the risk is acceptable to answer him. What do you think?"

"I agree, son. This is exciting to find another human in our solar system alive and kicking. But I would still be cautious."

Jacob turned on the ship's transmitter and set the controls to the appropriate energy levels. "This is Jacob, captain of the SIL11. We are very happy to hear your voice."

"And I'm very happy to hear yours. You are apparently not following the standard procedures for SIL spacecraft. That's good thing, whether it's intentional or not. Other SIL spacecraft have met their demise when they have entered Saturn's space. Demons and angels are apparently using our solar system as some kind of interstellar game. It's a long story but what be happy to let you in on what I know. Chiron is currently the farthest human outpost, of course we don't get a lot of visitors."

"I'm afraid the SIL7 has met their demise as you described," Jacob responded.

"I saw that you were harvesting some rocks from Chiron's rings for water, I assume. Did you get enough? And what course at you setting for now?"

Jacob kept silent. He was not yet sure of this fellow, Petrulov. He seemed almost too good to be true and wasn't too sure about showing all his cards as of yet. He looked up at his dad, but he only shrugged his shoulders. This was his call but this time he wanted his crew's feedback.

Petrulov answered his silence. "Your silence is telling me that you have some hesitation. Don't know who to trust after all you have seen, perfectly understandable. But let me be quite frank with you. I have been left here for quite some time. The rest of them followed these angels or Dimensionless Ones, which they have named themselves. I know that doesn't make sense right now but I was 'volunteered' to stay behind. My spacecraft is small though far superior than yours, but it was not designed for long interstellar travel as yours was. I will do anything to get off this rock and socialize with other humans. I will go as far as disabling your ship and take it by force. If you think I'm bluffing, think again, you have been gone for a couple hundred years, consider the improvement of weaponry and overall technology during those years."

Again Jacob answered his threat with silence. He was somewhat encouraged by his response. Not with the threat itself, but he sounded very human, and was showing his darker side. Petrulov answered his silence again, "Sorry about the threat but I am desperate. My request is to allow my spacecraft to dock with yours and allow me to come on board. I would not be a real threat to you once I'm actually on board your ship. Talk it over your crew. You have three hours, by four hours my small spacecraft will be unable to safely return to Chiron at our present speed. This is Petrulov, over and out. I believe that was what you use to say."

Petrulov lied which was something in which he had gotten quite good at. His spacecraft was not at all that limited and it was able to travel throughout the solar system. Neither Jacob nor Luther had detected the lie.

Jacob looked up again to his dad but he didn't shrug his shoulders this time. "What do you think, dad?"

Luther rubbed his chin and was in deep thought. "He has us over a barrel, and he knows it. His motivation sounds genuine. You have to let him know that you are in charge if he does come over. Besides, I'm sure he has information about our home. I would never totally trust him in any case." Then Luther added, "I think at the end of the day, it looks like we're going to take on another crewmember."

Jacob responded, "I think we need to show some trust with our first reintroduction to the human race. "

Chapter 15 - The Hitchhiker

When Jacob had the crew assembled to discuss allowing Petrulov to come on board, it turned out a rather short discussion. Nobody was able to suggest another course of action, other than allowing his ship to dock with theirs since nobody had doubted his ability to disable their ship. The crew was somewhat split on whether to trust him. Jessica and Sarah did not trust him as well as himself. Christina and Todd felt that he should be trusted and to Jacob's surprise, his dad remained totally silent on the issue.

An hour and half after Petrulov last transmission, Jacob ceased his silent treatment with Petrulov.

"You have permission to dock with us please use the aft starboard docking ring. We are assuming that you are the only one coming on board and there is nobody else on your ship. But we do have some prerequisites."

Petrulov answered, "Yes I'm only one on board and I'm not at all surprised about 'conditions'. What are they?"

"Once docked, you will power down your ship completely and allow an inspection of your vessel to confirm that there are no others on board. Two – you will enter our spacecraft through a decontamination process. Three – you will be accepted as a crewmember, and expected to work as one, since we are somewhat shorthanded. And lastly but not least, that you will recognize my authority as captain of the SIL11. Any questions?"

"Aye, aye captain. There is one slight problem, I can put my engines on standby, but I cannot shut them down completely, if we are ever going to use this vessel again. I will explain the details with you and your engineer but it would take some time. I hope you understand. Please, be aware that English is not my native language but I do know the language but I might be a bit rusty. Is anything else, sir?"

"Do you need any assistance from us during the docking procedure?"

"No problems there," Petrulov replied.

"Well welcome to the SIL11, my name is Jacob, which I prefer that over both captain or sir, if you don't mind."

"Yes, cap---, I mean Jacob. I'll be docking in the next 15 minutes, and by the way, my first name is Ivan."

Ivan followed all of Jacob's instructions precisely and without complaints. Christina and Todd entered his spacecraft. They confirmed that nobody else appeared to be on board. Ivan invited them to investigate his spacecraft till their heart's content; he wanted them to know that he had nothing to hide. Christina was an engineer but she felt like she was in Alice in Wonderland, since nothing inside was familiar. She felt like young girl in small toy store wanting to try everything out but there were no batteries in any of the toys. Surprising to her, there were no indicator lights on the ship accompanying by total silence with the lack murmuring from any type of equipment. First problem was to understand how the operator and ship communicated with one another. Both Christina and Todd realized there was going to be a sharp learning curve to enter into Ivan's century. Todd was even more lost and disliked the Spartan appearance on board. No wonder Ivan wanted to leave this ship, he would too.

Once through the decontamination process, Ivan was quite talkative and was surprisingly fluent in English despite his admission for the opposite. He said he hadn't much practice at normal conversation but it did not deter his exuberance. He talked about his outpost and the state of affairs in their solar system.

Ivan's spacecraft was a shuttle craft from their outpost which was a small complex situated on the sunny side of Chiron. Of course, the sunny side would be somewhat be a misnomer, since the sun was only a bright star that gave no warmth to his dreary world. The complex was large enough for about twenty-five colonists. Except for Ivan, there were no longer any other residents left on the centaur. SIL11 crew was amazed that human influence had stretched so far out in the solar system. Interplanetary travel was revolutionized when it was discovered that neutrinos could be captured and be used for propulsion. It allowed travel from planet to planet in months or weeks and not in years. This allowed them to send out other "SIL" expeditions after the original 18 missions to explore much farther targets, even those across the center of the galaxy. Ivan shared with the crew that Corporate felt quite confident that an inhabitable world will be found before their own planet would perish with age. Of course, this all occurred before 'they' came. The crew had no way to verify anything that Ivan told them but it seemed to truthful.

He told the crew that Corporate had done something never done in human history, and that was to unite mankind. It allowed peace and prosperity to reach levels never before recorded in history. There were massive colonization of Mars and the asteroid belt. Corporate was able to tap in the natural resources throughout the solar system. Of course, there were consequences to these historical changes, individuality suffered and soon became a thing of the past. There were jobs for everyone and all people were fed and kept comfortable. Disease and starvation was soon eliminated which bulked the power that Corporate acquired. Corporate instilled the message that everyone was free to seek out their own destiny, but that was a lie. People were measured and assessed before their teenage years and were assigned or condemned for some people to a life which Corporate had maneuvered that person into. Corporate also decided what people ate, where they lived and what their futures were. But Earth did rule supreme in the solar system, but that was all before 'they' came.

"They" referred to two different advanced beings. The first beings called themselves the "Dimensionless Ones" and were referred by some as man's guardian angels.. They communicated with people in most unusual and many cases unnatural ways. And they would often change their manner of communication depending where and when they decided to communicate. They didn't require a response; they seem to know what one was thinking after that person had deciphered the message or heard the message from another. Not everyone could decipher the message, but the people who did were willing to share the message it contained to anyone who was willing to listen. Nobody understood what their means of communications served except for some cerebral exercises. The Dimensionless Ones had some an effect on people's behavior to be that open and gregarious regarding the contents of their messages. Not even most secretive people seemed unable to control their enthusiasm for spreading the message. Occasionally they had appeared in physical form, or least they created a form that humans could see. The most widespread form was bright tiny pinpoints of light. The light did have any physical characteristics that equipment could register, so their existence was initially in doubt. But what was interesting was there was always more than one form, regardless the form used by the Dimensionless Ones. Therefore, it was believed they were an advance race and not the one advanced being. Their messages were quite simple but bundled in riddles. The most important one was a warning of another race of beings that would come after them which were hostile and second they gave instructions to build ships and to follow them to bring the human race to a new level of existence. They never gave details or answered questions. One had to take them on their word, or wait to see what would happen. Corporate had united the human race but now mankind was being torn apart. Some believed in the Dimensionless Ones, others could not decide if to believe in them or not. While others thought it was unwise to follow without more information, and others believed the Dimensionless Ones themselves were evil. Even some religious extremists believed that Dimensionless Ones were the anti-Christ, and Christ was going to follow. The Dimensionless Ones seem to know where all our colonies and outposts were that had spread across the solar system and delivered the same two messages to all. Human race was quite divided and the Dimensionless Ones gave individuals the right to choose. So many ships were built over the next two years and many people left. It was known as the Great Human Departure, to those who remained. Those who left with the Dimensionless Ones were never heard from again.

That following year, after the Great Human Departure, the others, or the "demons" arrived. The religious extremists who initiated the idea of the Dimensionless Ones were evil, had got it wrong. Christ was not among the second group that followed and all hell broke out wherever they went. They were superior to humans in physical strength, physical tolerances, and cognitive abilities and most importantly their technology was vastly superior to humans. But they were still hampered by physical bodies and relied heavily on their technology unlike the Dimensionless Ones. Their fleet of four battlecruisers entered the solar system and in matter of months had neutralized all of Earth's defenses, not only Earth's but on the Moon and Mars as well.

When they found out that the Dimensionless Ones had preceded them, they began slaughtering thousands of human inhabitants who had any contact with them and enslaved millions more. Within them, hatred festered for the Dimensionless Ones but their hatred remained a mystery to all. They broadcasted that noncompliant human habitants would be tracked down to be killed or enslaved, and eventually they would destroy all evidence of a human civilization. They were sadists, an apparent learned behavior, finding new ways of torturing and killing humans and maximizing the pain over longer duration, partly to incite fear into people. But sadly their abuse of humans was more than just inciting fear, it also appeared to give them great pleasure as well. They were not as advanced as the Dimensionless Ones, since they still had their physical forms and needed their technology to meet their ends. They were terrifying not in their behavior but in their appearance as well. They were insect or lizard-like but had no direct resemblance to any known Earth lizard or insect. They were bipedal with long thin legs and thin arms, which allowed great agility and speed. No one wanted them upset, since it typically resulted in instant death for any human nearby. They had lidless black eyes with no expression of emotion in them most of time. They also had some kind of inherent radar system, similar to Terran bats. No one would have been able to sneak up on them from behind.

They had a dark blue mucus covering most of their body except what would be called feet and they soon discovered to their delight that it was extremely irritating to human skin. They took small children from parent's arms and hugged them, and gave them back to the parents, as the children screamed and cried in extreme agony. Their dark black eyes would appear to momentarily glow blue when they witnessed this suffering or any other type of suffering bestowed onto humans. Humans interpreted it as a sign of pleasure, since their eyes would glow when they witness unbearable suffering from humans. They had a few long hair-like appendages that came through their ooze, which moved independently and apparently was some type of sensory organ. They had no typical mouths and nobody really wanted to find out how they ate if they did or how they replenished their bodies with energy.

The few that had survived their brutality and genocide went into hiding all across the solar system. Ivan informed the SIL11 crew that the residents of Chiron opted to leave with the 'Dimensionless Ones' but he 'volunteered' to stay at Chiron. He didn't expect the "demons" to look for him. But he took precautions nonetheless. For example, Ivan permanently rigged his transmitter to minimum power both on the outpost and aboard the shuttle since he didn't want to inadvertently send a locator beacon to them from his location at a time of possible weakness on his part. Chiron was a very remote rock from Earth with rare visits from any Earth vessels historically and would have been an unlikely target of the 'demons'.

The 'demons' referred to themselves as the Gatekeepers. There was no apparent connection to their name and to their behavior. They had an exceeding hatred to anything connected with the Dimensionless Ones. Of course, no human had any knowledge of the history between the Gatekeepers and the Dimensionless Ones. The Gatekeepers ferried enslaved people back to their home world and systematically destroyed all structures and technology on Earth, the Moon, Mars and other locations in the asteroid belt. They laid traps for human loners on Earth and Mars who they wanted corralled.

They were also set up to destroy any returning SIL spacecraft, once they knew of the program's existence. One of their first targets was Corporate's receiver and transmitter on the moon that were built for the SIL returning spacecraft. They must have thought this SIL program was some kind of threat or of significant importance, since they permanently stationed a lone battlecruiser in Titan's orbit to destroy any returning vessels. SIL7 was a demonstration of this set up.

Ivan was quite informative on solar system's current status. He expected that the SIL11 had been notified by the Dimensionless Ones, but wasn't really interested in the details of that communication as though he heard all before. He glazed over many details about himself, for example why he volunteered to stay behind or more likely why he was 'volunteered' to stay behind. His response was that somebody had to stay behind and it was before the arrival of the Gatekeepers. With most of the SIL11 crew, it didn't quite ring true and it gave the impression that he was hiding secrets about himself. Luther mentioned to other crewmembers that he was convinced that Ivan was definitely human with some inherent human flaws of his own. Subsequently, nobody pushed Ivan too hard on the matter.

Jacob heard the compelling stories that Ivan was telling his crew. He believed most of it, and was consistent with all their experiences since arriving back to their solar system as well as the story of the Tandoorians, that the SIL11 had encountered. But he still didn't trust the man. Ivan asked him, "Where are we going? And what are we going to do?" Jacob responded rather slowly to him, "I can tell you where we are not going, Earth, the Moon and Mars and definitely not Saturn as well." But Jacob didn't give him any more information than that. After Jacob's terse response to his question, Ivan replied, "I guess I'll be a hitchhiker then and see where our road leads, thanks for picking me up." He didn't bring up the subject of destination with Jacob again.

Chapter 16 - Reverse Subterfuge

To no one's surprise, Ivan was assigned to be under Christina's tutelage. Not only was it going to be a steep learning curve for Christina to learn this century's technology but for Ivan as well to learn this archaic and obsolete technology on board the SIL11. Christina had divided their time between the SIL11 and Ivan's shuttle craft.

Ivan was more interested in learning the systems and controls on board the SIL11 then teaching Christina the workings of his shuttle craft. As of now, Ivan realized that he would be scrutinized and watched, so he needed to become a model crew member, and hopefully shift attention away from him. He didn't like this captain, Jacob. He thought he was obstinate and arrogant for man coming from the past nearly two centuries ago. He knew that Jacob wanted Christina to become acquainted with equipment on board his shuttle, he so he did so he would appear totally helpful and transparent. Of course, he would not allow Christina to learn the inner workings of the security system on board his shuttle. If this captain knew all the capabilities of his spacecraft and the dangers it may pose to his SIL11, he would have scuttled him and his shuttlecraft at the earliest opportunity.

He would eventually find out where this SIL11 was headed. He knew the best course of action, is to leave this damned solar system and as quickly as possible. At least the captain was not entirely dense, since he was steering away from Earth and Mars, so he had time to plan in seizing the ship and escaping this solar system on his own. He should be able to convince Christina and the captain in making some important modifications to SIL11 for improved performance and longevity. He was certain they would be eager to take advantages of vastly new technologies, which they would be oblivious to them now.

He had time, so he needed to ring in his own demons at least temporarily. He had been alone for some time, and took notice of three women on board. They were all pregnant with same gestational period. Coming out of long term stasis does bring out sexual appetite in people, so he wasn't that surprised about it. Considering their current state, the women were not the most mouth-watering bait for him but these women were still young and attractive. They were the kind of women he loved to bring terror and pain to their lives; it was a hunger that he had which never seemed satisfied.

He could not help himself. He couldn't stop. It all started when he was a teenager. Girls were attracted to him for no apparent reason. In return, he enjoyed pinching them and pulling their hair. Of course he got in trouble in school and with the law, but he was a juvenile and was treated with kid gloves. His parents didn't do anything about his behavior, so he felt that he received permission to continue. His reputation seemed to attract some women even more. He strung two young girls and raped them both. He started cutting one of them with a pocket knife. She had cuts on her arms, her legs and breasts. The cuts were initially superficial but blood began to drip from the wounds, which excited him. He wanted more so he made the cuts a little deeper as he went. He left the face alone, but his enjoyment was interrupted by the girl behind him who began to scream wildly. Both girls were initiately gaged, but the one girl who was forced to watch had managed to get her gag out of her mouth. He enjoyed listening to the screaming initially, but realized that he would be discovered if she did not desist her screaming. So he plunged his pocket knife into her abdomen and continued stabbing her until the screaming stopped. He told the other girl with the cuts that he was out of time and needed to leave. She was allowed to live by his good graces. Of course, he never returned home and evaded the law enforcement for years to come. Finally his hunger would get the best of him, and eventually he ended in prison for a number of years. He became a model prisoner and was eventually released which was most likely an administrative error.

He learned to be a shuttle pilot, but very few were interested in his skills locally. He looked for work off world, maybe on Mars or the asteroid belt. When he assigned on Chiron, he started satisfying his hunger again by raping of two women. He allowed them to live which may have been his mistake since he was quickly incarcerated. He was monitored continuously anytime he was outside his quarters and was avoided by the crew, especially the other women. The only companionship was being roughed up a bit by Chiron security guards. His being 'volunteered' to remain on Chiron after the others left for the Dimensionless Ones was not quite true, but this SIL11 crew seemed naïve enough to accept his account of events. The fact was that he was marooned there by the rest of Chiron inhabitants. He grinned to himself to think that this fool of a captain had assigned him to his future wife. But he would have to refrain from the impulse of having his way with this woman until the time was ripe. Maybe he'll give it to them as a wedding present raping her and killing them both, which sounded quite delicious to him.

***

Luther found his way down to Christina's quarters and had asked Jacob to join him. He had concerns about their new passenger, Ivan. He did not regret in supporting taking him on board, since it was their only choice. In Luther's mind, they had been hijacked, and Ivan was a criminal until proven otherwise. He felt everybody on board was part of his family and Ivan was a threat to them all and it would be better to be rid of him, sooner than later. Before he decided he could the same to them. Luther and Jessica had been monitoring his activities 24/7 since he came on board. Luther had no qualms regarding personal freedoms or privacy; they were a far second to the security of his family. He was really quite surprise regarding his own reaction to this new crew member. Ivan was after all, very agreeable and very open about most things and most importantly, he was the first human contact since returning their solar system. It may not look good to others in this solar system if they did not take this refugee in. But his evasiveness on his being left behind on Chiron, and poor acting job about his acceptance and eagerness to please gnawed at Luther. Luther knew that Ivan hated his son, and might turn out to be a possible target for Ivan. Once the captain was disposed of, Ivan could think the biggest obstacle of taking over the SIL11 had been removed.

He felt that the shuttle should be off limits to Ivan, it was too large of a risk. He knew he would get an earful from Christina and probably from his son as well. Christina would feel that it was the only way to acquire an understanding of its technology was to have Ivan show Christina the systems on board. Jacob would be hungry for some of the technology to improve the SIL11. His largest concern was the Yamas, or Gatekeepers, and if the shuttle had technology that could help to disguise them, it was be his highest priority. They would suffer certain death if the Gatekeepers learn about their existence.

Gatekeepers seemed to be most inappropriate name for the Yamas but only the SIL7 captain referred to these beings as Yamas. So Jacob decided to refer to these creatures as the Gatekeepers. Regardless, the SIL11 needed to avoid any potential contact with them. He felt for some reason, the Ivan would be in complete agreement with him. He didn't think that Ivan had some alliance with this enemy. When he talked, he appeared to have a genuine hatred for Gatekeepers. It may have come from Gatekeepers killing one or more of his family members since it seemed very personal. Along with his hatred was a healthy dose of fear but he did not dwell or elaborate on his fears. The SIL11 crew knew where the Gatekeepers were, but Luther was more concerned about a potential enemy on board pretending to be a friend.

Jacob had caught up with him as they were nearing Christina's quarters. Christina would probably move in with Jacob in the near future, and free the quarters for someone else.

"Hey Dad, what's this about? I did notice that you were not very talkative at our last meeting discussing our guest. Do you trust him?'

Luther stopped in the tracks and turned to face his son. He put up a finger up to his mouth as if asking for quiet.

"Keep your voice down. He might be monitoring us right now for all we know. NO! I don't trust him at all. The sooner he is off this ship the better."

Jacob eyes grew large, "Why this reaction, he hasn't showed any ill will to anybody and seem to have accepted his role enthusiastically. Christina says he is slowly learning his task and willing answer any of her questions regarding the mechanisms of his ship. Why this sudden hostility towards him?" Jacob wanted to know.

"Look son, you know I had some training in psychiatry, right?" Luther whispered, "And Ivan has had practice in subterfuge or deception, but for me, he has been relatively easy to read." Luther paused and asked his son, "Do you think he likes you?"

"I don't think so, but he hasn't shown any aggression towards me."

"Son take my word on this, you need to absolutely watch your back on him. He really does hate you and has taken an unhealthy interest in your fiancé as well."

Jacob stood silent and reflected on his dealings with Ivan. He couldn't comprehend how his father could come up with such a conclusion in such a short time.

"Yes, I may be overreacting to Ivan, but only a little. Ivan is quite disturbing to my psychiatry side of me. And this crew, every one of them is now a member of my family! I will protect them at all costs, even you. First of all, he is lying about volunteering to stay behind at Chiron. I'm convinced the other Chiron inhabitants marooned him there, and he must have committed quite a treacherous crime for them to leave him behind, " Luther paused the continued, "when we reach Christina's quarters signal Christina to be silent and begin looking for any device or object on her person or clothes. Ivan has had too much opportunity not to have a listening or tracking device on her person for Ivan to monitor."

"Dad that sounds paranoid. Why would he do that?" asked Jacob.

"First of all, I don't trust him and he has almost two centuries of technology on us . I doubt very much that he trusts us, but views us as some cavemen found in some unexplored cave in Antarctica. Let's just take precautions. Don't send her anything electronically, that would make it too easy for him to track with his technology. Just use archaic hand signals as I did with you, to keep your voice down."

Jacob looked at his father, "What do mean cavemen and where is Anartica?"

Luther replied, "Never mind that now. It seems that geography has always been a waste on you. Anyway, go down to her quarters and bring her out here with minimal discussion. Then we will go to Jessica's quarters, where I know Ivan had not ventured. Jessica will use a microscopic scanner on her person to make sure he is not listening and we are not overheard."

"I have already arranged with Sarah to distract Ivan by taking him on a tour of the farm along with Todd. I don't really want my daughter to be alone with the man, but I needed someone I could trust."

"Wow, and I here I thought I was captain" Jacob laughed.

Christina, Jacob and Luther entered Jessica's quarters. Jessica indicated to Christina to lie still on her bed and then Jessica began to scan Christina's person and clothes for unidentified objects of any size or shape. To Jacob's surprise, Jessica found two different objects, one that looked like a single hair among her own hair that appeared to some sort of transmitter and another small adhesive cube, less than a millimeter in length stuck between her two toes."

The last one even shocked Christina. She had no idea how that the second device got between her toes, unless the device was able to move on its own. Jessica secured the two objects in a small carrying case and went down the hall to Luther's quarters and set them inside. They would have to come up with a story for Ivan, if he asks Christina where she had been and what she was doing. It was imperative to let Ivan believe that he still had the upper hand. She would also give those two items a closer look, and see what they were and how they operated. When she came back to her quarters, she could tell that both Christina and Jacob were angry.

"Nerve of that man!" Christina was yelling.

Jacob countered, "I think we should through him into the airlock without a spacesuit and see how advance he really is. Damn it Dad, you were right all along."

"Don't get too rash, son. All we know is that he is monitoring us. After all, we don't trust him, and I have no doubt that he doesn't trust us either. I don't think killing him is a good choice. I hope I don't regret saying that later though."

After a pause, Luther added, "At least, you and Christina know now what we might be up against. I think it's important, that we allow him to think he has the upper hand. I would highly recommend not allowing him access to his ship at all. I think he would understand that its precautionary on our part after all he would suspect that we would still be a little mistrusting, but he will cry out like hell to convince you otherwise and argue that it is his ship and rightly so. But regardless I think it would be a mistake to allow him free access to his ship."

Jacob turned to Christina, "I don't want you working with him anymore."

Luther quickly interjected, "Son, I think that would be a mistake. He would probably figure out that we were already on to him, if you did that."

Christina turned to Jacob, "Your dad is right, the SIL11 is currently safe from him as long as he thinks we are in the dark."

"What about your personal safety and our child's?" Jacob asked his future wife.

"Look son, Jessica and I have been monitoring him since he's been on board. You can see for yourself the Jessica's PCD has eyes on him from various cameras that were on board and few new ones that we recently installed. We are continuously adding more cameras. See for yourself."

Both Christina and Jacob viewed the PCD and saw Ivan and Sarah standing next to Todd who was bending over grasping at a bunch of grapes at the farm. When Christina put the earphones on attached to the PCD, she could hear them talking.

"Well I'm glad that not all of you are boring Todd," said Ivan, "How does your wine taste?"

"It tastes good to us, and Luther thinks it tastes similar to the wine he had when he was on Earth. But the rest of us don't really know what wine is supposed to taste like. Would you like some?"

Ivan answered, "You don't have to ask me twice, lead the way."

Christina removed the earphones, "Jacob if it's OK with you, I think we should try this reverse subterfuge as your dad proposes."

Jacob looked around to everybody. He hesitated in his response. He wanted his future wife and his child to be safe of course. The fear of course, was that none of them knew what Ivan was capable of, especially with his unknown technologies. Jacob also thought to himself, if they are wrong about him and he was just innocent, then he would be subjected to undeserved actions by the crew, which would be cruel. He himself, wanted to kill him after all, but that was rash response and not a well-conceived plan. His dad always had this sixth sense about people even before his psychiatric training. Now, he was quite formidable in reading people and as far as he knew, he never had been wrong about his initial read of people. But Ivan's conduct had been so far exemplary and his behavior appeared normal. Hadn't he told everyone that they should show a measure of trust in Ivan? His dad though had definitely had sabotaged any possibility of that. So he decided to rely on his own gut feeling, and the truth of the matter was that he didn't like the man.

He would go along with this reverse subterfuge plan but only until Ivan could be safely subdued and put into cryostatis. He told Jessica and his dad to keep monitoring him, and told Christina to be extra cautious around him but not to act like it. He asked his dad if there was a small subcutaneous injector that Sarah could conceal and when the time was right inject Ivan to render him immediately unconscious. Luther new exactly what to use and would prepare some doses for Sarah. Lastly he told them, but prepared for anything and always assume that they are being watched.

***

Ivan grabbed the bottle out of Todd's hands and poured himself another glassful.

Ivan looked at Sarah, "Don't you want to join in?" he asked offering the bottle to her.

77

Sarah was stone-faced. He was politely flirting with her, ever since they had left the farm and in front of her husband. She couldn't believe it since she was obviously pregnant, but he still seemed to care less about her pregnancy and lusted for her. She knew that Todd was just playing along and being a gracious host, but she could tell that Todd was not happy. She was a doctor, and understood that Ivan could be feeling some strong sexual desires again, now that he was among women again, so she was not going to make a scene. Maybe she should introduce Ivan to Jessica, since Jessica never met a man she didn't like. But it was complicated now with her father involved with Jessica, and Jessica had seemed much more subdued either because of her pregnancy or because of her dad's influence.

"Sorry, Ivan but as you know I'm with child," she said pointing to her enlarged midsection.

Ivan looked at Todd and said, "Well I guess it's just us then."

Ivan had come to find out that this woman was Jacob's sister. He could easily imagine her not being pregnant and shoving his fingers deeply into her and grapping her smooth neck with the other. Of course, the more he thought about it, it wouldn't matter if she was pregnant or not, just as long he could see her life vanish from her eyes. But not now, he had to slow down his drinking and becomes friends with this husband, Todd. He needed friends and needed to have some acceptance if his plan to take over the SIL11 was going to work. But this Todd fellow seemed like a complete imbecile, but no matter he was a good actor. Not only that but he had time, they were not going anywhere without him and his ship. Besides he had managed to put surveillance equipment on both Christina and Todd who have entered his shuttle, and soon they would be on everyone.

Chapter 17 - New Plans

Jacob notified Ivan that he needed to speak with him the next morning after his meeting with Christina, Jessica and his dad. Todd had done his job quite well, since Ivan was quite hungover for their meeting. Jacob hoped that his reduced mental status would hamper him in becoming overly exciting about denying him his ship.

Overnight, Jacob had put some new plans into action. He had Ivan's surveillance equipment that was found on Christina scattered in Christina's quarters; the cubic tracking device on the floor of the bathroom and the hair-like listening device under Christina's pillow. He hoped that Ivan would continue to feel confident about having the upper hand but of course Christina was not in the room. Jacob didn't want Christina anywhere near Ivan if he took exception. Christina was outside undocking Ivan's shuttle craft from the SIL side without disturbing the shuttle, since he was convinced that Ivan would be aware of any specific tampering with his shuttle. By now, the shuttle was only held to the SIL11 by two tethers which could be easily released if needed, but it was meant only as last means of deterrence. Meantime, Sarah was standing by in the spacesuit dressing room near Christina's quarters armed with an air gun that could stealthy launch a knockout hypo and put their guest to sleep. Sarah was the best shot on board and had the gumption to use it. It was a hobby she picked up from their mother who use to shoot single shot old fashion rifles for the Olympic trials. Their mom was truly the expert shot, one of her many talents, but Sarah was not far behind her in that skill.

***

Ivan received the captain's message to report to him in Christina's quarters. He cussed to himself about the amount of wine he had consumed just hours ago. Maybe the cute woman doctor, Sarah would give him something to relieve his self-inflicted headache. But, he was a crew member now and needed to follow his damn orders first and make a good impression on the captain. He dressed himself and wondered what the captain wanted since the summons did not include that information. He looked at his surveillance on Christina and Todd. Todd was in quarters, sleeping it off like he should be doing and Christina was surprisingly still in her quarters. Maybe it was some engineering task that he wanted Christina and him to jointly start. He was surprised that they had not asked about new technology from him sooner. This is where he would acquire more confidence in the crew by giving some well-needed technology to them. He already knew the routes to both Christina's and Sarah's quarters, so went on his way without an escort, at least he wasn't going to wait for one.

When he was nearing Christina's quarters, he received information from his armband that someone was in the ship's spacesuit dressing room. He took note of it but took no action, since he did not want to appear to be nosey to the crew. But he also was alerted that there was a small unidentified motion around his shuttle craft. He immediately set the autopilot for the shuttle to arm band command. It was probably some small space debris bouncing off his shuttle or a cloud of dust which caused the SIL11 to vibrate. There had been no tampering with his shuttle's systems, so he wasn't alarmed, so he decided to investigate the matter later.

He smiled when he arrived outside Christina's quarters. Antiquated intercom system was just left of the door, what a great museum piece. He hoped that Christina might be scantily dressed when he entered but he very much doubted that.

He pushed the appropriate button, "Captain, Ivan reporting."

Jacob immediately responded, "Please come in, Ivan."

Ivan strode in wearing a constructed smile. "What's up captain?" He looked around the room in a sudden panic, noticing that Christina was not in the room.

"Where's Christina?" Ivan blurted out.

"She should be in the spacesuit dressing room getting prepared," Jacob mildly responded.

Jacob could tell that Ivan was becoming agitated. He wanted Ivan less defensive, so he replied disarmingly, "Christina tells me that you have been quick learner considering since our controls and systems would appear quite antiquated to you. She also has said that you have been cooperative about teaching about your ship's systems and controls to her."

Ivan relaxed a bit and said, "Thank you, captain that means a lot coming from you."

"Only thing is, Christina is getting a little frustrated with herself for not learning quickly enough. Not sure what the problem, she is a gifted engineer, don't you think?"

"Yes sir, but all your people have almost 200 hundred years of catch up to do."

"Don't get alarmed Ivan, but I have decided to close off your ship from the crew until we understand its operations better. I do consider it a risk to my ship as well as a security risk."

"I don't understand, you don't trust your own crew with the shuttle?"

Jacob allowed some time to slip by watching Ivan intently, "I don't think you heard me correctly, I mean the entire crew, including you," Jacob clarified.

Ivan's smile disappeared from his face and was replaced with a small frown and dilated eyes. He made a small step towards Jacob but stopped suddenly. He wasn't ready for this confrontation. He felt that he could subdue the captain, but he didn't know where the rest of the crew was. He always felt that he was under constant surveillance himself since arriving on board and this might turn out to be a fatal step, if acted on his sudden rage and his thirst for violence. He replied, "What do you mean to keep me away from my own ship, CAPTAIN?" he asked between his clenched teeth.

"Yes I do. Hope you understand. But I consider your free excess to your ship without our knowledge, a risk that is currently unacceptable. Especially with a race of beings out there who want to destroy this ship without provocation on a moment's notice. In addition, we have no weaponry that could possibly deflect such an attack from the Gatekeepers." Jacob said hoping to sound genuine as if all his concern was about the Gatekeepers.

Ivan took a deep breath. "Captain, your concern with the Gatekeepers is highly warranted it. But you will not find a stronger ally against them then me."

Jacob responded, "Good, follow me then."

Ivan followed Jacob into the spacesuit dressing room, where he expected to see Christina and find out what moronic but noble task the captain wanted to accomplish. He didn't see Christina in the dressing room, but heard a female voice from behind say, "This is for your hangover."

He immediately activated his personal force field. And the dart with the strong sedative harmlessly bounced off him. He turned to Sarah saying, "You have a big mouth," and slapped fiercely across her face. Sarah fell in a heap.

Jacob began to move towards Ivan. But Ivan took out a small device under his armband and pointed it at Jacob and said, "I'll kill you if you take another step, captain."

Jacob froze. He didn't know whether Ivan was bluffing or not, but he couldn't risk it. Ivan bent down to pick up the dart and looked at Jacob.

"What was your plan, captain? I would really like to know."

"Ivan disarm yourself, or I will release your space shuttle from the SIL11 and let it float away in space. And you won't have a spaceship anymore."

Christina had been monitoring the conversation outside and said over the intercom, "I'm releasing the shuttle in 20 seconds unless I get orders from you captain to stop."

"Captain and Christina, both of you are being a bit dramatic, don't you think. I have full control of the shuttle right here. Watch as I maneuver the shuttle to other side of SIL11."

Chirstina gasped, "Sorry captain, somehow he does have full control."

Ivan responded to her, "You will need to come through this airlock, you fucking slut. All the other airlocks have been inactivated. How much air do you have left my pet."

He turned his glaring eyes onto Jacob. "You had a good plan but your sluts don't seem know how to carry them out. Now, I'll be taking over your spacecraft after I rape your sister and choke her to death, and rape your future wife. Of course, you will be knocked out with this drug you intended for me while I'm doing this," Ivan gloated waving the dart at Jacob.

Ivan added, "Actually I wish you could watch.me do your sister and your future wife before I kill you. But even us future people have limitations. But it will be quite a family affair, don't you think."

Ivan realized something was wrong when he began to collapse totally paralyzed. At the same time, Jacob was collapsing. Ivan thought he heard an unfamiliar voice before losing consciousness saying, "NOT WITH MY FAMILY."

***

81

Jessica and Luther watched Jacob and Ivan collapse on the floor. Luther released his finger from the intercom button and backed away. Jessica stopped injecting anesthesia into the room air and held Luther for one soothing moment and said, "He was worse than you thought." Luther held her and allowed himself to briefly allowed his lungs fill with air and slowly breathe it out. Jessica felt good to him, but they had things to do.

Both Jessica and Luther already had their gas masks on and quickly started making their way to the back of the ship. When they arrived, Luther immediately gave Ivan an injection of a strong sedative, which would have him unconscious for at least 3 hours. The anesthetizing gas was only temporary, but humans obviously still reacted physically to it as they 200 years ago. After administering the injection to Ivan, and went over to his daughter. He took out his modernized stethoscope out and listened to her heart and the fetus's. There was other equipment that would have accomplished the same thing with less effort, but it was comforting to him to hear their hearts directly. He grimaced at the sight of bruising on her right cheek and around her right eye, and continued monitoring them until Sarah began to stir. Jessica went over to Jacob to make sure that he didn't sustain any injuries from his fall but he was also beginning to awaken and seemed unharmed.

Jacob turned to his father and said in halting speech, "Wh--, whaaat happen?"

"Son, I hope you don't mind but I came up with another backup plan this morning."

Jacob could only smile and shake his head a little.

Jessica turned on the intercom, "Christina are you OK? It's all clear for you to come in, Ivan is laying on the floor in a heap."

"Wait till I get on board and kick that son-of-a-bitch in the groin a few times, then I'll feel OK," Christina responded.

Jessica responded with a laugh, "Sounds good, over and out."

Chapter 18 - Ceres

After Sarah had removed a few devices from Ivan's body and confirmed that what was left was just his tissue, bone and blood, Jacob and her put Ivan into a cryochamber for a long sleep. Sarah even scanned his body for potential nanoparticles or nano-devices but had found none. Even though, he was quite helpless, Jacob put restraints on him while he was in stasis which was of course quite absurd. Jacob just wanted to rest easier. The crew left him and went about their business, which was preparations for Ceres, free of anxiety about the man and bewildered that they had been fooled by him. But Jacob didn't stop at the restraints; he also programmed his PCD to monitor Ivan's stasis condition and would alert him instantly of any changes, no matter how minor.

Sarah performed a full physical on Christina, after she had her physical by her father on his absolute insistence. She put a brief fuss but nothing too elaborate. She actually enjoyed her father's attention, drawing it away from that woman, Jessica. She was kicking herself for opening her big mouth, when she had Ivan in her sights. Ivan did strike her rather hard, but it was a good lesson that she was glad to learn. Afterwards, Sarah went down to join her husband. He had missed another huge drama by sleeping it away. But he did his job that's what counts and Sarah wanted to reward the man. She was thinking of some succulent ways of doing so.

After Christina's physical, she left everyone in very irritable mood. After a brief hug with her future husband, not even Jacob wanted to venture to ask what was eating at her. She was not talkative to anyone. Christina was angry mostly at herself for not anticipating Ivan's moves. If had not been for Luther, the entire crew could have perished. She first wanted to know how Ivan had inactivated the airlocks except for the one, and she wanted to know how Ivan took control of his shuttle craft so easily. The second move, she may be able to forgive herself, since it was probably the technology that she had yet to comprehend. But Jacob was right during his conversation with Ivan that she was learning the technology to slowly. Christina understood that the conversation was just a poly of Jacob's part but now she was beginning to believe it. After Ivan became unconscious, the shuttle rotated itself to its original position and was appearing to allow itself to be docked with the SIL11 again. There was some discussion of scraping the shuttle but it may prove to be vital commodity in when they enter asteroid belt or the inner solar system. Even the idea there was on some self-destruct mechanism was considered, but dismissed by Jacob and the crew. She was planning to spend a great deal of time on board Ivan's shuttle and find a door through its security system. SIL11 needed that technology. But first, she was going outside, after a quick nap and bite to eat to investigate what happened to the other airlocks.

Jacob was also upset with himself about his misjudgment of Ivan. Ivan had more clever tricks then Jacob anticipated and it could of cost him; his ship, his crew, his future wife and his life. But Jacob did not have luxury of brooding over the past. Ceres had not yet become visible to the SIL11 but he had their course zooming towards it. He knew that there might be a whole host of possible problems when they arrive, so should they, the SIL11, consider other options.

How much stock did he have now in the general assessments of the solar system by Ivan, Jacob asked himself. The psychopath was definitely less forthcoming about his technology and directly lied about his situation at Chiron. But how he described the status of the solar system seemed more than just plausible; not only did his dialogue correlated well with all their data, and was consistent with the

Tandoorian story, but there was something more. Ivan held certain convictions and resolve when he talked passionately about the Gatekeepers, and there was no hint of dishonestly in those specific dialogues. Jacob's father agreed in principal with his assessment of Ivan's stories but did not discount the possibility that he had lied about everything just gain a small advantage for his attempted mutiny.

So if he believed in Ivan's assessment, should they, SIL11 continue onto Ceres? The Gatekeepers had ventured into the asteroid belt hunting down some of the larger human instillations accordingly to Ivan, and undoubtedly Ceres would have been target. Since Ceres had been a prior target, maybe they would be less likely to return there. It was the largest body that would on their side of the solar system before arriving at Venus and the best chance of assessing on their own the human situation in the solar system as well as collaborating Ivan's stories. But a stop at Ceres could be highly risky. Even if the Gatekeepers ships were not in the area, Ceres could be under surveillance or be set as a trap. If either scenario is true then, their ship would be doomed. According to Ivan, the Gatekeepers brought four battlecruisers into their solar system. One was orbiting Titan, another was in the proximity of Earth and still another should be around Mars. Ivan had mentioned that a fourth that ferried off human prisoners back to their own world or some other world, and had recently left the solar system. In the weeks that followed Ivan's attempted mutiny, he was able to pinpoint the location of the two remaining Gatekeeper ships with the ship's MDS; one indeed was in low orbit around the Moon and another in a low orbit around Mars. The enormous size of their ships made them easy to detect. It was if camouflage and deception was not part of their battle strategies, and it appeared that their boldness or arrogance did not allow for such cautious thinking. It was first time that Jacob sensed that this was a dent in their armor, a possible flaw or weakness than may someday be exploited. But for now, hiding was only strategy for SIL11.

Another two reasons for coming to Ceres were for a course adjustment for Venus and another less intense braking procedure to slow down the SIL11 even further. Ivan had indicated there were rumors of a possible human underground organization near Venus but most people discounted it as just rumors, since Venus was still one of the inhospitable places in the solar system even in this century. Ivan had agreed with most people's view that they were only rumors.

If they were to alter their plan, what would be an alternative course of action? Jacob didn't really know. Obviously, they could escape their solar system but where would they go? Ivan did not have a course that was used for the Great Human Departure, or he purposefully kept it to himself. Most of the crew on the SIL11 had lived their entire lives on board this ship. He asked himself, did he want his son or daughter or the rest of the next generation to also be trapped forever on board on this spacecraft. This solar system was their ancestral home. He didn't want to leave it, unless there were no other options. There was also the problem of obtaining more antimatter, which they didn't have enough, if they considering any long term interstellar flight. He wished the Dimensionless Ones would again contact them and provide another option to them. But nobody had experience or seen anything unusual that would correspond to an incoming message from them. They appeared to be on their own, the decision was theirs. Jacob though was fairly certain that they had not heard the last from the Dimensionless Ones. Even though they were still months away from Ceres, he needed to make a decision soon. He again called an all hands meeting but this time he allowed enough time for his people to prepare.

***

Christina flipped through her PCD organizing the data regarding the Ivan's shuttlecraft while waiting for the others. She had coined the name for the shuttle as IOSAC (Ivan's Orbtial Shuttle Around Chiron). She had learned a great deal about IOSAC operations and systems. She still didn't have security access to operate or control the ship but hopefully she would have it soon. She also didn't quite know how IOSAC harvested neutrinos for its propulsion. But it had obvious advantages over their antimatter propulsion aboard the SIL11. It was safer, had an endless fuel supply and was more efficient allowing for quicker acceleration to speeds approaching the speed of light. But IOSAC security system was the real stumbling block. There was something that she was missing.

Jessica and Luther entered the galley and prepared some syn-coffee for themselves.

"Hey Christina, do you want some?" Jessica asked.

Christina politely declined since she was already quite alert and felt simulated enough. "Hey Jessica, were you able to obtain any information from those devices we found from Ivan and on myself?"

Jessica responded, "The devices we found on you were quite simplistic. As we thought, one was transmitter and the other a tracker. Both were somehow hooked to the shuttle, IOSAC… isn't that the name you gave it?

"Yeah that's the name I chose. Anyway, what about those other devices, that was either in or on Ivan?"

"Those devices are totally in stasis, like Ivan himself. No activity. No power. No way of knowing their function or how they operated. I was thinking of taking them apart to see if I could learn more."

Christina looked at Jessica. Jessica was still quite pompous despite her recent mellowing either from her pregnancy or Luther's influence. This was not a decision just for her, since the captain needed to be apprised of Jessica's plans.

"Don't you think you should consult with the engineer and the captain before taking things apart?" she retorted.

"Wow, aren't we a bit touchy today," Jessica responded.

Luther broke in before a fight broke out, "Ladies let's focus on why your captain has asked us here. Right now, it's monumental decision that the captain has to make, regarding what our next steps should be. He deserves our energies to be focused on helping him to make the right decision."

Chrisitna gave a quick smile to Luther and a brief glare at Jessica. "How can we know what the right decision is? Any decision we make may damn us anyway. Maybe we are already damned."

"I hope you have something better than that for your captain," replied Jessica with a smug look. "After all he probably already knows what you think already, doesn't he? Just remember the rest of us don't know what goes on in that bedroom of yours, except for the obvious," Jessica said pointing to Christina's midsection.

"Neither of you are being helpful right now," interjected Luther.

Jessica turned to Luther. "I'm sorry. You know how I feel already about this."

"Yes I do, but nobody else does. Let's wait on the captain and everyone else before we start exchanging ideas."

Christina and Jessica exchanged looks and both nodded towards Luther.

Sarah and Todd came into the galley. Upon seeing the syn-coffee in front of Jessica and Luther, Todd decided to prepare a cup for himself and another for Sarah.

Sarah momentarily watched Christina and Jessica exchange looks at one another while Todd prepared her coffee. She witnessed a moment of exasperation on her father's face as well. Too bad she had missed the cat fight between the future moms, Sarah thought, it would have been entertaining. But she decided not to probe since she realized her involvement may have ignited a situation that was already volatile. Women did tend to get a little more emotional during pregnancy, or how did her husband put it, a little bitchier than usual.

"How are you two feeling these days?" Sarah asked innocently looking at Jessica and Christina.

She added, "Christina you are bit overdue for your examination. Your last one was when you were in your second trimester, but now you should be in your third trimester. Maybe we can set something up after the meeting? Or even better, I can give you exam after the meeting. Your choice."

Christina looked up from her PCD to Sarah. She felt perfectly fine, but she would acquiesce to her suggestion. She didn't want to snap at both of her women 'friends.' She smiled at Sarah.

"After the meeting, would be fine, Sarah. Just know I feel fine, and it will probably be a waste of your time anyway. But you're the doctor, and I'll comply," Christina responded.

"Nonsense! It's never a waste of time for telling someone that they are medically fit. It's much better than the alternative."

Luther smiled at her daughter. She had improved on her bedside manner. "I agree," he added.

"Hello everyone," Jacob announced as he entered the galley somewhat oblivious to everyone's eyes on him.

"You all know why we are here. I will like everyone not only give an opinion on what they think is our best course of action, but also to carefully listen to everyone else's opinion," he said as he sat himself at the head of the table and not next to Christina as everyone had expected. Christina was still buried in her PCD files and did react to Jacob decision to sit elsewhere.

"How about we start with the youngest and then go to the oldest. Sorry Dad. Christina?"

Christina put down her PCD and looked around the table. She knew the reason why Jacob was sitting the head of the table and she was not troubled by it. Jacob had explained that he wanted to demonstrate to everyone else that her opinions were her own by giving her the spotlight, and having it totally on her. Hopefully, they would all take heed on what she had to say. Christina also knew that on this particular occasion her opinion was not the same as his, but he still wanted everyone to hear her. She smiled also thinking that she was very bitchy this morning, and Jacob had the common sense of sitting away from her and that was the real reason.

"In my opinion, we should leave this place of death that we use to know as our solar system. It is obviously not ours anymore. The Gatekeepers will only destroy us or enslave us not if, but when they detect us. Of course, neither is a desirable alternative. We have the IOSAC, Ivan's shuttle, which we can learn from and hopefully transcend out limitations for space travel. Remember the Tandoorians had an entire kingdom after their massive exodus but all we found was a tomb when we had arrived."

Everyone kept quiet with everyone looking at everyone else.

"Thanks Christina," Jacob said breaking the uneasy silence.

"Jessica?"

"Yes, there is a high risk of being detected as we venture closer to the sun. But, with the good captain piloting us, I believe, we have a higher chance of escaping detection than not. I want to stay at our ancestral home, this is where we belong. I don't want to go into another deep sleep or my children to go into one. I'm also selfish, and I don't want my new found love to go into one and never waking again." Jessica reached out and grasped Luther's hand and then continued, "However, I do believe traveling to Ceres is an unnecessary risk. It has probably has been destroyed by the Gatekeepers and what we can learn from ruins is not worth the risk of being detected. Our recent experience with Ivan shows us not to underestimate our enemies. We got lucky because we had a lovable old-timer who gave us that one more layer of security. My choice is to travel directly to Venus. I am inspired from hearing of a possible underground, and maybe eventually finding ways to defend our solar system to repel these invaders. I would prefer to fight over running away," concluded Jessica.

"Sarah?"

Sarah decided not to be rash or overconfident in developing her opinion. She had spent long periods of time contemplating on what she was going to say to the crew. She thought she would bring in a bit of humor before suggesting her ideas to them."

"As probably many of you have guessed, I usually oppose whatever my twin brother suggests," to her relief there were a few small laughs from everyone.

She continued, "But the captain has managed for everyone to hear my opinion before his, even though technically, I'm the oldest. So, I'll just have to guess what he might say, so I don't disappoint everyone."

She paused and was thrilled to see large smiles on everyone's faces. She even got complimentary nod from her father. She continued, "I, too, don't want to leave our solar system. And it might be a shock to everyone, but I agree on the course that my twin brother has already had lain in for us. Ceres will be far away from Earth, Mars, and Saturn and far away from the Gatekeepers. I would suspect that any security net that the Gatekeepers use, would be between Ceres and Earth, not in the opposite direction. When I was hearing the stories regarding the Gatekeepers from Ivan, I was horrified at the extreme sadistic brutality they seem to hold for the human race but also they displayed absolute arrogance for their technology and sheer disgust on the limitations of our own. It was like that we were not even worthy opponents for their race and to obtain any gratification they had to torture our people to make it worth their while. Sadly to say, it almost sounds like man's darker side. Therefore, I'm with Jessica, I don't think we will be detected if we are careful enough. But, in my opinion, we should find out what's on Ceres and not avoid it. Once we leave the asteroid belt to venture into the inner solar system, we most likely will not have an opportunity to come back to Ceres. Hopefully we will run into others like Ivan, but these survivors would hopefully be sane, of course. The asteroid belt is the mostly likely location for survivors. I don't even think the Gatekeepers will consider survivors in deep space, a worthwhile quarry. Remember, Tandoorians were not visited by the Gatekeepers and why was that? Maybe the Gatekeepers already knew that their race was doomed and controlling the Southern sect did not seem like worthwhile endeavor from them," Sarah concluded.

Jacob smiled at his sister, "Well this is a first. Those were my thoughts too. Todd?"

Todd got up and poured himself a fresh cup of syn-coffee. He went around the room asking everybody if they wanted a warm up. When he was finished, he sat down and looked at everyone.

"Well as you probably guess, I agree with my wife. I won't want to add any more surprise than we have had already," he said grinning at Jacob. Then he added, "there is one thing I would like to add, not as an actual 'course of action' but more like just a thought. I firmly believe whatever we decide the Dimensionless Ones will contact us again. Whatever we were planning to do, it will probably change, if we still decide to continue following their instructions. I don't think whatever we decide will be wrong as long as we continue to follow their instructions. I for one am a strong believer in these Dimensionless Ones. Now, I think it's time for a glass of wine," Todd concluded.

"Sure Todd but let's hear one more opinion, my dad's," countered Jacob.

Luther began speaking, "You all have wise and well thought out ideas for what we should do. Todd is probably the most correct; we should accept the possibility that whatever we decide now could change on moment's notice. Christina you may have the wisest choice of all, and that is to get out of this dreaded solar system at all costs. You are not just thinking about your personal safety but the safety of your child as well. A mother's love is still one of the strongest forces in the universe. But I don't agree with you on this one, Christina, I tend to agree with my children, Sarah and Jacob. Sorry, my love but I think Ceres is worthwhile destination but at the same time I agree with you, it is highly risky. There is one thing we might consider to reduce our anxiety about Ceres being spied on and bobby-trapped. We do have another ship, the IOSAC , and a dummy passenger, Ivan. We can put Ivan in the ship with his cryochamber and remotely pilot the IOSAC to Ceres at a safe distance. Allow it to land, delay a day or two, and then remotely pilot it back to the SIL11. If nothing happens to the IOSAC, they we may assume it alright for a short term look at Ceres ourselves. But I would keep our visit short on Ceres and then head to Venus," Luther concluded.

Christina responded to Luther, "But we don't know how the IOSAC operates."

Luther smiled, "I'm sure you and Jessica can figure it out, before we get there. I have great confidence in the both of you and wonderful combination of science and engineering. Don't you agree, Captain?"

Jacob looked around the room. Everyone had their say and he just then decided to continue on their present course to Ceres and add in, his dad's suggestion. "Yes, I do, dad. I'm sure they'll have the shuttle operating soon. So we will continue on to Ceres, until the Dimensionless Ones tell us otherwise. Todd how about some wine?"

"Right away, captain," replied Todd.

Todd poured a glass of wine for everyone, even the women who had a small sample of wine. Everyone raised their glass and Todd made a toast for a safe journey to Ceres and that Dimensionless Ones had not forgotten about them.

It was strange, not only did Jacob and Todd felt it, but everyone else felt that the Dimensionless Ones were still nearby.

Chapter 19 - The Secret

Christina took her PCD with her to Sarah's infirmary. She had sent a message to Jessica to meet up with her at the spacesuit changing room where the IOSAC was docked after her appointment with Sarah. She didn't want to waste any time in attempting to unlock or circumvent the IOSAC security system. Luther was a wizard in getting people motivated, she marveled including herself. She did feel that this was an obtainable goal and did not want to disappoint the crew. She hoped that Jessica would feel the same way. When looking at the data she had collected regarding the IOSAC, it appeared the most systems, if not all were automated. If she could leap over the security barricade, she or somebody would be able to pilot the shuttle. Of course, she was not yet certified to pilot a spacecraft. Only Jacob and Luther on board had any experience in piloting a space vessel of any type, but knowing all the systems on board with all the specifications, she felt at least she could stumble through it. She felt that she needed to get some resolution to this problem, or the whole crew may end up disenchanted her including Jacob. She knew that she was becoming somewhat of a bitch with the crew, which was expressing it mildly. She didn't like herself lashing out at her fellow crewmembers, since they were her family as well.

Sarah was somewhat delayed in keeping their appointment. Sarah had messaged her that she was on the way and would be only a few minutes late. When Christina was walking to the infirmary, she had an idea about one or the devices found on Ivan. It was a device that had been placed just under Ivan's skin. If she was going to use it the same way, she would need a dermal injector. Fortunately, there were few secrets outside crew quarters on the ship, so she knew exactly where to find one before Sarah returned.

Sarah seemed rather smug, thought Christina when Sarah returned and examined her. Maybe it was because she had finally gotten her way. Sarah was very polite and seemed genuinely concerned about her and her baby's health. Maybe her own pregnancy was mellowing her out. Her examination resulted in a bill of good health from Sarah for both her and her baby. She left the infirmary in better mood than she went in with the dermal injector in hand. Maybe there's hope for Sarah being a doctor after all.

Christina imagined her father and mother would be quite excited for her and would have absolutely spoiled their grandchild. Christina was the only child of the former captain and the communication expert, her mother. The former captain, her father had died quite violently. He succumbed to his mortal wounds in battling Tom, Jessica's older brother just after her father had killed Tom. It was a heart-breaking event for the crew and particularly to her that left 6 people murdered at the hands of Tom, Tom himself, and Jessica's and Tom's mother committed suicide shortly after. Her father should have been considered a hero in giving his life to save the rest of the crew at the hands of Tom. But the crew wanted to put it behind them, and even though they could never forget, the crew wanted to others things to distract them from those events. She had already had lost her mother to advanced pancreatic cancer soon after giving birth to her. She felt quite alone. It wasn't until Jacob's mother took her under her wing and began training her to be an engineer that finally drew her out of her shell. But she avoided Jacob's father, Luther. Luther did not save her mother from the ravages of cancer or prevent her father from dying. She knew it was totally unfair to blame him. It was later discovered later that her mother already had early cancer when she was pregnant with her and probably was undiagnosed when she came on board. A more thorough examination of her mother may have prevented their whole family from leaving Earth. As for her father, he had unrecoverable wounds that could not heal in time for the severe trauma he suffered not to take his life no matter what Luther did. And she knew that was all Tom. But Luther was only one available to blame for being alone, there was no one else left. She could have blamed Jessica for having her father killed but she wasn't a grown-up at the time, and she wanted a grown up to blame besides she was left alone as well and she felt some kindred feeling towards her back then even though she dared not show it. Now, that she was getting to know Luther and Luther was to become her father-in-law, she was regretting for avoiding him and blaming him all this time. At least now, she had a second chance to make amends with Luther but she needed to solve this security mystery of IOSAC to prove her worth to him.

Christina found Jessica quietly sitting on a bench near the spacesuits. Jessica looked up at her when she entered and immediately moved over on the bench to allow ample room for Christina to sit. Christina accepted the invitation and sat next to her. Some unusual emotion stirred in Christina when she stared at those large pooled eyes of Jessica but Christina promptly dismissed it.

Jessica's dark eyes met hers with a sign of remorse, "I'm sorry Christina, and I should always consult with you on matters regarding engineering including instrumentation."

"No worries," Christina responded and added, "I could have said that a little better than I did. Luther must have thought that I was going to bite your head off."

Jessica smiled, "Yes, men can be so sensitive, especially older men." She looked quickly away as though she was thinking of something entirely different.

Christina enjoyed the pleasantries with Jessica but she still wanted to start the task at hand as quickly as possible. "Jessica, did you bring the items from Ivan's person?"

Jessica placed an intricate woven armband down between them with two other small devices, one was earpiece found in Ivan's ear and the other was a small cube which was similar to the one found on Christina's toes but much smaller. All of them had fine hair-like structures associated with them.

"And you have no ideas on what the functions of any those devices are?" Christina asked.

"Well not exactly, this one for instance is obviously an earpiece but it has not produced a single sound since we retrieved it. So our guess for it being an auditory receiver cannot be confirmed. This one," Jessica said, pointing to the tiny cube "is some kind of dermal device but again it has had no activity with it since we retrieved it. Lastly this armband, has been thoroughly investigated, even this miniature weapon that Ivan threatened Jacob with has had no activity. No power, no switches, no nothing!"

"What are these hair-like projections?" asked Christina.

"I thought they may be some kind of wiring to human nervous system. But when I attached them to myself, again, no activity, no power."

"I know this might seem strange, but I believe these devices are the key to the IOSAC security system. There is nothing on board the IOSAC to indicate that there is some kind of separate security system and these devices on Ivan were just communication devices. This shuttle probably was meant to be used by various Chiron inhabitants. And I believe that these devices gave the shuttle user access to shuttle operations. I have examined all the systems on board the IOSAC and there is no other security and no other way to operate the shuttle."

Jessica responded, "Well these devices are either dead or broken."

Christina looked at Jessica, "I have an idea. Could you come on board the IOSAC with me?"

Jessica quickly said, "Of course, I would love to have a look around."

Christina added, "But first I need to over some of the IOSAC schematics with you and tell you what I know about the IOSAC. If my idea doesn't work, then we will need to start from the beginning."

Christina told Jessica most of the basics of the IOSAC technology using the schematics as a reference. Jessica was quite baffled about the neutrino propulsion system but neutrinos were quite energetic and abundant. Ivan had blatantly lied about the range of his shuttle, it appeared that the IOSAC could collect neutrinos on demand. Like Christina when she first arrived on the IOSAC, Jessica got caught up with the wonders of advanced technology. It was like a fairy tale to her.

Christina injected herself with the cube near as possible to the same location as where Ivan had worn it. She put his armband on and inserted the earpiece into her ear. Christina could not see, hear or feel anything from the devices as Jessica indicated.

"Yep, I don't feel or hear anything just as you said Jessica, but let's go on board. She pressurized the bridge and the IOSAC with air from the SIL11 and opened the airlock door. She motioned Jessica to come through and Christina followed behind her.

Soon as Christina entered into the IOSAC's domain, the hair-like structures began moving on her skin from the armband and in her ear from the earpiece and anchored the devices to her. She became aware of another presence. The presence was not hostile or aggressive but was totally submissive, waiting. She became aware or the surroundings around the entire IOSAC, the course it was on, and the fact it was attached to the SIL11. It seemed to her that the IOSAC was there in her mind awaiting her commands.

Christina also was aware that this awareness not only filled her but it was also affecting her unborn child. Her unborn child began kicking and hitting the walls of her uterus. She had just told Sarah about her unborn moving around inside a bit, and occasionally giving a good kick, but this was karate fight in her uterus. The IOSAC itself began to jerk around violently. This was a mistake, an awful mistake

"Jessica get me out of here," she screamed, "and get Sarah down here right away."

Unexpectedly, her lower torso tightened and cramped up. Was this the beginning of labor but didn't she have two months to go? She asked herself. She stumbled as Jessica grabbed for her. The smaller shuttle was beginning to affect the SIL11 with its turbulent actions. Too much of this and the small shuttle will put a huge whole in the side of the SIL11.

"Hurry," she gasped as Jessica was holding her up and making their way back to the SIL11. Jessica turned on the intercom as soon as they were out of airlock. "All hands, this is an emergency at the IOSAC airlock. Sarah, we need you right away, it's Christina, she looks ill. Over and out."

The cramping momentarily stopped, and Christina focused on the shuttle to stop and asked to be released. The shuttle immediately became quiet. The hairs retracted and the presence was gone. She immediately tugged the armband off her arm. She lay on the bench and tried to calm herself and her unborn child.

Her unborn stopped the karate fight inside and he/she seemed to relax. Christina took out her earpiece as well and drew in a deep breath. The twins were the first to arrive. Sarah began to examine Christina immediately. Jacob looked panic and pleaded to Jessica, "What the hell happen?"

Sarah reassured Christina and Jacob that both mother's and child's heartbeats were again normal. The rest of crew, Todd and Luther had also arrived. Christina felt much better, and now she had solved the mystery or the IOSAC security system. The security system was rebooted to whoever was wearing the armband and devices in the shuttle craft and was allowed full control of the shuttle using the human nervous system. Not only hers but apparently her baby's as well. She only hoped that her baby's commands had not caused any damage to the IOSAC or the SIL11.

Jessica began to tell Christina's future husband about the events that lead to her first contraction, when again her abdomen began tightening. Christina bent over grunting when her underwear and pants became wet. Jessica stopped her explanation to Jacob and looked down at Christina's grunting. At the same time, Sarah looked up to everyone and said, "We need to get her in the infirmary right away; her baby is coming."

Jacob grasped Christina's hand and looked at her with concerned eyes. Her second contraction began to subside and her eyes sparkled. Christina's hand gently tightened around her husband's hand, she smiled and then whispered "Guess what, I found out its little secret."

Chapter 20 - New Life

Christina gave birth to her premature son. He weighed in at only about 4 lb but he was healthy and already thriving in his incubator. Jacob, the proud father, visited his son whenever his duties allowed him. Sarah wanted him kept in the incubator for at least 2 weeks until his organs had more of a chance to mature. Christina had recovered quite quickly from the labor and spent most of her time with her son. He was not even the size of her forearm but she held him periodically and beamed at the face of her first son. He was quiet and his eyes had not yet the ability to focus, but he reacted to Christina's touch and made faces to her voice.

Jacob could no longer hold onto his anger towards Christina. Initially, he was ready to explode at Christina for pulling such a reckless stunt. At least, she had some sense to have somebody with her. She not only endangered herself and their child, but she had endangered the ship and the entire crew. If it had been somebody else and not the mother of his son, he would have relieved her of duty for that stunt, instead he put her on medical leave. He knew that Christina regretted her actions and was apologetic to the crew, but he would not let her continue her experimentation with the IOSAC. Sarah removed the cube from her arm and Christina was ban from the vicinity of the airlock. He knew that this would infuriate her but he had to maintain discipline with the crew, and it was only a token punishment. But she wasn't angry with him, and matter of fact, she accepted her fate unconditionally. She was happy to be only a mother for a while, but to Jacob's surprise, she asked if she could start forming their wedding plans in the very near future. She expressed that she wanted her family whole. She also asked if they could name their son, Tobias, which was Jacob's middle name. After all that, Jacob couldn't remain angry with her and he agreed with her regarding the wedding and their son's name. They decided to get married as soon as Tobias was able to thrive outside his incubator.

Even though Christina's actions did not cause any damage to the SIL11 itself, it did produce some hairline fractures to the airlock connecting the IOSAC and the SIL11 and damaged some of the airlock's components. Jacob asked Todd to repair the minor fractures to ensure that the airlock was once again airtight, and replace the damaged components so the airlock would operate nominally.

Jacob was at first quite eager to discover for himself what Christina already had discovered regarding IOSAC. He also would have liked to pilot the shuttle himself. It would have been quite exhilirating to 'feel' a ship and then only think of an action and ship would immediately respond to his thoughts. But he reconsidered that option and concluded that he was not necessarily the best choice. Jacob realized that there may be occasions when both the IOSAC and the SIL11 needed to be piloted at the same time. Of course, the remaining women could not pilot the shuttle because of their pregnancies and the only other pilot on board was his dad. So Jacob announced that Luther would be the shuttle's pilot. As eager as Jacob was in piloting the shuttle, his father was just the opposite. Yes, he accepted his new duty and agreed with his son's assessment but he didn't have to like it. He told Jacob that he was repulsed with the idea of a foreign entity attaching to his nervous system and his own brain no matter how benign the connection. Also, he was only a fair pilot not an expert. But none of things mattered to Jacob. As time passed, Jacob assessed that his father's repulsion was only temporary, since his father expression was more often associated with a broad smile and sparkling eyes when he was connected with the shuttle.

Once Tobias was out of the incubator and on his own, Jacob and Christina wedding day came. Sarah officiated at the ceremony, as the ship's doctor, since the captain was the one getting married. Todd was Jacob's best man and Jessica was Christina's maid of honor. Jacob had decided that it would not be quite right to have his father as best man. Luther already had the more superior title of dad in Jacob's book. Only Christina could fit into an elegant dress from her wardrobe while both Jessica and Sarah of course could not. Todd had prepared a wondrous meal for the occasion and had plenty of his fine wine was available. This time Christina could partake in the wine while Sarah and Jessica still refrained from it. The talk at the reception was not on Jacob and Christina since the tying of the knot between them seemed inevitable, but on the possible union of Jessica and Luther. Both Jacob and Sarah had given their blessings to their father for marrying Jessica at the reception but Luther had not asked for any. When the topic came up, Jessica blushed and began talking excitedly about the possibility but Luther did not say much about it. Jessica knew that Luther would not marry her until she had told Jacob the truth about her child's father. Now that Jacob was married off, she would tell him soon but in only in private. Jessica was most definitely excited about marrying this older man while it still continued to bewilder Luther why this young beautiful woman would not only want him but to marry him as well.

In the weeks ahead, both Sarah and Jessica gave birth to daughters. Both daughters were full term and normal. Jessica named her daughter Nozomi which meant 'hope', which Luther totally endorsed. Sarah named her daughter, Rhiannon, which meant 'great queen' but had another meaning as 'witch or healer' as well. Of course, most of the crew assumed that neither father had much contribution to the child's naming.

After these events, Jacob began implementing longer duty lists. Sarah came up with a plan for a daycare to be set up for all three children; Tobias, Nozomi and Rhiannon. Each woman was able to nurse and so one of them was always available to nurse any child who was hungry. With the captain's endorsement, Sarah organized the day care so that all three children would be cared for by one of the couples that would rotate between all the couples' quarters. The remaining four crewmembers were on duty on staggered or consecutive 6 hour shifts, preparing for their interaction with Ceres. The day care couple was on a 12 hour day care shift duty which could possibly include eating and sleeping in the shift, but it had to be arranged internally with the couple themselves as long as one was awake to care for the children. Each couple would be allowed a 6 hour personal period for every 24 hours of either duty shift or day care shift. It was not a great deal of personal time, but it was all that could be allowed.

Jacob knew Sarah's schedule was demanding, but the general tasks that needed to be completed prior to Ceres were quite long indeed. They included; constant monitoring of the Gatekeepers position, constant ship maintenance, upkeep of the farm, continuing minor repairs from the water harvest and Tobias's brief piloting of the shuttle, and self-education of this century's technology. Then among them there were even more demands on personal time, which included Sarah medical monitoring of the crew including the newest members, his father's continuous experimentation with the shuttle, Jessica's preparation of the education material for this century and his goal of finding a good rock for the SIL11 to hide behind while the unmanned shuttle attempted to land on Ceres. And they all desired to be together with their new families and interact with their children as well. Jacob had again thought how wonderful this crew can be. He even gave his new wife, a wedding present; he lifted his ban on her regarding the IOSAC.

Jacob thought things were going quite well. Jessica was on duty and was coming up the bridge to meet him there. She had asked for a private audience with him and insisted that nobody be aware of their meeting. Jessica never gave him a clue on what this was about. He only remembered their only and last private meeting they had without giving much thought on what possibly she wanted to discuss him. Knowing Jessica, maybe she didn't plan a discussion at all and maybe she desired some younger meat for her sexual appetite. He tried to block out the memory of their last encounter out of his mind, but his enlarging penis informed him that he was failing miserably.

Jessica entered the bridge wearing a tight shirt and tight jeans. She was only a few weeks from her baby delivery but her shape was almost back to her pre-pregnancy form. She was very voluptuous and was wickedly smiling at him. She strolled up to him, watching him with her dark penetrating eyes. She whispered into his ear, "Do you remember the last time we were alone?"

Jacob stumbled back a step or two and responded, "What do you mean?"

Jessica inserted her finger into her mouth and wiped a small amount of saliva on her lips so they glistened. She strode up to him and with her other hand stroked his groin area. Jacob jumped back and quickly asked, "What are you doing? What do you want?"

Jessica's smile broadens and responded, "At least one part of you remembers."

"Look Jessica that was a long time ago. I don't want any part of this. I'm married now and you're involved with my father," Jacob said and turned his back to her.

Jessica laughed right out and responded, "Sorry Jacob but your dad is all the man I need right now, sorry to disappoint you and your enlarging member."

"Then what the hell is this about?' Jacob said as he turned towards her again.

"I just asked if you remember our last meeting alone together," she asked but her playfulness had disappeared.

"Of course, what is this about?"

"A natural result of such a meeting as ours is what?" she asked.

"More meetings," he tersely responded.

"Besides that," Jessica laughed knowing that she had riled him up enough and said quietly, "A child."

Jacob hadn't yet grasped the meaning until she said, "*Your* child."

Then he understood and was becoming quite irritated with her, "So you are telling me that I'm the father of your child. Why are you telling me this now."

"We both know our bodies took over the last time. I accept that you are Christina's husband and quite happy with your new family. But I'm also quite happy with your father. For me to announce that you are the father of my child would have spoiled everything for both of us. Don't you agree?"

"Yes but why tell me now? You didn't have to say anything and I and nobody else would have known the difference."

"Somehow your father knew right away, the first time I seduced him. But he promised to keep my little secret. In return, I promised him that I would tell you one day.

"Why now?"

"Well I know your dad well enough to know that he will not marry me until you knew that you are the father, regardless how happy we make each other. And I want him!"

"OK, you told me what else do you want from me?"

"Three simple things; one -your silence with the rest of the crew, two – let Luther know that you know and lastly allow Luther to raise my daughter as his own."

Jacob rubbed his chin and thought about the second child, Nozomi. He really did agree with Jessica, but he waited to find out how much she really loved his father. Jessica was not normally confrontational but he hoped this would light a fire under Jessica, and that was all the proof he needed. He didn't have to wait long. The short silence was broken up by Jessica, "My darling, if you don't meet all my demands, the entire crew will know about our little meeting that occurred almost a year ago, including your cute little wife."

He smiled at her in answer to her threat. "I guess you don't know me very well, I was in agreement before you threatened me. Remember I do not respond well to threats." He paused briefly but continued, "But in this case, I'll let it pass, I agree with everything you said. Instead of another daughter, I'll take a new sister, but I'll be damned in calling you mom."

Jessica laughed and her eyes sparkled with delight. She went up to him and hugged him fiercely and kissed him on the cheek. She turned and began to dance away. Just before she left, she turned to Jacob, smiled and added, "You know your father didn't teach you all his tricks." She laughed and skipped out of the room. Jacob just sighed with relief, and went back to the MDS scanner looking for rocks. But he couldn't concentrate. What he needed was to find Christina and hope she was in the mood for some naughty sex.

Chapter 21 - A Message

Todd was returning from his normal daily shift on the farm. His clothes were covered with both dirt and blood. He was more grossly messy than usual. He had his 'farm helpers' i.e. automated robots turn over the soil for a new crop of corn, and had the automated exterminator harvest four chickens. But as luck would have it, both malfunctioned, so he had to get quite grimy today. Fortunately, Sarah was delayed in retrieving the children from Jacob's quarters, so he had time to get cleaned up. After his six hours on the farm, Sarah and he had a half a day with the kids. He was not expecting to get any sleep on this day care shift. But he told himself he shouldn't be griping since Sarah was putting in longer hours than he was.

Todd was a product of blue collar workers. His father was maintenance technician and his mother, a botanist when SIL had departed Earth. Todd's claim to fame was that he was the first child born on SIL11. Todd thought how things do change, since now there were three generations on board the SIL11 and he was now the second oldest on board.

His family had been shielded from the terrible rampage of Tom, Jessica's brother. They were in far corner of the farm, where his parents were arguing over a piece of farming machinery. He just sat, listening to his parents while playing absentmindedly in the dirt. His parents did not argue or fight much, so he was listening intently to this rare argument. They loved each other desperately. They didn't have close friends on board and kept pretty much to themselves. His parents didn't complain about their jobs or being low in the totem pole in authority. Everybody else told them what they wanted and they just proceeded to do it. Neither one of them had any dreams or fantasies about being in charge, matter-of-fact, his father shied away from having authority, and his mother was never offered a supervisory role since they had been on board. His dad didn't want the responsibilities or the blame that naturally came with it. At an early age, he was indoctrinated to the chores of living on a spacecraft, his home. He didn't mind the work, he lost his closest friends to Tom's carnage and lost his desire for play. The other children were younger than him by a few years and he wasn't interested in playing with them, at least while they were children. His father died in a terrible accident which he suffered an electrocution which caused him stumble backwards into grabbling hook, which killed him instantly. His mother lingered for years after, but her exuberance for life had left her after his father died. Her mother was encouraged to have another child by artificial insemination or natural means to satisfy the mission's quota of 2 replacement children but it was a volunteer program that she wanted no part of. Todd did not know how to comfort her even though he tried but he was only a child unawares that there was little he could do to aid her. She became withdrawn and he lost his mother a couple of years before she actually died. She died quietly and alone.

When they got older, one of the young girls took interest in him. Only one had the boldness to come up to him and attempt to talk with him while he was working, her name was Sarah. When they spoke, she would ask obvious questions or ask about his work, and then giggle for no apparent reason at his answers. She had her way with most of the other children, except her twin brother who was also stubbornly independent. Todd imagined that Sarah liked him because he was older but he imagined that her interest would die away once she got older. Sarah became a beautiful lady as the years passed. She was still headstrong but he didn't mind, and so he returned her interest became apparent to her and everyone else. Sarah became quite excited that Todd had taken interest in her and started gossiping to the other teenagers that Todd was her new boyfriend and that she was in love, another passing feeling, figured Todd until she got older. He felt this way since she was obviously very intelligent; being taught the medical sciences, way above anything he could have potentially study. All his learning had been hands-on learning, or learning what he had to know to accomplish his tasks on the ship. But in his eyes, she was brilliant lady. Her feelings didn't pass though, and as soon as she 'graduated' as a doctor, Todd took the chance at asking her to marry him, even though both were rather young for marriage. As a pleasant surprise, Sarah accepted his proposal and they became husband and wife, a now first time parents as well.

He sat on Sarah desk chair, deciding whether to take his shower right away or have a glass of wine first. He did drink a bit more than anyone else, but it was their loss, not his. He closed his eyes for a moment and was struck hard in the head. He turned quickly and saw one of Sarah's book fall to the floor. It landed with the title of the book facing up. The title, <u>You Only Live Twice</u> by Ian Fleming, an old 20th century international spy novel seemed to shimmer, then the word, 'You' started to glow orange, as other words remained their original color. He thought to himself, that the hit in the head was a bit harder than he imagined, maybe he needed to contact his wife right away. The letters of '*you*' began glowing ever brighter and turned from a dim orange to bright red. The letters appears in the word became larger than the rest of title. He watched the book in disbelief. He looked away, rubbed his eyes and looked back at the book, the YOU was still growing and turning brighter. Just then, the lights of the room went out. He couldn't see the book anymore, and thought that there was a power outage, but that has only happened once or twice during his entire life. He noticed a pinpoint of light seemed to be emanating from the book shelf where the book had been shelved. The pinpoint of light grew in brightness without becoming larger, until the entire room was illuminated beyond the normal room lights. He looked down at the book, the letters, Y-O-U began to fade and shrink until the letter's original size and color returned. The pinpoint of light disappeared and the normal room lights turned back on.

He thought, what the hell just happened. Then his wife opened their quarter's doors pushing a stroller with infants, including their own Rhiannon.

Sarah looked at her husband and asked, "Are you OK? You appear very confused. You did remembered that I was picking up the kids?"

"Sarah, one or your books must have gotten dislodged and hit me in the head, I think I might be hallucinating," Todd replied.

She went over to him and noticed Ian Fleming's book on the floor. She sighed, "Really Todd, this is an old lightweight paperback. Maybe one of my larger hard covered books might affect you but this one?"

"Well, I am hallucinating. I'm seeing the letters on the book become distorted and a bright light appeared and disappeared."

"Are you still seeing these hallucinations?" she asked as she examined his head. "Well I don't see any bumps on your head. Maybe I should take you to the infirmary?"

"No, I don't see anything now. And I do feel fine but it was all quite strange."

Sarah frowned and said, "You don't make up stories, Todd, this is somewhat concerning."

Todd shook his head quickly, "I'm fine, no need for a trip to your infirmary."

Sarah looked him over and said, "Well, in the shower with you then. You're a mess and we have company."

"Sure thing, honey, but those guys could care less how I look," he said pointing to the infants.

"Well, I do!"

Sarah had thrown his clothes into laundry receptacle and had two of the three children asleep in their quarters. She informed him that she was going to take Rhiannon to the galley, and breastfeed her and eat something herself.

He dressed in some loose fitting pants and tee-shirt and quietly tiptoed to the desk chair as the two infants slept in their bed. He noticed that Ian Fleming's book was still lying on the floor. It was refreshing to get a shower in. He assumed that Sarah had nursed the other two infants to sleep. He had the opportunity for some quiet time. He carefully put his feet on Sarah desk and stretched out.

Another one of Sarah's books fell and landed on his groin. He gritted his teeth and suppressed a loud yell to a low groan; it was a hard-covered book. Again, the book was face up and the title of the book began to shimmer as before. This time, the title was Jacob Have I Loved by Katherine Paterson and letters of the word, H_A_V_E began to turn red and grow in size. Same thing was happening as with the other book. But this time the lights did not go out, and no pinpoint of light appeared. After about 15 seconds, the letters began to fade and shrink, until the book appeared normal.

He may not be the brightest occupant on board the SIL11 but he was no idiot. Something was happening to him; maybe the Dimensionless Ones were attempting to contact them again, but this time they were delivering a message to him for the SIL11 crew. The two words that had glowed red may be part of a message, 'YOU HAVE'. So far it was only part of a message but for some unknown reason he expected more of the message to come. He decided to keep this to himself for now until he could verify with someone else that the words were indeed glowing red and/or until he received the entire message. He put both of the books back on the shelf. He looked around their room in which three of the four walls were covered with shelves of books. Well at least, the Dimensionless Ones won't run out of ammunition, he thought. He wished he could communicate with these beings in some way, so not to endure another hit on his more vital body parts and to select less sensitive areas of his body to be targeted with the books. After all, they had his attention now

Sarah returned to their room with Rhiannon asleep in her arms. Sarah herself appeared to be sleepwalking into their room. She laid Rhiannon next to Tobias and Nozomi and motioned him to join her where she laid. He turned down the lights, crawled over next to her carefully so not to wake the infants, and cuddled with Sarah. Sarah was asleep in less than minute. Just after Todd had closed his eyes, another book fell between Sarah and Todd. Todd opened his eyes and Sarah stirred from her sleep. This book was a children's book with a sketch of a dinosaur in front. It was titled All My Friends Are Dead by Avery Monsen. Both Sarah and Todd looked down at the book where the word, F-R-I-E-

N-D-S began to glow red and become enlarged. Sarah sat straight up in bed and goggled at the book, but Todd only smiled.

"Do you see what I see?" Sarah whispered to Todd.

"Yes, honey, and this is the 3rd book that has fallen," Todd quietly replied.

After a quarter of a minute, the letter's red color began to fade and returned to their normal size.

"Did the other books have a word emphasized?"

"Yes honey, so far I have 'YOU HAVE FRIENDS' but I'm sure there's more to come."

"How do you know?"

"I don't really know why, but I'm sure of it and now I know I'm not hallucinating."

"You must be getting a Dimensionless Ones message."

"That's what I think," Todd responded and added, "Go to sleep honey, we can discuss when the babies wake up."

During the remainder of their day care shift, Todd received single words messages from three additional books with one of the books falling twice. They were Cricket on the Hearth, Men are from Mars and Women are from Venus, Not as a Stranger, with the Cricket on the Hearth falling off for a second time. The message thus far was, YOU HAVE FRIENDS ON VENUS NOT ON _____. But Todd knew the message was not yet complete. Todd and Sarah had their rest shift and spent most of it bed after Jessica had picked up the children, but no other books fell from the shelves while they slept.

Todd had gotten up before Sarah and decided to visit the captain who was working on the bridge. Todd knew that Jacob and Christina would start their rest shift in about an hour and he and Sarah would begin their first work shift at the same time. Even though the message was not complete, Todd felt that the captain needed to know. He didn't want to wake Jacob and Christina during their rest period and didn't want to wake up his wife yet either. Of course, Sarah might be quite upset with him for going to see her brother without her but Todd sometimes knows what's better for his wife than she did for herself. She needed all the sleep that she could get. He left her message on her PCD before he left their quarters.

When Todd entered the bridge, Jacob looked up from on his PCDs that laid on the counter.

"Good morning Todd, what brings you up here? You still have another hour before you start your shift," Jacob inquired.

Todd walked up beside Jacob and viewed his PCDs. He didn't quite catch what was on one but Jacob's second one caught his attention which had loaded an electronic book called the Atlas of Ceres by Andrew Mackins published in 2061. On Jacob's PCD, the printed title on the monitor began to shimmer. Jacob noticed that Todd was staring at his PCD, so Jacob thought that maybe Todd had taken an interest in what he was doing and said, "Oh yeh, I'm trying to find the most appropriate landing spot for our planned unmanned mission. Ceres has lot of variable topography and it will make for a ..."

Jacob could tell that Todd was not listening to him but continued to stare at his PCD. He looked down at what Todd was staring at. On his PCD screen, the word C-E-R-E-S had grossly enlarged and was glowing in brilliant red. Jacob snatched up his PCD, thinking that his PCD had some electronic 'hiccup'. The PCD did not respond to Jacob's commands and continued to display the distorted title.

"What is wrong with this thing?" Jacob asked rhetorically.

Todd finally responded, "So you saw it too?"

"What do you mean, my PCD's malfunction?" maybe Todd was trying to pull some kind of gag joke on him.

But Todd was stone-faced and serious, "Did you see the word, CERES enlarged and glowing red, captain?"

"Yes, why does that mean something to you?"

Todd paused and looked at Jacob and replied, "I received a message from the Dimensionless Ones, it says, 'You have friends on Venus not on Ceres.'"

Jacob was momentarily baffled and peered down at his PCD. The display monitor had returned to normal. He tapped on the image, and the pages of the book were sequentially displayed. His PCD was again operating normally. He looked up at Todd and asked, "How did you get all of that from this single malfunction. You haven't been sipping too much of that wine of yours?"

"No sir. But I think it would be best, if you come to my quarters. Your sister will collaborate my story. It has been an interesting day for us both."

Chapter 22 - The Solar Arrow

"Sarah, are you awake? The captain is here with me, can we come in?" Todd said into the intercom after adjusting to a minimum volume.

"Sure if he doesn't mind me being in grumpy mood," Sarah responded.

Jacob responded, "Not anything that I haven't seen before, besides this is important."

"Yeah I know, Todd told you about the falling books and the possible Dimensionless Ones message. Come in."

"Well not about the falling books at least not yet," Jacob was saying as they both entered the room. Sarah sat up in bed with a t-shirt on and her hair in total disarray. It had appeared that she had just awakened. Todd began his story of the events that put the message together. Todd was quite detailed and Sarah nodded at specific points during his monologue.

Jacob looked at his sister and asked, "Is that way it all happened?"

"For most of it, but I wasn't there for all of it, but Todd did tell me everything about the rest," Sarah murmured. "His details are quite accurate of the events when I was present and the recounting of events that I did not witness was the same for the most part."

"What do you mean for the most part?" Jacob inquired.

"Well, it's nothing ground shaking. But he added some details and omitted some others but the story is very consistent," answered Sarah matter-of-factly.

"We should tell everyone right now," Jacob said while going over to the ship intercom and announced, "All hands meeting in 15 minutes at the galley."

"Right now?" griped Sarah.

"Sorry Sarah, but a meeting at any time is inconvenient for somebody."

Luther and Jessica retrieved the children from Sarah's quarters and brought them down to the galley in a stroller. It was a good time for a meeting if there was ever a good time, Jessica thought. Maybe the mothers would want to nurse their own children while the meeting was going on, and beside it was right between the other couples' shifts. It would allow Jacob to acknowledge to Luther, the conversation she had with his son. Luther was pleased when Jessica informed him that she told Jacob about the whole truth of their daughter. He was a little hesitant about raising Nozomi as his own. He still needed confirmation from his son on that accord. Jessica didn't understand the big difference in daughter or granddaughter, it was still his genes. Soon she thought, she will be pregnant again. Luther had a healthy appetite for sex, and as long as his sperm had a motor in them, there shouldn't be a problem of her getting pregnant again. She was always available to him and encouraged him aplenty. She hoped that the new shuttle toy of his did not distract too much from her.

Christina came into the room, even though exhausted she hoisted Tobias up and held him in her arms. The baby gurgled and cooed at the sound of his mother's voice. Jessica looked up at Christina while Christina was talking gibberish to her son and asked, "Do you know what this is about?"

Christina answered while rocking her son, "Nope."

"Come on Christina, he is your husband."

Christina sighed and frowned at Jessica, "I said I don't know. There was nothing 5 hours ago when began our work shifts. Haven't seen him since."

Luther looked over at Jessica and a reprimanding look. Then Jessica apologized, "Sorry Christina, I just thought you would know."

"Well Jessica, tell you the truth. I'm just as curious as you are. But I hope it doesn't include any more work."

Luther smiled and responded to Christina, "I agree with you on that account."

Todd, Sarah and Jacob strolled into the galley together. Sarah immediately asked, "Didn't anybody make some syn-coffee." Seeing that none was made, she jaunted over to the machine and made herself a cup. "Anybody else?" When nobody responded, she took her cup of coffee, lifted Rhiannon from the stroller and sat across from her father.

Jacob announced to the group, "It appears that we have another message from our 'guardian angels'," Jacob continued, "Todd here will explain everything."

Todd recanted all the events that led to the completed message again carefully, this time not leaving out a single detail, and he concluded with the Dimensionless Ones completed message, 'You have friends on Venus not on Ceres'.

Luther chuckled, "these Dimensionless Ones appear to have some fun with these messages. What a way to entertain oneself, by throwing books at an unsuspected target."

"It's funny that you say that, after the first two books, with one hitting me in head and the other in my privates, I wondered how I could ask them somehow not to hit me in my sensitive parts. I was thinking they already have my attention. After that, not a single book hit me hard or in a sensitive spot. It was like they could read my thoughts. I bet they are telepathic or something."

Jessica was beaming. After all, she was the one to suggest going directly to Venus and avoiding Ceres all together in the first place.

"Looks like we are going to Venus," Jessica smiled.

Jacob looked at the faces of everyone and asked, "Does everyone agree with Jessica on skipping Ceres and heading to Venus?"

Everyone nodded in agreement, even with Sarah's small almost imperceptible nod.

Jacob paused and rubbed his chin which was his habit of attaining everyone's attention and then continued, "Then we will skip Ceres then. But it does produce a bit of a problem. Uranus had slowed us down considerably when we travelling in the outer solar system. But we were going to aerobrake in Ceres tenuous atmosphere to slow us down even further before navigating into the inner solar system. I hesitate to use more of the anti-matter propulsion, since we are critically low on anti-matter fuel. None of you will probably like this, but we should probably use Mercury to slow us down, it also has a light exosphere which should produce enough aerobraking similar to Ceres and quietly put us into a Venus orbit."

Todd interrupted and asked, "Isn't that going to get a little warm for us?"

Jacob smiled, "I'm not concerned about the heat, but the solar radiation will be more intense than usual especially if we get unlucky and a large solar flare erupts towards us. We may need to modulate our current magnetoelectric shields for radiation for that possibility; our ship was not designed for close proximity to stars. We may also need stop the ship's rotation and position our living quarters and farm on the opposite side from the sun. It's risky plan but hopefully the only inconvenience is that we'll be weightless for a while. But it will increase everybody's work load for a while. My wife, Christina will fill you in on the details later."

A smile that was on Christina's face while she was playing with Tobias had evaporated, as she turned and grimly looked at her husband. Tips of her ears began to turn red simmering in anger and she carefully lowered Tobias into the stroller. She didn't say a word, and she didn't need to. Everyone was quite aware that this was first time that Christina was aware of Jacob's plan or the Dimensionless Ones message, and she had no current plan in place. Jacob seemed unaware of the dangerous ground that he was walking on with his wife.

Luther hazarded a question, "Will we be out of sight from any of the Gatekeepers' ships? Will we appear like comets, like a solar arrow?"

"I will attempt to keep our trajectory the same as a comet like 'a solar arrow' as you describe, dad, but I don't know about the Gatekeepers. I doubt that the Dimensionless Ones would put us in harm's way."

He looked way from his dad, then scanned the entire crew and said, "Neither I or Christina have had time to work out any duty details. I will assign you new duties when we have them. But the Dimensionless Ones seem to imply that we are more danger going to Ceres, so I think its important to make course corrections now, which will minimize the risk of being detected."

Jacob's last response seemed to lessen Christina's tension, but she was obviously still angry.

Luther continued, "The Dmensionless Ones did not say to stay clear of Ceres, just that we won't find any 'friends' there. "

But Jacob disagreed with his father, "It's dangerous to take them literally. The first time we got their message it only said, 'Do not go home, there is a trap awaiting you.' The reality was that the Gatekeepers had ships at both Saturn and Earth. But the message didn't specifically say that. We decided avoid Earth as much as possible, which meant choosing Uranus over Saturn as our aero-braking planet. If we continued on to Saturn, we would have met the same fate as SIL7. I have the same feeling about Ceres, and we should avoid it as much as possible. Mercury has risks but most of those risks are known therefore more acceptable."

Luther nodded his head in agreement.

Jacob asked the group, "Anything else?"

Everyone remained quiet, until Tobias started crying. Christina instinctively picked him up and rocked him until he quieted down. Jacob adjourned the meeting and started to walk towards Christina and their son. But Jessica grabbed his arm, "Don't you have something to tell your dad?" she asked. Jacob turned toward her and looked into her dark eyes. Then he remembered their earlier meeting, he smiled to Jessica and whispered, "Sure thing" then turned toward his dad and said, "Hey dad, you have a minute?"

"Sure, son."

He looked across the room at Christina gently bouncing Tobias on her knee. She was waiting for him. He said, "Christina, I'll meet you back in our quarters in couple of minutes, I have something I want to talk with my dad about."

Christina's expression towards Jacob had softened but now she returned her grim face and marched out of the galley without giving a response.

Not the way that Jacob wanted to start his rest period. Jacob turned towards his father after everyone had left the galley except for him and his dad.

Jacob started, "Jessica told me everything about her, I mean, our daughter. What Jessica has proposed seems to be the best for everyone involved. Do you want to adopt Nozomi as your own daughter?"

Luther was staring at his hands, thinking about what he was going to say. He slowly replied, "Are *you* sure that you want another sister and not a daughter?"

"Look dad, I have my hands full with a new family including a new son. And I have this ship and this crew; I wouldn't have much time for a new daughter as well. Not to mention, the hellfire that would be started between Christina and me."

Luther nodded his head. "I understand son. But you know I hate secrets but everybody seems to think I can keep one. This will not be a secret."

Jacob looked confused, "What do you mean?"

"I mean secrets are things known between people that are kept from others for a *time*, until the secret gets out. Well this cannot be a secret because it will NEVER get out. You, I, and Jessica will take this to our graves. Even Nozomi will be unawares and she will take it to her grave as well. Nozomi will always think I am her dad till the day she dies. Do you understand and do you agree?"

Jacob was a bit stunned by the finality of what his dad wanted. But he understood. His father wanted to be all in as a dad, and not partially in. He was either all in or not in at all. Jacob nodded in agreement.

"Are you sure?" his dad asked.

"Yes dad, I'm sure."

Luther smiled and just then beamed like a new father. "You know Jacob, a few hundred years ago a new dad would give a rolled dried tobacco to his closest associates to smoke as a way to celebrate. I wish I had a couple right now."

"What do you mean, smoke? Do you mean you watched the dried tobacco burn up?"

"Now come on son, I know that you are not that dense in human history."

Jacob laughed, "You know there were other things to smoke other than tobacco back then."

"I'm afraid we don't have any seeds, that could produce any products to smoke," Luther said laughing back.

Jacob became subdued and stone-faced. He reminisced about his time with his mom and didn't want her memory to fade any more than it had already been. He wanted his dad also not to forget anything about her either. He realized that it was selfish of him to desire that and it was almost to the point of being cruel to his father. Jacob thought, how did Jessica measure up against his mother in his dad's eyes but instead asked his father, "Dad, do you love Jessica?"

"She is my fountain of youth, son."

"That's not what I asked," Jacob responded.

Luther realized that his son was thinking of his mother. Her death still weighed heavily upon him and still influenced his thoughts and feelings. Luther responded, "Look son, I loved your mother more than myself. I do not know if I will ever be able to love anybody like her again. But Jessica has filled a void in me. I feel whole again. For a middle-aged person like me, my situation could not be better, surrounded by a loving family and loved by absolutely stunning younger woman. That's the best answer I can give you."

"No worries, I understand. Anyway, talking about hellfire, I think I started some coals to glow with Christina, which I need to put out before a fire starts," Jacob said as he started his way out of the galley.

Jacob heard his dad's last comment, "Good luck with that," and him laughing away.

Chapter 23 - Pirates

Christina had realized that she may have over-reacted to Jacob's announcement. The SIL11 with its magnetoelectric shield was designed for sun-like exposure from stellar radiation at distances further than 75 million kilometers. Mercury was closer at 58 million kilometers, but not drastically closer. Yet, she did not know how to modulate the current system sufficiently to protect them for a possible solar flare while in a flyby with Mercury. Maybe the technology of the IOSAC could help them. She asked Jacob to assign Luther to her in this endeavor and have Todd on call if needed for any possible two-man spacewalking excursion.

Jacob also reluctantly assigned Jessica to himself. He needed much more surveillance on more multiple sources than was currently monitored and Jessica was best qualified with the MDS. Besides watching the Gatekeepers' ships surrounding Saturn, Mars and Earth, the Dimensionless Ones message suggested to keep an eye out for any activity near Ceres, since such activity could be hostile. But Jacob was not only concerned with Ceres, but the entire asteroid belt since they were already on the fringe of the asteroid belt and will be navigating through on their way to Mercury. There were numerous opportunities for concealment of hostile forces throughout the belt. He did not want to engage in any battle with their outdated weaponry, and it was clear that the Gatekeepers' technology was far advanced over any current human technology and their weaponry would be inferior to current human technology as well. So whether it was human hostiles or Gatekeepers, he was outgunned. But he would also like to start monitoring Venus for activity in an effort to inspire hope within the crew. And lastly, the outer planets other than Saturn still needed periodic glimpses. This required somebody full time on the MDS.

His immediate efforts needed to focus on navigating the best course to Mercury and a subsequent orbit around Venus. He needed to balance that with the desire to keep their distance from Ceres as much as possible without using all their remaining fuel. The best distance they could achieve from Ceres would be 1.7 million kilometers. Not near adequate enough to escape detection by the Gatekeepers if they were in immediate area but hopefully enough from hostile locals. In addition, the SIL11 may pass in closer proximity to some other asteroids during their journey, which could also pose a threat. He needed to create a map on the asteroids current locations and trajectories in this part of the asteroid belt to avoid any possible close calls. Again, he needed to make course changes in very small steps, so that it appeared imperceptible to anyone else watching them. He hoped that they would appear as a random comet hurdling towards the sun.

Sarah's task was to improve on celabite, the medication used to speed up the body's mechanism for DNA repair and protection against cosmic radiation. She also needed to synthesize enough for the entire crew for potential emergency use in case of solar flare activity. There was some medical information aboard the IOSAC of several improved compounds for human body to survive the cosmic ray or solar radiation onslaught during both Mercurian flyby and a Venus orbit. One in particular was exceedingly effective in adults and had early studies indicating that it should be safe for children, even though it had not yet been approved by Corporate Health Authority for pediatric use. With Tobias, Nozomi and Rhiannon, this was an important attribute. She was encouraged by its ease of synthesis which could be accomplished here on board the SIL11 with ingredients already on board. One of the steps, she took note of, was the removal of a particular impurity formed during the synthesis. This impurity was toxic but did not accumulate enough during the synthesis to pose a safety threat to adult humans; however, it was much more toxic to pediatric subjects. The removal of this impurity was imperative to ensure the safety of their youngest crewmembers. So though, the synthesis was relatively easy, the purification was going to be much more labor intensive. Sarah knew that Jacob could not afford any more personnel to this project, so she didn't even ask for help or notify him of the purification complication. She would have to tackle this on her own. It did mean a lot of hours in isolation, so she valued her rest shift and even her daycare shifts.

Todd was quite proud of the amount of food that he, Sarah and periodically others had raised since waking up, almost two years ago. The yields on the crops had only improved since those early beginnings. The production was beyond the needs of self-preservation, and reached a point where exporting was possible. So he continued to work the farm, but being between planting and harvesting on most of the crops, the farm basically ran itself. Todd needed to be on call for any required spacewalk excursions with Christina, definitely not his favorite activity. But he would be there, if Christina required it. He was responsible for overseeing equipment maintenance on board while the rest of the crew was working on other projects. Since his duties were relatively light compared to others, Jacob had added the task of redistributing the food around the ship and removing the bulk of it from the engineered food stores. Jacob explained it was precautionary move; in case of some military battle, where single hit could take out their entire food supply. Todd didn't mind the work, since he was not able to see Sarah or Rhiannon as often as he would like anyway. His rest periods and daycare shifts were now pleasures he highly anticipated.

Only during rest and daycare shifts did the armband and the earpiece for IOSAC ever leave Luther's wrist and ear. He felt somewhat guilty since his job felt more like playtime than anything else. The IOSAC was one the newer human creations which was totally controlled by human nervous system. There were no other controls except a fail-safe system for protecting the occupant, in case of a suicide attempt. Chiron was one the newer outposts in the solar system and therefore had the latest technology. Jacob did not want any more unmanned flights from the SIL11, because of the risk of being detected by hostiles. But Luther continued to find ways to integrate the technology of the IOSAC with those of the SIL11. When Christina had asked him if the IOSAC could contribute to the shielding power of the SIL11, he not only discover that the IOSAC could contribute but was able to protect the entire SIL at 5 times the intensity than that the SIL11 could shield on its own. The IOSAC was able to perform this task while attached to the SIL11 airlock. With the integrated shielding technology along with the medication Sarah was synthesizing, the crew should be protected from any small to medium size solar flare. A massive solar flare still could potentially kill them all, but one actually occurring while they were in the Mercurian flyby posed a very small risk.

Jacob also wanted to know about the IOSAC weaponry as well to supplement SIL11 meager arsenal. SIL11 weaponry consisted primarily of antimissile lasers, numerous non-nuclear missiles, a few small nuclear weapons, and a couple of powerful antimatter torpedoes. The torpedoes were useless in a dogfight at close range and the nuclear device may be effective but they would damage the SIL systems as well. The SIL11 also includes a magnetoelectric shield but it was designed to protect the ship and its occupants from cosmic rays not as defense shield. Luther doubted the SIL11 weaponry could defend them against any present-day weaponry and definitely not against the Gatekeepers. IOSAC had three fundamental weapons; a particle force field which no particle with mass can penetrate, high intensity laser beam emitter and an anti-graviton pulse cannon. Unfortunately, Luther could find no means to extend the force field beyond the IOSAC to shield the SIL11.

In the weeks ahead, Sarah had noticed a trend among the parents. Since everyone's schedule was more crowded with new duties, all the parents was wanting to have their own child be with them during their rest period. Therefore, only two children were in day care at a time and was making Sarah's schedule less efficient. The children were also getting less dependent on breastmilk for nourishment as the weeks went by, so one mother need not to be available all the time. Jacob could get more work out of his crew by scheduling more work hours. Sarah noticed this in herself, yes she got slammed by two 6 hour work shifts but typically it was followed by 18 hours of almost leisure time. She also noticed there was less interacting between the crew. While each crew member was partnered with different personnel for various tasks assigned to the crew at different times. It was less rare for the whole crew to get together.

Sarah had fewer opportunities to learn how to influence the crew in her favor. She felt that was a terrible disadvantage for her. Jacob was captain whom didn't need to influence anybody, her father had already demonstrated his ability to influence people and Todd, her husband, didn't try to influence anybody even though he did it effortlessly. She was successful in influencing the crew during the initial discussion of Ceres. It didn't matter much to her that it turned out to be the wrong choice, since the decision was made before the Dimensionless Ones last message. She recognized that she lacked certain means to influence the male crew members that both Jessica and Christina had. She felt that she was attractive but the males were her father, her brother and her husband. While Jessica and Christina could attempt sexual sway with other male crew members, Sarah could not. Jessica in particular was effective in swaying male attention and did not hesitate irritating the other female crew members when required. She was somewhat baffled at the fact that she no longer could sway Jessica and Christina as she once did when they were children.

So she felt that she needed more group activities to gain the crew's trust in her. She would try to convince Jacob, not easy task in itself, to allow her to set up an all-hands meeting to discuss everyone's current schedule of activities.

***

Jacob was both pleasantly surprised in Jessica's recent behavior. It appears that his reluctance in assigning Jessica to the bridge with him was not well founded. Mostly, she behaved herself and only occasionally allowed her blouse to become more opened than proper work attire or allowed her skirt to ride bit too high. Each time she caught him looking, she flashed a wicked smile in his direction, but other than that she continued to work and kept conversation to a minimum. She had set her PCD to continue monitoring several areas of the asteroid belt. On this day, she asked him if she leave a little early to prepare Luther's dessert tonight. Jacob assumed that she was her dad's dessert but allowed her to leave anyway. Minutes later, Sarah asked if she could talk with him privately. He also wanted to speak with her as well so he invited her to the bridge.

"What's up sis?"

Sarah gave a disarming smile and looked at the space charts and various PCDs scattered on his table. "I've noticed you and Christina are keeping Tobias with you when you are having your rest shift."

"Yeah, we want to spend as much time with him as possible, he's had a rough start in this life."

"Well, it seems that all the parents want to spend more time with their children including Todd and myself."

"So does Jessica and dad, but not all the time as with both of us," Jacob responded, "I guess it goes with being a first time parent."

"I guess," Sarah responded, "Figured out a course yet?"

"Almost."

Sarah asked, "How much of this new medication that I'm synthesizing for solar radiation is needed?"

"Hopefully, we won't need any, but I would synthesize no more than a week's worth for every member of the crew including the children."

"Well, I'm almost there as well."

"Was there anything else, sis?" Jacob asked, knowing there must be something else that she wanted to ask in person. The question of the amount of medicine could have been easily handled between their PCDs.

"I was wondering if you would support an all-hands meeting to discuss new schedules for everyone. Day care is not being utilized as much as it was when we first put adopted it. There appears to be more leisure time for the crew. I was wondering if we could possible use some of the time for group activities, it may help with morale."

Jacob countered, "I thought we were too busy to have a 'morale problem'."

Sarah smiled and said, "Well, we don't have one now, but a doctor doesn't just treat diseases but prevents them as well, right?"

Jacob didn't know what his sister was really after, but having a meeting to change the crew's schedule that would be acceptable to everyone wouldn't cause any harm, so he answered, "I don't see a problem on having a meeting. Go ahead and arrange one."

"Thanks, bro," she said as began to walk away. But Jacob stopped her, "there is something else I wish for you to do and it is not up for discussion, OK?"

"Yes, *captain*," she announced since it sounded like an order to her.

"I want you to officially seal the birth records of Nozomi and her DNA sequence. No inquires can be made in that regard, unless a medical emergency requires the sequence information. Any question, *doctor*."

"Don't worry bro, I have your back on this one. I have been expecting such a request from you or dad for a while now, and it's all prepared just need your command authorization. I'll send you link for your approval."

Jacob sighed that was easier than he thought it would be.

Sarah turned to leave the room, but before she got to the doorway, Jessica burst into the room almost running into her. She totally ignored Sarah and went directly to the captain and announced, "Sir, we have a problem."

"What is it?'

Jessica quickly responded, "There are three very small vessels following us. They are 400,000 kilometers away but they are closing. They should intercept us in about a day."

"What's their origin?" Jacob asked.

"Not sure right now, but I believe they were hiding behind one of the smaller asteroids," Jessica responded.

"Damn, probably pirates," Jacob murmured to himself.

Chapter 24 - The Separation

Jacob went over to the charts of local asteroids and quickly but intensely scanned them. After he found what he was looking for, he turned to the women, "Jessica, have my dad report to me on the double and keep monitoring the unidentified vessels but also lookout for any additional vessels in the area. Sarah gather all the children and take them to the infirmary and seal the door."

Both answered simultaneously, "Yes, captain," without a trace of sarcasm.

He then went to the intercom and announced, "All hands go to battle readiness." He had never issued that command since he was captain. It almost made him choke on the words, 'battle readiness.' He probably should not have been surprised, that he wouldn't need to issue that command until returned to his own solar system. This ship was by no means a military vessel, so discipline wasn't necessarily the highest priority in training. But he needed everyone's cooperation and hopefully everyone would follow his orders without question or hestitation.

He was outgunned regardless who they faced but he planned on tactics for human hostiles rather than the Gatekeepers. If they are the Gatekeepers, they would be dead in a manner of minutes, regardless of what actions he took. If the Gatekeepers were looking for prisoners, well after hearing what happens to human prisoners from Ivan, he was prepared to scuttle the SIL11 and its crew on a moment's notice even without the crew's approval.

Christina's frantic voice came over the intercom, "Jacob what's happening?"

"Christina, we are being pursued by three small vessels. Please bring up all ship's defenses and personally man the antimissile lasers. "

"What about Tobias?" asked Christina worriedly.

"Sarah will be in the infirmary with all the children," Jacob reassured her.

"Sorry for the interruption, I will be at weapons control and have all weapons ready in less than hour, is that soon enough."

"Yes Christina, over and out."

Luther walked into the room watching his son prepare his ship.

"Reporting, captain," he said firmly to his son.

"Dad, I want you get into the IOSAC and head for this small asteroid, "Jacob said, while pointing to the charts. "It's less than 100,000 kilometers away and we are nearly heading straight for it."

"What's going on, son?"

"We have three small vessels pursuing us. I believe they are human but hostile. Dad, you will be my last resort. But I want you to detach the IOSAC and slowly get in front of the SIL 11 to avoid detection. If there is stealth technology on board the IOSAC, use it. Get to this asteroid and attached yourself to it, allow us and these unidentified vessels to pass you unnoticed and then follow from behind at a safe distance to avoid detection. When you receive the transmission and you hear the word, 'Nozomi,' from me, that will be only the signal for all clear, any other transmission from me that does not include that word 'Nozomi', and I want you blow them out of the sky if you can, no matter what I say. Additionally, I want you to run on radio silence until you get the signal for all clear. I will try to resolve this situation diplomatically so nobody gets hurt, but I want your weapons readied and locked on them, while we are talking. And I want you disembark immediately."

Luther only responded, "Yes, captain," he turned and to leave the room.

Jessica yelled at him before he left, "You better kiss me before you go!"

Luther turned and they embraced and kissed her, then Luther departed quickly while she called out to him, "I love you, Luther. You better come back to me."

Jacob wanted to get Jessica back on track, he needed Jessica as well as the rest of the crew to be sharp. "Jessica, I want you to have constant surveillance on all three unidentified vessels, the IOSAC, the Gatekeepers' ships, and the local asteroid field all around with the MSD. Link my PCD to the unidentified vessels, position and course and only notify me if there are any changes in the Gatekeepers' positions," Jacob commanded.

"Yes, captain," answered Jessica as her teary eyes stared at the place where Luther had stood.

In a less formidable voice Jacob said, "Don't worry Jessica, my dad will be fine. I'm more concerned about the rest of us."

She brightly smiled at him and turned to the MSD workstation.

Again, Jacob was on the intercom, "Luther is taking the IOSAC on my orders," he announced to everyone, so that nobody would be alarmed about Luther's or IOSAC disappearance. "For the rest of you, we are preparing for a possible gunfight with these ships or a possible hostile boarding and takeover. I will explain, what preparations I wish to have completed in the next two to three hours. First, Luther has taken the IOSAC as our last resort. Second, I have Christina manning the ship's defenses, and Jessica will be monitoring the hostile ships' position, course and speed constantly and watching out for additional vessels in the area. Sarah has the children in the infirmary, the safest part of the ship. Todd, I want you to go to our armory and distribute sidearms to all the crew members and take a stockpile of heavier weapons to Sarah in the infirmary and reseal its doors. Then lock or seal all the remaining doors on board. I don't want anything to be easy for them."

Todd piped in, "On it. Do you want me to remain with the children after I lock everything down."

"Sorry Todd, but no. Sarah's is the best marksman on board. I have totally confidence in her defending our babies. I need you to find a secure but remote part of the ship with some extra weapons. You will be our cavalry if needed. If you hear me announce, 'Rhiannon' over the intercom then move towards the infirmary, if you hear 'Tobias' head for weapons control and if you hear 'Nozomi', then proceed to the bridge."

"I see, mother's child name will tell me where to go."

"Affirmative, but keep hidden and don't reveal your position until then. If I announce all three names at once, it will be the all clear sign, if you hear only two names, then we are in trouble and you will need to use your own best judgment."

"What kind of trouble?" asked Todd.

"Sorry, Todd, if I knew I would tell you!"

Jacob paused then continued talking to the crew, "I just want to make sure we are prepared for the worst possible scenario. I am hoping to resolve this without violence, since I'm sure their weapons are far superior to ours. Once they are in visible range, keep silent unless I call upon you and do not disagree with me at any time, regardless of what I say. Remember, I may tell them the truth or I may tell them lies. As I told Todd, I don't want to make anything easy for them. Does everybody understand my orders?"

There was a murmur of 'yes, captain' all across the ship.

Jacob waited a few hours, when Jessica confirmed that his dad had found an appropriate hiding place of the rapidly approaching asteroid on the opposite side from the approaching SIL11. His MDS image had disappeared and Luther and the IOSAC had become to be part of the asteroid surface. Hopefully, when the unidentified ships pass they will not be able to detect IOSAC presence on the surface as well. The relatively medium sized asteroid was about a kilometer in length and only half kilometer across but was amply sized for an IOSAC hideout. The SIL11 was bearing down on the asteroid with sufficient margin safety of a half kilometer, and their followers followed their trajectory and continued to close. They didn't seem unduly concerned for asteroid's close proximity. SIL11 would pass the asteroid in less than two hours and the unidentified vessels would overtake them in 10 hours. It was encouraging to see that these small vessels didn't overtake them much sooner. It was possible that their technology was relatively old as well, but he had to consider that it could be a ploy to direct them into a trap. Either way Jacob was not changing course or speed.

Both SIL11 and the unidentified spacecraft flew by the medium sized asteroid without changing course. Those vessels were close enough to pick a faint signal from the SIL11, so Jacob hazard a transmission to them, "This is Captain Jacob Wilson of the Space Intelligence Locator 11 to the approaching vessels. Please identify yourself and your intentions."

Jessica looked up from her monitor, "They have answered you, all three ships have launched a missile towards us."

"What type of missile? Do you know Jessica?"

"No sir, they have more modern weapons than us, but, they aren't that futuristic. They appear to have higher speeds than our missiles but they haven't doubled our missile speeds yet, and they're configuration suggest that they are non-nuclear. The distance at which they launched and type of weapon suggests that they're intention is to get our attention, not necessarily to harm us. I believe they are trying to intimidate us."

"Well it's working, but not unexpected. " He turned on intercom, "Christina, incoming!"

"Yes I already have them sighted and tracking them. Not within range yet, and they are not making this very difficult, captain."

"Jessica and I think they are just trying to get our attention. Launch a pair of guided missiles at each vessel after you destroy theirs, maybe we can get their attention as well," Jacob replied.

"Yes, sir."

As expected, the missiles from the unidentified vessels were easily neutralized by the SIL11 defense lasers, and the SIL11 missiles harmlessly exploded on the unidentified vessels' shields.

A low signal strength transmission from one of those vessels was being picked up and Jacob listed intently, "Captain Wilson is it? Well this is Commodore Fredrick, of the Totanus group. I admire your current evasion of the Gatekeepers but you will not be able to evade us. Stop you ship and allow us to board, and we will spare your life and the life of your crew."

"What is your business on board the SIL11?" asked Jacob.

Commodore Fredrick responded, "You can call it anything you like, my dear sir, perhaps an inspection." Jacob heard muffled laughter in the background. "But to be frank with you, Jacob, we would like to take inventory of our new ship. That ship should garner quite an exquisite price on the open black market. We don't get see a lot of these ships as you would probably guess."

Jacob smiled, he was right about them, they were pirates. He would play along.

"We have information for Corporate. Please do not interfere with Corporate business."

"My good fellow, there is no Corporate. Don't think I'm an idiot, I know that you know there is no Corporate or you would have not survived so long."

"If you are so well informed then you know that SIL spacecraft were designed for interstellar travel. And that SIL spacecraft is capable of extremely high speeds, but it would take an enormous amount of time to speed up or slow it down," Jacob lied. He was taking a gamble here. The SIL spacecraft was not designed for rapid acceleration or deceleration but the ship could do it, it would just use up all their current fuel to completely stop.

"Don't worry captain, we will just net our new ship."

"Christina launch a nuclear missile at them immediately and detonate just before it reaches their shields," Jacob commanded over the intercom. He wanted to attempt a nuclear strike before they got to close.

"Yes, captain," responded Christina.

The nuclear device went off but had no effect on their ships. Their shield protected them from the nuclear blast, and a mild shock wave would be hitting their ship in five minutes. He announced to the crew, "Brace for impact in five minutes."

Jessica said, "Captain we have two more similar vessels approaching, this time coming towards our bow. Time for intercept is less than 50 minutes."

"Track two new targets at our bow and launch a guided antimatter torpedo between them. Have several of the MCD scanners on those ships, if one those ships attempts to launch a missile detonate our torpedo, we may be able to cause some minor damage. "

The oncoming ships were much further away than the ships closing from behind and the SIL11 was still in the safe zone for the anti-matter weapon launch.

Jessica turned towards the captain, "The ships off our bow are creating some kind of electromagnetic netting. I think this net is the net that the pirate commodore was referring to. Maybe we got lucky and they did not detect our launch. The three ships behinds us, also may have not detected our frontal launch because of our ship's blocking their line of sight."

Minutes later, a bright flash erupted in front of the SIL11 bow. Jacob eavesdropped on their communication with the MSD. Obviously they didn't appear to understand the SIL capabilities yet.

"Commodore Fredrick, this is Bill, the captain of the Totanus 9. Both my ship and the Totanus 11 have lost propulsion, weapons and our shield from an anti-matter blast from that SIL ship but life support, communications and other minor systems are still functioning, awaiting assistance."

"Bill you are an idiot!! Didn't you monitor the SIL11 for a weapon's launch?" the commodore yelled.

"Commodore you ordered us to begin the weaving the 'net' at all costs. So the short answer is no, sorry commodore."

"For being stupid, Bill and Stef, I will send out a retrieval team for my ships. But, I'm afraid your life support will be well exhausted long before I send the message. I'm sorry too. Good luck to you both."

"Commodore please!" exclaimed Bill.

 But his call for mercy fell on silence of space. There was no further communications between the ships.

The three ships behind them were closing on them. It was going to be a bit bumpy going through the shock wave of the anti-matter/matter explosion but the distance was great enough not to cause damage.

Jacob transmitted this message to Luther, "Don't move, stay where you are."

The purpose of the message was simple. It was too allow the Commodore to become aware of another ship. But he hoped that the Commodore would assume that it was defenseless shuttle made in their ancient days and maybe divert a ship towards the IOSAC and split them up. If his dad followed orders then he would assume that his time had come to eliminate a few pirates.

SIL11 was receiving another transmission. "Captain Diller is it? No, I guess its Miller. Now you have made things difficult for me. I can no longer ensure your safety. You have damaged two of my highly prized spacecraft. Ceres will not be happy with me, and I'm afraid you personally will have to pay. If you stand down I will spare the life of your crew and your crew aboard your shuttle. One of my ships will be headed in their direction, if he doesn't hear from me soon, he will destroy your shuttle."

"You can't. Most of the *crew* on the shuttle are only children," Jacob lied.

"Oh yeah, the SIL program encouraged procreation on board. Now that makes sense. Ah, my dear captain, you will not resist our boarding, or you can good-bye to the products of your genes. Do I make myself clear?"

Good. The commodore took the bait. Jacob didn't answer the last message. Jacob had one single huge advantage over the commodore; the commodore did not want to damage the SIL11 because of its possible value, while Jacob had absolutely no qualms about disintegrating his entire fleet. Jessica informed him that one of ships had reversed course but two remaining Totanus ships were closing on their position. He announced to the crew, "Their will be a hostile and armed boarding party arriving in the next couple of hours. Do not abandon your posts and surrender if necessary. Todd remain hidden, you are the calvary and remember the mothers of our children. And Sarah, Jessica will be joining you in the infirmary. This will be no more communications on board except from me from this point on. Over and out"

He glanced over his shoulder at Jessica and said, "Jessica any changes with the Gatekeepers ships?"

"No sir, do wish for me to leave now?"

"Just one more thing. Can you rig the air supply around the door of the infirmary to release some anesthetizing gas like you did with Ivan and have the release controlled in the infirmary itself?"

"Yes, captain

"Good. Use the anesthetizing gas at your discretion. Now go join Sarah, and protect our kids at all costs."

Chapter 25 - The Battle for the Ship

Luther had settled into a short canyon on the far side of the asteroid. Even though, he had the IOSAC do some non-mobile tests and had some unmanned flights, it was nothing compared to the exhilaration of actually flying it. He also quite astonished at the ease for the data retrieval when actually sitting in the pilot chair. It was better than having information at your fingertips. All he did was wondered about any stealth technology; IOSAC responded with its capabilities and limitations, appearing in his head. The technology was available on board to divert light around the vessel, so that it would appear invisible, but it was limited in duration for up to 6 hours because of its huge drain on energy reserves.

When he wondered about type of spacecraft that were chasing the SIL11, he was informed that they were Totanus fighters, which were century old Corporate Type II fighters retrofitted with a modern defense shield. They were capable in repulsing his high intensity lasers for a short time, but they had no defense against the anti-graviton canon. The stealth technology was somewhat recent, so the Totanus fighters pursuing the SIL11 would not be able to detect him. At full power, the anti-graviton cannon would not only crush their defense shield and the fighter's hull, but would displace them nearly five thousands kilometers.

He thought that he would no problem overtaking all three of the fighters. But they could have surprises of their own. Besides, he needed to refrain from too much confidence, since over-confidence is a weakness, one that his own son loves to exploit. His son was never trained in military tactics, but his fascination for some of his books regarding famous historical battles were frequent reads for him. Luther was proud of him; this plan of his was well thought out. But their survival depended on the crew's execution of his plans, any misstep could be their last.

He learned a great deal about those fighters and the people that piloted them. The leadership of the Totanus mafia was a conglomerate of labor executives who survived the Gatekeepers sweep of the asteroid belt. Before the invasion, many of these labor bosses used the guise of representing the interests of mining workers of the asteroid belt, then defrauded Corporate large sums of money, which of course the miners never saw. The labor bosses used the defrauded money to invest in criminal activities that had huge dividends on their investments and controlled the masses of labor in the asteroid belt. Many of the structures on Ceres itself had been destroyed, so had the security forces, who kept the peace in the asteroid belt in the Gatekeepers initial sweep. The surviving labor bosses on Ceres and the much of the asteroid belt took advantage of this opportunity and formed the Totanus mafia. There was no authority to oppose them, and the Gatekeepers did not consider them a potential threat, so they left them alone for the time-being. There was only one other criminal family in the asteroid belt and they were the Vesta-Pallas consortium but they were not near large enough to vie for supremacy in the asteroid belt, so they kept a rather low profile, but they did occasionally surprise Totanus family.

He was able to track in the SIL11 and the Totanus fighters and allowed them to pass his position. He was quite sure that nobody would be able to detect him, when he made his shuttle invisible during their passing.

Now for the wait, but Luther had confidence in his son. Jacob was hopeful enough to make an apparent last attempt to reconcile this confrontation by peaceful means, but resourceful enough to survive if the attempt failed. He also began tracking two Totanus vessels in a collision course with the SIL11. It looked like the SIL11 would be trapped. But luck was on SIL11 side, since the two fighter pilots in frantic attempt to create an energy field net to stop the SIL11 became careless and allowed one the SIL11's anti-matter torpedoes to detonate, incapacitating the two fighters. That was a huge break for the crew of the SIL11. Finally, there was a message from Jacob, "Don't move, stay where you are."

Jacob thought, well it's time to rough up some Totanus fighters. He allowed his vessel to become invisible again and left the asteroid at flank speed. Jacob's gambit had paid off, since he could track one of the Totanus fighters breaking formation and heading straight at him. Jacob had managed to split up the enemy. The one fighter targeting him was doomed of course since he had no idea that he was approaching at rapid speed. Then he will be able to sneak up on the other remaining fighters. He would mourn for the four crewmembers on the Totanus fighter later, but for now they were messing with his family.

***

The two remaining Totanus fighters were well within visual range. A small bright flash appeared behind the SIL11 and the pursuing vessels. Again, he could eavesdrop on the Commodores communications.

"Simon, I told you not to destroy their shuttle. We needed their children are bargaining chips. Couldn't you have held off?" the commodore asked the captain of the retreating fighter.

There was no response.

"Captain of the Totanus 15, do you read?"

Again, no response. The commodore tried a couple more desperate attempts to reach his wing man, but there was no response. The last communication of the commodore was, "Damn!"

The commodore turned his attention to the SIL11.

"Captain Ziller? You don't seem to take us very seriously. Do you have some friends back there, that you don't want me to know about?"

A potent beam of light from the front fighter was directed towards the SIL11's farm. Obviously, at close range their lasers were quite effective. The glass roof of the arboretum instantly shattered and all the growing crops as well as the nourishing dirt vanished into the vacuum of space. The arboretum appeared to be a total loss. Fortunately, all the SIL11 doors were sealed, which minimized the loss to the rest of the ship.

"Captain Miller. Do you take me seriously now? Answer this question, or will target more sensitive areas of your ship, do you have friends back there?"

Jacob weighed his response and replied to the commodore, "You have destroyed our food supply. Commodore I take you very seriously, you didn't need to mutilate my ship! I do not have any targets except the two of you on our scanners? Check your own advanced scanners. Where is our shuttle? Have your destroyed it?" he frantically replied.

Jacob was quite disturbed with the damage on his ship, but he was not giving in, so he would continue with the charade. Todd was going to be quite angry about the loss of his grapes, Jacob thought.

"Be prepared to be boarded," the commodore responded and then abruptly ended communications. The forward fighter was about a half hour ahead of the second fighter. Jacob monitored the docking of the fighter to the aft starboard airlock. Four crewmembers disembarked from the fighter and blasted their way through the sealed door and onto the SIL11. Of course, there was no one to meet them appropriately. Jacob monitored their every move.

One of the four invaders was flashing hand signals to other three. Jacob assumed he was the commodore. They divided up heading in different directions. Commodore Fredrick gave cynical smile to the camera, giving him the finger and then destroying the camera. They all proceeded to impunitively destroy the SIL11's factory installed cameras with ease. Again, Jacob was in luck because they did not recognize the additional cameras that were installed while Ivan roamed the ship, so Jacob continued to monitor them. The commodore headed for the other aft port docking ring, probably to instruct the crew of the second fighter. Another was headed to his location, the bridge, and another to engineering and lastly one to weapons control.

Jacob was a little a relieved that none of them, was advancing to the infirmary. He opened up SIL11's intercom and simply said, "Tobias." At the same time, the blip for the second fighter disappeared from his monitor, and the IOSAC appeared on his scope, two thousand meters from their stern. The IOSAC maneuvered into the aft port side docking ring. The commodore seemed unaware that another one of his fighters had been neutralized and was assuming that his fighter was currently docking. Luther had properly prepared himself with his personal shield activated and Ivan's weapon on hand. After the docking ring had finished pressurizing, the commodore opened the door. Luther instantly killed him where he stood.

Luther's first instinct was to go to infirmary, where he assumed the children were being kept secured. But he hesitated, since his son would have adequately protected the children with one, possible two heavily armed crewmembers. Luther instead proceeded to the bridge, where he knew his son was located and probably was the least protected. Jacob smiled, watching his dad making the right choice and continued their radio silence.

***

"Stop right there missy. I will not hesitate to kill you if you reach for any of the controls," said the armed pirate.

Christina froze on what she was doing and acquiesced to the pirate.

"Stand up missy, let me take a look at you," snarled the pirate

Christina stood up and turned towards the man.

"Why you're quite a dish aren't you? I have to try you out before I sell you off."

Christina did not give him the pleasure of eliciting a response from her. She stood there watching him in silence.

"You don't talk much. Well that's fine with me, as long as you follow orders. Now, take off the silly outfit of yours and I'll give you a whirl."

Again, Christina didn't respond or move.

The pirate pointed his weapon at her and said, "I mean it."

Christina began stripping off her clothes. She hesitated when all she had left was her panties.

"Well missy, don't stop there," the pirate said pointing to her panties and then he instantly fell into heap.

Todd looked down on him from behind. He had just given him a silent lethal dose from his Taser gun. He looked up at Christina and smiled, "You do look nice, but get dressed. We can't let Sarah know that you have showing off your tits to me."

***

Jacob also surrendered to the pirate entering the bridge. Jacob didn't want a gunfight with a person he wouldn't hesitate to kill him and had the means to do so. The pirate seemed distracted; he was using his armband possibly to communicate with the rest of his crew and possibly the other fighter, Jacob surmised. He appeared confused.

The pirate irritably said, "Keep your hands and away from the controls."

"Of course," Jacob politely responded.

"Turn around," the pirate snapped, "the commodore wanted to do you in himself. But I can't reach him for some reason. Are you blocking our communications?"

"I don't think we have the technology to block your sophisticated communication system. Do you?" Jacob calmly replied.

The pirate was again using his armband, and Jacob thought he was probably to communicate with the others. He was totally distracted and looked up.

"Well I guess the commodore is busy. I'll just do you myself."

As the pirate raised his weapon, he fell in a heap. "You stupid bastard, nobody messes with my family," Luther said looking down at the heap.

Luther added, "Are you OK, son"

They briefly embraced and Jacob went back to monitor the remaining pirate on board. He identified another pirate heap at weapons control. Todd was there as well as Christina. Christina had half of her clothes off. Jacob gritted his teeth, and hoped that the pirate had not raped her before Todd had reached her. The only remaining pirate was scoping out engineering. Of course, there was nobody there for the pirate to subdue. He also started using his armband and he too looked confused.

Jacob looked at his father, "He has two possible choices; one to get back to one of the aft docking rings, or head to the bridge. I want you to go to the two docking areas and eliminate him if he goes there. I will circle around and try my best to block his path near the infirmary before he reaches there. I don't want him to be blasting doors past the infirmary, a couple of them leads to the vacuum of space where are farm once resided; he could inadvertently depressurize more of our ship. Ready?"

Luther replied, "Can I make one suggestion, use your command override to open the doors for me and you to get there, that might buy us the time we need."

"Good idea! I should have thought of that myself," Jacob replied.

"Are you kidding, you thought of everything else," his father laughed.

Jacob grabbed his sidearm and opened up the doors for them, and they proceeded to respective destinations.

As Jacob turned the corner as he was nearing infirmary, the pirate was standing at the doors of the infirmary staring right him with his weapon pointed to his head. He yelled, "Drop your sidearm and raise your arms, my dear sir."

Jacob had miscalculated by few seconds, the pirate had got here before he did. He dropped his weapon and raised his hands above his head as requested.

"Are you the captain here?" the pirate asked.

"Yes, I'm Captain Miller."

"Well, my commodore wanted to have some fun with you. You don't mind do you? After all, I will allow you to live a little longer, so my commodore can have his treat. But where's the rest of your crew, Captain?"

Jacob purposefully glanced at the infirmary doors. He was hoping that either Sarah or Jessica could see him and the perpetrator outside their door.

"In here? The infirmary? Well that does make some sense, it is the safest part of the ship, isn't it?" the pirate responded, mostly talking to himself.

The pirate continued, "You open those doors or tell them inside to open up the doors and toss their weapons out, or I will kill you where you stand. And don't try to be a hero to save your crew. If you don't to as I ask, I'll kill you and everybody inside that infirmary of yours. Do I make myself clear captain?"

Jacob nodded but it was directed to the concealed camera up above, which the pirate had not noticed and probably thought he was nodding to him.

As he approached the keypad for the door, he lost strength in his legs and the room darkened. He could hear the pirate collapsing as well as he hit the floor. Jacob had one last feeling before losing consciousness completely, and it was a sense of relief.

Chapter 26 - Squabbling

The SIL11 acquired another passenger, who was deep in cryogenic sleep and another spacecraft, which was docked alongside. The weapons of the pirates were confiscated and the bodies of the dead pirates were incinerated and their ashes were released into space. . The pirate's spacecraft even though inferior to the IOSAC, may actual pose larger obstacles in learning to fly it. Its systems were not connected to human nervous system for automated control as with the IOSAC, but it had one redeeming quality, it had no seemingly impenetrable security system. SIL11 course and speed had not changed significantly to attract attention of the Gatekeepers apparently. All the Gatekeepers ships continued their orbits around their respective planet or moon. So they continued their approach to Mercury for its last aerobraking maneuver. This maneuver would be nowhere close to the intensity as with the maneuver at Uranus, but it was still necessary to settle into comfortable orbit around Venus without attracting attention and save on their dwindling anti-matter reserves.

Jacob was quite relieved that the SIL11 was still functioning and none of the SIL crew was killed. It was quite a loss to lose the arboretum and their ability to grow food for now. They still had backup dirt and ability to reconstruct its roof, but it needed much labor and time, which was something that they didn't have in excess. Todd had been quite resourceful and industrious in redeploying the food on board. Only a fifth of their food had actually been lost during the pirate attack. The remaining food would be quite sufficient for the entire crew as least for the time being. Todd was quite protective of his wine supply since all the bottles were hidden in his and Sarah's quarters; not a single bottle was lost during the pirate's attack. The remaining food was still distributed in four other areas of the ship and so it was decided to keep the food in those locations and Sarah insisted to Todd's chagrin to keep the wine in those four locations as well. The factory installed cameras in the areas of the pirate infiltration were destroyed and needed replacing. But all and all, they were lucky with all other ship's systems still operating nominally.

Duties were again shuffled with Todd and Sarah working full time on the restoration of the arboretum roof. Sarah had finished her task for making anti-radiation medications for the children during their Mercury flyby, making her available. Christina project with additional radiation shielding was primarily completed as well, so Christina would act as advisor on the roof project and was assigned in replacing the cameras. She was also again assigned to figure out the futuristic systems of the pirates' Corporate Type II fighter. But this time, Jacob would not allow Christina in doing this alone. He had either Jessica or his dad to partner with Christina in investigating the fighter's on board systems. He also needed Jessica to spell him in monitoring the Gatekeepers' task force and monitoring the remaining asteroid belt for potential threats until they had passed Mars's orbit. Of course, they all were obligated to watch the SIL11's toddlers and squeeze in some rest and nourishment. This schedule unfortunately did not allow for any entertainment or recreation of any kind for the crew. This on occasion resulted in short tempers and some irritability among the crew. Even though the crew had a several lifetimes of sleep, now the crew couldn't get enough of it now.

On one occasion, Jessica and Christina got into it. Despite apparently being one big family, Christina still did not trust Jessica and Jessica refused to defuse her suspicions. Christina had little time with Jacob these days, and was actually spending less time with Jacob than Jessica was.

Jessica had moved into Luther's quarters, so Christina had thought that Jessica's quarters would be abandoned similarly as she abandoned hers when moving into the captain's quarters. So, when she was replacing the camera fixtures near Jessica's old quarters, she had carefully opened the doors to Jessica's old quarters without being observed. She could tell people later that she accidently opened the doors when she was fixing the camera. What she saw somewhat shocked her. Inside was Jessica's old brass bed with clean white satin sheets still on them but surrounding the bed were a myriad of chains and straps with old style handcuffs. The walls were draped with satin black sheets and candles placed generously around the room. There were belts and feather covered whips alongside an assortment of sex toys. As she looked around, she began to feel a little warm. So this was Jessica's fun room, Christina thought. Christina thought the old man, Luther must have more energy than she gave him credit for. She laughed out loud thinking about how Luther would assume that Jessica was in his clutches during one of their rendezvous when the reverse would be actually true. Then she questioned why another room, why not use their own bedroom for their fantasies. Then she considered that this was Jessica's room and Luther may not have any idea it existed, maybe it was for her other sex partners on board, like her own husband and possibly Todd. She wouldn't even exclude Sarah from Jessica's list.

"What are you doing in my room?" Jessica blurted out behind Christina, "Looking for some unspeakable pleasures?"

Christina was quite startled and jumped around. "I thought you moved in with Luther."

"Oh I have. But I thought I would decorate this room, most of this stuff was left by my mother. She must have brought on board with her when SIL11 departed Earth. My mother had a special relationship with my father, wouldn't you say," she said seductively while walking slowly to the edge of the bed. Her eyes were dark and penetrating, with a small smile directed at Christina. "What do you think about my interior designing skills? See anything you would like? Or would like to do?"

Christina was speechless, she honestly believed that Jessica was trying to seduce her. Jessica lay on top of the bed, extending her arms and played with one of the handcuffs near the bedpost.

She looked up Christina. "You are a quiet one, aren't you? You haven't answered any of my questions as of yet," Jessica added playfully. "I was going to get dressed into something more appropriate for this room. Would you like to watch?"

Christina assumed that she was right about Jessica, and she was trying to seduce her and assumed that Jacob must have also been here before. Christina marched over to Jessica and erupted, slapping Jessica hard across the face, "You fuckin' slut, have you been sleeping with my husband!"

"Your husband?" Jessica asked incredulously. But Jessica refused to diffuse the situation, instead she inflamed it. "He is quite buff, isn't he? He's a chip off the old block isn't he?"

Christina became infuriated and tried to strike Jessica again. This time Jessica was prepared and fended off Christina's blow. They began to shout and scream at one another. Luther who was heading towards that direction quickly sent Jacob a quick message about an altercation between Jessica and Christina in Jessica's old quarters. Jacob immediately responded he would be there in less than minute. Luther began to jog down to Jessica's quarters, and into his fun room.

When Luther got there, Christina had Jessica pinned to the bed and Jessica had grabbed both of Christina's arms to prevent Christina from striking her. They both were struggling with one another and cussing at each other's face.

"What the hell is going on?" Luther asked.

Jessica answered first, "I found this bitch in our room. When I asked what she was doing here, she wouldn't answer. Then she struck me across the face, the fuckin' bitch." She continued to struggling in a losing battle to keep Christina's arms in check.

While Jessica was speaking, Christina had managed to free her left arm and took a big back swing to let Jessica have it again. This time, Luther lunged out and grabbed her arm before she could deliver the blow.

Luther pleaded, "Christina stop!!"

Luther picked up Christina and separated the two. Jessica rolled off the bed on the other side with her face red from the blow, fists clenched and eyes burning hot. Luther struggled to keep Christina from attacking Jessica.

Then Jacob arrived. At first, he was somewhat shocked at the decorum of the room but quickly dismissed it when he saw his wife flailing at Luther and trying to escape to get at Jessica. Jessica was smoldering and had her fist clenched readying for the attack.

"Christina, stop and that's an order!!" Jacob wailed.

Christina stopped when saw her husband standing there, and yelled at him, "Have you been sleeping with that slut?" she said pointing to Jessica.

"And the hell gave you that idea?"

"Just look around you. This is Jessica's playpen and you know it. I know she attracted to you and you are attracted to her. Don't deny it!"

"There has been only you since a time before we were married! Now apologize to Jessica," Jacob replied.

"What??" Christina asked incredulously.

Luther interjected, "If it makes any difference to you Christina, this is *my* and Jessica's room."

Christina turned to Luther and stared at him as though she didn't know him. Jacob chuckled and scanned the entire room and said, "Dad, you have some extravagant tastes."

"Most of these are Jessica's *decorations*, I'll have you know," Luther replied.

Jessica smiled at Luther and then at Jacob, and asked, "Do you like them, captain? I bet you know how to use most of them."

Christina again struggled in Luther's grasp. This time Luther responded to Jesscia, "Jessica, stop enraging her and egging her on! And now you apologize to Christina."

Both women unclenched their fist and both took a deep breath of air. Jessica was the first to apologize. "Sorry, to stir you up like I did, while giving you the wrong idea. But you refused to answer my question, of why you were in the room, when I first arrived."

Jacob turned to Christina, "Christina?!"

A torrent of tears streamed down her face and her face turned red with embarrassment. Christina started, "Sorry Jessica, your door inadvertently opened when I was trying to isolate the connections for the camera I was installing. What I saw inside your room, gave me a double take with all the chains, straps and whips *decorating* the room. I couldn't help but to take a short glimpse."

Jacob again scanned entire the room and said, "I can understand that, but not striking a fellow crewmember."

Christina continued, "I do apologize for striking you. I do hope you are OK? I guess I didn't know I could swing that hard."

Christina turned towards Jacob and mumbled, "I'm sorry love, it's obvious you have never been in this room either. I don't know what got into me!"

Jacob smiled at her, and said, "Maybe it will give us some ideas about our own place." Then his smile vanished replaced with a concerned look. "Normally, a captain would throw the both of you in the brig for fighting on board. BUT, this ship and I cannot afford missing duty time from any crewmember. The both of you and particularly you Christina have put me into a precarious position. Therefore, the only retribution you two will have make is a sincere and I mean sincere handshake and hug between the both of you. You are daughter and mother in law after all, for good gracious. Do I make myself totally clear? And I mean NOW!"

Jessica and Christina walked towards the foot of the bed. Christina extended her hand and Jessica accepted it, the she grasped Christina's shoulder and pulled it towards her. For a brief but extremely difficult hug.

Christina quickly left the room and scampered back to her quarters, with tears streaming down her face. Luther turned Jessica towards him and examined the redness under her eye from Christina's roundhouse right.

"Is she OK?" Jacob asked his father.

"It might be black and blue for a while, but I think she will be OK" answered Luther and looked at Jessica and lovingly asked, "Are you feeling OK? No dizziness?"

"Don't worry about thing, I'm absolutely fine," Jessica said and deeply kissed him. She smiled at him and added, "Should we get started?"

Jacob stood at the doorway and scanned the room again. Luther noticed him there standing there and said, "Captain, I believe you were a bit too lenient towards the women, I think that Jessica here needs some more punishment which I plan to administer as soon as you leave," Luther said surveying the *decorations* in the room. "Maybe Christina could use same kind of punishment after all you don't want to be too easy on the crew, after all you are captain," Luther laughed.

Jacob looked around the room and smiled. Then shook his head at his father and left the premises. He walked towards his own quarters to find Christina. He was somewhat shocked at his father's play room. He never thought of his old man as an old dirty man. But he totally understood though, especially when it came to Jessica's revved up sex drive, he knew that Jessica would have lots of ideas, which only his dad would be privy to. Lucky man, he thought and now he had to deal with his wife. He considered his dad's suggestion, but he decided to let Christina make that call. For the time being, he would be stern but supportive of his wife. He would go to her now and only show his supportive side to her for now.

Chapter 27 - The Dreams

SIL11 did not encounter any more pirates prior to crossing Mars's orbit around the sun. Both Mars and Earth were on the other side of the sun and Jacob had planned to keep the SIL11 in that relative position to those planets unchanged as long as possible. Hell was on the other side of the sun and Jacob did not want any part of it.

He kept a careful eye on those enemies. He had confidence that the vessel orbiting Titan would not be able to detect them now, so his biggest concern were the two large Gatekeeper ships that still orbited both Mars and Earth, not to mention possibly another appearing out of nowhere. He was fortunate that Earth and Mars were near perihelion, scant under 75 million miles apart and on the opposite side of the Sun. Once they make their brief pass around Mercury, and hopefully they will have stationary orbit around Venus. Once around Venus, they could be detected by almost anybody, unless they could submerge under the cloud tops of Venus, which of course was impossible with this ship. Jacob was totally relying now on the Dimensionless Ones last message. He had no plan once they arrive at Venus. If someone or something did not help them, they would be at the mercy of the Gatekeepers. A last resort was planned which was to abandon the SIL11 and split the crew and use the IOSAC and Corporate fighter, as life rafts. It was possible that the Gatekeepers would only destroy the SIL11 and ignore the two smaller life rafts. Eventually, they all would either die or become fugitives on Earth or Mars. Jacob of course realized that this was a poor plan, which is why the Dimensionless Ones or possibly new friends on Venus were the only recourse to a more viable option. In both Ivan's story and the Tandoorian's history, it was mentioned that the Dimensionless Ones offered each civilization an opportunity to build specific ships and follow the Dimensionless Ones to who knows where. So did the crew of the SIL11 already miss their opportunity? Jacob asked himself. He didn't know for certain if he would choose the path of the Dimensionless Ones, but he sure would like the option to be available to him. The only crew member that he knew who would absolutely go, would be Todd and most likely his sister. But he couldn't be sure how his dad, Jessica or even Christina would choose.

He knew his crew was on edge, but he even needed more from them now that they were entering the inner solar system. Communications would be limited to PCD messaging, hand signals, or voice. Stray radio waves from spacesuits could possibly be detected by the Gatekeepers therefore radio communications were disallowed. Of course, the SAMs could not be utilized since they relied on radio signals. Ship to ship communications between the SIL11 and its two small vessels would be silenced. Even the ship's intercom system would only be held in reserve for emergencies only. He had ordered the portal views blocked so that any room light would not escape the SIL11. Only minimal lighting was allowed on the reconstruction of the arboretum roof and it was only allowed in terms of need. He made course corrections so they had their course pinpointed to Mercury and then he took the engines off line. He would have to restart them once he got closer to Mercury. If the Gatekeepers were tracking them, he only wanted to appear to be rock speeding it's way towards the sun, like hundreds of other space rocks.

The crew accepted the new changes but of course none of them actually liked them. Sarah gave Jacob weekly reports on the crew's less than optimum demeanor and their poor morale. This ultimately led to arguments between Jacob and Sarah. But instead of Sarah being the instigator, Jacob was often than not the one who started the arguments.

Their haven and escape was the care of their children. Tobias, Nozomi and Rhiannon began to enter the educational phase of walking and talking. They not only interacted with their parents now but began to interact with each other. This by itself reduced some of squabbling and arguments between the adults, after all one must be a good example for the next generation. Occasionally Luther would become melancholy with thoughts of these two generations that may never have an opportunity to run along a sandy beach in the bright sun, or feel the rain splatter on your face then soak your clothes. He was reminded by his two children that they could not miss what they never experienced. And they had endless of other opportunities that other children on Earth would never be able to experience and from what they have gathered; they had been saved from possible torments of the Gatekeepers. How many Earth children have seen another planet up close and one that actually had an ancient and different civilization on it? Or experienced periodic weightlessness or the seen the brilliant stellar sky without being obscured by an atmosphere? To save face, he allowed his children to outwardly cheer him up but the sadness of not having the ability to share your own childhood experiences with his children or his grandchildren still lingered in his mind. It seemed to him that it was all too altruistic; maybe his true sadness came from the thought that he would not be able experience those childhood moments again.

He was quite proud of the accomplishments of this crew, not only have they survived which in present circumstances was a daunting task, but to do what's right for the remaining human race. They still had on board two sleeping enemies who would not hesitate to destroy them all if it meant saving their own skins. He hoped the crew's mercy on the two would pay dividends down the road, but he didn't think that the crew was actually expecting such a reward. Instead most of the crew had only hope in the Dimensionless Ones, who have been guiding their steps. He personally not had an encounter with them, Jessica, Sarah and Todd had experienced theirs as rudimentary as they were. The Gatekeepers were in almost all aspects just the opposite. They were cruel, savage and merciless but they were also quite arrogant. They were technologically far superior and physically superior to the past and present human race, and they knew it and capitalized on it. Their overconfidence will be their doom, Jacob mused.

He wondered what life on Earth would be like right now under Gatekeepers' rule. It was said that the Gatekeepers had killed tens of thousands of people and had enslaved millions more. What was the Gatekeepers' purpose for such atrocities? Did their arrogance blind them to a possibility that the eventual result from such torture would be a rebellion? And why did the Gatekeepers hate the Dimensionless Ones as accounts had suggested? It was his understanding that the Gatekeepers had no means to battle and even influence the Dimensionless Ones. They were in a totally different reality, and they could easily change others observed reality to suit their own purpose.

Like his son, Luther was also filled with thoughts of Dimensionless Ones and Gatekeepers swirling in his head, as he lay down in his bed. Luther was more interested in their possible origins and how those origins had shaped their separate purposes. Jessica still had a couple of more hours of duty left before she could join him. And knowing Jessica, she would playfully wake him up and stir up his desires. He was tired from his own shift and Nozomi was sound asleep in her own small bed. He let sleep overtake him in matter of minutes, and a couple of peculiar dreams invaded his mind.

In his first dream, he was a Dimensionless One on a surreal planet where life had ceased to exist centuries ago. But their energy and life force seem to still emanate from this planet. They had survived all those centuries on their planet with help from something they called the Ancient One. The Ancient

131

One guided them to evolve into beings of energy and losing the necessity for their material bodies. They no longer ate, slept, breathe or reproduce at they had millions of years ago. As a final step in their evolution, the Ancient One instructed them to seek out other civilizations that had become aware of their possible finite existence on their own planet and lead them to a place the he has prepared from them. With this final instruction, the Ancient One left their planet for all eternity. The Dimensionless Ones became divided. Some followed the Ancient One's will, believing that they could sustain their life force outside their own planet sphere of influence and become aware of other talents that have been latent until they left their planet. Others however, were afraid to leave their home planet since it has always sustained them for thousands of centuries. Their beliefs were reinforced when none of the Dimensionless Ones that had left ever returned. These Dimensionless Ones that stayed became known as the Gatekeepers since they believed that they should stay or die. As centuries passed, no Dimensionless Ones ever returned and the Ancient One's instruction was lost to them. Those who stayed noticed that their energy began to decline. They began to believe that they needed a body to sustain their energy force. So they manufactured physical bodies since them they had technology to do so, so over decades the remaining Dimensionless Ones or Gatekeepers became enslaved into material bodies again. They became more and more reliant on their technology as their enslavement gave way to the needs of their bodies. However, their technology allowed them to venture away from their home planet and became independent of their home world. During the centuries that ensued, the Gatekeepers with highly superior spacecraft would on occasion encounter groups of true Dimensionless Ones. The Gatekeepers were angry with them since they never returned to tell them that they survived and had incurred new talents to deliver their messages to other civilizations. Instead they had allowed themselves to become irreversible enslaved to their material bodies once more. The Gatekeepers became so angry that they targeted their weapons on the Dimensionless Ones, anytime they saw them. Of course, any physical weapon was totally ineffective against them. The Dimensionless Ones were sad about the destiny of the Gatekeepers but they left them, never reveling themselves to the Gatekeepers again. In addition, they would not interfere with Gatekeeper's interactions with other beings.

Luther's mind briefly awoke as he felt Jessica crawling into bed next to him. To his surprise, Jessica left him alone and quickly fell back into sleep. Luther's mind began to wander once more as a second dream invaded his consciousness.

In this dream, he was not a Dimensionless One but a Gatekeeper. They were an amiable race. They had no history of wars between themselves or among nearby civilizations. Their planet was situated nearby a small but dangerous black hole. This specific black hole was difficult to detect and they had observed alien spacecraft losing themselves in it early in their history. They took it upon themselves to be guardians of the black hole and diverted alien spacecraft from it. Their home planet was a part of league of planets in this more densely populated part of the galaxy. They were the best at developing spacecraft among these planets. In this league of planets, they became known as the Gatekeepers and were highly regarded among the other members. Their spacecraft was prized among all the members. But they did not share this technology with other planets in their League in fear that one member would use these ships and this technology against another league planet or even against themselves, the Gatekeepers. This did not deter some members from trying to steal their technology but other members supported their decision and considered it a wise choice by the Gatekeepers to preserve peace in their League.

The Dimensionless Ones started to come one by one to the different planets in the League. Most of the planets considered them as benevolent beings to rescue them from their perilous density of their finite existence. However, the Gatekeepers did not trust them and thought their own technology would allow them to escape their finite existence and didn't need these advanced beings. However, the other planets did not support Gatekeepers' view and since the Gatekeepers kept their technology to themselves, the other planets in the League felt this was their only alternative.

The Gatekeepers decided to monitor the evacuation of their fellow planets in oddly designed spacecraft that had designed with instructions given to them by the Dimensionless Ones. Dimensionless Ones never appeared to Gatekeepers since they stirred an ancient mistrust among the Gatekeepers. To the Gatekeepers disbelief, the Dimensionless Ones lead the entire evacuation to another similar black hole situated many light years away as the former League members disappeared from existence. Billions of intelligent life forms were being wiped out of existence by the Dimensionless Ones by guiding them blindly to black hole's death grip. The Gatekeepers were shell shocked and swore that any race that accepted the Dimensionless Ones guidance would suffer the anguish and horror that they were now experiencing, maybe in time, that race would come to realize the Dimensionless Ones were not their friends.

A black figure with sinewy arms and legs and expressionless black eyes turned towards Luther in his dream and spoke angrily into his mind, "You are not one of us! You are a Dimensionless One!" The Gatekeeper paused changed the tone of his voice inside his head from anger to threatening. "Ahh, you are not trained and have not endured the crucible of change. I will have you one day!"

Luther awoke with a start with Jessica intently watching him.

"Are you OK?" she asked.

Luther noticed that the sheets around him were slightly wet with sweat and he was breathing rapidly. He calmed himself by taking a deep breath as he went over the details of his two dreams. He didn't want to forget anything about them. Of course, we would never forget the last face he saw in his dream even he wanted to.

He looked up Jessica, "I'm fine, just had a couple of vivid dreams. The last one had quite a terrifying end!"

Jessica responded seductively, "Were you dreaming about me? About the naughty things you want to do to me?"

Luther ignored her remark and concentrated on the details of his dream. But unlike other dreams, the details of these two dreams did not diminish after he awoke and unlike other dreams, they seemed plausible in the real world.

"Are you playing hard to get?" Jessica asked as her hand stroked his testicles under the bedsheets.

"You don't always have to do that, you know," quipped Luther.

Jessica's eyes turned to concern and her voice echoed that concern, "Are you OK, sweetheart? What have I done to upset you?"

Luther sighed, "Nothing's wrong. I just want you to know that you don't always need to be a sex toy or a sex kitten all the time. I would love you regardless whether you were trying to seduce me or not. Occasionally and any only occasionally, 'not' is what I would like."

Jessica smiled brightly and non-seductively. She moved her hand onto his chest and laid her head on his shoulder. He in turn, wrapped his arm around her and played with her hair. A tear rolled down her cheek. "I love you, Luther with all my heart. I would do anything for you."

"I know," Luther smiled and responded, "but sometimes nothing might be all that I want."

They lay together very still and enjoyed the warmth and closeness of their bodies. Jessica twirled the small hairs on Luther's chest while Luther described his dreams to her in vivid detail. Jessica was somewhat surprised at the exuberance that Luther displayed telling his tales. When he was finished, she asked, "Did you think those dreams mean anything?"

He replied, "I don't know but they have my attention. Maybe I just had a conversation with the Dimensionless Ones, but I don't really know."

"Well there, let's have a reality check shall we?" Jessica whispered into Luther's ear, "How would like to be a father again? I'm pregnant again but his time, it's with YOUR child."

Chapter 28 - A Revelation

Both Sarah and Todd were working feverishly on the arboretum roof. They had three hour biweekly meetings with Christina to work out the engineering aspects of the reconstruction project, but Sarah and Todd were doing most of the construction duties themselves. They had succeeded in the construction of a temporary roof that was airtight to allow the actual roof to be constructed. Besides Christina, both Luther and Jessica helped out when they could and cared for Rhiannon whenever Sarah and Todd needed them to. But most of the time, Sarah and Todd had Rhiannon nearby in a temporary constructed play area near them. Despite the farm being blown away by the pirates, the rotating mechanism had only needed minor repairs, so the construction was done in normal g gravity. Gravity tended to make the repairs less difficult since tools and parts tended not to drift away from you. And larger parts did not become large battering rams to the rest of the fragile ship. There were plenty of cranes and devises to lift heavier parts. For both Sarah and Todd, the farm had become their home. Once the temporary roof was in place, they had decided to proceed with filling the farm with dirt again. This is where Rhiannon played most of the time, she was always a very dirty girl but as long as she didn't eat the dirt, neither Sarah or Todd cared about how dirty she got as long as she got a good scrubbing at the end of the work day. Of course, that was Rhiannon least favorite part of the day and she let everyone know about it.

Jacob was cooped up on the bridge most of time. He kept MDS, the eyes and ears of the SIL11 pointed towards the sun most of the time. Since behind the sun, were two gigantic Gatekeepers ships that hovered over the most inhabitable planets of Earth and Mars. Of course, the cradle of human civilization was the Earth and reports of expanding human colonies on Mars probably necessitated the need for monitoring human activities from up above and parley out punishment whether deserved or not to the two sets of human inhabitants. One of the larger corporate projects according the records on board both the IOSAC and the Corporate fighter, was the terraforming project on Mars. Large nuclear reactors were melting the polar caps of frozen carbon dioxide and also releasing underground stores of frozen water into the atmosphere. Over the last couple hundred years, the atmosphere on Mars has dramatically increased in pressure from the released carbon dioxide and water Prior to the Gatekeepers arrival, Martian authorities were already introducing various plant life to Mars and in some small areas, and vegetation had actually began to proliferate but were constantly threatened to be snuffed out by large dust storms on the planet surface. Jacob would have liked to fly by Mars to see for himself, man's progress in colonizing the planet, but of course the presence of the Gatekeepers would not allow any such visit.

Jacob also kept an eye on Venus but her veil of thick brilliant clouds did not give away any of her secrets. This was planet was poorly named, after the God of beauty when it was one of the ugliest and inhospitable places on a planet's surface anywhere in the solar system. And yet they were heading straight for it. He challenged both Christina and Jessica to come up with ideas to survive on the planet, but the challenge was no more than a prayer, one he didn't expect to be answered. He feared that he was developing into a recluse and shied away from social gatherings. Any spare time he had, was spent with his son and wife now, and really nobody else. Both Sarah and Luther mentioned this withdrawal at every possible opportunity, but he ignored them for the most part. He diverted their attention to the ship and to their current situation.

In addition, a chasm was developing between him and Christina. She was a model crewmate, always eager to please and resolute in her efforts. But two events stuck in his mind, her putting their son at risk prior to birth with the incident of the IOSAC and her jealous rage towards Jessica. Her hard working efforts never faltered but prior to those two events, she was always been a model of strength and common sense. She had always been his rock since the passing of his mother. Her support always gave him the needed strength for command, and was always there to be his confidant. He didn't talk to her anymore about personal strategies, not only because everyone seemed to know everything, but also uncertainty had crept in regarding her reactions. That was one professional wedge between them but also personally they were drifting apart. Even though together they spent their free time as a family, most if not all was spent interacting with Tobias and not really with each other. Christina would still come to him when he needed her, but her enthusiasm and passion for lovemaking or simple sex were not as strong as they once were. As a consequence, he didn't seek out intimacy as much as he once did. Did she know about him and Jessica when they had first awakened from their cryogenic sleep? After all, half of the crew had known about their sexual encounter. His immediate family knew about it, and they also knew that Jacob was Nozomi's real father. But he felt certain that his secret was kept safe by them, and Christina and Todd were still kept in the dark. Maybe Christina didn't hear about it from anybody; maybe she only sensed it. Women did seem to sense somethings without the support of any evidence. Then this may have been an attempt by his imagination to understand his wife's behavior. She was genuinely charming and totally engaged with Tobias, there was no doubt about her love for their child. Maybe her feelings for her child had just put Jacob on the backburner temporarily and she doesn't even realize that she was doing it or maybe she did.

Jacob even questioned his handling of those two events with Christina. Being Christina's husband has made it difficult for Jacob to be totally detached and render a fair judgement on her. When he gravitated back to those two past events, it did not appear to him that he had any better approach then the ones he had chosen. Maybe Christina actually felt that the consequences were not severe enough and he had lost some respect and credibility in her eyes. Maybe the loss of trust in allowing Christina to work alone on the alien technology had manifested itself with this attitude towards him. He didn't know and did really didn't want to speak to her directly about it, with the possible fear of losing the special time they had together with Tobias and losing all intimate contact with his wife. So Jacob encouraged the belief among the crew and especially Christina, that he was quite overwhelmed with his responsibilities and channeled all his efforts in devising a plan once they reach Venus. It was the truth, but there more than one why for his withdrawal.

* * *

Christina felt a chasm developing between her and Jacob as well. In her mind, the crack had been initiated by Jacob, but not only with her, but with the entire crew. Both Jacob's sister and father had failed to encourage him to socialize more with his extended family. He would always change the subject towards more pressing matters in regards to their ship and mission. She felt reluctant in pursuing the matter herself too far after all she did not want to jeopardize her short but wonderful family times with Jacob and Tobias. Both Jacob and she were self-proclaimed workaholics, but not to the extreme that Jacob was demonstrating now. She wouldn't blame Jacob to be disappointed with her recent behavior. She deserved the public chastising from Jacob after she almost lost their son because of her

136

blind passion for solving the IOSAC security problem and her unexplained and uncontrollable rage towards Jessica in her play room. She hadn't reached such levels of passion or emotion in the past, Jessica and Sarah had always been more emotional. She was supposed to be the most rational among the women if not the entire surviving crew. She doubted she held that title now.

Not only was Jacob working long hours on the bridge but she was registering some rather long hours herself. She had to put together the engineering plans for Sarah and Todd and show them those plans twice a week. At first it was difficult, since neither one were engineers, and the project was quite complex. She would have on many occasions suit up herself and show them what to do. But the temporary roof was holding and the task of reconstructing the roof was becoming less arduous for Christina, with Sarah learning the terminology and possessing natural skills for mathematics and Todd being quite practical and perceptive about the construction project and asked questions on mattes that she had overlooked. Before long, a simple review of schematics was what all the two needed in their biweekly meetings. As time went by, her primary task became the unveiling of the Corporate's technology on their short range fighter. But to Christina this was not work but more like play. She would have spent more time on deciphering the technology but was limited since Luther had to be present. But she planned to be at the fighter anytime Luther could spare time away from his precious wife and his own duties.

She thought that maybe another pregnancy may bring her and Jacob closer together. But another baby would have to wait until she had more energy than she had now. Tobias took all her remaining energy after duty hours. She still made herself available to Jacob, so he shouldn't complain about sex but he tended to want that less and less as the days and weeks passed.

Luther was always open to hear her complaints regarding her relations with his son during the times they worked together. He would have proven to be an extremely good psychoanalyst if he had decided to pursue such a career instead of being this ship's doctor, when they had initially launched from Earth. But for crew's sake, Christina was glad that he had not made that other career choice. He was not judgmental and assumed nothing, he was the ultimate listener. He appeared to be genuinely unconcerned about her vicious attack on his wife, Jessica. Instead, he encouraged her to spend time with her and become friends with her.

Jessica accepted an invitation for breakfast with Christina. Christina did inform Jessica that they would be alone but promised not to punch her in the face again. Jessica laughed out loud which put Christina at ease. As Christina made her way to the galley, she wondered what she would say to Jessica, besides apologizing to her again but this time it would be a genuine apology. She wondered if she needed to explain herself to Jessica or just leave the past in the past. She was a bit nervous in seeing her again, but couldn't place why that would be. They had been together since they were children. Often they would stick together and allow themselves to be directed by Sarah in some make believe game or journeying to some distant planet, including Earth. Sarah promised them that she would protect them from evil boys but that was until Sarah herself got interested in an older boy. They were close when they were small, but Jessica's brother, Tom had changed all that. Christina had become fearful of Jessica. Looking back at the aftermath of Tom's massacre, she felt a twinge of regret and guilt in not going to her and comforting her old friend, Jessica. Jessica was becoming an outcast as she delved into her books for escape. She was very studious type and showed great promise for sciences and mathematics. She also had a propensity for learning languages. She would later become Jacob's science officer and was probably the smartest person on board. As Jessica became older, she also became a very beautiful woman, and she knew it. She took advantage of her charms and persuasiveness with men. Christina never liked that side of her being able to manipulate men but she did admire Jessica's beauty. So, maybe she would apologize to Jessica not only for the slap across the face but for deserting her when she was young when her brother died along with her father and eventually her mother. But to be truthful, she didn't know what she was going to say.

When she entered the galley, Jessica was already there drinking some syn-coffee. Jessica smiled broadly to her and asked, "I hope you're more talkative today."

Christina responded immediately, "Oh yes, and let me start by genuinely apologizing in hitting you across the face. I am truly sorry."

"Nonsense, Luther was right, I did egg you on. And if I had known that you bring quite some punch to the swing of yours. I would have behaved rather differently. Everybody on board knows that Jacob loves you and not me. I was just rather surprised that you would be that jealous, since you know that too."

Christina frowned and said, "Yes, I do believe Jacob loves me."

"Good. I would like to talk to you about something entirely different if you don't mind."

Christina was relieved and quickly responded, "Of course, what is it?"

"I'm pregnant again!" Jessica proclaimed.

"Really? How wonderful," Christina said as she embraced Jessica. Jessica returned the embrace emphatically. Jessica's face was radiant and tears of joy streaming down. Jessica seemed more excited about this pregnancy than her previous one. If Christina recollected correctly, Jessica was rather subdued when she talked about her first pregnancy early on. Maybe Jessica just needed to get use to the idea of being pregnant, since she was going to lose her figure. Or maybe since she was so excited about her own pregnancy, her own emotional state and perception might have been distorted. Anyway, Jessica was extremely happy now and Christina was truly happy for Jessica. Christina added, "Who else knows?"

"Well Luther knows of course and Doctor Sarah, since she needed to confirm my condition, but nobody else until you!"

Christina reflected on her own thoughts of becoming pregnant. "How did Luther react to your good news?" she asked Jessica.

"He was quite astounded at first but he was definitely joyous! At least, his grin was so large that it broke out into a wide smile. And it was bigger than when I give him some pleasurable and very wet oral stimulation."

"Well I guess that would be a pretty big smile, Jessica," Christina laughed.

"Just telling you how I see it. Well should we start preparing some breakfast, since I'm eating for two now."

"Sure, but there is one more thing, I wanted to say. No, that's not it, there is one more thing I need to say," Christina said as she gently held on to Jessica's hands. Jessica's dark penetrating knowing eyes turned towards her.

"I would like apologize to you for something I failed to do before we even before we went into our cryogenic sleep."

"There's no need for that," Jessica retorted, "that was long ago."

"Yes there is, so please be quiet and let me get this out!" Christina demanded.

Jessica clasped Christina's hands and continued to look into her eyes, "Of course," Jessica murmured softly.

"I'm so sorry that I was not there for you when your family died so many years ago. You were like a sister and I abandoned you with your grief and your fears. I was not a friend then, but I would very much like to become friends, no… sisters again with you."

A lone solitary tear had escaped Jessica's large pooled dark eyes and ran down her cheek. Jessica's murmured back, "Then as sisters, we need to forget the past. The past is poisoned with deeds done by strangers who are no longer with us. Those strangers don't exist anymore, even the one who gave me a slap a few weeks ago. Agreed?"

Christina was first spell bound by her eyes and her calming voice. She heard the words but only could nod. Her own eyes began to swell in tears. Jessica smiled pleasantly and kissed her firmly on her lips. "Shall we break some eggs and have a couple of omelets with cheese," Jessica finally said.

Again, Christina was mute but nodded enthusiastically.

"You do become quite quiet as some interesting times," Jessica said as she smiled at Christian.

Christina asked awkwardly, "What else should we have?"

"Well let's stay on the healthier side, shall we have some berries and or some sliced tomatoes to go with it. What do you think?"

"Sounds good," Christina managed to answer, but all she could think about was the kiss that Jessica gave her and how much she enjoyed it.

Jessica offhand asked Christina while they were preparing breakfast, "How are things between you and Jacob. Have you thought about getting pregnant yourself?"

Christina could not answer, not because of the question but because of her haunting kiss. It was the only thing that she could think about.

Chapter 29 - The Disappearing Act

"Jessica, please report to the bridge," Jacob punched into his PCD. He was tempted to use the ship's intercom, but he had introduced certain limitations to the crew for protection from being detected by the Gatekeepers, and one of them was to not use the ship's intercom unless it was an emergency. His observation was quite important but it was not an emergency. So he opted for the normal lines of communications and decided not to use the more desirable line of communication, which was the ship-wide intercom system. He needed to make a good example to his crew, but he didn't like it. He added, "That is if you are awake." He also didn't want to wake Jessica needlessly, the whole crew was suffering some degree of sleep deprivation.

Both Gatekeepers ships orbited Mars and Earth like clockwork. But today when both ships entered the far-side of their respective planet, they failed to reappear at the pre-determined time. Instead, they appeared a half-hour later and then resumed their clockwork orbits around Earth and Mars. He double checked his observations and there was a definitive 30 minute gap. Where did the Gatekeepers go in such a short period of time? He discounted the possibility of the Gatekeepers ships entering the atmosphere and landing on the surface and then relaunching to its former orbit. It just wasn't enough time for such a maneuver even for their impressive ships and simultaneously was quite improbable. Was it possible that the Dimensionless Ones were again up to their old planet antics? He didn't think so, since this appeared to be a one-time event. Something happened that he could not explain and did not like mysteries when it came to his ship and crew. Since both planets were on the far-side of the sun, he could not extract out exact measurements of altitude, speed and position of the Gatekeepers to see if there was a change. In several minutes he received a reply from Jessica that she was on her way to the bridge.

'Hello captain," Jessica announced as she entered the bridge.

"I hope that I didn't interrupt anything important," Jacob replied.

"Actually I was enjoying some eggs with your wife; she seems to be very concerned about you and your recent behavior."

"She didn't try to take a swing at you again, did she?"

"Oh no, captain, she was quite friendly. Anyway what's up?"

"I have some abnormal readings regarding the Gatekeepers ships, I wondered if you could verify them?" Jacob asked.

"Of course, captain, right away."

Jessica sat down as Jacob downloaded the MSD readings on the two Gatekeeper ships to her PCD. He told her about the 30 minute gap and asked her if she might know what could cause such a phenomenon. Jessica went carefully through the files.

As Jessica gathered the data, she asked Jacob, "She says that you are becoming a recluse."

Jacob didn't want to respond to inquiries about his relationship with Christina or with the rest of the crew for that matter. He just responded, "Don't get distracted, this gap could be very important."

"Yes, captain. It does appear that there is a 30 minute delay in the ships reappearing. That is peculiarly remarkable since the gap is the same from our vantage point, but the orbits around the two planets are totally different. In some ways, the gap around Mars was even longer since its orbit is much shorter," Jessica replied.

"What do you think it means?" Jacob asked.

"At this point captain, I don't know. Do you mind if I study these readings a bit longer? And do some investigating on my own?" Jessica inquired

"Of course, Jessica. Anything you need, just let me know," Jacob responded.

"By the way captain, I'm having another baby. This time, you will have a true half-brother or sister. I have told most on board including your wife."

"Congratulations, Jessica. You are good at this motherhood stuff."

Jessica whipped her head around. For some reason, his last comment did not set well with her. But she only studied him for a moment and added, "You're pretty good at making babies too, you know. I know this from firsthand experience. Maybe you should make some more with Christina? But maybe she hasn't been in the mood lately?"

At that, Jacob turned and quietly left the bridge. He knew that her last comment was either some sort of dismissal from her or a prelude for partaking in one of her games. He didn't have time for Jessica or himself to be distracted by such games, so he left.

He knew Christina was starting one of her engineering meetings with Todd and Sarah. She had initially complained that were more 'classes' than meetings. But as of late, she informed him, that she was impressed with their progress and the two of them were catching on to the engineering lingo quite quickly. She even said that his sister would have made a fine engineer. He knew that Sarah must have been very impressive for Christina to admit to such an assessment.

He hoped he could get a quick tour to see their progress on rebuilding the farm and also see if Tobias would be as dirty as Rhiannon in less than hour. If Jessica was starting to notice his anti-social attitudes from him, he would need to make necessary adjustments. Jessica had some anti-social attitudes herself until she hooked up his father, so if she noticing then the whole crew was probably noticing it. Tom had displayed some anti-social attitudes prior to his rampage as well, so the crew was probably very sensitive to any similar behavior. Maybe, he'll grab a bottle wine from Todd's stash and have a date with Christina under the temporary roof. But he would need to bring a PCD with him, in case Jessica had some further information but maybe it was time to get reacquainted with his wife.

When Jacob arrived at the dimly lit farm, he saw Christina, Todd and Sarah gathered around table with their PCDs and some printed out schematics. He also noticed that Todd and Sarah were already encouraging a worthy career to both Rhiannon and Tobias as farmers. Each child each had a plastic shovel and a small bag of seeds. Now neither one walked extremely well, but a small bucket of water was available for them a couple steps away to water their planted seeds if they got that far and if they decided they wanted to. He decided not to interrupt the adult meeting, and instead walk towards the children.

Tobias recognized his dad and squealed, "Daddy!" Tobias stiffly walked towards his dad with a large dirty grin on his face.

"Hey Tobias, what are you up to?" Jacob asked as he put down his bottle of wine, then reached down and lifted Tobias up to hug him.

"We're farmers! Rhia and me are planting stuff." Jacob took hold of Tobias's bag and saw that it contained wheat kernels.

Rhiannon came over and shouted, "Hi Uncle Jake, we're planting wheat!"

He put Tobias down and hugged Rhiannon as well. "Well, you two show me how to be a good farmer," he replied.

The both of them started talking at the same time, neither one was irritated with the other for speaking out of turn. But they were both quick to correct one another. No etiquette rules applied here, the communication was very efficient and nobody's feelings were hurt. Somehow before adulthood, kids started to fear speaking out and social rules needed to be applied, so everyone's voice could be heard without a quick dismissal or cruel criticisms from the listeners. Fortunately, these two were still years from that change in communication style.

They explained that needed to put holes in the dirt about a finger length and cover up the kernel with dirt. Tobias stumbled over to the bucket water and tried to pick it up but was unable to do. So, Rhiannon noticing his struggle, quickly went over to help him. Together, they managed to lift up the small bucket of water and walked towards their seeds. Tobias stumbled and both Tobias and Rhiannon fell forward with their bucket of water soaking into the dirt. Fortunately neither was hurt. They both laughed out loud and began to stomping around the mud where the water spilled. A sudden contest on which one could get muddier ensued. Jacob decided to take their bucket and stroll over to the small water reservoir and filled their bucket again about half full, and brought it back where they were still stomping;

"I don't think this is what good farmers do, do you?"

Both shook their heads with wry smiles on their faces. Again, they managed to pick up the bucket together but this time a little slower, managed to get the bucket where the seeds were. They cupped their hands and started throwing water onto their respective dirt hills.

The adult meeting concluded and Sarah, Christina and Todd came strolling over. Todd was the first to speak.

'Hey Jacob, rumor had it that you were chained up on the bridge. Did somebody unshackle you?"

Jacob smiled and responded, "It turns out I had that key all along, wouldn't you know."

Both Christina and Sarah smiled back at him. Sarah looked at the two children throwing water on the dirt and of course themselves and said to Jacob, "Well you managed to figure out a way for the kids to reach a new plateau of dirtiness."

Jacob quickly responded, "Hey now, I didn't put the water bucket, seeds and shovels out here for them. Besides they need to know to be a good farmer you have to get a little dirty, don't you agree?"

"Absolutely, who's the bottle for? I am getting a little thirsty," Todd answered eyeing Jacob's bottle of wine.

He looked up at Todd and then at Sarah and answered, "You can get your own bottle at anytime, Todd. But by the way, would you two mind if you watch Tobias for a while and let him bathed with Rhiannon. I would like to take my wife here out for a date. It's not an order but if you two didn't mind, I would really appreciate it."

"A date?" Chrisitna asked.

But Sarah interrupted Jacob before he could respond, "Of course we will, and it's about time you had a date. Come on Todd, pick up Tobias and I'll take Rhiannon. They may need two baths."

They walked away before either one could say good bye to Tobias. Christina looked at her husband and dared to say, "What kind date were you thinking about?"

"Well let's just start with some wine and giving me a tour of the farm project. OK?"

Christina walked over and extended her hand. Jacob reached for the bottle and the two of them walked over to the now unoccupied table to open his bottle.

Christina and Jacob sipped a couple of glasses of wine and then walked around the farm. Christina discussed the complex roofing project with Jacob. The arboretum roof consisted of two layers; a movable high reflective layer that served to maximize the amount of light on the dirt surface which could then retract to expose the clearly transparent roof above it, which served as the nighttime sky. Despite its complexity, Sarah and Todd had nearly finished with the new roof and in a couple of weeks, the new roof was due for pressurization tests, prior to removing the temporary roof. The temporary roof was totally opaque, which Jacob had insisted on to minimize the amount of light escaping the SIL11, but right now he somewhat regretted his decision since the spectacular stellar view was unavailable to him and Christina presently, which he would have if there was a fully functional roof. He passed that information to Christina who only smiled in response. Most of the major farming equipment was locked down during the pirate assault and therefore was spared. The plumbing of the irrigation systems were damaged during the sudden decompression, but Todd had nearly finished replacing most of the damaged pipes and valves.

After Christina had finished her tour, they returned to their table and finished what was left of the wine. Jacob then told Christina about his recent observation regarding the temporary loss of the Gatekeepers' vessels and currently Jessica was confirming and studying that phenomenon. Jacob noticed a slight twinge in Christina's facial expression when he mentioned her name. He decided to ignore the twinge and he made an erotic suggestion to her.

"The kids got plenty dirty. Do you want to get down and get dirty as well?"

Christina smiled, "What did you have in mind?"

Jacob went over to her and began removing her clothes. Soon, he had her on her back in the dirt. She opened up herself to him. Jacob quickly removed his clothes and got on top of her, with his hands and knees in the dirt. Christina whispered to him, "You'll have to wash me when we are done here." Jacob pounded her hard and gasped when he climaxed. He rolled next to her and studied the roof construction. A minute later, his PCD was ringing for his attention. Jacob assumed it was Jessica.

"I'm sorry honey, but I have to take this, it's probably Jessica" Jacob murmured.

"I know, don't worry," Christina whispered with a look that seemed to be far, far away.

He got up and retrieved his pants. He took out his PCD and saw the message from Jessica as he had thought.

"I have confirmed your observations and I have made another astonishing observation myself. I will update you when you return to the bridge. –Jessica."

"Christina, I need a real quick shower and get back to the bridge, Jessica has something for me," Jacob paused then continued, "Sorry again, but if you would like why don't you come with me? It might be quite interesting."

'That's OK honey, I need to take a long bath, not a quick shower. I probably have dirt up my ass. I also need to get some food and shut eye, since Luther is expecting me in less than 6 hours down by the Corporate fighter," Christina replied quickly. She did not want to confront Jessica right now. She was very distraught about the sex she just had with husband. She enjoyed it but she had her eyes closed most of the time, and she was imagining being with Jessica and not with her husband. Not only that, but she felt a twinge of jealously not towards Jessica regarding her husband but just the opposite, a twinge of jealously towards her husband for going to see Jessica. What is wrong with me? Christina asked herself, I never had homosexual tendencies before. She definitely intended to have a long bath but also an another glass or two of wine.

Chapter 30 - Deception

Jessica had two large photos of the stellar sky on the table when Jacob entered the bridge. She was all business with her eyebrows drawn in, studying the photos intensely.

"Hello captain," she said, "I think we have been duped."

"Hi Jessica, what did you find, did those two Gatekeeper ships disappear for 30 minutes or is something else going on?" asked Jacob.

"I repeated the confirmation of your findings, which I initially performed that last time we spoke," Jessica mused, "but something else came to my attention, when I studied some other photos towards the sun."

"Well get to it, Jessica. What did you learn?"

She pointed to a faint star on one the current photos, "This is Jupiter in this current photo, but captain it's not supposed to be there. It's was not in this position a few hours ago. She placed an adhesive small white dot nearly a hundred centimeters away from Jupiter, nearly on top the sun. This is where Jupiter is supposed to be from all our previous data. All the other stars align exactly to the previous positions and mapped out correctly."

"Is it possible that you misidentified it, maybe it's an unmapped asteroid. After all this is just a photo," asked Jacob.

"Come on Captain, give me more credit than that," Jessica said irritably, then continued, "When I magnified that faint dot, it shows me the planet, a large gaseous giant with many moons." Jessica pulled out from under the photo, a smaller photo of Jupiter with its moons. "See here," she said pointing to the photo of Jupiter.

Then Jessica pointed to larger photo next to it that was taken from the exact position but was taken a couple of days earlier. The sun and all the other stars aligned including the planets, Earth and Mars with the other photo exactly, except for the absence of Jupiter."

"I also calculated what the position of the Gatekeeper ship around Titan based on our previous observations of Saturn after it had destroyed the SIL7. The predicted position is exactly where it is currently now when I focus on the Saturn system. So there was no gap with this Gatekeeper ship position around Titan. And if I look at the positions of all the other outer planets of the solar system, none of the others had a shift in position, none of them, only Jupiter!"

"So what else did you find?," asked Jacob pointing to a photo with the dots of Earth and Mars on it, which Jessica hadn't addressed yet.

Jessica immediately responded, "Oh, yes, if I look at a magnified photo immediately of Earth just prior to your observed gap and immediately afterwards," Jessica said as she pulled out a photo from under it. "You will see that both continents' positions and cloud formations are entirely different in the two photos. And if I do the same for Mars, I'm certain that I will find differences in the Mars' topography as well, which is what I was just preparing to do."

"You don't think this is a communication from the Dimensionless Ones, do you?" asked of his science officer.

"No sir. As I said we have been duped."

"So you are saying, that our current image of the inner solar system is not a true image but a false projection of some kind? This projection looks exactly as the true image, except for a few inconsequential minor flaws, which we happen to stumble on."

"I would agree captain, and I would add that this projection is probably not the work of the Gatekeepers, since I doubt that such flaws would be included if it was."

"Human work?"

"Yes, I would agree with that, Captain."

"Question now, for what purpose is this projection?"

"Don't know captain."

"Well, confirm what you saw on Earth is also true with Mars. In six hours, we will have crew meeting to discuss our observations. I assume that's enough time for you?"

"Yes, captain, more that enough."

***

Jessica got to the all hands meeting early. She wanted to meet Todd to tell him firsthand about her pregnancy. She had told everyone else and she didn't want Todd to think that he was left out, since she didn't think that Sarah would tell him due to her doctor-patient privilege. She rather liked Todd, just as most of the crew did. He spoke what was on his mind but never sought the center stage, as did most of the crew, even herself admittedly. And she couldn't help herself, but she was attracted to him, as she was to all the male crewmembers. He was quite handsome with a bold jaw with piercing blue eyes. It was no wonder that Sarah had tight reins on him. She did admire them as a couple; it was if they each had won a sweepstakes when they had committed to each other. Sarah defended her trophy well by minimizing Todd being around the opposite sex alone. But Todd, defended Sarah in all matters, but at least he had no concerns regarding competition from the opposite sex.

Her husband, Luther was with Christina presently, going over some of their last minute notes, to support an announcement from them. Most likely, they had enough information about flying the Corporate fighter. They didn't discuss duties among themselves, so he didn't know of this deception that Jacob and herself had discovered and she didn't know about the progress on the Corporate fighter. If they talked at all, they focused on Nozomi and her soon to be sibling. They both rather enjoyed the physical intimacy they shared, where conversation was not required and only volunteered. When they did talk, they never discussed duties and only on occasion other crewmembers. A conflict between them and one

146

of the other crewmembers or if there was a serious personal problem that a crewmate was facing, would be the only topics of conversation outside their immediate family. At times, he would talk about Jacob and Sarah, but it was unavoidable since they were his children as well. So, as of late, when they weren't talking about their child or her pregnancy, he still occasionally brought up her conflict with Christina. He was still somewhat miffed at her still for antagonizing Christina, as if she had thrown the first punch at Christina and not the other way around. She realized that a bit of immaturity from her, raising its ugly head when she was antagonizing Christina. But all that was well into past, Christina and Jessica had come to mutual understanding. Jessica wondered if their understanding had caused to Christina to become somewhat out of sorts. She couldn't put her finger on it, but Christina was acting a little strange, not aggressive or angry, just different. She noticed her intense eyes on her, but they did not burn of mistrust and hatred but of something entirely different.

Jessica saw Jacob come into the galley with Christina in tow. Jacob came to her and asked if she wanted to present the deception that they were experiencing regarding the 30 minute gap of the Gatekeepers ships' orbits around Mars and Earth. She smiled gratefully but indicated that he should present the findings. Jessica smiled at Christina as well, but she only gave a quick grin and sat on the opposite side of Jacob, so she didn't have to say anything. Jessica thought that with her bouts of jealously, Christina would put up interference and sit between Jessica and Jacob but she did just the opposite. Sarah and Todd came in next, with Todd carrying a bottle of unopened wine.

"Todd," Jessica began, "I wanted to tell you before you heard it from others, that I'm pregnant again."

Todd smiled at her. "Well congratulations. I knew there was some reason to bring a bottle of wine to this party," Todd replied. He added, "Hopefully, Sarah won't be far behind."

Sarah turned to her husband with a little irritation in her eyes but was rather quickly replaced with fondness, but she didn't speak.

"I have no doubt about that," Jessica replied.

Luther came in and took a seat next to his wife but brightly looked over to Christina, "Are you ready to tell everyone the news?"

Christina shot Luther a look of anxiety and quietly replied, "Do you mind, if you tell everyone our news."

"Not at all. Are you sure? Most of it was your work," Luther asked.

"Yes I'm sure," was all Christina said.

Jacob had concern written on his face. His eyes were downcast and his attention was preoccupied with information on his PCD. When everyone had settled in, he looked up from his PCD and painted on a cheerful, friendly face with a smile that wouldn't even fool his own son.

"Hello everyone, I would like to thank everyone for the tremendous amount of work that has put in ever since we were awakened. I know, it appears that our work load is increasing, well I'm not here to dispute that, matter of fact, I know how many hours in this gallant crew puts in. Sorry present circumstances require your best efforts, and needless to say, it's a matter of life and death," Jacob started.

Everyone was slowly nodding towards him but they were all wondering why he was stating the obvious.

Sarah popped in, "Ok bro, want to tell us what's really on your mind?

Jacob paused with sigh and then continued, "Now that's out of the way, I would like to bring up three different issues from three different people, which we either need to discuss or to inform you."

He looked over to his sister, "OK Sarah, do you have a general update regarding our farm?"

"Yes Jacob," Sarah said smiling to everyone. Unlike her brother, her smile appeared genuine and was infectious. Soon everyone was smiling back to her. She continued, "First of all, thanks everyone for pitching in rebuilding our farm, everyone here had a hand to its progress. We are only 10 days to our first of two pressurized tests. The first test will still have the temporary roof in place and then 2 days later, the true acid test will be conducted when the temporary roof removed. Both Todd and I have high expectations for the tests and believe we could be planting again in 14 days. "

Todd added, "I brought some wine for us to celebrate this achievement of all SIL11 crewmembers, and after the meeting, I'll even open it."

Small chuckles erupted around the room followed by a small applause

Jacob smiled at both Sarah and Todd, "Nice work!"

Jacob stare left his sister's eyes and went to his wife's. But Christina, was pointing over towards his dad and shaking her head. Jacob's eyes left Christina and settled on his dad's face.

"Dad, I guess you have an update for us as well," Jacob asked.

"Yes, with mostly Christina engineering know how, we have deciphered most of the technical operations of the Corporate Fighter. With the captain's permission, we are ready to launch a test flight for the fighter."

"I don't think that would be a good idea," Jacob responded, "You know we are probably being watched."

Luther continued, "We all know about the Gatekeepers, and we are taking great pains to conceal ourselves from them, but I think it is important to find out if we can actually navigate this vessel, especially if we are in dire need for it. Your only plan right now if the Gatekeepers do spot us, is to abandon the SIL11 and split ourselves between the IOSAC and this Corporate fighter. I'm not disagreeing with your plan, since it is the only possible one I can see, but I think that we need to take the risk to test the fighter first. But it is your decision, captain."

Jacob looked at his dad, "Even if we did such a test flight, it would be quite simplistic. It would have to be launched on the side of the ship away from the sun, and it would need to be masked by the SIL11 continuously to avoid detection by the Gatekeepers."

"Yes sir, I would agree. We only need to know if we can pilot the ship," Luther responded.

"We will discuss but first we should discuss one other piece of information," Jacob replied, "We are being deceived, the image we are observing from the SIL11 of the inner solar system towards the sun is a false image, and not a true image. Jessica has all the details."

Jessica laid down her photos that Jacob had seen before and she explained their observations to the crew. When she was finished with explanations, she added, "We have no information at all regarding the source of this subterfuge, any conclusions on its source would be foolish."

Sarah ignored Jessica's last comment and asked her brother, "Is this a result of the Gatekeepers' technology? Have they detected us? I know this was your primary concern all along."

Jacob replied, "I don't have any idea for the source of this deception. Matter of fact it may not be the Gatekeepers."

Luther countered, "The IOSAC has stealth technology; this could be advanced human technology."

Jacob replied again, "It could be but it's beyond even IOSAC 's technology."

Todd spoke out, "What purpose would the Gatekeepers have in using such subterfuge? They don't need to hide themselves, they could be in range to destroy us in a matter of hours and we would be defenseless to stop them. Anyway from the stories I hear about the Gatekeepers, they would want to inflict some fear into us anyway, by showing themselves to us long before they destroyed us."

Luther interjected, "Good point, Todd. This deception is not consistent with Gatekeepers typical behavior. Wouldn't we receive some type of warning from the Dimensionless Ones? Since we are following their instructions to the letter so far, and they haven't let us down yet."

Christina finally put in her opinion, "If this is some Gatekeeper's ploy, then we are done for, if it isn't, then all we know is that no harm has come to us so far. So why, would we want to change our plan? I, of course, agree with Luther that the shuttle needs to be tested."

Jacob looked around the table at his crew's faces. They all had spoken out, and all had plenty of opportunity to add to any of topics. Now, all their cheery faces were squished into consternation. Jacob put back on his painted face and spoke to the group.

"If there are no other comments, the following plan will be executed: We will not make any navigational changes presently, and we will continue to monitor the Gatekeepers' ships even if it's only a projection. Dad, you can test fly the shuttle but it will be simplistic test as I indicated before, but I would like the test flight to occur the same time we remove the temporary roof off the farm. It might be advantageous to have a small maneuverable spacecraft out there when we are finishing the farm's roof. Christina will monitor both the roof completion and the test flight at the same time from the bridge."

Everyone responded with unenthusiastic nod. Todd added, "I brought the wine for celebration. We still have good news to celebrate, a new farm and a new shuttle. We all should still have a glass."

Jacob finished, "I couldn't agree with you more, since wine is also good at alleviating anxieties as well. Open it up, Todd, let's drink up."

Chapter 31 - Luther's Test Flight

Luther was up early when he heard Jessica suffering some minor morning sickness. He was glad he was awakened since he ready to start the day. It was going to be a big day for him and the entire SIL11 crew. The first static pressurized test of the new arboretum roof passed with flying colors and the true test was coming in a few hours. He wanted to go over the operations of control module aboard the Corporate fighter before actually detaching from the ship. There was more that could go wrong with the fighter than with IOSAC, despite the fighter having more familiar technology. Nozomi was up already as well building with her large Lego blocks. Some toys never go out of style. He remembers his toys, especially his favorites, such as his wagon and bike. He doubted very much if those toys were around on Earth anymore, except in museums. Nozomi had dark penetrating eyes like her mother but weren't quite as large as her mother's. Unfortunately she had inherited his facial shape and features and not the exquisite features of her mother's face. She drop her blocks and ran to him, once he began to move about. He hugged her fiercely and then wanted to explain that she was building a farm as well. But her farm was not on a spacecraft but she explained that she was emulating an old style farm on Earth that she had saw in one of children's picture books that Sarah had collected.

Jessica came out of the bathroom with just a tee shirt on. Her face was slighter paler than normal but her eyes were large and penetrating as ever and her hair was perfect.

"Feeling OK, honey?" Luther asked her.

"Nothing more than usual, I clean up well, don't I?" Jessica answered.

Her pregnancy was early so there were no detractions from her beautiful figure. In addition to her figure, she was a self-professed nymphomaniac, add in her penetrating gaze and seductive voice resulted in a very desirable wife. He still couldn't figure out how he ended up with such a beautiful spouse. Obviously, she was very fertile as well considering that his sperm count wasn't what it used to be. But he intended not to be lead astray away from his task today, not even by her.

"I'm going to the Corporate fighter, are you OK with Nozomi?" asked Luther.

"No worries, I'm fine. Are you ready for your big test flight?" Jessica responded.

"I hope so. I just want to go over a few things for the umpteenth time. I don't believe you can ever be over prepared," Luther answered.

Jessica sat next to Nozomi and started looking at her proposed farm. Luther walked over to the two of them and gave Jessica a prolonged kiss and then gave Nozomi a tight squeeze. When Luther was about to leave, Jessica piped up, "The kids and I will be watching you! Have fun and be safe. Love you."

Luther turned to his wife and responded, "Love you too." He turned and left their room to have another opportunity to be a test pilot again.

**

Everyone was preparing for the big day. Christina and Sarah dropped off Tobias and Rhiannon with Jessica for the day with little or no small talk with Jessica. Christina went to the bridge and Sarah headed to the new farm where Todd had already begun to prepare for the removal of the temporary roof.

Everyone was looking forward in removing the temporary roof but no one was more excited about it than Todd. Farming had become his passion. He never thought that farming would be such a rewarding endeavor. When the pirates had blown away the farm, most everyone was somewhat relieved that they had not hit a more vital or sensitive part of the ship and the fact that no one died in the attack. But Todd was horrified. It was like another crewmember did indeed had died for him. Somehow his passion had rubbed off on his wife. Sarah, chief medical officer getting her hands dirty with her husband. During the reconstruction of the arboretum, she spent almost her entire time either at the farm or in their quarters as he did. Yes, Sarah was assigned to the farm by the captain, but if she hadn't liked the idea, her brother would have had an earful. And if Jacob had assigned someone else, she would have vehemently protested and all most likely disobeyed his order. Jacob was wise to assign Sarah to the farm to avoid any more conflicts with his sister.

Since they entered the solar system and been awakened, their marriage had matured. They had become more of a couple than a sum of individuals. Sarah had become less dominating in their relationship and Todd more assertive, until equilibrium was established which the unity through their bond made them an almost indestructible force and an unwanted opponent to anyone else. Others knew or sensed this bond, and were taken back in some awe that this had indeed occurred since the awakening and showed profound respect for their new gelled relationship.

Christina could easily tell that her husband was quite nervous. He paced the floor and constantly checked the MDS for any changes, whether projected or not, on the Gatekeeper ships. He was in contact with the Luther who was now on board the Corporate fighter. He confided in her that he didn't like not being in control and taking gambles with his ship or crew. He admitted that unexpected events still could occur that could change an outcome even when he was in control with a well thought out plan. But this time he lacked much information which increased the risk to his crew. He didn't like the number of unknowns that he was facing with this plan but he could not see any other alternatives. Christina focused her attention on the farm crew of Sarah and Todd. They were separated, probably the first time in weeks, with Sarah inside with hands on control of cranes situated around the arboretum including the roof, walls and the ground while Todd was space walking outside. His job was to monitor and assist the retraction of the temporary roof material. He was to roll it up and store it in one of the outside storage bins. Nothing was ever wasted on this mission, a learned necessity for interstellar travel. The entire crew except Jessica was on full duty and Jessica was sure to have her hands full as well in care of all three children. Christina was somewhat relieved that Jessica was not involved in this operation, considering her recent feelings towards her. It was a distraction that she could do without. She knew that Todd was taking a gamble of having much of dirt already in place after the first static pressure test. Christina knew that if this new roof project failed for any reason, she would be accountable for it. She had confidence in her engineering ability and had virtually checked all the work that both and Sarah and Todd have been producing over the last few weeks. She was confident that the roof would function flawlessly, but things happen and she needed to be totally focused on the task ahead. If anything goes wrong, she wanted to be aware of it first and initiate the appropriate response.

Jacob was quite endearing when they had both reached the bridge. He said that he very much enjoyed their date and hoped in the near future they would have more and this time with a transparent roof. Christina smiled at him in response and agreed wholeheartedly. She concluded afterwards that her responses were a bit short and without the expected fervor. Christina was sure that Jacob would be suspecting something, but present circumstances did allow for any elaboration on his part, and Christina did not know how she should respond.

Luther had some feeling of dread. Everyone else was working in tandem but he was totally alone. He knew it was unavoidable, everyone had a significant role to play and Jessica was needed as the babysitter. He was alone, when pirates came to call and that resulted well for the crew. But in that instance, he had total control of his ship, IOSAC and he knew it. This Corporate fighter was a different story. He was very familiar with its controls but was ill-practiced in actually piloting an alien ship. Also the corporate fighter was showing its age, and wasn't as pristine as was the IOSAC. He wished that Christina was here to aid him if an engineering problem should occur but she was also needed for the arboretum. Christina and he had tested all the essential functions of the fighter and the fighter appeared to be operating nominally. He had gone over the controls so repetitively that he could operate fighter in his sleep, but simulations were not the same as actual flight time. He was confident in his role as long as everything went as planned, but nothing for this ship or the crew had gone as planned thus far. He laughed to himself, well there is a first time for everything. Jacob and Todd had already adjusted the receiver gain and transmission power for their communications devices, to allow very low power transmissions yet fully understand one another. Along with Todd, he would be the only one in direct communication with Jacob or Christian. Both Sarah and Jessica would be communicating using the PCDs. It was his turn to adjust power levels of his transmitter and receiver. He estimated that the second lowest level of the transmitter would be sufficient for their communications, and he turned up his receiver to near maximum.

Luther announced to Jacob, "Hey son, are you picking me up?"

"Loud and clear, maybe we can lower your setting one more increment?" Jacob replied.

Luther set the transmitter at its lowest setting. "Still read me, son."

"No problem, your end?"

"It's a little more difficult to hear you but definitely manageable. You know hearing is one of those human functions that decrease naturally over time. There will be no engine or mechanical noises that I'll be picking up, so I think we are good!" Luther answered.

"Christina, can you hear me as well?" asked Luther.

"No problem, you are good to go. I'm monitoring the fighter's systems on the PCD, so it looks good for a go. You are free to detach once you are on the shady side of the SIL11. Good luck!" Christina responded.

Luther laughed, "And here, I thought that captain was in charge."

Jacob interjected with a laugh as well, "Just get that thing off my ship and quit being a nuisance." After a short pause he added, "Have a nice flight, dad and don't do much wild stuff out there."

"NOBODY will know that I'm even out here," Luther laughed.

Luther's plan was simple, he was going to perform some basic maneuvers on the shady side of ship and when it was time for the roof to be detracted, he would be in a very tight synchronous orbit in close proximity of the arboretum around the SIL11 in case he was needed. That way he would be observed as part of the ship to anyone even if they were in close proximity. The plan was simple but he couldn't shed his feeling of dread.

Luther began to think his feeling of dread was a byproduct of something he ate or from simply not eating. He actually could not remember if indeed he had breakfast. But his sense of dread seemed to dissipate during his test flight. His initial maneuvers were flawless. The fighter performed much better than their original SIL11 shuttle which was destroyed during the mission. That feeling with IOSAC he piloted began to return to him. All thrusters were amply functioning. He headed his fighter on plane away from the SIL11 in a direction away from the sun. Its acceleration was considerable in such short distance was only inferior to the IOSAC but better than anything else he flew. He was about 10 km out when Jacob decided he needed to reel in his father. So he ordered his dad to prepare for synchronous orbit with arboretum and to signal when he was in place.

Both Sarah and Todd were already beginning to retract the roof, which were anchored by large electromagnets. Christina was fixed on the pressure detectors within the arboretum.

After a time, Jacob noticed a huge smile appear on his wife's face and her eyes sparkled. The new roof is sealed properly with absolutely no change in pressure. "We did it!!" Christina exclaimed to everyone listening. "Todd will be growing his grapes again!"

"I never had a doubt about that," Todd laughed.

Everyone was cheering. It was time that something had gone as planned. But just then Todd noticed that the old roof was hung up on the gears retracting it into its storage bin.

"Captain," Todd began, "I have a situation here, the gears must have come misaligned as a result of the pirate attack and the old canopy is getting caught up with those gears. Only about half of the canopy is in storage. Please advise."

Christina immediately got on the intercom, "I'll shut down those gears from here. See if possible to rethread the canopy back in alignment, so we can bring it all into the storage bin."

But the gears failed to stop. The canopy was beginning to be ripped apart and in a manner of seconds, a large piece of the canopy was drifting freely into space in the opposite direction from the SIL11 trajectory and Todd could not stop it. Luther responded, "I'm on it!" as he maneuvered his fighter to grab onto the drifting canopy. He was close enough to the canopy that it should be easy for him to grab on to it before it was beyond the SIL11, which it would act as a waving flag for anyone who was watching including the Gatekeepers. It would be a horrendous event, if indeed the Gatekeepers would detect them, so their lives held in the balance.

At the angle of his fighter, he extended his left receptacle arm to grab onto the canopy. The canopy was nearly aft of the SIL11. He was there, he operated the control to grab it, but the pinchers failed.

Jacob yelled to his father, "Grab with the other arm it's beginning to drift beyond the SIL11. Please hurry!!"

Luther maneuvered his fighter so that he could extend his right pinchers. He should have known that pirates probably did not maintain their spacecraft appropriately. Both the remaining canopy and his fighter were now clear of the SIL 11. He was almost there with the right pincher which did operate normally.

Both Christina and Jacob could see that Luther was nearly there. And Jessica was holding Nozomi near the monitor, telling her daughter that her father was going to be a hero again. The other children felt the intensity of their parent's voices and looked up at the monitor as well.

The canopy suddenly and instantly dematerialized and then a second later, so did the Corporate fighter jet. An alien transmission came over the MDS in the low range, "This is the Venusian vessel, NN2. SIL spacecraft DO NOT eject further debris. You are being camouflaged from enemy ships orbiting Mars and Earth, detection would be suicidal for the both of us. Any further ejections and I will have to eliminate the SIL 11."

Only response that Jacob could muster was, "Oh, my God!"

Chapter 32 - The First Encounter

Jessica frantically grabbed her PCD and immediately texted the captain for an explanation regarding the disappearance of the Corporate fighter. Even though her fingers were putting in the letters for her question to the captain, she in her heart knew the answer and that Luther was gone. Tears dribbled freely down her cheeks, as the captain's response came back, "So sorry Jessica, but dad is gone." There were no other messages on her PCD, except for the captain's.

She went to her knees fiercely hugging Nozomi. Nozomi gazed into her mother's eyes but she did not understand. She only knew that her mother was very sad. The other children sensed Jessica's torment, and Tobias and Rhiannon began to cry. Jessica did not attempt to get up to console the other children like usual but only open her arms, allowed both Tobias and Rhiannon to come to her. Father, grandfather and husband had instantly died. There was no time for even a quick good-bye, he was already gone. Instead of consoling the children, Jessica cried wildly with them.

Jacob's eyes welled up, after the initial shock of his dad's disappearance. He managed a quick command for Todd to come back on board and another quick text to Jesscia. But afterwards, he couldn't move and he couldn't speak. The power of command was lost to him. Christina came quickly to him as she tried to console her husband. "I am so sorry honey, he was a father to us all," Christina paused, firmly hugged him and continued, "But you need to respond to this Venusian vessel in whatever way you see fit."

Christina's arms around him began to melt his frozen state. Christina was searching in his eyes to see if he was still there. He began to look back at his wife's eyes, there was sadness, pain but also determination in her eyes. He heard his wife's question, 'Jacob, are you still in there?"

Jacob blinked the tears from his eyes and nodded slowly. He released Christina, and went to the intercom, taking in a deep breath. "Venusian vessel, NN2, this is the captain of the SIL11. We receive you and will comply. Any further communications will be delayed, you have just killed our fellow crewmate on board the disintegrated corporate fighter or 'debris' as you put it. He was also my father. Over and out." He had not intended to have anger in his voice but there was plenty there all the same.

Jacob's eyes sought out Christina. She was there, with an emotionless expression nodding her approval of his message.

"Christina, please go to Jessica and the children. Jessica cannot be alone right now. We will meet up with the crew in the galley within the hour."

Christina nodded and grabbed onto him, burying her head into his chest. "Are you OK, my love?" Christina asked knowing full well that he wasn't as her eyes also began to well with tears.

Jacob nodded and added, "Go, quickly, I have to let my sister and Todd know what happened as well. "

Christina nodded again but now with tears flowing down her face. Then she abruptly turned and left the bridge.

***

Todd was very upset with himself to allow the torn canopy escape his grasp. It was only a matter of a few meters, but he realized that his self-preservation instincts were still intact. If he had managed somehow to grab onto the canopy, he realized he would be drifting out with it. He watched it drift to the back of the ship and watched Luther quickly pursue it. Despite Luther's quick response, it appeared that he was having problems latching onto the torn canopy. Then suddenly both the canopy and the fighter disappeared instantly. There were no explosions or laser fire, he couldn't explain what had happened. Then he had the idea, that the false projections that the captain and Jessica were speaking about, had something to do with these disappearances. He never had a genuine thought that both were actually gone. He was anticipating Luther's return with the torn canopy in tow at any moment.

He received a quick order from Jacob for him to return back to the airlock immediately and end his spacewalk. When he inquired to the captain, on what was happening, he received only silence and Luther never returned. Something was wrong, so with a sense of urgency he went to the nearest airlock. He didn't mind ending his spacewalk, he didn't like these ventures anyway. He always felt more comfortable on solid ground than floating about but even more so outside than inside. Despite being just a brief separation, he wanted to see his wife again.

***

Sarah was quite pleased on how the new farm turned out. She gazed up at the closed roof and turned on the solar-imitated lights. The arboretum was instantly flooded with bright light, then she turned them off and began retracting the reflective panel to reveal the transparent roof above. The immense stellar sky twinkled in her eyes. Christina will be in seventh heaven when she finds out how well the new roof was functioning, Sarah thought. She sent her a message but oddly she didn't receive a reply. Christina was probably either busy having some fun with Sarah's dad playing with their new toy, the Corporate fighter or having some alone time with her brother on the bridge. That gave her a thought on how she wanted to have some "alone" time with Todd. She knew that he would be coming in soon, and wanted to have everything secure here to meet up with him.

Her PCD went off, letting her know that she received a message. She assumed it would be Christina but instead it was her twin brother with the message. "On my way to the farm, I'll be a there a couple of minutes. Please wait for me, sis." It was a quite an odd message. First, it wasn't an order which was typically the only communication she received from Jacob over the PCD. Secondly, he addressed her as sis and not just Sarah. Something was amiss here. She ignored the implications since she would be finding out what was going on with her brother soon enough. She finished securing all the cranes and she was hoping her meeting up with her brother would not take too long, she was eager to find Todd. She thought it would be delightful to be a mother again.

She was surprised to find Jacob already waiting for her as she climbed down from the small cubicle arboretum control center. But instead of finding him smiling, Sarah found him with sad eyes and a wet face. Well this couldn't be good, Sarah told herself.

Jacob managed to say in broken speech, "Dad is gone."

"What do you mean, 'gone'?" Sarah replied in a thin voice.

157

"He's dead," Jacob said meagerly. Then he came over and hugged his sister tightly.

Sarah shoved him away, "Dead?" she yelled, "What do you mean dead, what happen?"

Sarah's whole world was just shaken. Yes, she was amiable with the entire crew and enjoyed being with them all, but she really only loved two people, Todd and her dad. Now, one of them was gone?

"TELL ME WHAT HAPPEN?" she screamed at her brother. She didn't want her brother's hug, she wanted an explanation with the hope that her brother was wrong. Jacob looked at her sister's eyes flaming with fury. He expected this from his sister. She was closer to no one else except maybe and only maybe, Todd. He was here for her, but he didn't have the strength to calm her storm that was brewing.

"He was killed in the Corporate fighter, which just disappeared." Jacob replied meekly.

"Was there a malfunction on board the fighter?" asked Sarah.

"No, he was disintegrated by a Venusian vessel that is hidden but appears to be in close proximity. I'm afraid it was only accident, they appear to have no hostile intentions. "

"No, hostile intentions, what the hell are you talking about, they just killed our DAD!" Sarah screamed back.

"I know, I will explain what I know to everyone in the galley in a few minutes," Jacob started but Sarah interrupted him, "Oh yeah, have another useless meeting, is that all you are going to do?"

Jacob incredulously looked at his sister, "You are not the only one the lost a father."

Again Sarah interrupted, "Well, obviously, I'm the only one who cares." The fury was still smoldering in her eyes, but now her face was awash with tears.

Jacob was not going to participate in a sibling fight with his sister, "If you want to find out what happen to dad, come to the galley with me! Now!" Jacob turned and hiked away from the arboretum Sarah clenched her fists and marched right after him.

Jacob typed into his PCD for Todd, "You will find your wife in the galley with the rest of the crew. Come as quickly as you can." He wanted somebody there for his sister, since he had no sagacity for dealing with her right now. He was enduring his own torrents of grief, and didn't want to be target practice for his sister. He understood her feelings. He had the same feelings to lash out towards his father when his mother died. When he thought back on that episode of his life, he realized that those regrets will now never disappear from his life.

But he needed to grief later. He needed to address the crew regarding establishing contact with inhabitants of Venus and inform them that the Venusian vessel was protecting them, so they claim, from detection of the Gatekeepers. Despite his anger at the Venusian ship, the NN2, for killing his father, he realized they were more likely protecting them and they were the best hope for their survival. He did not understand why the Venusians had not revealed themselves sooner, and why they deceived the SIL11 as well as the Gatekeepers. The loss of his father would have been avoided, if the SIL11 had been informed of their presence. It was not the time to ask "what ifs" though and he would not be only one with outright anger towards to the Venusians. The whole crew thought of the Luther as family, and everyone would have some degree of trepidation towards these Venusians. He must convince the crew that the death of his father was only an accident, and these Venusians were now their "friends". After all, the Dimensionless Ones had informed Todd of new friends on Venus and not on Ceres. Well, the entire crew came away unscathed from the pirate attack near Ceres and an encounter with a psycho killer, but now the most experienced crewmember was gone at the hands of the Venusians, their 'friends'. Some friends, he thought.

***

"Captain, was that necessary?" asked Julio incredulously. Julio was the navigator aboard the NN2. The NN2 was a human vessel built and serving from Venus; however, it had Veeder technology to mask this ship and other ships from detection using their incredulous projection system. Julio was born and raised on Mars. He was an explorer in the secluded areas near Mars's southpole. His captain, Antwan was pure Terran, raised in western Asia, formerly known as Ukraine and was a member of intelligence unit in Corporate's military arm. Julio had no family but Antwan had lost all three of his girls and his wife to the Gatekeepers. Antwan knew firsthand what those 'devils' were capable of and their inherent evil. Antwan did not fear the Gatekeepers but he had abundance of respect for their technology. He was the one that fired the disintegrators onto the unidentified object and an old Corporate II fighter. Both objects were out range of their projections and were a threat for detection. Antwan could not allow that to happen. It would not only threaten his ship and this SIL spacecraft but their bases on Venus. No, he could not allow it to happen, so he fired the Sausian's weapon at them, not leaving a single trace. Sausians were willing to aid the humans in their fight against the Gatekeepers, and allowed their technology on board human vessels. However, the technology was a guarded secret with the Sausians. There was still some mistrust between the Sausians and humans, which originated from their first encounter when a human SIL spacecraft that visited their home world.

Stewart, the communication officer and first officer on the NN2 informed both Antwan and Julio that the SIL11 would comply with their demand but also told them that they had killed the SIL11's captain father and the captain would delay further communications between the two ships. Stewart was a former first officer himself on board the SIL3 but had several years training with the Venusian military. Julio was a fool, Stewart thought, Antwan was only following standard procedure, which was to prevent detection at all costs, including human costs.

Stewart understood the undertones from the SIL11 captain. The SIL11 captain was hesitated in answering probably because of a healthy dose of mistrust since he had experienced it himself several years ago when he had returned home. The SIL captain probably had no idea of what was happening to their solar system but he prayed he had the wisdom not to start a battle with NN2. The NN2 was not large ship, only one fifth the size of the SIL11 and only 4 crewmembers but its abilities were was well beyond the SIL11's technology. The fourth crew member was Janice Gilmer, she was part time medical officer and full time engineer. Destroying a ship the size of the SIL11 with the Sausian weapon was risky in itself which would create some residual energy that the Gatekeepers could possibly detect. It was a gamble to help them, but it was a principal directive among the Venusian military to save as many of the returning SIL space vessels as possible. Any new alien technology would add to the technologies that they have already accumulated from other SIL missions to counter the threat of the Gatekeepers. A few of the SIL had actual contingencies of new intelligent species that were assigned ambassadors returning back with them. The Veeders, Sausians, and Tiahians now shared Venus with the humans from both Earth and Mars. There were originally 18 SIL missions with an additional 18 more missions added by Corporate. Of those 36 missions, only 6 SIL had returned safely, another 12 were not due to return yet and half of all the SIL missions were either overdue or were destroyed by the Gatekeepers. SIL7 was the latest victim of the Gatekeepers in what they refer to as the 'sterilization process'.

"Understood, Stewart, allow them 2 Earth hours before contacting them again. Julio adjust course to minimize the distance between our ships within a kilometer. It is time we show ourselves to the SIL crew," Antwan commanded. Antwan hesitated and added," Stewart you will be our ambassador to this SIL craft if they decide not to launch missiles at us."

"Yes sir," Stewart replied and he expected to be just that. He knew what questions that this SIL11 crew would have and what information they needed to know. He would only be giving them information they needed to know. The whole Venusian colony was based on the premise of a need to know basis. He listened to Antwan's last command to Julio. "If they use any weapons or launch another shuttle, disintegrate them immediately," the captain commanded and added, "you do understand the meaning of the word 'immediately'?"

Julio sighed and replied, "Yes captain."

Chapter 33 - A Choice

Sarah was breathing heavily as everyone began to gather at the galley. Jacob had arrived first for once, closely followed by Sarah. Todd came next and rushed over to her and swallowed her up in his arms. She allowed Todd to hug, kiss and fuss over her, but her attention was elsewhere. Todd told her of his spacewalk and what he saw from outside. He told her that he didn't understand what had happen and that he thought the alien projection was only hiding Luther. His story only pushed her towards greater thralls of anger. The fact that she was last to know fueled her anger. She needed to come back from this precipice. She was on the verge of outright vile irrational anger at anyone and everyone, and only two threads were holding her back; her reason and how her dead father would have reacted to such behavior. The latter thread was very thin since her father was not there, but that was not to say her reason was much stronger. Then something happen she didn't expect to pull her back the precipice. Jessica and Christina were bringing the children into the galley with Jessica and Christina each holding one of Rhiannon hands. Her eyes were wet and painted with uncertainty as her eyes searched for someone. Sarah bolted to her daughter and lifted her into her arms. She smiled at Rhiannon, something she didn't think she was capable of at the moment. Then it snowballed; Rhiannon's face brightened and retuned a broad smile back to her mother which caused her mother to smile even more so. When Rhiannon saw her mother's smile swell, she laughed and hugged her mother.

The room remained somber as Sarah went back to her chair holding Rhiannon. When Sarah lowered herself on the chair, Rhiannon jumped out of arms and onto Todd's lap. Todd returned his daughter's laugh with a small smile and said, "Now you hold still my princess, the adults need to speak about somethings. OK?"

Rhiannon smiled back, and replied, "OK, daddy."

Jessica watched the interaction between Rhiannon and her father, Todd with tortured eyes. She gripped tightly onto Nozomi. She became aware of another presence deep within her womb. Luther had left her with two constant reminders of their love together. She was not alone but the bitterness of his departure consumed her whole self. It would be some time for her to get over her grief, but it was soothing to know that she was not alone. It was not like that ill-fated day, when her own mother took her own life to leave her all alone. There were going to be brighter days ahead.

Jacob addressed the gathering, "I know that everyone knows by now, that about an hour ago, we made contact with Venusian vessel, who has been camouflaging us from the Gatekeepers ships here in the inner solar system. In order to protect that camouflage, it disintegrated both the wayward temporary canopy and the Corporate fighter which my dad was piloting. One of our own has now been killed. I apologize for not foreseeing this and take full responsibility for our loss." Jacob stopped and fought the returning tears. He surveyed the faces of everyone in that room and settled on his sister's face. The rampant fire that was burning in his sister's eyes was beginning to run out of fuel but dangerous smoldering coals still remained. He continued, "They ask us not to eject anything else from the ship, or they would have no choice but to eliminate us as well. My only response to them so far, is that we would comply but any further communications between us will be delayed."

Jacob again surveyed the room, this time settling on Jessica's face. Her typical penetrating dark eyes were now only reflections of her own inner sorrow, morning for her deceased husband, but hatred had not taken hold of her, at least for now.

"Ever since we have returned to our solar system and have awakened, we have been searching for other human beings. But those we found were either trying to kill us or attempting to commandeer our ship. But now, I believe we may have found our home with these Venusians, which unknowingly was facilitated by my dad. He has given his life, so we may be protected. We should honor my father's last action to stay protected by accepting these Venusians, despite their swift destruction of the Corporate fighter."

After a brief pause, Jacob continued, "But as before, I want the crew to freely give their opinions of our situation and how to proceed."

The galley was quiet with only the sounds of fidgety children disturbing the solemn silence. Jacob sat and was apparently quite willing to wait for the crew to speak up. His dark eyes were grieving for his lost father, but his voice had steel in it and a conviction of what he telling the crew. Jacob needed to hear his own words to convince himself, and not only the rest of the crew.

Christina knew it was her turn to speak out. She believed in her husband and his words, and she needed to show her support of her spouse. She typically waited for others to speak but not this time. So in a calm voice she began to speak: "I am truly sorry to everyone whom has lost a family member, a husband, a father and grandfather." As she was speaking her eyes fell in turn on Jessica, then on Sarah and Jacob. Then she looked down at Tobias and tenderly squeezed his shoulder with her gaze returning back to Jessica. "But I believe wholeheartedly with my husband. It was a tragic death in losing Luther. But if the Venusian had not done what they had done, then one of the Gatekeepers ships may have spotted us and we would be now engaged in a futile and hopeless escape." There Christina said her peace and received a grateful nod from her husband.

Todd spoke out, "I agree with you captain. The Dimensionless Ones said that Venus was where our friends were. I still have faith in the Dimensionless Ones. We should introduce ourselves to them in the hopes that they will be our friends."

Jacob looked at Todd and gave him slight nod, but his eyes went to his sister and then to Jessica. Both women were battling demons within themselves.

Jessica looked up at everyone with teary eyes. "I'll agree with the captain, because I know in my heart, that this is what Luther would want us to do."

Everyone nodded to Jessica but she returned to her downward stare. Everyone else was looking at Sarah in anticipation. Everyone had known about her close relationship with her father and actually, everyone was somewhat astonished that Jessica had not thrown her hammer and not already demanded an assault on the Venusian ship. Sarah's eyes were dark and smoldering and her face was wet. She turned and had a brief fond smile for Rhiannon and her husband. After a couple of very tense and uncomfortable moments, Sarah began to speak loudly and venomously, "I want everyone to REMEMBER that those bastard Venusians killed MY father. I will never forgive them for that, NEVER."

Her voice remained solid but she took off some of its edge and said, "It would be useless to start a battle with them which would only end with our demise. And it would be pointless not to cooperate with them, since if we didn't would also most likely end with our demise. So I have to agree with my half-wit brother. But I for one will watch them carefully at every turn and it will take some time before any amount of trust could be built between them and me. But as for that specific Venusian captain that either ordered my father's death or had done it himself, I will NEVER FORGIVE HIM!" She gazed around the room and took measure of everyone's reaction. Everyone seemed to accept in what she had to say and then she concluded, "We need to look out for our own children, it is their future that we are deciding on. That's all I have to say."

Jacob waited a handful of seconds to be sure everyone had their say and then again addressed the crew, "Thanks everyone. I will then go up to bridge and establish a rapport with the Venusians. Before I do, I would like everyone here to sit here in a moment for silence to remember my father."

All the adults bowed their heads and even children stopped fidgeting and lowered their heads to mimick their parents. The total silence was interrupted by everyone's PCD playing a tune in unison,

It was an old tune was called Taps, historically it was a tune played by the bugle at military funerals in the former United States. Sarah and Jacob recognized the tune but the others had not heard it before. None of them had ever heard a bugle played before, but the music coming from their PCDs sounded as if was being played a bugle. While the tune was being played, the operator of their corresponding PCD had no control, therefore could not stop the playing the tune until it concluded. Once the last note was played, everyone saw two attachments on their PCDs with no documentation of where the computer files had come from or even more interesting of when they were sent. The files were simply there.

Jacob announced, "Let's just have one person open the files on their PCD. I don't want a virus infecting everybody's device." Even though computer viruses had become relatively scarce when they had launched from Earth, but viruses could have had renaissance in this new era. Jacob turned towards Christina and asked her, "Open up the attachments on your PCD, one at a time, and see what they are."

Todd exclaimed, "I know where the files came from, I don't know how I know, I just know. They came from the Dimensionless Ones."

Christina looked up from one of her PCDs to her husband's face, "I think Todd is right, the two files are some sort of sophisticated technical schematics and instructions for modifying either the SIL11 or the IOSAC vessels. Both files were associated with two words, 'FOLLOW US'." Christina happened to be carrying two of her PCDs with her, so she checked her other PCD for the attachments. The other PCD had same files but a different message which read, "YOUR FRIENDS."

Everyone else in turn, open the files up on their own PCD. The two same files were on all the PCDs but each had a different message at the end. Jacob also happened to be carrying two PCDs; one had the message, "VENUSIANS MAYBE," and the other PCD, "EXPECT HELP." Jessica's one PCD that she had on her person had the message, "BUT DON'T", Todd had "BUILD YOUR" and Sarah's "SHIP AND".

There was a general discussion within the group, exchanging messages and trying to build one single message that included all the two words messages on each of the PCDs into one without breaking up the two words. Everyone was more at ease, playing this simple word game. Everybody knew this game had indeed originated from the Dimensionless Ones. The anxiety of the Venusians was now reduced since it was included in the message. After a couple of minutes, Todd had figured out the message not because he was smartest at word games, but he expended more exuberance and energy and therefore infused more effort into the task. Everyone agreed with the content of the message from Todd. The message read:

"BUILD YOUR SHIP AND FOLLOW US. VENUSIANS MAYBE YOUR FRIENDS BUT DON'T EXPECT HELP."

Jacob asked the crew not to react to the recent message from the Dimensionless Ones. They obviously would allow time for people to choose. He needed to establish a rapport with the Venusians and that was his first task at hand. Christina told Jacob that she would go with Jessica back to her quarters with the children. Jessica would be dealing with this loss of her husband for some time. Todd guided Sarah back to the farm. Todd was excited about the Dimensionless Ones reestablishing communications with the SIL11 crew, but that exuberance needed to take a back seat since his wife needed him now. He thought the best course of action was to get Sarah busy again with her hands and make some easy decisions. Of course, that would be planting new crops. He would let Sarah decide on what crops should be planted and participate in the planting itself. He thought the necessity for such crops was questionable, it would excellent therapy for his wife. The SIL11 had now been given the same choice that the Tandorians had centuries ago and the human race had years ago. He was certain what his choice would be but the rest of the SIL11 crew would need to be convinced. He had this distinct feeling that not many on board would want to follow the Dimensionless Ones after Luther's passing.

Chapter 34 - The Reception

The Venusian vessel was now visible to the SIL11 crew, but only faintly. The NN2 had position itself above the SIL11, it was small vessel but was alien in form. The skeleton of the ship was obstructed by a slight nebulous material that made the scaffolding of the NN2 to appear to be inside a milky bubble. The Venusian ambassador was on his way from the NN2 to the airlock of the SIL11 where once the Corporate fighter had once docked. The ambassador, Stewart Hemlock, was also inside his own bubble and was carrying another denser bubble with him. He had no spacesuit on, so his bubble must have provided life sustaining environment for him. Once the crew had learned that Stewart was a former first officer on board the SIL3, they all wanted to have a look at their assigned ambassador. Sarah was not eager to greet this stranger but her curiosity got the best of her and Jessica decided on excluding herself from the ambassador for now and remained in her quarters with the children. So the whole crew, except Jessica was standing outside the airlock anticipating his arrival.

When the airlock door swung open, Stewart was not enveloped in a bubble but still held a more milky bubble with him. He set down the bubble the extended his hand to anyone who was willing to accept it and said, "I'm Stewart Hemlock, first officer of the Venusian vessel, NN2, let me be one of the first to welcome you back to your solar system." He was an average-size black man, less in statue to either Todd or Jacob, and was least 10-15 years older than the pair. He would have been still younger than Luther, therefore most likely a second generation first officer on the SIL3.

Jacob stepped towards Stewart and shook the first officer's hand saying, "I'm Jacob Miller, the captain of the SIL11. Let me introduce you to my crew."

Jacob introduced everyone and their function to Stewart except for Jessica. The last person present he introduced was his sister, "This is Sarah Wilson, Chief Medical Officer and my twin sister. It was our dad that was aboard the Corporate fighter. "

Stewart extended his hand to Sarah but she refused to accept it. Stewart said to Sarah, "My deepest condolences to you and your brother. I am very sorry for your lost. Please believe me, if there was any way to avoid his loss, we would have."

Sarah did not answer him but did give a brief nod. Stewart turned towards Jacob and asked, "Was your dad first generation on board the SIL11?"

"Of course, he was, what else would he had been?" Jacob replied.

Stewart answered him, "Most of the SIL missions have a mixture of second and third generation when they return but there were two SIL missions, one with a mixture of first and second generations like yours and another with third and fourth generations on board."

Jacob answered, "We were a mixture of first, second and third generations, we have three small children on board."

Stewart smiled and asked, "Where are your children? I would love to see them. Venus has only a few children and most were born off-world."

Jacob answered, "My first officer is in her quarters with the children. She is not ready to receive you as of yet. You have to understand my dad was her husband."

The smile on Stewart's face escaped and he replied solemnly, "I understand."

Stewart looked at everyone's faces, and said to Jacob, "You have a rather small crew. How do you keep this ship running?"

"I'm afraid this crew has had more than its share of adversity during our mission. I believe they are the finest crew in the galaxy and that's how we keep this ship running," Jacob replied. He looked at Stewart eyes. He appeared very friendly but he had been fooled before and continued, "You are not the first to greet us back to our solar system. But we have been rather unlucky with our new acquaintances."

Stewart raised an eyebrow and replied, "You have had other contacts within our solar system? Do you refer to some messages that you acquired by extraordinary means?"

"We have been in contact with Dimensionless Ones since we have entered the solar system. But no, that is not what I meant. We have had contact with humans since we have been back. I'm afraid our 'getting acquainted' was rather disappointing. I will fill you in later and let you meet these acquaintances who are now guests of the SIL11."

"Indeed," Stewart replied. He paused then continued. "I'm afraid us Venusians are not very contusive to pleasantries. We are a direct people with very little patience. My captain has a request of you captain, which he would like implement immediately."

"What is it ambassador?" asked Jacob.

"Captain Antwan would like you to change course for Venus immediately," answered Stewart and added, "Please captain call me Stewart."

Christina piped in, "Stewart we do have the necessary fuel to settle in an orbit around Venus without using Mercury for a small dose of aerobreaking."

Stewart turned and faced Christina and said, "Ah, you are the chief engineer." He lifted his bubble and offered it to Christina and added, "This is our gift to the SIL11."

"What is it?" asked Christina.

"It's rather large dose of anti-matter for your fuel under a strong magnetic field. I assume your engines still run on anti-matter? Well if they do, there is enough here for you to return to the Leonis star system, if you wish."

Christina took the bubble from Stewart. It was surprisingly light. "But how do I insert it into our protective magnetic field with this bubble material around it?"

Stewart answered, "Just set it in close proximity of your remaining anti-matter fuel cell, and I will remotely incorporated it into your fuel cell automatically."

Christina turned to Jacob, "Captain?"

166

"Do as he asks, Christina," Jacob responded and then turned to Stewart, "OK, we will comply, but you will need to start answering a few hundred questions from me and the crew. OK?"

"Yes captain, that is why I'm here," Stewart responded.

Jacob turned towards his crew, "Todd you go to engineering and assist Christina and then escort her back to the galley. Sarah, you go to Jessica quarters and have her and the children brought to the galley. Tell Jessica this is an order not a request. After our show and tell session with the ambassador here, Sarah you will prepare for a full physical examination of Stewart and Todd you will prepare a fresh dinner for ambassador with the crew as an apology."

They all nodded and replied, "Yes, captain."

Jacob then pointed towards Stewart, "You, accompany me to the bridge."

Stewart also answered, "Yes, captain."

Jacob sighed with a breath of relief since he had no disagreements from anybody. He was in command again and he needed to ensure that he would not lose that ability again. He would mourn later for his father, but not now. He needed to be totally aware of everything around him and be ready to act and also find the wisdom of whether to act or not. He saw no reason not to change course to Venus and comply with the NN2 captain. With the fuel they just received, it would make no sense not to proceed to Venus directly since it was there terminal destination. He decided he would relate all that has happened to them to the ambassador, if he answered their questions directly and honestly. His father was always able to sense when others were lying and when they were not. That trait had not rubbed off on him, but there were indications that it may have rubbed off on Sarah. He wanted a medical exam to make sure he was human of course, but also wanted Sarah to ask some direct questions in private with the ambassador and get an assessment of his mental state, specifically his honesty. It was a risk that is she may not have enough of his dad's trait to get an accurate assessment, or Sarah in her present frame of mind, might just end up killing him for retribution. He could only hope that she would make the correct decision, but it was hers.

***

Stewart allowed a complete physical from Sarah and answered her questions as well as he could. He also initiated the inclusion of the anti-matter fuel, he had brought with him that incorporated into the SIL fuel without incident. Then Stewart welcomed all inquiries and tried to answer as many of the crew's questions as possible, the even personal questions in particular one from Todd and another from Jessica. Todd wanted to know if he was offered the chance to go with the Dimensionless Ones and if so, why didn't he accept their invitation. This prompted Stewart to tell his story of returning to the solar system.

In many ways, his story was similar to their own. They had arrived back to the solar system much sooner than would be expected, since the world they explored had advanced technology in ship propulsion systems. With very few structural modifications, they were able to implement some of those systems. This allowed them to accelerate and decelerate to near light speed much more quickly than the original SIL systems. The system that they had explored did not have any inhabitants left, not because of any natural causes that they could detect but they had simply abandoned their world. There was a black hole nearby their planet, but their planet was not in any immediate danger. It would a several thousand years before the black hole would threaten their world. There were no references to Dimensionless Ones in their records but they when they left, they thought of their mission was one with galactic importance.

When they arrived back to the Solar System, the Dimensionless Ones did indeed contact them through one of the crew member's dreams. The dream could not be discounted as just 'a dream' since the dream in its entirety was repeated each night in explicit detail for nearly a week. This crew member did not appear to have any mental abnormalities, even though most of the crew seemed dubious of its meaning, until other members began to have the same exact dream. The message was simple, "Ride the icy rock until its flames a bright lengthy tail, and do not go to the ringed planet." A comet was spotted only 50,000 km from their position. The captain thought it was too much for coincidence to come in such close proximity of the comet, so they 'hitched a ride' on that specific comet. When the tail of the comet began to elongate, a Venusian vessel spotted them and escorted them back to Venus, where they settled in city among the Venusian clouds high above the surface. Just prior to arriving at Venus, another message came from the Dimensionless One describing modifications to their SIL3 vessel and their shuttle with an invitation to come and follow them. More than half his crew accepted the invitation, while the rest of the crew enlisted into the Venusian military. The Venusian authorities allowed the rest of the crew to depart and follow the Dimensionless Ones, who were never heard from again. Stewart personal decision was based that he had never had this dream that his crewmates had shared. He also reached his decision on the lack of evidence that the Dimensionless Ones were truly benevolent. The story was the same in all cases from many different worlds and different times that once people followed them they were never heard from again. Did the Dimensionless Ones lead those races to their demise? It was true that the Gatekeepers were anything but benevolent, but some alien histories suggest that they were not always evil and treacherous. The Gatekeepers did not trust the Dimensionless Ones and punished races that had accepted their invitation. The sadistic behavior towards other intelligent species appeared to be a learned behavior that was increasing more terrible with each passing century. Stewart's own first-hand knowledge of the Gatekeepers' behavior and the terrible stories from other Venusians motivated him to fight against them. But strangely, while the Gatekeepers' thirst for blood and fear increased, ancient evidence suggests that even though their technology was vast and highly advanced, it has also been stagnant for thousands of years. A growing belief was beginning among the Venusians that pooled technologies among the various intelligent species may actually threaten the Gatekeepers. And it was thought that the Gatekeepers themselves may actually feel threatened by such cooperation, and therefore dedicated much of their effort in their sterilization program which included destruction of the SIL vessels and their ability to communicate with other humans.

Stewart was product of a military family with both his father and mother being part of the Corporate military arm, when the SIL3 had left the solar system. His military upbringing by his parents therefore led him to become the first officer of the SIL3. He needed purpose and repulsing this invasion by Gatekeepers became his firm conviction, so he stayed and watched many of his crewmates disappear into the outer reaches of the solar system. He earned respect among the Venusians and his career advanced to the first officer of the NN2. None of the Venusians vessels were large in size, matter of fact, .the largest vessels were a couple of dated SIL spacecraft. But that this is not to say that these Venusian vessels were poorly armed or lacked a sophisticated propulsion system. Venusians never congregated in large groups as well when venturing outside the Venus atmosphere. A basic Venusian directive was that Venusians were to take their own life if capture by the Gatekeepers was imminent as well as the self-destruction of any Venusian vessel outside the Venusian atmosphere if pursued by the Gatekeepers.

Venus of course was unlikely place for hiding. Its surface is the hottest in the solar system and did not allow for any habitation. Its atmosphere was composed for a dense carbon dioxide with some sulfuric acid. In addition even though wind speeds are mild on the surface, they were extreme in higher altitudes at more than 700 km/hr but temperatures were dramatically lower. Near the top of the clouds, wind speeds were much lower with very mild temperatures. With the help of alien technology, the Venusians were able to build habitats especially near the south polar that were still well hidden from the Gatekeepers. The Gatekeeper ships had not ventured any closer to the sun than with Earth, so it was hoped that Venus would not be under the Gatekeepers' watchful eye, but few Venusians actually believed they were not being watched.

After his story, Stewart was confronted by Jessica's question. Of why, his vessel had not contacted the SIL11 earlier, which would have prevented the accidental death of her husband, Luther. He had a simple answer, 'it was the captain's prerogative.' He knew this would not suffice so he elaborated. His captain, Antwan was a very conservative individual. He knew and had experienced the atrocities of the Gatekeepers. It was his decision not to expose themselves to the SIL11 until they were at the proximity of Venus's orbit or until it was absolute necessary. He suggested that he may have made a different decision if he was captain but he needed to support his captain's decision.

Sarah was satisfied with both Stewart's physical exam as well as his mental exam. Stewart was aware that Sarah was the daughter of the deceased fighter pilot, so he went beyond typical pleasantries to make her feel as ease, and allowed more rude behavior on her part. But he had his limits, so he made her know that he would tolerate any more senseless rudeness. He might have allowed it, since he willing to secure their cooperation but it was more important that he didn't lose her respect. Sarah accepted his admonishment silently. Once Sarah realized that this specific individual had no hand in the decision for the destruction of her dad's fighter, she did actually admire him, but not to the point of trust.

Sarah reported her results to her brother. Jacob seemed to also admire the Venusian. He decided to introduce him to his two other guests; Ivan Petrulov and the pirate, who became known as Blackbeard among the crew. First Stewart was rather surprised that they had met any other humans in the solar system and somehow the crew of the SIL11 managed to survive meetings either one of these characters. He apologized for their first encounters with humans since returning and he admittedly stated they had been welcomed had been less desirable since returning. He was aware of the Ceres pirates. They were a dangerous lot and played into the Gatekeepers hands. He reluctantly admitted that he did not know this Ivan Petrulov but he would do thorough background check on him. He was impressed that they were able to commandeer the IOSAC, which he referred to as the MT Corporate shuttle, which was somewhat sophisticated for its time. Jacob invited him to follow him and escort him to his room.

He turned to Jacob after his visit with the other guests and said, "There are always inherent dangers of being an ambassador. I have accepted those, so do you have for me another empty cryostatis chamber for me?"

169

Jacob replied, "Nope sorry, just a bed and bathroom, I hope that will do."

Stewart stood still quite relieved, "Thank you captain, it will more than suffice."

Chapter 35 - A Trip to Venus

The captain Antwan was indeed conservative and careful, Jacob observed. Antwan had continued projecting false images to both sides of their ships and minimized the distance between their vessels. Antwan had informed Jacob that he wished Stewart to remain on the SIL11 for any service that he or the NN2 could render. When Jacob appreciably accepted his offer, Antwan suggested, but only suggested, that an individual from his crew would come and be the SIL11 ambassador to the NN2. If Jacob decided to send an ambassador, Antwan suggested that maybe Jessica and her daughter could become the ambassadors. He would like to attempt in making amends to the widow and the daughter of the deceased fighter pilot. Jacob told Antwan, he would consider his proposal and let him know his decision in a couple of days. Jacob saw no need for a rush decision since they were still weeks away from Venus. He wanted the crew to weigh in on Antwan's proposal but most importantly he needed Jessica to decide for herself if this was something that she was willing to do. In Jacob's eyes, the decision was not his, the crews; or Antwan decision but hers and hers alone. Antwan's proposal was sound, Jessica was the first officer just as Stewart was, and she was also a fine science officer, who may be able learn the nuances of their technology in this century more rapidly than anyone else on board, but again it was her decision.

The crew also needed to make their decisions on whether to accept the Dimensionless Ones' proposal. Stewart was not at all surprised when he was eventually informed about the Dimensionless Ones' files and message to the SIL11 crew. Stewart immediately informed them that none of the Venusians will interfere with their choices, since many Venusians had that same choice given to them in the past. He did make it clear that the Venusians would only assist and aid the individuals who decide to stay on Venus, but they could not provide the same for individuals travelling with the Dimensionless Ones. The Venusians had discovered that these ships when modified by the Dimensionless Ones were of no value unless the Dimensionless Ones were present. Somehow the guidance and propulsion systems were not part of the Dimensionless Ones technical instructions and diagrams, and were only supplied by the good graces of the Dimensionless Ones at the time of departure. The actual modifications to existing vessels or the construction of new vessels were rather easily installed or made but the functions of the various systems of these new ships were a mystery to all who constructed them. Once constructed or modified, the time frame for departure was rather short which precluded any study of the systems and in addition, any experimentation with the new systems prior to departure would render the systems inoperative and the occupant would lose their chance to depart with the Dimensionless Ones. These warnings were included in the Dimensionless Ones instructions. The acceptance and rejection of the offer from the Dimensionless Ones was also a one-time offer. If an individual rejected their proposal, it was never be offered again as far as the Venusians knew and this was consistent with all the historical recordings from other intelligent species that had been encountered these beings. Some speculated that the Gatekeepers behavior stemmed from a sincere regret that they too had not accepted the Dimensionless Ones one-time proposal and now were damned in a universe, which distances would always prevent meaningful interactions between intelligent species. Of course, the Venusians were bound to prove them wrong, if this was indeed their reason.

***

Todd was pleased that Sarah had chosen five crops to plant besides his beloved grapes, which were; corn, tomatoes, carrots, lettuce and wheat. Since Sarah's physical and mental examination of the ambassador, her duties were centralized around Todd. She was still the SIL11 medical doctor but only occasional visits from the pregnant Jessica interrupted her duties with Todd.

Todd allowed her to till the soil and plant the seeds while he collected the fertilizer which was a byproduct from the crew and repaired and maintained the automated water sprinkler system. Rhiannon danced around the farm imitating the chores that her parents were engaged in. The other children, Nozomi and Tobias did not come around as often as before. Jessica still would not let Nozomi out of her sight and Christina and Tobias spent more time with those two. Todd sensed that Rhiannon missed her two friends but she did not verbalize her feelings, after all she did have her mom and dad almost entirely to herself. Sarah was still glum over the loss of her father, but his suggested treatment of working the farm did appear therapeutic effect on her. They occasionally experienced bouts of intimacy which did chip away at her sullenness, but for Todd there was no need to rush. His experience in watching the crops grow had taught him patience for the reward was in the harvest. Soon his wife will be totally with him again, but on this day which she was planting crops, she surprised him.

Sarah directed a question to her husband when Rhiannon was out of earshot, "What do you think, Todd, should be go with Dimensionless Ones?"

Jacob responded, "Sarah I believe in them. I have no proof but I sense a wonder awaits us if we allow ourselves to be led by them. But with that said, the most important thing for me far and away is that we three stay together."

Sarah replied, "I totally agree that we should stay together. And I'm quite relieved you feel that way about the Dimensionless Ones. I had a sense that you were with them since my books flew off the shelves to deliver a message to you, but I was never sure. We haven't come straight out to talk about it."

"I didn't want you to feel threatened in my view of the Dimensionless Ones," Todd shared.

"Todd, even though we apparently agree to go with the Dimensionless Ones, but are reasons are very different. You believe in them and you seem eager to go. But for me, my mistrust and ill feelings towards the Venusians may never go away. I would eventually become a threat to them, intentionally or unintentionally. I have to leave before somebody else gets hurt, maybe I can gain redemption with the Dimensionless Ones."

Todd smiled and gazed at his wife. Sarah smiled back, but a contentious thought gave her pause. Then she continued, "Do you think we are being fair to Rhiannon? She really doesn't have a choice. We both could be wrong, and the path with the Dimensionless Ones could be one for self-annihilation."

Todd answered, "Sarah, I don't think you need to worry. I know it's only a belief without proof, but the Dimensionless Ones will be the answer for all of us. I truly believe it in my heart and soul. So be at ease wife, I believe our daughter will be in good hands."

Sarah stood up next her husband. She embraced and kissed him and whispered, "So our decision has been made. Your job will be to convince the others to come with us and my job is not to allow others to ignore our decision, no matter who they are."

***

Christina's engineering prowess was not as necessary now as was before the ambassador arrived. The anti-matter fuel seamlessly combined with their remaining fuel, which was not even visible to the naked eye. Now the amount of fuel they had would allow them for interstellar travel again. The need for extra shielding for the ship against the sun radiation near Mercury's orbit was no longer necessary and the arboretum roof was operating nominally. Now for the first time since her awakening, she had much more spare time then she knew how to fill it. She was torn in spending time with her husband and the Venusian ambassador, and consoling and talking with Jessica.

Christina still had those foreign feelings for Jessica but refrained from expressing them to her. Somehow, Christina felt these feelings where inappropriate during Jessica's time of mourning. Besides, Jessica was enjoying her company while Nozomi and Tobias were constant companions.

"Why are you being so nice to me?" Jessica asked Christina one afternoon, when both Tobias and Nozomi were sleeping, "I don't want to be taking time away from your husband, I'm sure he misses you."

Christina countered, "Jacob prefers to mourn for his father alone and anyway he has been with the Venusian ambassador constantly since his arrival. I doubt he misses me much."

"Look he better miss you, he chose you over me," Jessica said teasingly, "and I can see why, you are a quite a beautiful woman."

Christina did not reply directly but was surprisingly pleased with her compliment. So Jessica continued, "You don't have to worry about me; with Nozomi here with me, I'm beginning to feel better. I should be taking better care of myself now since I'm carrying a child. I fairly certain this pregnancy will result in a son. This pregnancy has been more of a challenge than my previous one."

"You can't be sure, maybe you want a son more than another daughter and it has clouded your judgement," Christina offered.

"You might be right Christina. But I still don't know why you are here so much," Jessica paused then continued sternly, "You don't think I'll go crazy to do? Did Jacob put you up to spy on me and make sure I'm not a time bomb, like my brother, ready to go off?"

This conversation was not going well for Christina, she quickly replied, "No Jessica, Jacob only asked me to comfort you the day your husband died. I would have come myself anyway, but all these return trips to your quarters have been on my own volition."

"I don't understand, I thought you didn't think you like me. Your right cross gave me that impression."

Christina again offered, "I'm so sorry about that blow across your face. Sometimes even friends can rub you the wrong way."

"Come on Christina, we were never close friends, so what is it with you?"

173

Christina did not answer but only looked in those deep dark penetrating eyes of Jessica's. A small smile crept onto Jessica's face. She got up never taking her eyes off Christina and sat next to her. She bent close and whispered into her ear, "So I see, you have some desire for me?"

Christina senses were heightened. Before she could respond, Jessica was kissing her with an open mouth allowing her tongue to caress hers. Her hands caressed Christina' body as Christina began to moan. Then Jessica stood and slowly removed her clothes, then reseated herself and began to methodically undress Jessica. Christina finally managed a response, "Yes!"

Both Christina and Jessica were lying on their sweaty back sides once they both had quenched their appetites. Both knew that this lesbian experience was a first for both of them. Christina immensely enjoyed the pleasures that Jessica was able to give to her and hoped that she was sufficient for Jessica. She didn't want to say anything to spoil her mood and the ambience. The children were still sleeping soundly and her body was wet with sweat and tingled. Jessica rolled over towards her and smiled.

"Christina you were very pleasurable and it was nice to be close to someone again," Jessica said but then she sighed and continued, "But I'm afraid that to be honest I still prefer men over women for sex. Please know that this is nothing personal, it's just the way I feel."

Christina's heart sank. Her eyes welled up and she could not respond to Jessica right now. Christina was heartbroken. Jessica looked at Christina but Christina diverted her eyes elsewhere.

"I'm sorry Christina," Jessica added, "I do like you but I did enjoy myself but I just wanted to be very frank with you."

Christina finally managed to respond, "This was a mistake! I should have not enticed you by coming here all the time." Christina began to weep, but she tried to hide her tears from Jessica. She began to dress herself and wiped the tears from her face.

Then Jessica suggested, "Maybe if you can entice your husband to come here with you, we all could get what we want."

Christina began to get angry, "I thought you were the grieving widow, was this just a ploy of yours to get to my husband?"

"I didn't mean to get you angry," Jessica said, "I was just exploring options. In a threesome, you have me and your husband at the same time, isn't that appealing to you."

Christina finished dressing and responded, "As I said before, this was a mistake!" Christina picked up Tobias who was still sleeping and left the room without saying another word. She was ashamed, she was not only had been unfaithful to her husband but it was with another woman. Jacob must never know.

***

Jacob planned a formal funeral for his father, which the entire crew was of course invited as well as the new ambassador. Luther's body was to be ejected into space then incinerated. Jacob had asked Stewart if he thought this would alarm the Gatekeepers. Stewart reminded him that their projection shield will protect them and they should remember their crewmate in any fashion they thought appropriate. Jacob had asked Jessica and Sarah to present a personal artifact of his dad's including one of his own to be boxed as part of the funeral event. Sarah had chosen an old relic of his, a bronzed stethoscope, Jessica had his reading glasses and for himself, a picture of his mother that he kept with him even after her death. But before the funeral, he needed to speak with Jessica about her and her daughter becoming ambassadors, so he sent a PCD message to her that he was coming to her quarters.

Jessica was somewhat ashamed that she had led Christina on. It was a pleasurable experience to be with another woman, but it was not what she really wanted. Christina was now again very upset with her. She would need to watch her back. Christina could appear any time and give her another right cross. She dressed but allowed Nozomi to continue to snooze. Her PCD went off letting her know that she had a message. When she picked it up, she saw Jacob's message that he was coming down to her quarters but did not explain why. Jessica began to panic. Did he know about her and Christina and her already? Did Christina spill her guts to him? Christina had a hefty right cross, but Jacob could cause her some real serious damage. A notion of taking flight did cross her mind, but where was she to go after all they were confined in the SIL11. She decided to let events proceed and see where they will take her, she need not to assume anything.

Jacob arrived and requested to be let in. Jessica complied and watched him enter her room. Jessica was somewhat relieved that there was not anger in his eyes.

"I hope I'm not disturbing you, but I needed to ask you something," Jacob began.

Jessica was taken off guard this was not how she thought the conversation would proceed. She would try to remain calm and innocent. She replied to Jacob, "No captain, you're not interrupting anything, what can I do for you?"

Jacob eyes were downcast as he responded to her, "I know that you, well, all of us have suffered a great loss recently, but the captain of the Venusian vessel had a request. He asked me for an ambassador from the SIL11 to come to his ship and he suggested you and Nozomi to be those ambassadors. Stewart would remain here on board the SIL11 while you are over on the NN2. The captain said he wanted to make amends to you and Nozomi for the inadvertent death of your husband."

Jessica released a big sigh of relief since this conversation was totally unrelated to her and Christina.

Before Jessica could respond, Jacob added, "Before you say anything, let me tell you that as far as I'm concerned this is totally your decision, regardless of what I may think, the crew might think, or what Antwan, the NN2 captain might think. And, if you need time to decide, take all the time you need but I would like an answer prior to sooner than later. But personally I could not have chosen a better candidate than you."

This was the escape that Jessica needed to avoid Christina and Jacob in the future, and of course wherever she went Nozomi would be accompanying her. She just wanted to ask a couple of questions, so that she did appear to make this decision in haste.

She asked first, "Do they have a doctor on board? You know that I am pregnant."

"Yes, Jessica they do have medical officer on board, how knows you may actually benefit from their advances in medical science."

Then she asked, "Captain, I trust you, do you think it will be safe?"

Jacob paused before answering, "You know as much as I do. In my humble opinion, I do not believe that the Venusians mean us any harm. I think we are important assets to them. I know that we did not get off on the right track and our experience with humans in this current solar system has been less than stellar, but I do think it will be safe."

Jessica had already decided on leaving the SIL11, but she did not want to appear too eager on getting off the SIL11, so she hesitated. The opportunity was perfect for her. She was thrilled to become educated to this century and would be an ideal opportunity for both Nozomi and her unborn son. She could then educate the SIL11 crew, if she returned. She had already decided that she was not going with the Dimensionless Ones, so despite her first deadly encounter with these Venusians, they were her future. Obviously, it was a way to escape the Christina calamity.

Jessica replied after pretending to mull over her options, "Captain, I would be honored to be SIL11 ambassador to the Venusian vessel and of course Nozomi will accompany me. Thank you, captain."

Jacob was somewhat surprised at her willingness to serve as ambassador and more so at her quick decision. It was as though she had already decided to go before the opportunity was actually offered to her. He will be sorry to see her go even if it's for a short period, after all she became family to him. But, he smiled at her, "Thank you, ambassador. You are allowed to depart whenever you are ready after Luther's funeral. Agreed?"

"Of course captain, I will be ready the next day."

Chapter 36 - The Funeral and a Decision

Christina huddled in her quarters the day before Luther's funeral. She received a message from Jacob that he wanted her to join him for dinner and then take a walk in the new arboretum. She was confused, ashamed, worried and perplexed all at once. She loved Jacob but now her marriage was stained with adultery. Her fling with Jessica was truly a mistake, but now it threatened to unravel her whole world. Was she brave enough to face Jacob and tell him the truth then watch her life go up in ashes? Or hide the truth and watch as their relationship become infected which may fester because of her dishonesty.

She knew that Jacob wanted to discuss their future before meeting with the rest of the SIL11 crew to decide on the Dimensionless Ones proposal or the Venusians offer. They had not discussed it between themselves as of yet. It was very quaint of Jacob in framing their discussion as a date. He was romantic to a fault. The last time they had a date, they shared good conversation, good wine and good sex. But it was an illusion, they talked about their mission, it was the only wine, and she thought about Jessica when Jacob was making love to her. Now, Jacob wanted another date, she hoped it would be different except for the wine.

The galley was somewhat smokey when Christina entered. Jacob had grilled chicken that was served with country gravy, mashed potatoes and green beans, one of Christina's favorite meals. It was of course complemented with a bottle of Todd's red wine. She gave Jacob a small smile as she sat herself down at the table.

Jacob began, "Hey sweetheart, in seems like months ago since our last date. So much has happened since then, wouldn't you say?"

"Of course, sweetheart. I know you want to discuss about our choice; the Dimensionless Ones or the Venusians," answered Christina.

"You could always read me as a book, Christina. But I also think it's time to confess our sins to one another, and start with a clean plate before we discuss our future," Jacob said as he put down clean plates on the table with emphasis.

Christina did not answer and could not move. Somehow, Jacob knew about her one night affair with Jessica. She had no choice now, she must confess as Jacob indicated, and stop this infection of their marriage. Before she could begin, Jacob said, "Let me start."

Jacob paused and sat across from Christina then he continued, "I probably should have told you about this long ago, but there was never a good moment. Soon after we awoke from our long slumber and before we got together, Jessica came to me. As you probably well know, how seductive and provocative, she can be. Well, I had sex with Jessica, which was a needed release for me. It was only a sexual release for Jessica as well. When we done, we both just walked off and continued our duties, never seeing each other again in that manner."

Christina interrupted, "Was that the only time?"

"Yes, sweetheart," Jacob answered as he searched into Christina's eyes.

"My dear husband, I must confess that I too have had sex with Jessica. But it was a mistake, since I love you husband."

"What, you had sex with Jessica?"

"Remember when I landed a punch on Jessica's face?" Christina began, "It was the first time that Jessica was being sexually suggestive with me."

"Did my dad know about it?"

"I don't think so, but I'm certain that he had his suspicions."

"Would you rather have Jessica than me?" Jacob asked.

'No, and you? Would you rather be with Jessica?"

"Me neither."

Christina replied, "I'm enjoying this date much more than I did our last date. I needed to get this off my chest."

Jacob looked at Christina, "There is more," he said.

"More?" asked Christina incredulously, "You said it only happened once and that was long before we got married."

"That was my only sin, but there is more you need to know."

"Well what is it?" Christina asked.

"Nozomi is not my dad's. She is actually my daughter."

Christina was flabbergasted. "You're the father of Nozomi! Did your dad know?"

"Actually, he was the one that convinced Jessica to tell me. He told Jessica that he could not marry her until I learned the truth. We made a pact to keep this a secret to our grave. I'm afraid I have broken their trust and only because I love you and I felt it tainted our relationship. But Nozomi must never know!"

"But now she doesn't have a dad, even though her father is alive," Christina spoke mostly to herself.

"Christina, Jessica will not have any problem finding a dad for Nozomi if she wishes. She is going to be the new ambassador to the NN2 and Nozomi will also be an ambassador."

Jacob went over to the stove and the grill proportioned out their meals onto their plates and said, "I hope you agree that it was nice to start with a clean plate again."

Christina grabbed Jacob arm and said, "I'm so sorry about my affair with Jessica after all you had rendezvous with her was well before we were married, however, I have been unfaithful, this only happened a couple of days ago."

He smiled and said, "Well, I am somewhat surprised. However, that just proves that Jessica has superior sexual prowess which can affect the whole crew, except for most likely my sister. My poor dad never had a chance."

Christina laughed out loud and the first time she smiled genuinely at Jacob in weeks.

"You know she wanted me to bring you with me the next time we had a rendezvous," Christina proclaimed.

"Did she now? Two for the price of one!" Jacob laughed, "It will be difficult when she is on the NN2 and we will be here".

"Should we tell her that both of us know about each other's secret," Christina asked.

"Oh no, Jessica is very good at keeping secrets, but there is something else I want to discuss."

"Is it about the Dimensionless Ones' offer? I assume you want to know how I feel about it." Christina responded.

"Yep, that would it, Christina. Well?" Jacob asked impatiently.

"Be honest, I'm personally on the fence. I will go wherever my husband decides, along with Tobias of course," Christina answered.

"You would not have any regrets regardless of which way I may choose?"

"No, none at all."

Jacob remained quiet as he chowed down his grilled chicken followed by a generous heap of mashed potatoes and gravy. Christina followed suit with a bit of chicken and some green beans. Christina thought that this date's conversation was much more inspiring than the previous date, and watched her husband eat with abandon. She still felt somewhat guilty, since her husband's confession was not that earth-shattering as hers, and hers probably hit her husband right straight at the heart and shook him up a bit. But Jacob took it in stride instead of lashing out at her. She was able as he put it, 'clean off her plate." She felt much better as though the ceiling on top of her was removed, and she was able to breathe free and easy. The infection was gone. She decided to ask the question even though she already knew the answer.

"So what has my husband decided?" Christina asked.

Jacob looked over the table at her as he swallowed another helping of potatoes and gravy. He put down his fork and said, "I would have liked to see the entire crew of the SIL11 go one way or another, together. I'm sure my father would have been able to broker such a deal among the crew, since it was his family. But my dad is gone, and I don't see a path forward that could unite the entire crew. I'm fairly certain, even now, that Jessica and Todd are on the opposite sides of the fence, and I'm sure Sarah would be inclined to go with Todd especially now with the death of our father. As for myself, I am not certain about these Dimensionless Ones, especially since I do not yet understand their motive. I guess they don't need a motive since it's more of a human trait, but I'm still uncomfortable with it. The

Venusians on the other hand are fighting for our solar system by keeping themselves alive and growing stronger to fight another day. I have no doubt about the Venusians motives, and I want to be part of that fight to prevent our extinction at the hands of the Gatekeepers. But if this is the path I wish to proceed, then I will be putting both you and Tobias in harm's way."

Christina smiled at her husband, "We were born into harm's way, and with you at the helm we have come through with shining colors. I, and probably the whole crew, believe in you. You have saved us in multiple scenarios. I'll always be behind you. You just have to convince the crew to come with us."

"Thanks for the vote of confidence, but I'm fairly certain that Todd feels just as strong or stronger in going with the Dimensionless Ones. Anyway, are you a ready for that walk in our new farm? Todd told me that it was all ours tonight, and Sarah and he would watch Tobias for the next 8 hours. He told me that he thoroughly watered the seeded areas, and we shouldn't disturb them. Shall we go?"

"I'm all yours tonight," Christina mischievously responded.

***

The funeral was a solemn event. Except for Stewart, there was not a tearless one among them. Sarah, Jessica and Jacob had all put their personal innuendos into the cubed box. Jessica had drawn the words 'SIL11 CREW WAS MY FAMILY' on the side of the crypt. Jessica planned a brief eulogy at her own request, but promised Jacob that she would be very brief. The box was ejected and incinerated in space as Jessica began her eulogy:

"Luther was truly family for everyone here. He was a protective but cultivating father for both Jacob and Sarah, especially after the loss of their mother. He welcomed in both Todd and Christina with open arms to his family. He was father and grandfather to all the children here. He found ways to save everyone in his family at times of great peril, even in his last act turned out to be an attempt to save everyone on board."

"But for me, he was my friend, my lover and my savior. He was not blinded by my human shortcomings but he saw me through them. What he found was a scared little girl, agonizing over an event she felt guilty for. Over time, he taught her that she was not responsible but was unintended victim herself in that tragic event decades ago. He allowed this girl to be herself but wanted her honesty and trust to be above anything else. Well this little girl, finally learned to be an adult, a wife and a mother. In doing so, he had become my life."

"I thought that my life was over when I found out he died. He was everything to me. I didn't know where to run to and where to hide. But Luther even in his death would not allow me to run and hid. Nozomi and her unborn brother depend on me and to honor Luther, I will raise these children as he would have, after all they were his family."

"I love you Luther, and good-by."

After the funeral, everyone remained as Jacob had requested. First, Jacob introduced Jessica and Nozomi as the new ambassadors to the NN2 then wanted to know what everybody thought about the Dimensionless Ones offer. Jacob offered a heartfelt speech about his deep desire to keep everyone together. He told everyone that in his heart, his father would have wanted 'his family' to stay together. He suggested that they should follow the Venusians and defend their solar system.

Todd agreed with Jacob that they should stay together as Luther would have liked. But they should go with Dimensionless Ones. In a fiery speech, which was unusual for Todd, he proclaimed that this was an opportunity for the human race to transcend above the Gatekeepers and for them to become more that just flesh and blood. It was time for their destiny to be fulfilled. Jessica and Christina agreed with Jacob to go with the Venusians. Jacob asked his sister to speak some sense into her husband.

Sarah responded, "NEVER! You will all end up in one hell or another. The Dimensionless Ones were the salvation of the human race. I WILL NEVER GO WITH THE VENUSIANS FREELY. NEVER!"

As Jacob feared the crew was splitting up; Jessica, Christina and Jacob with the Venusians and Todd and Sarah with the Dimensionless Ones. Their decision was made.

Chapter 37 - Details

As Jessica promised, she and Nozomi were prepared to disembark the SIL11 and venture to the NN2 the very next day. She only had a few belongings she wished to take. As a parting gift to Christina and Jacob, she left her decorations and toys in hers and Luther's old 'fun' room. She had hoped that the room would inspire them as it inspired her and Luther. For Todd and Sarah, she left most of Luther's possessions in her old quarters; which notably his books, which Sarah coveted.

As chief medical officer, Sarah insisted on one final examination of her unborn child before letting her disembark. Sarah wanted to make sure that both mother and the fetus were normal and thriving. She informed Jessica that during their voyage to Venus that she would be available to her at any time; since they were heading to the same place, and they were within a kilometer of each other. Her unborn son was the only connection she had left with her father and he was also her second brother. She had known for quite some time that Nozomi was not her brother but her nephew. She felt that she had failed by not coercing the crew not to join Todd and her. She would have liked very much to have the crew stay intact. But her decision and Todd's could not be converted. During their travels through the solar system, she had grown to admire Jessica. In Sarah's mind, she had to be quite a woman to have her father interested in her. Yes, Jessica was sexually provocative but it would have taken a lot more than that to have her father to take Jessica as his wife. Her final examination allowed for her seal of approval to let her leave, even though personally she would have liked her stay.

Stewart had left a device in the airlock that would surround Jessica and Nozomi in a bubble for transference to the NN2. Stewart informed her how to use the device and the small ring that was used to control the 'bubble.' When she entered the airlock, she followed Stewart's instruction and placed one of several rings on her index finger. Immediately, the bubble substance surrounded both Jessica and Nozomi then they began to immediately drift towards the NN2 after the outer latch was opened. Their belongings followed in separate a bubble which Jessica could also control with her ring. The ring somehow connected her neural network and both bubbles reacted to any command or even thought that Jessica had. Minutes later, the NN2 hailed the SIL11 informing Jacob and the crew that the new ambassadors had arrived unscathed.

Soon after Jessica and Nozomi had left the ship, Todd came to visit Jacob on the bridge. Stewart was also there when he arrived. Todd was eager to start modifying the ship, but he needed to know from Jacob which ship was he modifying. He had no claims to either ship but it was apparent from the Dimensionless Ones' message that a ship was going to be provided. He assumed that he would take the smaller ship with the Dimensionless Ones.

"Hey Jacob, could I disturb you for a moment," asked Todd.

"Sure, Todd, what can I do for you?" answered Jacob. Jacob gestured to Stewart to leave, so they could have some privacy.

But Todd responded, "Stewart you can stay, this won't take long."

"With your permission captain, do you mind if I stay? I would like to hear what he has to say." asked Stewart.

Jacob nodded his head towards Stewart, and then asked, "What is it, Todd?"

"Just a couple of things; first and foremost, I wanted to extent my sincere condolences to you regarding the loss of your father. I have so preoccupied with your sister that I have overlooked that Luther had more than one offspring. I have been delinquent in extending my hand to you, now that the funeral is over," Todd said as he extended his hand to Jacob.

Jacob replied shaking his hand, "There is no need for this. Besides, I much appreciated the help and time you have spent with my sister. I don't know what she would have done without you. You have been her rock! But thank you for the gesture." Jacob released his hand.

"I know we haven't seen eye to eye on this big decision we all had to come to, but you should know that it was my hope that you all would have decided to come with us," Todd paused then continued, 'I have never felt so strongly about something, as this quest with the Dimensionless Ones."

Jacob replied, "You made that quite apparent in you speech after the funeral. Is there something else you needed?"

"Oh yes, which ship should Sarah and I start initiating modifications on?" asked Todd.

"I hadn't considered which ship yet, let me think a second," said Jacob.

Stewart interjected, "If I may captain, offer any opinion?"

"Of course, ambassador, what do you suggest?" offered Jacob.

"Thanks, captain. Your MT Corporate shuttle, or as you refer to as IOSAC, would be more valuable to the Venusian colonies, than another SIL spacecraft. You have fine vessel but it is too antiquated to be of value in our struggle against the Gatekeepers. So if your intent and Christina's is to aid our cause against the Gatekeepers than I would recommend allowing Todd and Sarah to take the SIL11," said Stewart.

"Wouldn't the modifications be more cumbersome with the SIL11 than with the IOSAC?" asked Jacob.

Todd responded, "Captain, the modifications are only slightly more difficult from what Sarah and I could gather from the schematics and instructions. It would take Sarah and me more time to understand the operations of the IOSAC even with your wife's help. Sarah and I of course are much more familiar with the SIL11."

Jacob looked at both Stewart and Todd, "I am quite attached to this rust bucket, the SIL11. It is the only home that any of us have ever had. I suppose it's time for me to relinquish my childhood attachments to this ship. It is never easy to give up one's home, especially when it's the only home you know. But both of your arguments are solid. I see no reason for you, Todd and Sarah in not keeping the SIL11 as your home. Take good care of her. Todd, it looks like you'll be able to keep your farm and your valued grapes."

Todd replied, "Thank you, captain." Todd waited impatiently until the captain dismissed him so he could start his work. But the dismissal was delayed.

Jacob then turned directly towards Stewart, "The two prisoners will have to be transferred to your vessel. Please notify your captain. If you don't have room, make room. Since Ivan is well known serial killer as you told me, I am sure you would want to bring him to justice. What will you do with Blackbeard, the pirate? Sorry I don't even know his real name."

Stewart replied, "Of course captain. I am sure that we will be able to convince Blackbeard to become valuable addition to our Venusian army. We have been successful on several accounts, especially with foot soldiers to condition them to join our cause. They will be better protected than with their previous bosses and usually eat and sleep better. Gang bosses are typically more independent and also more well off thus typically more difficult, but I'm sure your prisoner is only a foot soldier. And as far as Ivan is concerned, he has been human Gatekeeper, no punishment will be sufficient for him but will try. You should be quite proud of your crew in apprehending him."

"I'm afraid my father had the biggest hand in that," Jacob quickly responded, "One more thing, ambassador, my father was also the only one here, except of course Ivan, to pilot the IOSAC. My wife is familiar with the operations of that ship, but she has never piloted a ship before. Will your projection screen be sufficient to hide her from the Gatekeepers if she takes the IOSAC out for a couple of test runs?"

"Yes captain, your wife can take your shuttle for a test flight but she will be very restricted in the space she can fly. I can give her those restrictions. Please aware that if your wife goes beyond the limitations we set forth, that she will be immediately targeted by the NN2 for disintegration. Are you sure you want to risk your wife's life to pilot the shuttle?" Stewart inquired.

Jacob reflected on allowing Christina to pilot a vessel which had lethal spatial limitations. Christina had never piloted any spacecraft in her life. This may not be the best opportunity for her to develop her skills now with her life in the balance. In fact, she was not the best choice, he was. He had more experience than anybody on the SIL11. Even though, she was the one familiar with the IOSAC operations, she was not the best choice to pilot the IOSAC. Christina will not be happy with this decision, but he was captain. The consequences of a pilot error would have been catastrophic; he couldn't take that chance with his wife.

Jacob answered Stewart, "You are quite right ambassador, I will pilot the shuttle."

Jacob turned to Todd, "Are you still here? Don't you think you and my sister should get started?"

Todd gave Jacob a large smile and then ran off to search for Sarah and tell her the good news. He had his ship, his wife, his daughter and now his farm and home. He wouldn't even need to change the locations of hidden stashes of wine he had on the SIL11. The random events of the universe were now in his favor. He hoped that his luck would last until the Dimensionless Ones were guiding them to their new home.

***

Jessica arrived in her bubble to the polished ship known as the NN2. The airlock was totally alien to her; it was also composed of this 'bubble' technology that the Venusians had skillfully rendered. Her bubble seemed to merge with this new bubble on the side of NN2 ship. As her ring began to glow, she understood its simple message, 'take a couple of steps forward.' It was not a command but a request in her mind, so she compiled. The bubble surface that was once in front of her from her bubble began to reemerge behind her, and the new bubble she was in began to slowly dissipate and then disappeared altogether. In front of her were the three of the four NN2 crewmembers; Antwan, Julio and Janice.

Julio was the tallest and palest of the three. He was very tall in human terms almost 95 cm in height, taller than any human she had ever seen. Jessica suspected that Julio characteristics may have been characteristics of Martians in general. They were human but generations on that planet had led to changes to their appearances. Since Mars was smaller and was further away from the sun, the reduction of gravity may have allowed for greater height, and the dimmer sun required less melanin protection. Next to him, in contrast, was a short dark-skinned man, but was quite muscular. While Julio was clean shaved, Antwan had a full beard and mustache. His hair was dark and curly. Antwan's eyes were penetrating as he gazed into her own eyes. There were signs of significant intelligence and discipline behind those commanding eyes. On his right, was Janice. She appeared to be Asian as Jessica was, but the similarities ended there. She was short with short black hair and much more thick-limbed than Jessica. She also had several scars showing, one that extended from her right ear across her neck and another scar across her left cheek bone. Jessica decided that a right hook from her would absolutely crush her skull. So she decided not to upset her new doctor.

Antwan extended his hand and said, "Welcome to the NN2 and your new home, ambassador, I'm Antwan, the captain." He turned towards the Martian and said, "This is Julio, the ship's navigator. He is also a Martian, I doubt you have had any opportunity to meet a Martian before. And to my left is Janice, your new doctor." Jessica nodded to each in turn.

Jessica accepted Antwan hand, "Thank you, captain. My name is Jessica and let me present to you, Nozomi, my daughter."

Antwan reached down and extended his hand to Nozomi, but she didn't take it. Her large eyes were transfixed onto Julio. She did glance at Antwan and Janice but they quickly returned to Julio.

Jessica admonished Nozomi, "Nozomi, you are now an ambassador, please shake the captain's hand."

Nozomi looked at her mother and then at Antwan's hand and then briefly shook it. But her eyes again returned to Julio. All three, Antwan, Julio and Janice were staring in wonder at this little girl.

Jessica noticed the three of them staring, "It appears that children are not that common among the Venusians."

Antwan glanced up to Nozomi's mothers face and said, "Our planet may have been named after the god of beauty and love, but children have not been its blessing."

But while Nozomi's eyes were transfixed on Julio, she asked, "Captain, did you know where my dad is? My Aunt Sarah said you would know."

Again Jessica admonished her young daughter, "I told you that he is gone and will never be coming back."

But Nozomi continued despite her mother's glare, "Do you know where he went to, captain?"

"I'm afraid he is dead," Antwan responded.

"Did you kill him?" asked Nozomi, who finally turned her eyes onto the captain.

Antwan kept silent. Jessica interjected, "You are ambassador, you need to act like one. You need to show the captain our respect."

But this did not deter Nozomi and she repeated her question.

Antwan finally responded to her, "I'm sorry but he did die because of my actions. So I guess, you would say that I killed him."

Nozomi deliberately went over to the captain and then kicked his shin as hard as she could, and then unexpectedly grabbed onto Julio's hand and gently asked him, "Could you show me to my new room?" She went with him without glancing back at Antwan and ignored her mother's shouts of her name.

Chapter 38 - Second Thoughts

"So you are leaving this entire ship to Sarah, Todd and Rhiannon?" asked Christina.

"Venusians consider it no more than an old relic, just a museum piece and no more," answered Jacob.

Christina circled around the bridge, looking at it as though it was going to be the last time she would see it, despite that fact they were still a couple of weeks from Venus. She stared at the controls and lightly touched them. She absentmindedly allowed her finger trace the edge of the console as if she assessing for the amount of dust accumulated. She considered all the hours that she had spent both inside and outside the ship to keep the vessel functioning smoothly. She had pride in this ship and it was the only home she had ever known. They had defended it with their lives without hesitation. Now, they would be just walking away from it.

"Have you asked yourself, why the pirates wanted it so badly?" Christina replied, "And why Ivan wanted it as well. Both were willing to kill us for this ship."

"I don't know Christina, maybe because it's a self-sustaining interstellar ship with the ability to travel around the galaxy," Jacob retorted. He paused then continued, as if trying to reassure his wife, "The Venusians don't seem to want it, they rather have the IOSAC. Besides without the anti-matter fuel which Antwan and Stewart provided, this ship would be no more than space debris in few weeks."

"You do have a point regarding the fuel, I'm just surprised you gave up your ship so easily," Christina surmised.

"Christina, we have to think like Venusians from now on, to understand what is best for the colonies on Venus and the future of mankind."

This rankled Christina, she said, "So you want to see your son in the Venusian military, taking orders, going off to war he cannot win and cheaply lay down his life."

Jacob inquired, "Why are you like this? You agreed the Venusians was going to be our future. Are you having second thoughts?"

"Second thoughts? How about third, fourth and fifth thoughts! How can we be so certain of our decision? How can Todd and Sarah be so wrong?" Christina asked.

"You already know the answer, which is simply is that we don't know. And we may never know."

Jacob was surprised to Christina's reaction to his news. He thought his wife would be upset that she was not piloting the shuttle. That part of his news, she took that in stride, admitting that she had never flown a spacecraft of any kind before. She knew how most of them operated but openly admitted that she never was a pilot. Instead, she was lamenting over the loss of her home. He did have to admit, he was little apprehensive in leaving the only place that he was familiar, but he was going to a new home. She had to see the logic, in taking the IOSAC and instead of this monstrosity, known as the SIL11. It was the only logical choice, maybe just not a personal one.

"Whatever! I'm taking Tobias down to the farm to play with Rhiannon. See you for dinner later?" asked Christina.

"Absolutely! Are you going to be OK?" answered Jacob.

Christina gently smiled, "I'm OK. Later then." She calmly strode off the bridge.

When Christina and Tobias arrived at the farm, only Sarah and Rhiannon were there. Todd was quite busy these days with the modification that the Dimensionless Ones required, and now spent little time at the farm. Sarah helped when she could with the modifications but she needed to keep an eye on Rhiannon and the farm was the easiest place to watch her. While watching Rhiannon, Sarah would tend to the new seedlings that were springing up. Sarah smiled when she saw Tobias run in the dirt towards Rhiannon, who was already as dirty as a little piglet.

"Hi Christina, It's probably looks a little ridiculous," Sarah said greeting her.

"What does?" Christina responded.

"Taking time-consuming care of these seedlings," answered Sarah.

"Why?" ventured Christina.

"Well, Todd and I have a lot of work with these Dimensionless Ones modifications. And these seedlings will probably not bear fruit in time, at least not for us. Yet I still baby them."

"You don't know that," exclaimed Christina.

"Are you excited about going to a planet, a new home," asked Sarah ignoring Christina last comment.

"Excited would not be the word I would use to describe my feelings; more frightened than anything else."

"Me, too," Sarah responded, "Hell, Todd, Tobias and I might be heading off to commit suicide."

"Come on, Sarah," Christina said, "You wouldn't sign up for this if that is what you really believe."

"It's hard to know what to believe. I use to look to my dad for help with these types of questions, but Todd has become my anchor, my pillar, now."

"I don't know about that, Sarah, when we were girls you always put Jessica and myself in our place. You never doubted yourself."

Sarah chuckled and responded, "That was years ago, things change. Now it seems that all I have is doubt."

Christina laughed, "I came down here to be consoled by my big sis, not watch her stagger in self-doubt."

"Are you having second thoughts?" asked Sarah.

"Are you?" Christina responded.

"Now, you shouldn't be answering a question with a question. That is a sign of avoidance behavior according to my dad. But to answer your question, no, I'm committed with Todd. Beside, you know that I could never trust the Venusians. Actually, it may be the other way around, the Venusians shouldn't trust me. And you?"

"Neither am I. I am mostly committed to your brother. Just hard to leave the only home you ever knew."

"Homesick already, uh. And you haven't even left the ship yet. Sounds like a terminal case of homesickness to me," chuckled Sarah again. Sarah added, "I'm afraid there is no medical treatment for it."

Christina only smiled at Sarah. At one time, Christina had only considered Sarah a manipulating bitch and unsympathetic doctor, but now she was a friend as well as family. She was going to miss her sister-in-law.

"Christina, come over her and check out the corn with me. The corn should be well drained, and not sitting in standing water," Sarah said and she waved her hand for Christina to come with her. Christina decided to tally along.

***

After Christina left the bridge, Jacob pondered her question regarding the pirate and Ivan, and that was 'why did they want their ship so badly'. He contemplated a possible scenario for obtaining the actual truth. Most direct approach would be to ask the prisoners himself. Even though their response may have some elements of truth but for the most part, their response would be an attempt to use this opportunity to gain favor with their captors or better yet gain their freedom. It would be difficult to separate the truth from their charades and in addition, questioning the prisoners without a Venusian present would be a great risk. This risk was not only because of prisoners' knowledge of present technology that he totally lacked, but also might be construed as a slap in the face by the Venusians for his lack of faith in them. Jacob also considered asking the Venusians, but their truth maybe mired with their belief that his ship had no strategic value. Jacob decided he would ask Stewart directly why their prisoners had considered his ship such a valuable prize, and discover if he could not only hear Stewart's words but formulate from them the actual truth. Jacob questioned what his motives were of why he wanted to know the inherent value of his ship; was he having second thoughts as well?

***

Jessica apologized profusely to the captain, "I'm terribly sorry for my daughter's behavior. I do not know what got into her. Obviously, she has a lot to learn about being an ambassador."

"Nonsense," retorted Antwan, "It's the behavior I would expect from an outstanding ambassador. She let me know where I stood since I was responsible for her father's death. She is letting me know that she has a chip over me or if you like a favor of me that she could cash in at any time."

"Your daughter needn't worry though, I do know the score," Antwan added.

189

"She needs to learn diplomacy as an ambassador," Jessica answered.

"No, I like her approach, sometimes diplomacy only clouds the issue for everyone," Antwan answered. "May I escort to your room, ambassador?" Antwan finished.

"Of course, captain, and thank you for your understanding," Jessica responded. But Jessica wasn't sure she liked Antwan reaction to her daughter's misbehavior. She would have been more comfortable if he was outraged at her daughter. But right now she needed to educate her daughter in certain civilities and mannerisms of being an ambassador. This was not proceeding as anticipated, Jessica mused. She hoped that she had made the right decisions for her and her daughter. She immediately realized that how much she was missing Luther right now and utterly alone she felt. She was hoping that she will see some of her husband in Nozomi when she matured, which seemed to be far in the future.

***

Since the Venusians had arrived, the crew of the SIL11 had become lazy and ambiguous about ship duties, Todd thought. He was not going to change the constant hours of working that the crew of the SIL11 had endured since they had entered the solar system. He was going full speed ahead with Dimensionless Ones modification plans.

The modifications plans were puzzling. It required cannibalizing most of the functional operations of the ship, except for life support and any type of sensors. Apparently, the Dimensionless Ones wanted the occupants to stay alive and witness their trip, but were not allowed to affect course and speed, or communicate with anybody on the outside. This was consistent with his knowledge of previous exoduses by other intelligent species. Eventually, the SIL11 was to be sealed tight, all thrust ports, the ice collector ports and even the airlocks were eventually to be permanently sealed. The plans were in two stages; one was mostly preparations and then final execution of the plan. The Dimensionless Ones allowed all functions of the SIL11 to continue while phase I plans were implemented. Included in those plans are two medium size rooms juxtaposition with each other with a polarized transparent medium in between them. Each would be sealed in the second phase. The one room was to be lit and contain breathable air while the second was to contain the vacuum of space and be in total darkness. Todd was guessing that the one room was for his family and the other was for accompanying Dimensionless Ones. Both rooms together were highly supported with intricate network of frames around both rooms. They were to be located near the center of the ship. From the structure, one would suspect that this support network was for some kind of material but that material was not mentioned in the plans.

Sarah aided him when she had Rhiannon asleep but only half-heartedly. She spent time with her brother, Christina and Tobias when she could until her guilt brought her back to Todd and the reality of actually modifying the SIL11. She hated not understanding the instructions and wanted to question all the instructions from the Dimensionless Ones, but she knew nobody would give her explanations and if a possible explanation was given, it may be beyond her comprehension anyway. So, she did her duty and followed those instructions but she still refuse to like them.

Todd was excited. Even his wife's attitude did not detract from Todd's exuberance for the plans. It was quite possible that he could complete the entire project himself if he had to. He felt there would be nothing that could keep him in seeing this through.

190

Venus was becoming extremely luminous in the stellar sky and began rival the sun in brightness as the NN2 and the SIL11 approached the planet. The surface was highly reflective that was the result of dense cloud formations around the planet. Venus was now in direct opposite side of the sun from Earth, and the Gatekeeper ship orbiting Earth could no longer be detected even without the projection system. Mars be only beginning to emerge from the sun's corona. Likewise, Mars was also still too close to the sun to be able to detect the Gatekeeper's ship orbiting that planet.

Jacob had been taking out the IOSAC for his test runs. It was a sheer pleasure to pilot. The ship reacted instantaneously to his thought commands, he needed to be careful though and stay focus while the piloted the IOSAC. Scattered thoughts could doom him and the test flight. He had no doubt that the Antwan would stay to true to his word and disintegrate the IOSAC if he advertently strayed beyond the set limits.

Stewart and Jacob initiated and then supervised the transfer of prisoners to the NN2. Sarah heavily sedated both prisoners and then removed them from their cryochambers. Both Todd and Stewart brought the pirate to the airlock system, while Sarah and Jacob managed to bring Ivan to the airlock system. Ivan and the pirate were then encapsulated by a bubble, only this time Stewart put on a ring to control both bubbles. Jacob and Stewart watched as the bubbles drifted towards the NN2. Minutes later the Antwan notified Jacob that the prisoners were successfully transferred and were now on board the NN2 in a security bubble. Jacob was very relieved that he was no longer responsible for those prisoners particularly Ivan, which he would have sooner had him killed. Stewart's investigation of Ivan disclosed that he had been a well-known rapist and later a sadistic killer but his whereabouts were unknown until now.

The voyage of the SIL11 was nearly at a close. Soon, the IOSAC would depart the SIL11 with Jacob, Christina and Tobias on board heading towards the cloud city sanctuaries high in the atmosphere in the southern polar region of Venus. It was time for him and his family to join the human race again and feel the pulse of humanity. He hoped the best for his sister, his niece and brother-in-law on their new venture, as well, but only felt sadness in their future departure, and the time was near.

Chapter 39 - Departure

The projection system of the NN2 was terminated and true vision of the solar system was now returned to the SIL11. As a matter of habit, Jacob pointed the SIL11's MDS towards Mars to locate the Gatekeeper's ship, but Mars was too close proximity to the sun's corona for its detection.

Todd and Sarah asked the all the crewmembers of the SIL11 to one final banquet before going into orbit around Venus and then initiating their venture with the Dimensionless Ones. No one had any contact with the Dimensionless Ones since receiving the blueprints and hearing a rendition of taps, but both Sarah and Todd expected them to appear on board once the captain and his family had left the ship.

An invitation was also sent to the NN2 for allowing Jessica and Nozomi to return the SIL11 occasion. Of course, Antwan had no objections whatsoever for their feast and recalled Stewart back to the NN2. It was decided that the Jacob's family would be the only occupants of the IOSAC because of limited size when venturing into Venus's atmosphere, which was only days away. Stewart had done his task and had managed to recruit some new Venusian's citizens. Surprisingly, Sarah received a personal message from her niece, Nozomi, who wanted to bring a new friend with her to the feast. Nozomi explained to Sarah that her friend, Julio was not a Venusian but a Martian, and wanted Tobias and Rhiannon to meet her new friend. Sarah was hesitant and reluctant but eventually agreed to allow this Martian on board.

Stewart said his good-byes to the SIL11 crew and decided to give one last try to persuade Todd to come with them. He distinctly avoided Sarah since he knew quite well that her feelings towards Venusians had never changed since their approach to Venus. Stewart met up with Todd who was preparing Jessica's and Luther's old quarters as a galley. Modifications to the SIL11 original galley were completed and a stove and oven was now relocated into a new galley. There was only purpose to the quick renovations to the Jessica's and Luther's old quarters was to have a functional galley, there was not going to be much of an atmosphere for this new galley.

"Hey Todd," Stewart began as he entered the construction zone, "I've been recalled to the NN2 and wanted to give you my last regards before heading over."

Todd smiled and said, "You can hold your breath ambassador, I'm not changing my mind about the Dimensionless Ones, but I would have credit you on your persistence. I take it you haven't tried your persuasive powers on my wife, have you?"

"You have to give me more credit than that, I really wanted to say good-bye. And no, I haven't spoken to your wife. She has made it quite clear that she wants nothing to do with me."

"If you wanted her cooperation, you have been better off killing me, her husband than her father, I'm afraid. But don't take it personally because I don't. Besides, she would have been a potential assassin for your captain. He would have to watch his back constantly with Sarah around. You and he are better off without us."

"Can't help myself, in saying that you would be a fine addition to the Venusian colonies," Stewart added.

Todd walked up to Stewart and extended his hand, "Thank you ambassador, but I, Sarah and Tobias are staying. But you watch out for the rest of my family though. We have had enough surprises getting to your planet. "

Stewart responded, "Don't worry; they are part of our family now."

Stewart also said his good-byes to Jacob, Christina and Tobias. They all felt they would be seeing each other real soon. Jacob felt that he acquired a true friend in Stewart, which was made easier with the fact that he had not been directly involved in the death of his father. Jacob could see why he was not only an effective ambassador but a SIL captain as well. He was well liked and soft spoken. Despite his skin color, Stewart reminded him of his own deceased father. Stewart then left the SIL11.

***

All six that remained watched as Jessica's bubble approached the SIL11. The bubble had three occupants; Jessica, Nozomi and another human life form who towered over both Jessica and Nozomi. Todd and Sarah had finished their preparations for the banquet as best as they could without the familiar galley. When they exited the airlock, Jessica was smiling wearing an extravagant gown that the NN2 crew provided for her to match her new station as ambassador. Nozomi was also wearing a colorful new dress. She sought her old friends, Tobias and Rhiannon holding her new friend's pale white hand.

Nozomi was the first to speak, "May I introduce all of you to my new shipmate, Julio. He is a representative from the planet Mars. I thought he was giant that I have read in some of Sarah's books, but he says that all his people pretty much look like him."

Julio extended his hand to Jacob, "Thank you, captain for allowing me on board. It is an honor to be here."

"No problem Julio, but forgive us for our stares since we have never met or even seen a Martian before."

"Don't worry captain, I understand."

Sarah moved up to Jessica and kissed her on the check. Todd followed suite. "How are feeling?" Sarah asked as she placed her hand on Jessica womb.

"Just great, maybe a little tired at times, but great," Jessica responded, "I know how Julio feels, I don't think these Venusians have seen a pregnant woman before."

Jacob and Christina squeezed each other hand. They had a special greeting for Jessica prepared and it was time to spring it on her. First, Christina walked up to her and gave her an enthusiastic kiss on Jessica's painted lips, smiled and stepped aside. Then Jacob came up to her grabbed her with both arms and kissed her deeply, which took Jessica's breath away.

Both Christina and Jacob said in unison, "Welcome back, Jessica!"

Jessica was totally unprepared for this welcome and her face exploded in crimson. Jacob and Christina laughed out loud and held each other's hand. Todd and Sarah were quite perplexed at their welcome but after seeing Jessica's embarrassment also began chuckling. It was not often that Jessica was seen that disconcerted.

However, Jessica quickly recovered from her embarrassment and looked into Jacob's and Christina's eyes, "Not in front of the children you two, maybe later," she cooed seductively. The expressions on Jacob's and Christina's face became frozen but Sarah and Todd again erupted in laughter.

Julio lightly squeezed Nozomi hand and whispered, "What was that all about?"

"I have no idea, you'll have to ask my mom," Nozomi quietly replied.

"Come on everybody, let's go to our feast and let the wine begin to flow," Todd announced. Sarah and Todd lead the way to their bountiful feast, followed by Jacob and Christina then Julio holding on to three little hands with his fingers.

After a night of feasting and drinking, the adults slept while the children confiscated the Martian until the very early morning hours. They led him to the farm which the roof was still retracted showing him the stellar sky. At each revolution, he attempted to point out his planet, so they would know where he was from but failed. He explained to them that his planet, Mars was now hidden by the sun. His revelation caused a torrent of new questions from the children that avalanched out of the children's mouths. Julio had a difficult time keeping up. The children were asking questions all at the same time, but they didn't seem to be aware of this being a problem.

Jacob awoke first among the adults and squeezed Christina's shoulder who was lying next to him while holding an empty bottle of wine.

"Christina?" Jacob whispered, "It is time for us to depart the SIL11."

Christina began to open her eyes and nodded her head in agreement. She looked around and quietly asked, "Where are the children?"

Jacob looked around the room and responded, "They must have kidnapped our new guest from Mars; he's not around either."

Jessica awoke next. She refrained from the wine for the most part, but she had her fill of food. Venusians may know more than they did about most things, but they didn't know what good food was, so she had her fill. Along with being pregnant, she felt absolutely fat. She looked up and saw Jacob leaving the room and Christina slowly getting up as well. Christina looked at Jessica and said, "Should we save our children from that Martian of yours?"

"You have it backwards, Christina, we need to save that Martian from our children," Jessica laughed.

Both Todd and Sarah had gotten up and surveyed the table which was full of empty and half-filled plates, unwashed pots and pans and several empty wine bottles scattered on the floor. Christina looked at Sarah, "You want to join our rescue mission to save Julio from our children?"

Sarah sighed and then responded, "Well since he is a Martian and not a Venusian, OK."

The women found the children drilling the Martian with questions when they entered the farm.

Jessica spoke first, "Julio could you bring Nozomi with you, it is time for us to leave."

The other two children said a quick good bye to their new friend, the Martian and ran into the waiting arms of their respective mothers. The group was reunited near the airlock. The children had somehow convinced themselves they would see each other again, so there were no tearful good-byes from any of them. However for Sarah, Christina and Jessica, their eyes cried freely as Julio lead Nozomi into the airlock. The men as well did not have dry faces though their tears were carefully restrained. Jessica, Julio and Nozomi floated in a bubble back to the NN2. The remaining group went across to the other aft airlock where the IOSAC was docked. It was then that Tobias stomped his feet, refusing to leave his home.

When Jacob lifted him up in an attempt to calm his son down, Tobias violently struck his father repeatedly in the chest, screaming, "I don't want to go! I don't want to go!"

Rhiannon walked over to his uncle and tugged at his pants. Jacob bent down towards his niece still holding onto Tobias. Rhiannon pulled out a shovel she had hidden into her back pocket when she was at the farm last.

"You'll need this Tobias," Rhiannon started while Tobias was still hammering at his father's chest, "You'll need to start your own farm on Venus". She reached into her other pocket and offered him some corn seeds as well. Tobias immediately stopped struggling against his father and stared down at Rhiannon with tearful eyes. He gestured to his father that he wanted down. Jacob complied and watched his son take the offered seeds and shovel from her.

"Thank you," said a tearful Tobias.

Rhiannon kissed Tobias on the cheek then stepped away saying, "Good-bye Tobias, happy farming."

Jacob holding Tobias and a tearful Christina stepped into the IOSAC waving their good-byes. Todd, Sarah and Rhiannon watched out of their portholes as the IOSAC joined up with the NN2 and began their descent into the Venusian atmosphere. Todd and Sarah realized that they would be the last to depart from the SIL11.

After watching the IOSAC and NN2 depart from their sight, Jacob and Sarah with Rhiannon in tow went to bridge to prepare for their departure. When they arrived at the bridge, two shining points of light hovered in the air giving off brilliant radiance of light. All three of them instinctively covered their eyes.

"What is that?" Rhiannon asked.

Todd answered, "They are our guardians; we call them the Dimensionless Ones. They will be guides to our new home."

Chapter 40 - The Gatekeepers

Todd spread his hands to two shining points of light and said, "Welcome." Both of the Dimensionless Ones reduced their luminosity so they no longer hurt human eyes. They did not use riddles to get their message across as they had done in the past, this time they allowed their thoughts to be mentally visualized by Todd, Sarah and even Rhiannon.

"*Thank you,*" one of the lights responded, then the other added, "*Are you ready to proceed?*"

"Yes of course, we all are," Todd responded as both Sarah and Rhiannon nodded their heads.

"*Good, to confirm your commitment to this journey, all communications with others will be severed, do agree with this action?*"

"Is that necessary? We would like to talk with our friends as long as we can," Sarah asked.

"*I'm sorry that is not possible,*" said the second light, "*Do you agree with this action?*"

Todd said, "I agree," and then turned his head towards his wife and daughter. Rhiannon immediately nodded her head in agreement after seeing her father's gestire, but Sarah hesitated for a moment before she nodded her head as well.

"*You do not have to speak or nod, we can hear your thoughts as well when they are directed at us, but like many others before you, they were more comfortable when they actually spoke. We just want to give you a choice.*"

"If it's OK with you, I'd rather keep speaking. Are we not allowed our own private thoughts?" Todd asked.

"*Only thoughts directed to us, will be read by us but be careful we will tolerate being deceived either, so don't attempt to be dishonest with us. But when you wish to have your own private thoughts or even an actual private conversation with your wife or daughter, we will not interfere or eavesdrop on those thoughts or conversations. Promise!*"

"What would you like us to do next?" asked Todd.

"*I will you give you a course and an acceleration vector for your ship using your conventional controls for the time being. You will not be visible to anyone in this solar system, so don't concern yourselves about being detected. We will finish the preparations to your and our cocoons so that your family as well as us will be safe during our last leg of our adventure ahead; we will also finishing sealing your ship. By the time we reach the asteroid belt, we will have taken full control of your vessel including propulsion and navigation and you and your family will stay in your cocoon with us next door to you. You are welcome to monitor visually our voyage using your own sensors. By the time we reach Jupiter's orbit, we will be for all intents and purposes will be travelling at the speed of light. I already know that have you enough provisions of food and water for the trip inside your cocoon.*"

Sarah asked, "There will be no cryogenesis for us?"

They responded, *"No, that will not be necessary."*

Sarah went to the console and implemented their course and acceleration vector. The course took them towards from Mars but a few degrees away from the planet. Sarah had no doubt at least not much doubt, that the Dimensionless Ones will shield them successfully from the Gatekeepers orbiting Mars. It was a great opportunity for them to see these immense ships of the Gatekeepers up close without the concerns of being noticed. The Dimensionless Ones must have already known about their new fuel stores, since their acceleration vector was quite steep, and the SIL11 would be rapidly burning through their anti-matter fuel. She hoped that NN2 and the IOSAC would be able to see them leaving Venus orbit and then disappearing in front of them at least that would give them some indication that the SIL11 was OK and didn't just explode in space.

Sarah wondered about the food and water, they had no more than 1 to 2 weeks of provisions for the three of them. Where ever they are going even at speeds near that of light would require more reserves than what they collected for their cocoon and so their destination would have to be nearby. She knew that would be quite presumptuous of her, anything was possible, including the possibilities that the speed would be so great that time itself would be nearly at a standstill for them. These beings, the Dimensionless Ones were probably not restricted by the dimensions of time and space, therefore for them anything was possible. But she, Todd and Rhiannon were part of this universe and were restricted to its dimensions. Sarah asked herself, whether the Dimensionless Ones were capable of transforming them into beings not restricted to time and space like them. She could have asked them but decided that she rather find out on her own. So only time will give her that answer.

***

Antwan contacted the IOSAC, "You will be following me to the Cloud City 8C. We will orbit the planet one last time before entering the atmosphere. You will be engaging winds of 150-250 km/hour near the city besides the normal sheering from re-entry. Those winds are quite mild compared to the winds on the rest of Venus. We will not be going too far into the Venusian atmosphere before reaching the city. Lower latitudes in the atmosphere are not survivable for your spacecraft, so don't miss my mark. Understood?"

"Understood Antwan," Jacob replied. He was glad that he was not piloting the SIL11 into this hellacious planet's atmosphere. He somewhat marveled when thinking that a couple of SIL pilots had somehow successfully maneuvered their vessel to the Venusian cities. The three of them, Jacob Christina and Tobias were all glued to the bridge window of the IOSAC as details of Venus's cloud formations could be deciphered as they disappeared into Venus's night side. In about an hour, the IOSAC and the NN2 would see the sunrise again. Minutes earlier, the old rust bucket, the SIL11 disappeared from all sensors on both the NN2 and the IOSAC. The NN2 was equipped to detect most sophisticated stealth technology but not this. The SIL11 along with Todd, his niece and his bull-headed sister were now gone. He was sad to see them depart and hoped for the best for them.

***

"Are you certain," asked the grey-bearded heavy set general to the terrified lieutenant. The lieutenant eyes were as large as dishes and perspiration dripped down the left side of his forehead.

His response was almost a squeal, 'Yes general, it has been confirmed that the Gatekeeper ship has left its Martian orbit."

"And its heading, lieutenant?" asked the general in cold icy voice.

"It's heading our way," squeaked the lieutenant.

'Has this been confirmed?"

"Yes as best as we can."

The general did not have time to weigh his options. That had been done for him already. Plans had been devised many years ago in case of possible detection by the Gatekeepers. The captain of the NN2, Antwan had reported that a Corporate fighter from a SIL vessel was beyond the projection screen for about 1-2 seconds at which point Antwan had disintegrated it in accordance with the Venusian code. But there had been no reaction by either Gatekeeper ship orbiting Mars or Earth. The Gatekeepers probably stayed patient, and found a way to track them to Venus. He hoped that this new deception of theirs would be enough to detract them from searching Venus. He stared at the awaiting lieutenant. "Commence General Order 34 immediately!" he commanded the lieutenant.

Thirty percent of the Venusian fleet prepared for an immediate launch out of the Venusian atmosphere. This contingent of 60-70 vessels, composed of some older warships, fighters, but mostly shuttles, tankers and frigates was programmed to leave Venusian space and immediately with all speed with a course towards the asteroid belt. The purpose of this contingent was not to save 30% of the fleet but act as a decoy for the Gatekeeper ship. This number of ships was of no threat to the immense Gatekeeper ship, and from prior experience there has never been a coordinated attack by more than one Gatekeeper vessel anyway. It appeared they were very confident of capabilities of one vessel and two would be overkill for any task, at least within this solar system. Also, with this number of vessels, it was quite possible that the Gatekeeper ship orbiting Earth would not be notified. The crews of this contingent understood more than too well that this was a suicide mission to save the remaining 70% that remain in the Venusian clouds, but like all Venusians their life were dispensable for the survival of Venus. This contingent fleet would rendezvous on the dark side of plant in synchronized orbit to remain hidden as long as possible before launching towards the asteroid belt.

***

Jacob and the IOSAC were nearly out of the dark side of Venus when Antwan contacted them again.

"Immediate abort! We will be turning around! Head back to the dark side. Follow my lead!" Antwan was shouting in outright panic. Jacob didn't like hearing that panic in his voice.

"What's happening?" Jacob asked.

"No time to explain but we are part of General Order 34! There will be a large contingent of vessels launching from the cloud cities, and they with us will rendezvous at Aphrodite point. Sorry I don't have more time to explain things to you. Cloud control has detected a Gatekeeper ship leaving Martian space and heading towards us! Just follow my tail for now, over and out!"

Jacob was absolutely stunned. They have been awake for years and extremely careful not to be noticed by the Gatekeepers. Now finally, after reaching their destination, they are told to flee because of the strong possibility that they have been detected. Jacob glanced over at Christina and saw her eyebrows swished together to signify deep concern. Jacob brought the IOSAC about and followed the NN2 to whatever destiny awaited them, which now appeared to be certain death.

***

All Venusians that had stayed behind were now on severe restrictions including minimal power usage and absolute radio silence. They hoped their remaining armada, their cities and their people would go unnoticed as hopefully the Gatekeeper ship would pursue the contingent of vessels fleeing towards the asteroid belt. The ships would fan out once they reached Earth's solar orbit and become exiled or destroyed depending on whether the Gatekeeper's ship had targeted them.

***

SIL11 was gaining speed rapidly as it hurtled towards Mars. Sarah watched a Gatekeeper ship leave Martian space headed towards them. The Gatekeeper ship was also accelerating at high speed. Sarah motioned Todd come next to her as she pointed out the Gatekeeper ship to Todd. The two Dimensionless Ones were in the newly built cocoon and modifying it so it would be survive any assault or mishap to the SIL11, so they were not present on the bridge.

"We have some serious issues, the Gatekeeper ship is heading our way," Sarah quietly announced to Todd, so not to awake Rhiannon.

"Dimensionless Ones are aware of them, Sarah. They are not in least bit concerned about the recent developments. They say that the Gatekeeper ship will pass the SIL11 within a thousand miles, but will not detect us."

"So you are having private conversations with the Dimensionless Ones now?" Sarah asked raising an eyebrow.

"Sarah, relax, I just asked them a question about the Gatekeepers; and they answered me immediately," Todd replied, "If you like you can ask them the same question and I'm sure they will give you a quick reply as well. I believe they are being honest about allowing us our own private thoughts and conversations. You have to ask them directly, if you have doubts though."

"No that's quite alright, I do believe you. So if they are not coming for us, where are they going?" Sarah said more as a statement than a question. Sarah added, "So obviously, they are heading for Venus and our departed friends!"

"Not our friends, but our family!" Todd responded. "Not just Venus but the last contingent of free human beings! We need to do something."

"Todd, DO NOT seek help from the Dimensionless Ones. Or inform them about our dilemma. Do you understand me, Todd?!" Sarah pleaded.

"OK, but why?" answered Todd.

199

"From everything that was have learned about the Dimensionless Ones, the constant is that they do not interfere with the affairs of other species regarding their interactions with the Gatekeepers once their choice has been made not to leave, don't you agree," Sarah asked her husband.

Sarah observed the nimbleness and speed of the Gatekeeper ship, despite being at twice the distance from the sun, the Gatekeeper ship was going to cross paths with the SIL11 near the sun.

"Yes, I would agree, so there is nothing we can do?" Todd asked with panic in his voice.

"Yes, there is one thing we could do. But it may not work, it might not even slow the Gatekeeper ship down, and it will end with our certain death."

"We still have navigational controls, when our ships are nearly at the point of crossing paths, I will plunge the SIL11 right into the Gatekeeper ship."

"Yes, that would do us in, including Rhiannon. Let me remind you that they made their choice just like us."

Sarah grimaced at the thought of sacrificing her only daughter and her husband. Sarah responded, "We could save the human race. But you would have to agree with this plan. You have had your heart set in following the Dimensionless Ones, do you want to turn away now?"

"The Dimensionless Ones may not allow us to plunge into the Gatekeeper's ship anyway. We too have made a choice. But we do have surprise on our side that I'm sure of. So, your plan may work if the Dimensionless Ones don't interfere," Todd surmised, "I'm with you, love, It's not every day, you get to save the human race."

Sarah then responded, "Here is the rest of my plan, I will quickly program the maneuver for the SIL11 to collide with the Gatekeeper ship at latest possible time and then rupture the magnetic fields holding our anti-matter fuel at the same time, and we will leave the bridge and get to the cocoon just before the collision, so the Dimensionless Ones don't suspect anything. It should be enough energy in the collision and the antimatter-matter reaction to annihilate a small moon. A disabled Gatekeeper ship would most likely plunge into the sun and destroy itself if the blast doesn't do it. It may also appear to the other Gatekeeper ship orbiting the Earth, that there was a malfunction near the solar surface that led to its sister ship's destruction."

"Brilliant plan, sweetheart. I will miss you and I love you!!" Todd replied.

"I love you too husband."

Sarah murmured under her breath, "Damn those Venusians, they killed my father and now I'm trying to save them! And at what cost, my husband, my daughter and my life. I must be absolutely insane!"

***

Lieutenant Beasley was carefully monitoring his screen. He was young and had just joined the Venusian military after being rescued from a derelict ship drifting in the asteroid belt. He thought he was saved, and now with the Gatekeepers bearing down, he removed that fantasy from his mind. His

200

last encounter with the Gatekeepers, resulted in the death of his parents, leaving him a young teenager to etch out an existence for himself. His fantasy was now over and it was time to visit reality again. His perspiration was dotting the screen underneath him. He marveled at the way the general could keep his cool; he didn't even raise his voice with him even though he, himself could barely talk. He supposed that is why he was a general and he was still a lieutenant. He felt fortunate to serve the general to witness his abilities to deal with crisis. He knew that this wasn't the general's first, he just hoped it wasn't his last.

The object that represented the Gatekeeper ship near the sun on his PCD screen had simply vanished. He had no explanation for its disappearance. He risked a message to the other side of Venus to obtain confirmation of its disappearance. It would have been something that the general would have ordered anyway. The response was quick and confirmed that the Gatekeeper ship had suffered a lethal malfunction and had plunged it into the sun's atmosphere vaporizing it. There had been reports of some solar activity near the area but no specific solar flare could be confirmed. The Gatekeeper ship was destroyed. He ran out of his cubicle and buzzed down the hall to the general's office. Finally, he would able to give the general some good news.

***

Jessica felt a tug on her dress from her daughter. She had just short experience with something she did not understand. The experience had captivated her, it was something familiar and loving. It was there for a brief time, but now it was gone. She didn't understanding her feeling but it was one of joy and love. She wrapped herself around that emotion but Nozomi persistent tug on her sleeve unraveled it. She looked down at her daughter with loving eyes despite the loss of that incredible feeling she had just experienced.

She asked, "What is Nozomi?"

Nozomi ignited her face with a bright smile and said, "Daddy was here."

***

Jacob was miles away from Jessica and Nozomi on the NN2, when he also felt a familiar presence. He felt a warmth and gentleness he hadn't experienced since childhood. He had fleeting thoughts of books, stethoscopes and his mother. But the feeling went away as quickly as it had come. He reached out for that feeling again, but it was gone and his PCD went off with the latest Antwan message.

"Crisis averted. Return with me to the Venusian atmosphere. The Gatekeeper vessel has been destroyed," was what the message contained.

He should have been ecstatic over the news but he yearned for that lost feeling. He thought about the presence he felt, and turned it over his mind how familiar it was. At least on this day, the Venusians had avoided oblivion, but his sister and her family were now on their way to their oblivion.

"There is only as much space, only as much time,
Only as much desire, only as many words,
Only as many pages, only as much ink
To accept all of us at light-speed
Hurrying into the Promised Land
Of oblivion that is waiting for us sooner or later."
— *Dejan Stojanovic*

Epilogue

The SIL11 was totally destroyed but somehow this cocoon with the Dimensionless Ones next to them was now tumbling into space intact and best she could tell was still in the general direction of their original heading. The Dimensionless Ones had installed a translucent material in the framework that she and Todd had installed. Opposite from the Dimensionless Ones chamber where a wall once stood was now a large window out into space. Todd and Rhiannon were next to her and out cold; either they were either in deep sleep or unconscious. Both were still alive and uninjured as best she could tell without a complete physical examination. She was grateful that somehow the Dimensionless Ones had saved their lives.

The two Dimensionless Ones were in their compartment shining brightly, but she noticed a third faint light was with the pair. This light was different; it was warm but was very dim and somehow familiar. She knew the presence. It had been a presence that had been with her since as far back as she could remember. Then, she concluded that it must be Dad. But as soon as she came to this realization, the presence was gone as well as the third faint light in their cocoon. She yearned for that presence again. Even though the presence seemed to be her dad, she couldn't believe it. Her dad was killed at the hands of the Venusians.

She asked the two remaining Dimensionless Ones to stop the tumbling of the cocoon, since she was getting nauseous as the cocoon continued to tumble.

"You have some nerve, asking us for something after the stunt you pulled," answered one of the Dimensionless Ones. She was sure of the words that the Dimensionless Ones had chosen but she also sensed it was given with understanding and some humor.

The tumbling began to slow and eventually stopped all together. She watched as they passed near Mars which was at one point the size of a small pie that she had prepared on their last banquet with their crewmates. She wondered if the Martians were celebrating with the destruction of the Gatekeepers' vessel. The image of Mars disappeared quickly, and their next stop was into oblivion.

Made in the USA
Middletown, DE
12 August 2018